LUMI'S HEART

Also by Ulana Dabbs:

Storms of Tomorrow

Lumi's Spell

LUMI'S HEART

Ulana Dabbs

LUMI'S HEART

For more information, contact:
ulana@ulanadabbs.com

Cover Artwork © Mario Wibisono
Content Edit by Philip Athans
Copy Edit by Lauren Nicholls
Proofreading by Rebecca Reed

Connect with the author on:
Website: www.ulanadabbs.com
Twitter: https://twitter.com/ulanadabbs

Bonus Content:

Get your free fantasy adventure!

"An emotionless warrior.
A journey across four lands.
A quest to uncover the power of the human heart."

Visit ulanadabbs.com to subscribe and receive your free copy of:

Storms of Tomorrow

To Steve.

You came into my world and you made it better in every way. Thank you for always cheering me on.

I

The sound drifted from afar. At first, I thought it was the remnant of a dream, but then my mind regained its focus. I rubbed the sleep from my eyes. The wood muffled the vibrations, but I was sure it came from the ship's deck. A voice whispered my name: *Jarin*, and its seductive tone sent a shiver up my arms and legs. I slipped from the berth and donned my boots and cloak to guard against the chill. Through the round window, the surface of the Great Atlantic rose and fell in a steady rhythm, but the light of dawn was stripped of grey and stained with yellow. The water turned the colour of salmon's flesh, and even the quality of air seemed different—it gained a faint shimmer that transformed the scenery outside into a mirage. And there was the sound. It came in faint waves, a mixture of play and song. None of my friends had the skills to make music, and Mirable's many attempts induced heavy sighs.

I fastened the sword to my waist and pulled the door open. A creamy, clove-like scent washed over me—a blend of summer flowers and winter spice. It made me lightheaded. Another door creaked, and Fjola sprang onto the deck, her daggers glinting in the amber hue. She cocked her head, as if trying to establish the source of the song. It was the sweetest melody, an echo of a mother's lullaby, or a gentle caress of a lover's voice. I felt this way as a boy when my mother pulled me safely into her embrace. My muscles went lax, and any worries I had floated away.

Fjola seemed unaffected by the tune. 'Is that Mirable?' she asked. Her hair fell down her back in rusty tangles, and the yellowish-pink colours shifted across her face and neck in waves. In the light of this beguiling aura, she looked like an alluring ghost, and it took me a moment to turn in the direction she was pointing.

Mirable stood with his hands open wide in a welcoming gesture, his turban partially undone, the loose strands flapping about him like crimson wings.

'This can't be good,' I said. Mirable treasured his headwear, and only under dire circumstances would he be this careless with it. That same realisation in Fjola's face sobered me up. We hastened to his side.

I placed my hand on Mirable's shoulder, but he didn't even look at me. I leaned over the rail and the pink air hovering over the ocean's surface passed through my nostrils, leaving a spicy-sweet taste of cornflower on my tongue. Mirable's brown irises were fixed on a shape writhing in the yellow blaze, and the foam bubbles clung to his greying beard.

'What's wrong with him?' Fjola asked, scanning the waters.

Mirable looked like a man in a stupor. His lips parted and spittle gathered in the corner of his mouth, a sign that he had stood here for some time, fascinated by the shape only he could recognise.

'I wish I knew.' I shook his shoulder. 'Mirable, what is it? What can you see?' I wanted my voice to sound firm, but the peculiar hue in the air muffled it. It was like speaking through a thin wall of crystal.

As if awakening from a long dream, he angled his head my way. The look on his face was pure bliss. If not for the circumstances, I'd have enjoyed this rare expression.

'She's magnificent,' he whispered. His brow furrowed. 'You can't steal her away from me. I won't allow it.'

'Steal who?'

In response to my question, the melody, so sweet and harmless moments ago, took on a darker tone. Even the shade of the ocean turned deeper, more clandestine pink. The colour was mesmerising, and just below the surface was a tantalising whisper, a secret desperate to be unveiled. *Come*, it murmured, *taste the sweetness of the world beneath.*

Mirable pointed at the ocean. 'She who came to heal me, of course.' His face softened. 'My place is with her. Together, we'll rule the waves.'

Fjola ventured closer to the rail, her daggers raised. She sniffed the air. 'A ghost?'

The silhouette that enthralled Mirable was little more than a shadow veiled in yellow hue, but the song it played touched us in different ways. While Fjola appeared deaf to the melody, I heard it well, and part of me wished to follow the notes into the black depths of the Great Atlantic, but something kept me on the sane side of the threshold. The same couldn't be said for Mirable. The creature that stalked the waves cast its spell over him, blinding my friend to reality.

'Oh, my beloved saviour,' Mirable chanted, 'take me, for only in your arms may I know peace and salvation.' He placed his left foot on the rail to climb it.

'By Agtarr's shadow, he's gone insane,' Fjola said. She sheathed her daggers and grabbed Mirable's arm.

I searched the waters. 'We must find the source of his attraction. We can't fight what we can't see.'

'And fast.' Boots thudded against the deck, and Fjola whipped her head around. 'Thank the gods. Njall, we need help!'

Njall came running, spear in hand, but before we could breathe a sigh of relief, he halted mid-stride. He turned his head from side to side and a look of wonder stole over his face. He dropped his spear and made his way across the deck to the ship's rail, hands outstretched.

Fjola cried her brother's name but to no avail. 'What's wrong with them?'

Gripped by delirium, Mirable struggled against her hold—the fool braced himself to jump ship. 'I've waited all my life,' he said. 'What's mine is yours. Here, take it. Take all of it.' He grabbed the purse from his pocket and thrust the contents into the water. The coins he was so protective of spilled in a rain of gold and silver. They hit the surface and sank into the depths.

Fjola gasped and slapped her hand over her mouth. We had just witnessed the true face of madness.

I seized Mirable's other arm and dragged him off the rail. The force behind my pull pushed us back, and we crashed onto the deck. Mirable's chant turned into a frenzied cry. He snatched a handful of my hair. A tearing pain shot through my scalp, and I cursed.

Fjola caught Mirable's hand and pried his fingers apart. He kicked her, and she staggered back.

'You can't stop me, you wretch,' he screamed, scrambling to his feet. I never dreamed he was capable of such rage. The apparition, or whatever it was, possessed his mind and there was no power strong enough to hold him.

I shot a glance in Njall's direction. Fjola's brother fared no better—he was halfway up the rail and ready to plunge into the pink waters.

'Can you manage?' I asked Fjola. Njall was twice the size of Mirable, and if the merchant was this strong, I dreaded to think what Njall would be like.

'Save my brother,' she said, and took hold of Mirable again.

I darted across the deck and wrapped my arms around Njall's waist. He strained against my grip. His body was pure muscle, making it impossible for me to get an upper hand, but I couldn't let go. He was the only family Fjola had left. She lost Skari, her betrothed, because of me, and I refused to be the cause of another loss in her life.

'Njall, you fool, you'll get us both killed,' I shouted into his back.

His chest vibrated with laughter. 'Killed? Nothing can harm us. The gods sent her to grant us eternal peace. Let her come to you, give in to the song and fulfil all your heart's desires.' He twisted in my grasp, his hands falling upon my shoulders like two slabs. 'Rejoice, brother, for all our struggles have ended at last.' The otherworldly colours slid across the deformed side of his face.

The shackles of dread fastened around my throat, and my lungs struggled to make use of the thick and viscid air. 'What are you talking about?' I croaked. 'Whatever's out there is deceiving you, trying to lure you to your death. Don't give in. The warrior I know would never succumb to the ghostly temptations.'

Njall's nostrils flared, and he pushed me away with a force that knocked the precious breath out of me. 'The God of Life offers us salvation, but you're unworthy of this gift.' He faced the ocean. 'I offer myself freely.'

It was useless. Whatever enchanted both Mirable and Njall was more powerful than any words we could say. The song it created ebbed and flowed, becoming darker or lighter in response to the emotions felt by those it captivated. Only Fjola and I didn't succumb to the charm. The formless shapes in the yellow haze had no influence over our minds, but this didn't make them any less dangerous. As if bolstered by Njall's desire to rejoice, the amber shroud of deception wrapped around him more tightly. The cloy scent of spice and flowers intensified, sickly and oppressive. Bile formed in my throat, and I had to swallow the urge to gag.

Njall climbed the last rung of the railing, leaving me no choice. I had to stop him before he plunged into the depths of the Great Atlantic and the arms of the ghosts that haunted it. I drew my sword from the scabbard, praying for forgiveness. My intention was not to hurt him, only to generate enough pain to snap him out of the illusion. The weapon's steel trapped some of the colours, making it gleam like a precious ornament. I feared the creatures charmed it and the sword wouldn't accomplish its task, but the only way of making sure was to test it.

I stabbed Njall in the upper thigh.

He roared, and I pulled the sword clean of his flesh. He lost his balance and fell over backwards. Blood spilled onto the deck and the melody ceased. The overwhelming sweetness turned sour and the mesmerising colours fell away like a curtain, exposing the weavers of this illusion.

'Have you gone insane?' Njall bellowed, clasping his hands around his bleeding thigh. Dark liquid pressed through the gaps between his fingers.

I paid him no heed—the creature poised above the waves had my full attention.

It took on a female form, its lower half engulfed by the waves, and the upper covered in scales that shimmered with various shades of yellows and pinks. Its hair was the colour of sand. Sea shells trapped in the loose strands clinked with each movement of its diamond-shaped head. The eyes that regarded me were pure white, with no iris. The creature opened its mouth, exposing a line of needle-sharp teeth, and hissed like a furious feline. I imagined those teeth stabbing through flesh, and recoiled. How something so hideous could charm my friends was beyond me.

The beast plunged into the depths of the Great Atlantic, taking the last of the colour with it.

I left Njall to nurse his injured thigh and raced across the deck to where Fjola stood, panting, with Mirable sprawled at her feet.

'Is he dead?'

'Unconscious.' She raised the hilt of her dagger. 'He's stronger than he looks. I hit him hard.'

I jerked my thumb in Njall's direction. 'He got a similar treatment.'

We looked at each other and burst out laughing. Perhaps it was tension leaving my body, or maybe the laughter came from a simple realisation that between the two of us we brought Njall and Mirable to their knees. Either way, my heart relished this rare moment. Fjola's voice was sweeter than any melody. There was no malice hidden behind it, and the song of it suffused the air with a warmth and honesty no illusion could rival. A familiar urge to embrace her came over me. It was becoming harder and harder to ignore the images of a future filled with Fjola's laughter. Moments like these were precious and unsettling at the same time. Her eyes fell to the black pearl at my neck and something like hope flickered in them.

Mirable groaned.

The noise sobered us up, the vision of a sweet future giving way to grim reality, and Fjola's laughter faded. Her face hardened and the expression of hurt returned to her deep-set eyes.

Njall hobbled our way, one hand pressed to the back of his thigh, the other sticky with blood. 'I'm glad you find it so amusing.'

'I stabbed you,' I said.

Njall snorted.

I patted Mirable's cheek, and he moaned again. His eyelids fluttered, and then parted. There was a dazed look in them. 'I had the strangest dream,' he said in a voice full of awe. 'For the first time in my life, a beautiful woman begged me to have her.' He pressed his finger to his chin. 'I think I refused her.' The frown on his face deepened, and the whites of his eyes grew large. He looked from me to Fjola to Njall. 'Did I?'

'Fjola did, with the hilt of her dagger,' I said. 'But not before the subject of your affections robbed you clean.'

Mirable uttered a sound that was a mixture of shock and horror. As his left hand flew to his turban, his right patted the pockets of his cloak. 'My coins are gone!'

I nodded. 'You offered them. *Freely*.'

He sprang to his feet and rushed to the railing. Halfway there, he staggered.

'Take it slow,' Fjola called after him. She bit down on her lip. 'Maybe I should've used less force.'

'His head will recover,' I said, 'but if he'd jumped off that rail…'

Mirable curled his fingers over his turban. 'Outwitted by a serena. My days of pride are over.' The misery in his voice was deeper than the Great Atlantic.

Njall shook his head. 'There's plenty of coin in this world. You'll make more.'

'What do you mean by a serena?' I asked.

'We've been lured by the maidens of the sea. Their nest must be somewhere nearby.' He leaned over the railing. 'Perhaps we can storm their lair and recover the gold.' He shook his fist at the waves. 'Those wretched thieves.'

'We're not storming anything,' I said. 'You and Njall barely escaped with your lives.'

'Thanks to our quick thinking,' Fjola chimed in.

I searched the waters, but there was no sign of the creature. Dawn cast its lure to the east, fishing for the golden sun. It would soon emerge with a promise of a new day and another chance at locating the mysterious island of Shinpi. Our ill encounter with the serena seemed more like a dream than reality, but something about it bothered me. 'Why did only you two fall prey to the song?'

Mirable twisted his head. 'For all your wit, you truly know little of the world. The serena is a fiend that feeds on the breath of the living. First, the music lures you, for it contains memories, and memories are bonds of the past. I was fast asleep when the melody stirred me to wakefulness with a tune my mother used to sing when I was only an offshoot. The sweet sound of her voice drew me out onto the deck. By then, it confused me enough for the serena to exert her influence over my mind.'

Njall looked deep in thought, his wound momentarily forgotten. I couldn't help but wonder who it was that sang for him.

'That doesn't explain why Jarin and I were immune to the creature's call,' Fjola said. 'There are many songs from my childhood I cherish, but the melody you two speak of sounded like a gurgle to me. There was nothing alluring about it.'

Mirable wagged his finger at the Great Atlantic, as if to scold the serena for her wicked ways. 'Oh, but it makes sense. She can only influence those with the hearts free of attachments.'

Fjola glanced at me.

'My mother used to say that women chased after the wealthy suitors. So it's no surprise the serena chose me as the object of her affections.' Mirable stared at the horizon, a peculiar longing touching his face. 'To see such beauty was worth the loss.'

'I have no coin to my name,' Njall said.

'But you're strong in body and mind. If only all of us could steal such qualities with one breath.'

Njall's brow wrinkled. Mirable wasn't one to shower him with compliments. 'My sister's blow muddled your mind.'

'No matter the reasons, let's put this unfortunate event behind us,' I said.

'Agreed,' Njall said, giving me a sidelong glance. 'Your sword cuts deeper than you think.'

Fjola offered Njall her arm for support. 'I have witch hazel. It'll help to stem the bleeding.' She helped him across the deck to her cabin.

Mirable cast one last look at the ocean and padded after them. I refused to dwell on the reasons behind the serena's choices. If the creature called to those free of attachments, it meant Fjola's feelings for me were deeper than I realised. By pushing her away, I scarred her heart the way Lumi scarred mine. I had to believe there'd come a day when I no longer troubled Fjola with my presence, the day of my soul's reckoning. She deserved a man who would be there to watch over her the way my father watched over my mother. Someone who would fill her life with joy and affection. Fjola deserved better than a man who was marked for death.

II

The heart beating inside the pocket of my jerkin became my obsession long before I cradled it in my palms. Even through the layers of clothing, I could feel its shape and the chill emanating from it. The glass box that held it captive for so long lay at the bottom of the Great Atlantic, for I preferred to keep the mystery of Lumi's heart close to my chest. From within its crystal shell, the voice of my mother's killer whispered my name over and over. This incessant call urged me forth, across the ocean, and into the unknown. Deep down, I knew Lumi awaited me in Shinpi, and this knowledge drove me.

When last I saw her, she mocked and ridiculed me, then disappeared into the snowstorm, leaving laughter and death in her wake. Lumi—the ghost of my past, the shadow haunting my dreams, my life's greatest sorrow. I had the power to destroy her right here in my pocket. To shatter her heart would give my mother peace. As long as Lumi walked the earth, Mother too would remain lost in Agtarr's shadow, for only those avenged in life could find peace in death.

So why couldn't I bring myself to crush the heart? What stayed my hand every time I reached for it? At nineteen, I could no longer blame the powerless child, the lonely boy blinded by the need of acceptance. Maybe it was my desire to look into Lumi's blue eyes one last time. I wanted her to see me, to know the pain she had caused, and to grieve for every life she turned to ice. My fingers curled around the taffrail. She was a heartless ice demon, who only I could make whole.

The Great Atlantic stretched before me, constant and fathomless. The glow of the sunset paved a golden trail, shimmering into the horizon. These were the last nights of summer and the cooling air settled on my skin. From the ship's deck everything appeared serene, but I knew better. During the months of sailing, I tasted the fury unleashed upon us by the way of storms and high waves, not to mention the terrible creature that accosted us only days ago. Mirable called it 'serena,' and I hoped I'd never hear its song again. The heart of the Great Atlantic was a formless chaos, and I couldn't understand why Nords longed for it so much. Our vessel was the one stable thing in this vast emptiness, and despite the many challenges, it cut the waves with the strength of purpose. Unlike me, it belonged here, with the ocean as its plinth and the stars for guidance. The figurehead in the shape of a serpent coiled around the prow, its deadly fangs on display, tongue split like a fork ready to stab the eastern horizon.

At the sound of footsteps, my hand travelled to the hilt of my sword. Out of habit. The blade of Stromhold Guardians belonged to my father, Eyvar, and brought me great comfort. It was like having him at my side, guiding me with his fortitude and wisdom. As a boy, I wanted to be like Father—the mighty Guardian of Stromhold, leading a band of formidable warriors, but that was not my fate. Only after Eyvar had fallen, I'd learned the truth about my destiny, but I refused to accept it then, and I refused to accept it now. Skaldir, the Goddess of Destruction, forged the blade and through it she gained the ability to control the wielder. Or so everyone thought.

Njall came to stand at my shoulder, his steel-blue eyes fixed on the horizon. 'Do you think we'll ever find it?' he asked, running his fingers down his beard.

Its length never ceased to amaze me. For this journey, he weaved it into a braid and secured the lower half with a leather band. The loose tip brushed against his belly, and unlike my scruffy stubble, his was a sight to behold. Tied into a warrior's tail, his hair fell past his shoulder blades, the length of it matching my own.

I followed his gaze. 'Our sail will stay up until we do.'

His hand drifted to the dressing Fjola wrapped around his thigh. 'I can't help but wonder if the God of Life approves of this quest.'

When I left Hvitur in search of Hyllus, my father's killer, Njall was at my side, and I trusted him with my life. He was eight years my elder, and the calm that emanated from him never failed to ease my anxious thoughts, but his unshakable trust in the gods divided us. It reminded me of my mother, Aliya.

My jaw clenched. 'I care not for Yldir's approval,' I said. 'Besides, I doubt he bothers with the desires of mortals.'

'Your contempt for those who created life is troubling.' He turned his head, exposing the scar on the left side of his face. Deep and jagged, it pulled at his eyelid, obscuring the upper half of his eye. It was a taint earned for trying to save a friend.

I snorted. 'You sound like my mother.'

'She sounds like a wise woman.'

'Wise and dead,' I said, wrapping my cloak tighter about me. The setting sun took the warmth of the day with it, leaving the world at the mercy of the chill that rose from the depths of the Great Atlantic. 'The gods are asleep, locked in the eternal dream, and of no use to anyone. My parents prayed to them all their lives, but when Agtarr's Warrior of Death knocked on their doors, the almighty Yldir wasn't there to answer.' I drew in a slow breath. The memories were still raw. Talking about my parents was like scratching a fresh wound. Yldir was Aliya's beloved god. My mother had an altar in her room devoted to him and spent hours on her knees, whispering prayers. To enter the Fields of Life, where the warmth of Yldir's grace melted the snowflakes of mortal sorrows, was her greatest desire. By keeping Lumi's heart beating, I denied her wish.

'You know what you must do,' Njall said, and his voice dispelled the shadows of my past.

'And it will be done.' I felt Lumi's heart react to my words with an irregular beat, as if it sensed the seal placed upon its fate. My companions trusted me to follow the customs of our land. In Nordur, a wrongful death called for vengeance. The God of Death set this law, and to break it was to defy Agtarr himself.

'Curses!' Mirable yelled from behind us.

I spun around. The merchant sat on the deck, cross-legged, his turban flashing like a crimson beacon. An empty purse rested in his left hand, and a small pile of silver lay scattered before him. When I passed him earlier, he was hard at work counting what was left from his generous offering to the serena. Since the events in Vester, I'd noticed changes in my friend. Hyllus imprisoned Mirable in his citadel, where he used the transformation magic to mutate his flesh. If not for my quest to avenge Father, the merchant would've joined the ranks of Varls, but despite his lucky escape, he was not the same man. Following the ordeal, Mirable became subdued, and his cheery disposition dampened somewhat. There was an aura of secrecy about him. When pressed, he became agitated, refusing to talk or even show me his right arm, so I resolved to let the matter rest for now.

'What's wrong?' I asked.

Mirable thrust his empty purse at me.

I rolled my eyes, and Njall shook his head.

'You've counted your wealth, or what's left of it, at least four times today,' I said. 'Why keep at it? You won't find more than there is.'

He grimaced. His umber skin was grooved like the outer side of a seashell, and his suffering in Vester added another ten winters to his forty-three. But it was only an illusion. I saw Mirable fight the ice guardians in the Lost City of Antaya, and there was nothing frail about him as he scaled the frozen shards and cast a dagger into the giant's eye. In agility, he surpassed even Fjola.

All at once, Mirable's expression lightened, and he raised his finger. 'My coins are to me what your sword is to you. Counting them gives me comfort.' He nodded, as if pleased by this conclusion. 'Besides, there's always an opportunity for a bargain. I'm yet to meet a merchant who takes no delight in a good sale. In addition, we know nothing of Shinpi and its customs, so I brought gold with me to buy us passage, but now…' He looked at his empty purse, and his expression soured. 'That rotten sea thief.'

Njall crossed his arms. 'Coin means little in the face of discipline and order.'

Mirable's hand flew to his turban. He patted it and breathed a sigh of relief. 'For a moment there, I feared the wind had snatched it again.' He pinched his full lips and looked at Njall. 'Obedience is a desirable quality indeed, but I've met many disciplined men whose control waned at the sight of gold. Someone's greed may be our opportunity.' He grinned, exposing a set of irregular teeth. 'I'm a merchant. I should know.'

'Not all of us find comfort in earthly desires,' Njall countered, nudging the few silver coins scattered on the deck. 'Besides, you have little left to bargain with.'

Mirable answered with a harsh squint.

I glanced to the other side of the ship where Fjola sat with one hand propped on her knee, gazing into the distance. I left Njall and Mirable to their squabble and crossed the deck to join her. She must've heard me coming, but she didn't look up. I lowered myself next to her, thinking of words to help me break the silence, but nothing came. The laugh we shared on the night of the serena seemed like something from a distant past. Today, Fjola tied her russet hair with a green band. Being so close to her, I felt the urge to wrap the soft waves around my fingers and smell the lavender. I pushed the longing aside. To succumb to it meant entrusting my heart to someone else's keep, and that would come with a price. I paid it once, and it left my life in ruin.

'Why are you here?' I asked after a time, thinking of Mirable and his words about the serena and hearts free of attachment. When we fled Antaya, Fjola wanted me to make good on my promise to shatter Lumi's heart, but I couldn't do it. Not for me, and not even for my mother. My unwillingness to fulfil the oath of vengeance turned her admiration into disappointment, and she walked away from me. On that day, a shadow dimmed her bright and curious eyes, the shape of it not so different to the one Lumi cast over my own heart. But when we set sail for Shinpi, I found Fjola aboard our vessel. When I asked Njall about her sudden change of heart, in his typical fashion, he shrugged. 'She's my sister, not my confidant.' And so I never spoke of it. Until now.

'For the same reason you're chasing after the demon,' she said at last.

I felt myself tense. 'You know my reasons.'

She snapped her head my way, her eyes a green blaze. 'How long are you going to deceive us and yourself? We almost died in Antaya so you could find that cursed heart and crush it. She killed your mother, destroyed everyone you cherished, and still you long for her.' Her shoulders drooped, and she looked at her hands. 'Perhaps she was never just a demon to you.'

I wanted to tell her how wrong she was, to prove that Lumi had no hold over me, but we both knew better. During my first visit to Hvitur, Fjola shared with me her intent to join the Stromhold warriors. Argil, my dear departed friend, taught her how to wield daggers, and she proved herself an excellent fighter. Her abilities, combined with her determination to make Nordur a safer place, would've made her a worthy addition to Stromhold, but Nordern customs forbade it. This didn't deter her. She resisted the union that my uncle, Torgal, arranged for her and fled Hvitur to join me on my quest. Now, my chest shrunk a little every time I looked at her downcast face.

I touched the black orb at my neck. I found it on the beach in Hvitur and kept it for good luck. My mother too wore one around her neck. Long before the custom of silver bands, men of Nordur used black pearls as a way to pledge their hearts to their chosen companions, but I wasn't planning on offering mine. To me, the pearl served as a reminder that I needed no one.

'What happens when we get there?' Fjola asked, licking her lips. The salt in the ocean water dried them out, giving rise to tiny grooves prone to cracks and bleeding.

'I won't rest until Goro-Khan joins Hyllus in the Agtarr's Chamber of Torments.'

'You don't know if the demon was telling the truth. She fooled you once. Would more deception be so surprising?'

With Fjola, everything came down to Lumi. But maybe she was right. Maybe Lumi did lie to me when she told me about Goro-Khan amid that fateful blizzard. She said he was her master and called him the Laughing God. I saw him in my vision in Antaya. He was the one who ordered Hyllus to create Lumi and used my weakness for her to lure me away from Stromhold. 'The way to know for sure is to find him, and Shinpi is the only clue I have.'

'We've been sailing close to three months now, and we're nearing the end of summer. Only four moons separate us from the Night of Norrsken. Shouldn't your concern be with the Goddess of Destruction?'

At the mention of Skaldir, my stomach knotted. 'How can I not think about her when you and Njall remind me of my destiny every chance you get?' My fingers found the left side of my temple, the place where Skaldir scarred me. It was Fjola who uncovered the mark, at my request. She told me it looked like an alignment of stars, but I never wanted to see it. My hand fell away. 'The scar on my temple is reminder enough. Believe me.'

A flash of crimson touched her high cheeks. 'If you took your responsibilities seriously, we wouldn't have to. Your refusal to accept the inevitable puts everyone at risk.'

I drew in a steady breath. The last thing I wanted was to answer Fjola's anger with my own. It'd drive the wedge between us deeper and accomplish nothing. 'Why do you think I'm in this forsaken boat in the middle of the Great Atlantic? You all keep telling me my fate is sealed, that no matter what I do, the Goddess of Destruction will prevail. But here I am, fighting my destiny, trying to prove that I'm stronger than this curse.'

'You're here because you're running. From the moment Torgal revealed the truth of your birth, you denied it. Chasing after phantoms, going against the gods.' She looked up at the sky, where the first stars exchanged places with the dying sun. 'None of this'll save you or make you strong enough to resist Skaldir's call. By fate or circumstance, the goddess chose *you* to bring about her awakening. *You* are her Valgsi, and the quicker you accept it, the easier it'll be to fight the urge to obey.'

I turned on her. 'What would you have me do? Sit in Hvitur and wait for the Night of Norrsken like an ensnared rabbit? I'd rather be out here, trying to find the man responsible for my plight instead of fretting over things beyond my control.' I stood up. 'My mother was a slave to the gods, but they spared her no grace. I refuse to follow her path, to let the dreamers decide my fate. Of all people, I thought you'd understand.'

'I'm not enslaved by a sword and neither am I the one with my soul under covenant,' she retorted. The challenge in her voice dared me to dispute her.

I opened my mouth to do just that, and then thought better of it. Over the course of three moons, I'd grown used to the constant reminders of my duties and the inept way I was trying to fulfil them. Instead, I marched to my cabin. The door screeched as I pulled it open. I hesitated. One glance over my shoulder assured me that my friends were still there.

Njall stood at the helm, manning the ship's wheel. Torgal built this boat for the crew of four and put Njall in charge. Like most Nords, he was a skilled helmsman but didn't shy from taking up oars when the need arose, and thanks to his knowledge of navigation, we remained in control of the waves. Mirable sat on the deck, still counting his coins. In his colourful garb, he reminded me of some exotic bird. From the moment our paths crossed in Vester, he became a constant presence in my life. Thanks to his quick thinking, Lumi's heart was safely tucked inside my pocket. Fjola was a silhouette against the nightfall, and I couldn't help but wonder what she'd be like if I stood firm and stopped her from following me to Sur those months ago. I had a sinking feeling she'd be leading a happier existence. Perhaps all of them would. Despite our differences, I considered the three of them my friends, and more than anything, I wanted to prove I was worthy of their devotion.

* * *

Fjola glared at Jarin's back. Hot tears burned beneath her lids, threatening to spill and flood her fractured heart. What was wrong with her? Since she set foot on this ship, her mood turned dark. When she walked away from Jarin on the day they fled Antaya, she was so sure of herself. Before then, she believed they shared a deeper connection. Like Jarin, she loved Nordur and wished to make it a safe place, and her own ambitions to become a Stromhold warrior made her feel that much closer to him. On the night at the hot springs, she rejected the Nordern traditions for good, refusing to accept her fate as Skari's wife. She wanted more from life and knew that staying in the village would make her a prisoner to routine and habit. Jarin's quest for revenge offered freedom and a chance to experience the world. Throwing caution to the wind, she ran after him, only to discover he was caught in his own prison of winter ice.

When Jarin refused to shatter the crystal heart of the demon, he shattered the budding dreams Fjola had about the future with him. Skari was dead, Stromhold had fallen into ruin, and Jarin cast her aside for a demon who destroyed everyone he loved. Maybe this was the gods' punishment for her defiance.

But that didn't stop her from boarding the ship.

Until its departure, she avoided Jarin and any talk of Shinpi, but as soon as the sail went up, her foolish heart betrayed her. Now she sat here, her head filled with the low hum of resentful thoughts. Every day at sea took them closer to Shinpi and to Lumi, the demon who stole the most precious years of Jarin's life. But still he chased after her, and even the vast expanse of the Great Atlantic was powerless to stop him. The encounter with the serena proved as much.

What made Lumi so special?

Like a windstorm, fury swept through Fjola, clamping her teeth. She despised the demon's wretched heart. She could see its shape weighing down Jarin's chest, and all she wanted was to rip it out and stomp it with the heel of her boot until it turned to crystal dust at her feet.

Fjola faced the horizon, glad for the cool breeze that dried her tears. In the face of Skaldir's awakening, her troubles seemed trivial. The world was alive and she was at its centre. A small part of her shivered at the prospect of discovering Shinpi. To set foot on the legendary island and return home to tell the story would earn her respect. They would stop questioning her decisions and accept that she was made to do more. To be more.

The world stretched before her, full of mystery and wonder, begging to be explored, but for all its greatness, without Jarin, it felt like a barren land. Before she knew of his existence, the road of her life forked and twisted with possibilities, but now it ran straight and narrow. The cool air turned razor sharp, straining her lungs. She pressed her hand against her breastbone. Inside, her traitorous heart pulsed and throbbed with Jarin's name.

'Enough,' she said.

The Night of Norrsken was fast approaching, and if Jarin succumbed to the call, the Goddess of Destruction would scorch the world just like she did on the Day of Judgement.

'Yldir, the god of all life,' Fjola whispered. 'Give me the strength to endure.'

* * *

Torgal's shipbuilders had little room for expansion, which resulted in a cabin that struggled to accommodate one person. I pulled the wooden berth free of the wall and spread a blanket over it. It was a bed in name only. Sleeping on it bruised my bones, but I accepted the discomfort the way I accepted stale bread each morning. I removed my cloak and boots and unfastened the belt that held my sword. I climbed onto the berth and set the blade within easy reach. A musty smell lingered inside the cabin, and the timber boards groaned like a crone pressed down by age.

I stretched on my back, using my left hand for a pillow, while my right found Lumi's heart. I took it out of my pocket and placed it on my chest. It was the size of a clenched fist and felt solid and cold against my skin. Blue veins spread across it in a set of branching rivers, forcing dark blood through the crystal that expanded and contracted in the way of a human heart. The rhythmical sound of its beating soothed my mind and woke the memories of Lumi. We were both cursed. She was forced into a heartless existence, and I would be stripped of my soul. I thought of her bluish lips sealed in silence, her obsidian hair, and her striking eyes. It was the storming blue in them that led me astray, mesmerised me, and made me want to follow her to the edge of the world.

My eyelids grew heavy, and I forced them open. I feared the night, for it was a realm of shrieking nightmares, but the pull of sleep was too strong to resist. It split my consciousness in two; one part dreaming, the other fighting to stay awake. I struggled to recall a time when I slept easy. Since the witches of Sur laid claim on my soul, my dreams conjured up images of Hrafn—the white raven that granted the two witches a gift of foresight. He poised his curved beak over Kylfa's eye, but the witch didn't shrink from it. Worse, she welcomed it. I watched in horror as the raven plunged the beak into her socket. The eye popped under the pressure, turning the cavity into a bloody mass. Hrafn screeched and stabbed again, only this time it wasn't Kylfa's eye he aimed for but mine. The pain was greater than Hyllus's magic and more revolting than Trofn's teeth against my skin.

'It's a reminder of your oath,' Trofn whispered and cackled.

I screamed, and the primal quality of the sound jolted me awake. My left eye twitched, and my nostrils flared like that of a horse in flight. I clapped my hands over my ears, trying to silence the remnants of that ancient voice. The walls of the cabin pressed down on me, and Lumi's heart pounded against my chest. I picked it up and pressed it to my forehead. The ship rocked on the waves like a dancer led by a skilful hand while the silver light of the moon pointed at me through the round window. Sweat drenched my shirt and the stink of it made me think of Elizan, the village where I first tested my sword in battle, and where Hyllus scorched my father with his magic. His death was the reason I'd damned my soul. I'd offered it to the witches of Sur in exchange for the power to kill Hyllus. Njall urged me to refuse them, but it was the only way to avenge Father. The witches fulfilled their end of the bargain, and soon I'd have to fulfil mine.

When my breath returned to its natural rhythm, Lumi's heart resumed its steady beat. I placed it back into my pocket—a cold rock against my warm chest. I rolled up my sleeve and pressed my palm against the symbol on my right wrist. Trofn used her magic to place it there and imbued it with a throbbing pain that was everlasting, pulsing under my skin like some black creature. The mark was a circle with a black eye in its centre. A series of lines connected the two. It served as a reminder of the covenant I'd forged.

Kylfa said that on the Night of Norrsken, Valgsi's soul would absorb Skaldir's magic and use it to wake the goddess from her dream. Two centuries ago, the mages from the Lost City of Antaya summoned Skaldir to help them win the battle against humankind, but the goddess did not come bearing gifts. Her wrath was mightier than their plight, and she unleashed it upon the world. The raging goddess crashed and burned everything until her brothers, Yldir and Agtarr, lured her to sleep and spent their powers to keep her dreaming. The witches desired my soul, for once surrendered, it'd feed the evil dwelling in the forests of Sur. Trofn marked me with black arts, and there'd be no cheating my way out of it. The witch said when the time came, I'd return to Sur by free will. What would happen to me after that, I couldn't tell.

I reached for my sword. The green jewel embedded into the rain-guard glinted in the dark like a jealous eye. My father knew the origin of the blade, but he concealed it from me, hiding behind the excuse of protecting his son. Perhaps he believed the lie would keep me safe, but it was foolish, and for all my love for him, his actions planted a seed of resentment in my heart. I ran my fingers across the ancient symbols etched into the fuller. They were inscribed by the Goddess of Destruction so that one day the Valgsi could use the script to stir her from her slumber.

I was the one who bore Skaldir's mark, the Valgsi she so eagerly awaited, destined to bring the world to ruin. Fjola accused me of ignorance, of evading my responsibilities, but to trust the tale was to accept my fate, and I wasn't willing to do that. No matter how much my friends fretted about the future, I was determined that on the Night of Norrsken, I'd resist Skaldir's call by the power of my free will. With no awakening, my soul would remain pure and thus useless to the witches. By rejecting my fate as the Valgsi, I'd save my soul. Or so I hoped.

III

'Jarin, look,' Fjola said in a voice sparkling with excitement.

To escape the stuffiness of our cabins, all four of us were out on the deck. The summer tried to reassert itself once more, resulting in a scorching day. My clothes stuck to my body like a second skin, and my nose was full of the sultry air. A dark stain bloomed on the back of Fjola's green shirt, and judging by her flushed cheeks, she struggled with the heat as much as I did. Njall manned the wheel, a waterskin in one hand. He drew his hair into a coil at the top of his head, exposing a heat rash on his neck. Mirable sat in a triangle of shade cast by the prow, his eyes half-closed, trousers rolled up to his knees, displaying a set of hairy legs. His right palm flapped like a fan in front of his face, and his expression was that of a man who relished the heat.

Fjola leaned on the railing, squinting into the distance, where the heat turned the air into a shifting haze. I dreamed of the day our feet would touched solid land. Time spent at sea convinced me I wasn't cut out for the life of a sailor. I missed Blixt, my beloved horse, and the icy wind on my face as we raced through the plains of Nordur. Torgal promised me he'd look after him until I came back, but some days I wondered if that return was a fool's wish. After all, no ship had ever come back from the voyage to Shinpi.

I crossed the deck to see the cause of Fjola's excitement. My back ached from the lack of exercise and days of stillness. There was a scant comfort to be had on a ship. Njall took it upon himself to ensure we could still wield weapons when we arrived at our destination, and I welcomed his efforts to keep us on our feet. Without this practice, the inertia would've been impossible to bear. Only Mirable shied away from our gatherings. He gave an excuse that sleep was more essential than flapping your arms on the deck at the crack of dawn, so he did not wish to be disturbed. I doubted his reasons. Merchants didn't strike me as people who snored until midday, and Mirable himself would often remark that coins didn't fall into the hands of those unwilling to work for them. On a few occasions, I caught him mumbling to himself when apart from the others, but when I ventured to ask, he'd shrug his shoulders and scold me for prying.

I followed Fjola's gaze and my breath caught. 'Do you think this is it?'

'It must be,' she said. Her eyes shone like green gems in my mother's jewellery box. She ushered Njall and Mirable to join us.

Visible in the distance was a dark line that peaked and fell in an unmistakable shape of a mountain range. It was only a shadow concealed behind the cloud of heat, but it was there, a sign we were nearing solid land.

'Yldir be praised,' Njall said. His shoulders came up, as if an immense weight lifted off them.

Mirable wetted his lips. 'So it is true.' He wrapped his hands around the taffrail until his brown knuckles turned white.

'We must prepare,' Njall said. 'Make ready your weapons.'

'A sure way to make enemies,' Mirable said. 'It's a pity my gold is at the bottom of the Great Atlantic.'

I was eager to get this voyage over with, but the voice of my father sounded in my ears, advising caution. 'Violence should be our last resort. Can you see the harbour?'

Njall shielded his eyes with his hand and scanned the horizon.

'It may be a little late for that,' Fjola said.

I blinked against the sun. Like a dark flower, a boat blossomed into view. Even from a distance, I glimpsed the peculiar structure of its sails, pregnant with the wind. They were rectangular and shaped like a gable roof tilted sideways. Their colour reminded me of the yellowing scrolls in Stromhold's library. The ship slit through the waves at a steady speed, and watching it advance, my mind ran through the possibilities. In Nordur, people thought of Shinpi as a land of legends—a view reinforced by the number of ships that put to sea in search of the place only to vanish without a trace. A veil of mystery enveloped Shinpi, and if I was to believe Lumi's words, Goro-Khan, her master and the man who played a part in the destruction of Stromhold, ruled this land.

My right hand curled around the hilt of my sword, while the fingers of my left sought after the coolness of Lumi's heart. The months of sailing had bridged the gap between us, and I could smell vengeance in the air. First, I'd seek her out and force the truth from those blue lips, and then I'd hunt Goro-Khan and drive my father's blade through his heart. So help me Agtarr.

The oars of the incoming ship splashed the ocean's surface like an array of slender fingers. A figurehead was affixed to the bow, and there was no mistaking that angry scowl—Skaldir, the Goddess of Destruction, with her hair carved into thick braids. This representation of the goddess wore a circlet sculpted into a crescent moon. Skaldir's hand rested on the hilt of a sword—the blade of Stromhold Guardians—the same weapon I inherited from my father. At the opposite end to the prow, a small green sail flapped in the breeze. The ship itself curved outwards and lacked the narrow prongs typical to the Nordern vessels.

A score of men dressed in green lined the deck. They reminded me of wooden figurines my father kept in his study and used to mark Varl's movements on the map of Nordur. As the ship drew closer, I could make out the leather scales of their armour, fused together to form a protective shield over the upper half of the body. Tied around the waist, wide iron plates secured the lower half. The men's headgear resembled a cone decorated with a jade crescent. When their ship anchored parallel to ours, I looked into the faces of these lifeless warriors and my mind prickled with recognition. Their features bore a resemblance to Lumi's—eyes lifted at the corners and thin lips locked into a straight line. The only difference between them was the skin colour; hers was icy-pale, while theirs a shade of desert sand.

I raised my hand in greeting, but the men of Shinpi did not return the gesture.

'They don't look a friendly bunch,' Mirable said, opening his palms wide. 'We come in peace to bask in Shinpi's beauty. We have no coins to offer, but—'

I nudged him with my elbow. This was not the time for elaborate speeches. Mirable scowled and crossed his hands over his chest.

Njall and I exchanged glances, and in his face I read the same unease.

With her fingers on her daggers, Fjola took a step back.

Five of Shinpi's men leaped onto our deck. The iron plates of their armour sent a shiver through the air. One of them spoke in a high-pitched tone, but the words came out in a jumble of unfamiliar syllables. I shook my head in response, berating myself for my lack of foresight. When I travelled to Vester in pursuit of Hyllus, I was familiar with the language of my enemies, but no man in Hvitur, or the whole Nordur, knew the tongue of Shinpi. Instead of rushing into the unknown, I should've listened to Torgal and put more effort into understanding the ways of my enemies. Marus, the scholar who served my uncle, suggested a journey to Eydimork Sands in search of answers about the mysterious land of Shinpi, but I refused him. Now, listening to the unfamiliar string of words, I regretted my hasty departure.

'You're a merchant,' Fjola said to Mirable. 'Do something.'

He pushed out his lower lip. 'I was trained to haggle not to study tongues of the world.'

'But you know ours.'

'I had business in Nordur.'

I hissed at them. 'Quiet.' Faced with this threat, we had to stand united and not be seen squabbling.

The men watched our exchange with stony expressions. No muscle twitched on their faces, making it impossible to guess their intent. Curved, single-edged blades with long hilts hung at their sides. I had no doubt these men would use them if we didn't explain our business here.

As if reading my thoughts, Mirable stepped forward, and this time I said nothing to stop him. He placed his palm against his chest and bowed so deep that the strands of his turban brushed the deck. The warriors showed no reaction to this demonstration of respect, but in his cheery fashion, Mirable offered them a wide grin. He swept his left hand at us, pointing at the shore with his right. Witnessing his gestures brought back memories of my childhood. When Lumi came to live with us, she pretended to be mute, and I was the one making words with my fingers. We developed our own silent language. It was like sharing a sweet secret, but when the curtain of her deceit fell away, the sweetness turned sour.

Mirable went on flapping his arms; first at the warriors, then at us, and back at Shinpi. At first, the men regarded his display with flat eyes, but a short time later, their facial expressions changed from indifference to disgust. One warrior wrinkled his nose, as if Mirable's gesticulations brought about an offensive smell. A man next to him curled his lip.

'I don't think it's working,' I said.

'Like a charm,' Mirable answered, offering another bow.

The warrior closest to him grabbed his turban and pulled him up. He issued a chain of words that sounded like an order. In response, his companion handed him a set of iron shackles. At the sight of them Mirable began to tremble. His eyes grew so large it was a wonder they didn't roll out of their sockets.

'Anything but this,' he pleaded, pressing his palms together.

The warrior was unmoved by his plea and fastened the iron around Mirable's wrists. Mirable shrieked, and my chest squeezed at the sound. When I first travelled to Vester in search of the witches, Mirable showed me the way to Sur. We parted at the crossroads where he promised to wait for me, but when I returned, there was no sign of the merchant. Later I'd learned that Hyllus's Varls apprehended Mirable and dragged him away into the Citadel of Vester. When I found him weeks later, Hyllus's foul magic was already at work inside of my friend's body, twisting and changing his muscles and organs. I wasn't there to stop it in time, but I was here now, and I refused to stand idle.

Assuming the warrior's stance, I drew my sword. The blade of Stromhold Guardians shimmered with green light. Sometimes I wondered if it was alive, working its way into me like a scorpion's stinger, for brandishing it filled me with sick pleasure. Njall and Fjola followed suit by drawing their weapons. Their presence bolstered my courage. Seeing our readiness to make a stand, Mirable struggled against the shackles.

The Shinpi's men took a step back and drew blades that looked nothing like Nordern weapons. They held them in both hands, and judging by their balanced posture, knew how to make them lethal. Five of them, plus another score on their ship, against the three of us—the odds were in their favour.

Emboldened by the Skaldir's magic cursing through my blade, I charged.

My godly sword clanged against the foreign weapon, sending tremors up my arm. I pushed against the warrior with force, but the man never lost his balance. The edge of his blade slid down my steel with a shower of tiny sparks.

We sprang away from each other.

Out of the corner of my eye, I glimpsed Njall with his spear poised against the two warriors. Fjola backed away. The steel flashed in her hands like two vipers ready to inflict pain, but the length of the foreign blades made it difficult for her to get close enough to use the daggers.

Mirable twisted under the arm of the man who held him, and with one swift motion, wrapped the chains of his shackles around the warrior's neck. The man cried out. As the merchant tightened his grip on the iron, his arms bulged through the layers of clothing.

Heartened by this sudden display of strength on Mirable's part, I uttered a battle cry and let the rage take over me.

Like an incoming tide, adrenaline surged through my muscles, washing away all traces of hesitation, and tripling my strength. A veil of green mist obscured my vision, and my head pounded like a drum. The images around me dissolved: the Great Atlantic, both ships, and the shores of Shinpi all faded away. My senses screamed blood, and I let Skaldir's wrath guide my sword.

I stabbed at the warrior.

Standing little chance against this unnatural strength, the man lost his balance and fell over backwards. He gasped, and tendons stood out on his neck. His expression sent a current of excitement through me. Visible through the shimmer of green, the figurehead of Skaldir bared her teeth. Her expression was that of a vulture descending to feed on corpses, while the blade in my hand thrummed with her need to destroy.

I laughed, bringing the sword down.

Darkness came next, as something sinister possessed my body and mind. Its need to dominate and punish was stronger than any human desire, and it filled my soul with the song of violence. To enter Shinpi was my right, and no man would stand between me and vengeance. As I delivered thrust after thrust, Agtarr's Warrior of Death rode on my shoulder, while the Goddess of Destruction whispered her encouragement.

I couldn't tell how long it lasted, but when I finally regained my senses, five of Shinpi's men lay in a heap of flesh and bone at my feet. More warriors sprang onboard from the adjacent ship. One had his arm wrapped around my neck, and two of his comrades held my wrists in a tight clasp. Everyone, including my friends, stared at me. When that ancient rage took over, the warriors must've overpowered all three of them and forced them to their knees. Even Mirable sat on the deck, his fists pressed to his temples, panting like a beast in the midday heat.

'Fight them,' I shouted, spittle flying from my lips. The world was a hue of green, and I wanted to slice the arms of those who held me hostage, but their grip on me was iron, and no matter how hard I strained, I couldn't get free. Another warrior made a leap from their ship to ours and attempted to pry the weapon from my hand. I shrieked at him, and my fingers tightened around the hilt until it felt like they'd snap under the pressure.

The man doubled his efforts. He stabbed my knuckles with a pocketknife, and the pain loosened my hold just enough for him to rip the blade free. The sound that came out of me wasn't a cry of defeat, but a guttural howl that would put the fiercest of Varls to shame.

'The sword is mine,' I roared. All rational thought was gone. Father's blade was the only thing that mattered. Apart from a small tease from Fjola on our way to Vester months ago, no one ever tried to stand between me and my sword. It was a keepsake, the source of my pride, and the only memory of my father I had left. I was the Guardian of Stromhold, and the blade was mine by right.

I snapped my head forward then back with such force that it connected with the nose of the warrior behind me. A sickening crunch filled my ears, and the grip around my neck loosened. I ripped my right hand free and thrust my elbow into the chin of my other captor.

He uttered a sharp cry.

I twisted to the side, kicking the third man, and creating an opening to freedom.

I lunged after my sword, but before I could grab it, a boot slammed into my shin. The force knocked me sprawling onto the deck. My chin hit the timber, sending waves of pain through my jaw. The weight of a heavy heel pressed upon my back. My hand reached for the sword, but another boot stomped on it. I laid there, the right side of my face pinned against the deck, my mood darker than the Agtarr's Chamber, my mind burning. I made another attempt at freedom, but something blunt struck the back of my head and a shawl of blackness wrapped itself around me.

IV

I came back to my senses with a deep groan and a taste of copper in my mouth. The back of my skull throbbed, and my nostrils filled with a stink of bodily odours—a revolting mixture of puke, urine, and faeces. I sat up, trying to focus on something other than nausea that rolled in my stomach like a mammoth seal.

'Thank the Yldir,' Mirable said. 'I feared you were gone for good.'

My vision cleared enough for me to read the frown of worry trapped in the grooves of his face. I tried to piece together the events that transpired, but my mind stumbled over them. When we reached the shores of Shinpi, the guards apprehended us. A memory of a struggle… then nothing. I shook my head to dispel the fog. 'What happened?'

'Perhaps it's for the best that you don't remember. Your reckless bravery tossed us in this jail.' Mirable shook his hands—a set of iron shackles bound them. 'This isn't an ordinary prison.'

The cell was a hollow box, with a layer of squalid straw covering the floor, which explained the reek of human excrement. It lacked windows of any kind, and the only way to freedom was through a door fashioned from thick wooden bars.

Affixed to the right wall was a set of fetters connected by a rusty chain, which made me think of Varls shackled in the Citadel of Vester. Above them, the only source of light didn't come from a simple lantern but a globe of energy that burned atop a shallow dish, casting a greenish glow over the stone walls.

Mirable followed my gaze and recoiled. 'It's foul.'

'We're in the right place,' I said, remembering the figurehead of Skaldir. It seemed the people of Shinpi worshipped the Goddess of Destruction and used her arts as a source of light. The laws of Nordur forbade the use of magic, and seeing it at work stiffened the hair on the nape of my neck. I still remembered the trouble Lumi had caused with her frosty tricks, for which Mother forever admonished her.

'I wouldn't go as far as the *right* place,' Mirable said.

'Do you know what happened to Njall and Fjola?'

'We were separated. They must be here somewhere, but I can't see anything beyond those bars.' His bottom lip quivered. 'They stripped me of my turban.'

Indeed, Mirable's headwear was gone, leaving his hair exposed in a mass of curls. 'First, we'll find the others, and then we'll recover your turban,' I said, testing my strength against the shackles on my wrists.

Mirable grabbed my hands. 'Truly?'

I nodded. His solid grip made a job of pulling them free. The memory of him apprehending the Shinpi guard flashed before my eyes—the way he twisted from the man's grasp would've impressed any warrior in Stromhold. I considered him for a moment. 'Are you well?'

He rolled his eyes. 'At a time like this? Look around, we're trapped here, in a place where people quack in a tongue that sends even my mind into a dizzying spin. For all we know, our friends might be dead, and you're worried about a small display of strength.' He pressed his fists to his temples. 'Imprisoned, with all my possessions at the bottom of the Great Atlantic. If any of those clods at the Merchant's Circle got a whiff of this, there'd be no end to their mockery.'

'Fjola and Njall aren't afflicted by Hyllus's magic. You're trying to deny it, but I saw you fight against the crystal giants and the way you pinned that man on the deck… Something's changing inside you, but you refuse to speak of it. Why?'

'It's a curious question from someone who's challenging his own destiny.'

I had a better chance at getting an answer from Blixt. 'Fine, have it your way,' I said, patting the front of my shirt. To my dismay, Lumi's heart was gone, and so was my sword.

'They took it, along with my turban and most of our clothes.'

I got to my feet, and the cell swivelled. I closed my eyes to regain balance. When the dizziness faded, I walked to the wooden bars and pressed my face into the gap between them. The shadows consumed the corridor beyond. 'Fjola,' I whispered into the dark.

No answer.

I clenched the bars tighter. They had no right to take my sword, not to mention the heart I'd managed to keep safe throughout the storms of our journey here. The thought of it shattered by the reckless men who knew nothing of its value sent a current of panic through me. What's worse, the absence of it left an aching void. I'd grown so accustomed to the constant beat inside my pocket that stillness felt like a prelude to death. I needed something other than my defeat to focus on, and since I got my friends into this plight, I had to get them out.

'Tell me exactly what happened,' I said, inspecting the walls. If my father found himself imprisoned, his priority would be to understand the world of his enemies. I didn't have his blade, but I still had the memories of him to guide me. The stone felt rough beneath my fingers, full of cracks and ridges. Near the fetters, claw-like indentations scarred the wall as if someone, or something, had tried to scratch its way to the orb of green light.

‘After you fell unconscious, the guards chained us and brought us here.’

‘Have you seen much of Shinpi?’

Mirable shook his head. ‘They fastened sacks over our heads, but I smelt fish and heard people talking. From the way their voices rose and fell, I’m certain they were haggling.’ His eyes glazed over. ‘If I understood the language, I’d teach them a thing or two.’

‘A market then?’

‘And a lively one at that.’ That dreamy look stole over his face again. ‘I could almost taste salted fish on my tongue, feel the silk—’

‘None of this is useful.’ I rattled the chain binding my wrists. ‘We must find a way to get these off. Look for something sharp. A loose nail, a splinter, anything that would help pry open the locks.’

We searched the cell inch by inch and came up empty. I ran my hands up and down the prison bars, hoping for a sliver of wood, but their surface was smoother than the inside of a seashell.

‘It’s no use,’ Mirable said, flopping back onto the floor.

I sat beside him. The silence stretched between us, flat and hopeless. It was unnatural to be locked in prison this quiet. I expected to hear other prisoners or guards, but the place lacked any signs of activity. The orb glowed in its dish—a green eye that made me think of the sneering goddess. An idea formed in my mind, but even as it took shape, I had to take caution in how I voiced it.

I leaned towards Mirable. 'There's one thing we could try.'

He blinked but said nothing.

'I know how much you detest the idea of transformation, and if it wasn't for the gravity of the situation, I'd never ask it of you—'

'Let me stop you there,' Mirable said, showing me the flat of his palm. His lifelines were a shade darker than the surrounding skin, like trails on a leather map. 'Don't you think I've suffered enough? You insist on the truth, but have you ever stopped to consider my feelings?'

The heat caught the tips of my ears and burned down my neck as I berated myself for even entertaining the idea that Mirable's transformation could be our salvation. He was right to be angry with me. Since our escape from Vester, I did nothing but question the changes in his behaviour, seeking clues to confirm my suspicions.

'Since that forsaken night in the Citadel of Vester, I no longer feel like myself,' Mirable said, and the misery in his voice reached the depths of my damned soul. 'I'm tainted. My ill fate will follow me into the afterlife, and the gates of Himinn will remain shut to me. I'll turn into an outcast, eschewed by the living and shunned by the gods.'

'Mirable…'

He glared at me. 'You wish to know what ails me and insist on prodding this wound, so let me satisfy your curiosity.' He sprang to his feet and pulled his shirt over his head. Deep blotches marked the skin of his upper torso. At first glance, they looked like simple bruises one can get from an unlucky fall down a staircase, but upon closer inspection, there was nothing ordinary about them. The marks I took for bruises were four inward-growing tumours. The smaller three inhabited his chest in a cluster of black lesions, with the largest of them blooming on his abdomen, its centre pulsing with dark matter. More tumours grew on his arms, and his flesh bunched around them, exposing a swelling of veins as dark as those on Lumi's heart. I had an inkling about Mirable's change, but seeing the effects of Hyllus's magic with my own eyes shook me to the core. My muscles tightened, and my first instinct was to recoil, but I resisted the urge.

Mirable must've spied something in my face because he turned around and fished for his shirt in the straw. By doing so, he exposed his back, and at the sight of the shrivelled skin and protruding discs of his spine, I had to stifle a gasp. The tumours on his chest and abdomen pulled the flesh, stretching the skin on his back. It was easy to imagine that with time the ongoing transformation would twist his back further, forcing him to use his arms for support. Like the Varls of Elizan, my friend would turn into a four-legged creature with an unparalleled sense of smell but little in terms of human sensitivities.

Mirable put his shirt back on, letting the loose material conceal the horrors that lurked beneath. 'I'm becoming one of them, turning into a mindless Varl, and no amount of pity from you will change that. My sight will deteriorate, and to compensate for that loss, my smell will become dominant. Who knows, maybe it'd help me sniff out profitable bargains for you.' The cell filled with the sound of his bitter laughter. 'Mirable, Jarin's trusted hound. It has a nice ring to it, don't you think?'

I sprang to my feet and put a hand on his shoulder. 'Don't say such things. It may be true that you're turning into a Varl, but it changes nothing in terms of our friendship. I'll never forget our first meeting and your poor attempts at saving my hide from those rogues in the tavern.' The memory made us both chuckle, but then my voice grew serious. 'It hurts to see you this way, but I'm glad it's no longer a secret. I was lost in my pursuits and failed to see your suffering for what it truly was. When we get out of here, I promise to do everything in my power to find the cure.' The moment I uttered the words, a memory of another promise whispered in my ear, the one I made to Lumi when she was still pure and innocent. To break the spell and give her voice back. Little did I know she wasn't the one who needed saving. I squeezed Mirable's shoulder. 'We'll stop the transformation before it's too late.'

'That's the reason I'm here. If there's a cure for this wretched change, Shinpi is the place to look.' He wrapped his hand around his right bicep. 'But I fear it's too late. You saw the tumours…'

'As long as you remain Mirable, the merchant we've grown to love, it's not too late.'

His deep-brown eyes filled with tears, and he embraced me. I hugged him back. The bones of his spine pressed against my palm, and I pushed down on them. I wanted to remember my friend's pain and the promise I'd made.

A lone cackle echoed inside my head. '*How can you save the soul of another if you cannot save your own, Valgsi…?'*

I startled. It was Trofn's voice. The mark on my wrist throbbed and tingled—a reminder of the curse the witch placed upon me. My days were numbered, but as long as I had enough of them to help my friend, it was all worth it.

'Get out of my head, witch,' I said under my breath.

Mirable released me from his grip. Tears left trails on his cheeks. 'What was that?'

'We'll find a way to stop the transformation. Together.'

He nodded and inspected his hands. 'I can break these chains.'

'Are you sure?'

He curled his hands into fists. As his concentration deepened, the veins on his neck stood out, and the tip of his tongue poked through his lips. His chest expanded with a large intake of breath, and then stilled. He strained against the links that connected the chain to the shackles, the beads of sweat glistening on his temples. The iron groaned and gave way with a sharp snap.

'There,' Mirable said, dangling the loose chain in front of me. Despite the origin of his strength, his voice rang with pride. 'Your turn.'

He set to work on my hands, and a moment later, another snap announced my freedom.

'You did well,' I said.

'Don't thank me yet. We still have the bars to conquer.' His shoulders hunched. 'Every time I use this strength, I'm choosing the Varl in me. I detest magic with all my heart. I always have, yet I'm the one with affliction. If my mother saw me now, she'd disown me. Do you know what it means for a merchant to be stripped of his father's name?' His hand travelled to where his turban used to be to find a sea of curls in its place. 'I'd rather fall into the arms of the serena than have this right taken from me.'

I searched for the words to comfort him, but each of them rang hollow. Mirable was transforming into something foul, a creature designed to follow orders and execute them with the help of its primary instincts. We fought enough Varls to know they had no need for logic or compassion. Their main task was to stalk the prey and use their mighty jaws to tear it to pieces. But who would become the merchant's prey, and by whose orders? The way Mirable absorbed Hyllus's magic impressed the mage, but my pact with the witches ensured he wasn't here to witness his finest creation. The thought filled me with a deep sense of satisfaction.

'We shouldn't let the magic defeat us,' I said. 'We're alive, and to some extent, still in charge of our thoughts and actions. Let's put our energies into finding the way out of this stinking pit, and then help our friends do the same.'

Mirable wiped his eyes with the back of his palm. 'You're right, but before we move on, I need to ask a favour.'

I felt myself stiffen. It never boded well when those closest to you asked favours in that tone of voice.

'If I lose myself, promise me I won't be running loose. We must protect the market streets from beasts.'

'Why are you asking this of me?' My mind worked on the reasons to refuse him. I killed my share of Varls, and it was a loathsome task, but unlike Mirable, those Varls were just creatures to me.

'You and I, we went through much together. You're the only one who can do it. Even though it pains me to say it, there's darkness in you, and I hope to appeal to it when the time comes. Fjola and Njall are too noble. They'd never harm me.'

His words fell like an axe. 'You believe *I* would?'

'I saw what that sword did to you on the deck. It possessed your mind and body. Watching you fight was like watching Skaldir herself. Her fury drives that blade, and you're her conduit.'

I rolled my eyes at him. 'Enough with the Valgsi nonsense.'

'It's not for me to convince you otherwise, but the longer you deny your own self, the more power you give to those who control it. My request is simple—when the time comes, use your sword to cut me down.' His round eyes peered into mine. 'I need your word.'

'Do not make promises you cannot keep, Valgsi…'

The voice of the witch trickled like ancient poison, but I refused to be overcome by it. I clasped hands with Mirable and squeezed hard. 'If, and only *if,* it comes to it.'

A deep sigh escaped him, and he looked up at the ceiling. 'Gods have blessed and cursed me in equal measure.'

I didn't feel so blessed. He exacted a promise, that if fulfilled, would leave a dark stain on my conscience, not to mention the heavy burden of grief I'd be forced to carry for the rest of my days. Mirable was like family, so how would Agtarr judge my actions? Would he consider them a provision of relief or murder of kin? I hoped I'd never need to find out.

I turned my attention to the cell door. 'Will you manage?'

'I'll certainly try.' He crossed the room and wrapped his fingers around the bars, then just stood there, his right ear cocked to one side.

'In need of help?' I asked after a few beats of stillness.

'Shhh… I think there's someone here with us.'

I walked to stand beside him, listening to the sound of silence. 'Maybe it's your imagination playing tricks on you.'

He ignored my remark and pressed his face further through the gap.

Now I could hear it too—shuffling footsteps.

'Guards?' I whispered.

We backed away from the door, adopting a defensive stance. Mirable had the Varl to aid him, but I only had my naked fists. My fingers itched for the hilt to wrap around, and I clenched them tighter.

The sound of footfalls drew closer.

V

Fjola pressed her forehead against the wooden bars, trying to see into the adjacent cell. The absence of sound made her assume it was empty. Or worse. 'Do you think they're dead?'

Njall sat with his back to the wall, beads of sweat glistening in the dips of his temples. Jarin's wound wasn't deep, but judging by the frown on his face, it caused him a great deal of discomfort. If they were in Hvitur, he'd call it a scratch, but here, far from the Nordern healers, the recovery would take longer. Back on the ship, Fjola did all she could for him with the supply of herbs she brought from Hvitur, but the guards took them along with their weapons, leaving her brother with no choice but to endure the pain.

'Doubt it,' he said.

Sometimes she wished she had a sister instead, or at least a sibling who spoke more than three words at a time. She glanced at the glowing orb in the corner of their cell, and the leafy glow sent gooseflesh crawling up her arms. Her senses urged her to put as much distance as she could between herself and the magic, but the confines of the cell didn't give her much choice. She sighed and paced the length of the room.

Njall's brow furrowed. 'Safeguard your energy.'

Fjola scraped a hand over her face. Motion made it feel like she was doing something, and however irrational the thought, she was sure the moment she stilled, her skull would explode from the tension. 'I can't just sit here pretending all is well.'

'I'm not asking you to.' His eyes fell on the burning orb, and he spat. 'Seeing how far we strayed from our laws, I'm surprised Agtarr is keeping us alive.'

'We haven't used the magic.'

'Our presence here is enough to anger the gods.'

She shared his distaste but understood that to accomplish some tasks one had to forgo the laws. 'He's going after our enemy. Those who worshipped Skaldir brought the Day of Judgement, and we can't let the mages repeat the same mistakes. Besides, if this Goro-Khan exists, he needs to pay for what he did to Skari and all those who died by Hyllus's hand.'

'Jarin's refusal of his fate concerns me more than Goro-Khan.'

'I believe in him.' Despite their quarrels, she trusted that in the end, Jarin would make the right choice. 'To free Nordur from the Varls, he offered his soul. I can't think of a greater sacrifice.'

Njall grunted and closed his eyes. Fjola slumped next to him, her back pressed against the wall. The chill from the stone seeped through her clothes, making her shiver. A child of Nordur, she was used to the cold, but unlike the sharp air of her homeland, the air in the prison was dank and musty. In the glowing light, her brother's skin looked sallow, and she felt a stab of concern.

'Let me look at it.' She reached for the makeshift band she had tied over his thigh prior to their capture. Dried blood coloured the material dark red.

Njall caught her hand, his palm sleek with sweat. 'Best leave it alone lest it starts bleeding again.'

She shrugged but did as he asked. Her brother endured much greater pain when Skari's father maimed his face.

After a few moments of silence, Njall said, 'If the witch has her way, you know what will become of him.'

The words startled her. She never stopped to consider the full extent of Jarin's oath. The soul was a gift from the God of Life, no human could exist without it, and by giving it away, Jarin lost his right to enter Himinn. Her heart went out to him, and for the first time, she felt a pang of guilt because her obsession with the demon made her blind to Jarin's plight. Consumed with the need to see the crystal heart shattered, she lost sight of his burden. Passionate but selfish, the witch told her. Could it be the crone was right? Fjola pressed her palm against her heated cheek. Since the moment they left Hvitur, she had wallowed in self-pity, rejecting Jarin's attempts to pacify her, and worse, deflecting his kindness with hurtful scorn. Her mouth filled with a bitter tang.

'I failed him,' she said.

'You care for him. It's easy to get lost in the thicket of emotions.' His words came as a surprise because her brother wasn't one to bear his heart.

'While *she* holds the spell over him, there's no future for us.'

'It's not for you to judge his choices. Don't make Skari's mistake.'

Fjola flinched. Skari's name came wrapped in layers of guilt she could never hope to unravel. The memories of him burned every part of her, and there was no way to douse the flames, for the one who could grant her forgiveness was long dead, his corpse torn apart by the Varls, left to rot in the dank corridors of the citadel. She refused Skari at every turn, and when he blamed Jarin for her lack of affection, she laughed in his face. Now she was forced to drink her own medicine and endure its sour taste.

'A heavy weight rests on Jarin's shoulders,' Njall said. 'If he fails, there'll be no future for any of us.'

The words were cruel, but Fjola couldn't deny the truth of them. Their days were numbered, and none of them had the power to see into the future. Not even Valgsi. The realisation filled her heart with a new resolve. No more wallowing. No more jealousy. Jarin was free to love whomever he wished, and she'd stand by him to the very end, whatever that end might be.

Fjola didn't know how many days she had left with him, and she refused to sacrifice another one to anger and resentment. Let him chase the demons and fight his battles. Jarin was the Guardian of Stromhold, and her duty was to follow him. Fjola got to her feet and wrapped her fingers around the bars. All of them were trapped in their own prisons, but the key to unlocking hers was within her grasp. To get it, all she had to do was stay true to her heart.

VI

I drew my breath and held it. To my left, Mirable uttered a growl that stirred the hair on the nape of my neck. I was glad to have him on my side, feeling pity for any guard unfortunate enough to cross him. Mirable didn't need weapons. The power he so despised coursed through his muscles, and even as he admonished the source of it, it granted him unparalleled strength. The footsteps halted on the other side of the wall. I balled my fists tighter, jerking them higher. My last brawl was the scuffle in the tavern where Mirable and I first met, seemingly a lifetime ago. Everything was different then—my mother alive and my foolish heart still prey to Lumi's illusions.

The intruder stepped into view. Enfolded in a black cloak, face concealed by a hood, the stranger approached the cell door. Hovering there for a moment, the visitor then threw a glance over their shoulder.

Mirable and I looked at each other.

Satisfied by whatever had drawn their attention, the intruder retrieved a set of keys from one of the robe's pockets. They jangled—the sound impossibly loud in a tense stillness. I glimpsed a pale hand as it tried each key in the lock. I craned my neck, straining to see into the shadows of the hood. It made me think of Trofn, the witch with no face who cursed my soul.

‘Do you mean us harm?’ Mirable asked in a trembling voice. A quivering chin replaced the mighty Varl that gave way to a simple merchant. I wished he had better control over the two. To show your fear in the enemy’s presence was the warrior’s greatest sin. Feel it, yes, but keep your wits about you while measuring your chances against your foe. These were my father’s words, and I’d give anything to have him at my side. His task was to defend Nordur from the Varls plaguing our villages, and like the true Guardian of Stromhold, he never faltered. If my companions knew him, they’d never have agreed to follow his doubt-riddled weakling of a son.

The door to our prison cell creaked open, and the figure threw the keys through the gap. They clattered across the floor and tangled in the filthy straw. Mirable lunged after them, and I cursed under my breath. It could’ve been a trap, an attempt at misleading us with a false promise of freedom. As the stranger turned away, something blue flashed between the folds of the robe’s hood. The mysterious figure hurried down the corridor, and I followed, sprinting to catch up. Halfway down, I was able to grasp a hand, and the chill pierced me like an ice shard.

The intruder struggled in my grip, but I held on, forcing them to face me.

‘You shouldn’t have come, Jarin Olversson,’ the familiar voice said, and all at once, my mind flooded with memories: knee-deep snow, Stromhold gates ajar like a mouth of a giant, inviting the fool to taste the horrors beyond, Argil's body splayed across the threshold to my mother's chamber, and Mother, with her glassy stare, precious life frozen by the magic that would never thaw.

'It's you,' I said, and the long-suppressed pain exploded anew in my chest. I snatched the hood with my free hand, pulling it down to reveal Lumi's face. Her hair spilled across her shoulders in a thick and lustrous mass, as black as Agtarr's cowl. Lumi's eyes met mine, and the familiar blue ignited in them. I blinked at the shapes swirling in the sapphire of her irises, alluring and dangerous. Willing them to still was like trying to catch a rushing stream, the water so alive between your fingers but impossible to grab hold of. When my father brought her inside the walls of Stromhold, I felt the effects of Lumi's magic firsthand. She mesmerised me, and I was still helpless in the wake of her power. Her soul was a blizzard, a raging snowstorm of frozen dreams. Lumi lured me into it, and I followed without question, only to find myself lost in the white plains, with no hope of finding a way out, for every path I carved for myself led me back to her.

Unable to stop myself, I reached out to touch the pale of her cheek, her skin under my fingers icy and smooth like freshly fallen snow.

'Why?' I asked. A great lump of flesh swelled in my throat, arresting the reminder of my words.

Lumi parted her bluish lips as if to scold me, but no sound escaped them. She blinked instead, and the spell binding me was broken. 'Your ship is anchored in a cove east of the harbour. Take it and go.'

Her voice was a peal of wind chimes, a sound I longed for as a child. It was this wish that set me on the path that ended in destruction of my home. While I chased the dream of breaking the curse that made her mute, she put my mother to death. I returned to find Stromhold turned into an ice cavern, its occupants frozen, and to learn there was no curse only cruel deception. Lumi used her magic to cast a veil of silence, creating an illusion of a voiceless girl. The memories lanced the wounds inflicted by her betrayal, causing the eruption of anger. I snatched my hand away from her cheek. 'I came here to seek retribution.'

Something rippled across her face, a grimace of regret perhaps, but I wasn't so easily fooled. Remorse was a feeling reserved for those with a heart, and Lumi had none.

'That's what Goro-Khan wants,' she said. 'He used me to lure you here.'

'You think highly of yourself. Do you really believe I sailed all this way just to find *you*?'

A faint smile touched the blue of her lips. 'I know you did. You can't hide your feelings from me. We've known each other for too long, weathered too many storms together. You shattered the magic of Antaya to retrieve my heart. I felt the warmth when you held it in your hands and every time after that. You brought it here, and it's calling out to me.' She looked aside, and her eyes became distant, dreamy.

'I intend to crush it,' I said, but the words lacked power.

'I can feel it. The void in my chest longs for a reunion.'

I grabbed her chin, forcing her to look at me. 'Where is Goro-Khan?'

'The Laughing God awaits the Valgsi. He dreams of restoring Antaya and bringing back the age of mages. He wants his son to be Skaldir's chosen.'

'Too late for that.'

'Not if you're within his grasp.' She grabbed my wrist. 'Leave now, before his plans are realised. You can still save yourself and your friends. Everything here is an illusion created to keep the mystery of Shinpi alive. Don't believe the things you see.'

'Every word that leaves your frozen lips is a lie. My mother warned me, but still, I trusted you. She paid for my foolishness with her life.' I grabbed Lumi's shoulders and shook her. 'You turned my life into a lie. You destroyed my peace and any hopes for the future.'

For a heartbeat, something like remorse glistened in her eyes, and then it was gone. She jerked away from me. 'If you stay, he will own you the way he owns me. Little by little, he'll strip you of your will with the sound of his laughter, and you'll descend into madness.'

She was asking the impossible. 'My mother died by Goro-Khan's order, and for that, he must pay. Nords don't leave their dead unavenged. But to understand such things, you'd have to be one of us. A human with a heart.'

Lumi's face turned as cool as the winter slopes of Nordur. She put the hood back on. 'You've always been stubborn. Do as you please, but remember, battle breeds many losers but only one true champion.' She rushed down the corridor and became one with the shadows.

My first instinct was to run after her, see her to her knees, and force the confession of guilt out of her. But Fjola and Njall were trapped somewhere in this prison, and we had the keys to their freedom. My chase would have to wait. I was certain that our paths would cross again, and I promised myself that next time I'd be holding her heart in my grip. I intended to make her feel everything I wanted her to feel, and more. Lumi didn't realise how lucky she was, for the absence of her heart allowed her to act without the fear of consequences. When Fjola asked me why I didn't smash the crystal when I first retrieved it, I didn't know for sure, but looking into the vortex of Lumi's eyes, I understood. There'd be no satisfaction in shattering the heart of someone who couldn't feel it break. She was the cause of my greatest pain, and I wanted, *needed* her to feel the extent of it. To live in torment over something you've done was worse than death. I knew that better than anyone.

I hastened back to the cell where Mirable waited with keys dangling from his fingers. 'Let's find the others,' I said.

'Was that—'

'Not now. Just because we can't see any guards doesn't mean we're safe.'

Mirable asked no more, and I was grateful for that. To speak of Lumi now would be unbearable. The encounter with her rattled me to the core, but I needed to stay sharp. The lives of my friends depended on my ability to think clearly.

We left the stink of our prison behind and edged along the corridor. It was long and narrow. The spheres illuminated the dark passageway with light that had no visible source. Unlike the erratic flames of an actual fire, their emerald glow held steady. Who kept the magic burning? The odour of waste and mildew hung thick in the air, mingling with another scent I struggled to place. Despite the cold emanating from the walls, I felt a trickle of sweat down my neck. The place was too quiet.

Mirable stopped at the door leading into a cell and whispered my name. I peered through the bars. The room resembled ours, except for a sinister cage suspended from the ceiling on a rusty chain. The bottom of it gaped open, and on the floor a human form lay twisted beyond recognition. I swallowed against the bile that rose in my throat, recognising the smell I tried to place earlier. It was the stench of burned flesh.

I placed my hand on Mirable's shoulder. 'Let's not linger.'

He backed away from the cell, his wide nostrils flaring. As we slinked further, more rooms came into view, each with a unique device: from racks with huge rollers on both ends to iron coffins spiked with thorns of steel. Some contraptions held people in their clutches, while others were littered with the charred bones of past residents. Suddenly, the silence made sense, and I understood that this was no ordinary prison but a dungeon designed with torture in mind. The dead couldn't scream for help.

With every cell we passed, Mirable's face paled a bit more, and his breathing became rugged. He scraped his nails against his left cheek over and over, leaving angry tracks. I had to get him out of this place and fast before the terror overtook him. We reached the corner where two more corridors stretched before us, one leading left and the other right, each lined with cells. I dreaded to think what lurked inside them.

A faint cry drifted our way, its source a nearby cell. Before I could stop him, Mirable leaped forward and grabbed the wooden bars with both hands.

'Help meeee…' the voice whistled.

‘We will. We will.’ Mirable sounded like a man afflicted by a fever. The keys rattled in his trembling fingers as he tried each in the lock.

I caught his hand. ‘What are you doing?’

‘What does it look like? I’m saving a life.’ The keys clattered to the floor, and he bent to pick them up.

The prisoner was a skeletal heap. Whatever crime caused his incarceration led to punishment by starvation. He lifted his head and stretched a weak hand towards Mirable, his gaunt fingers scraping against the stone. His skin bore long green lashes, as if someone whipped him with a strap made of magic.

Mirable retrieved the keys and resumed his rescue attempt. I cast a look over my shoulder, but the green-lit corridors stood empty. For now.

‘Even if you free him, what good would it do? He’s beyond help.’

‘No one is beyond saving,’ Mirable snapped. ‘The man speaks Vestern. I’m not going to leave one of us in this wretched pit.’

The prisoner ceased his desperate clawing, and his body stilled.

I took the keys from Mirable’s shaking hands. ‘We might get caught,’ I said, trying the first key. It went halfway into the lock but didn’t turn.

He crossed his arms against his chest and said nothing. There was no reasoning with him. I suspected the sight of this captive woke memories of his own torture at the hands of Hyllus, but just by looking at the prisoner, I knew he was bound for Himinn, and there was little we could do for him. He spoke Vestern, which meant he sailed here only to be captured and tortured. It didn't bode well for us. The worry for Njall and Fjola rose in me, and the images of them shackled and exposed to the magic made my fingers work faster. The second key I tried turned with the unmistakable sound of release. I pushed the barred door, and it creaked open.

Mirable darted past me and collapsed to his knees beside the dying man. He curled his hands over his head. 'What do I do?'

With a final glance at the two corridors, I stepped into the cell and crouched beside him. 'Let's turn him over,' I said, not feeling sure myself.

The man moaned. His skin was like a withered parchment under my fingers. His bones were on display, and I could feel the bands of his tendons. Green lacerations covered his entire body in a pattern of multiple zigzags, too many to count. The captive's eyes were closed, but his eyelids fluttered, chasing nightmares known only to him.

Mirable patted the man's sunken cheek. 'Can you hear me?' When there was no response, he slapped him. 'Can you tell me your name?'

The prisoner's eyes flew open, and he uttered a weak, shriek-like sound.

'We're here to help.'

I felt a prickle of unease. We lingered far too long. 'The man needs a healer, and I doubt we'll find one here. If we aren't careful, we'll get trapped with him. Do what you must, but make it quick.'

'So utterly callous! The Jarin I know would never abandon a fellow man in need.'

'I'm trying to save us while you're preoccupied with a stranger marked by Agtarr's Warrior.'

He winced. 'I'm not leaving without him.'

I took a deep breath. A part of me cursed the merchant's stubbornness, while another part respected him for it.

Mirable pushed his left hand under the man's back, his right below his knees, and picked him up with little effort. The prisoner looked like a cornhusk in his arms, the lifeless limbs dangling.

'Lead the way,' Mirable said.

A biting remark itched the tip of my tongue, but something in his face made me squash it. Mirable's jaw was set, his lips pressed together, his gaze alert. Rescuing this man meant more to him than our freedom, more perhaps than finding a cure for his transformation. It seemed most of Mirable's wounds from his time at the citadel festered on the inside. Maybe he saw himself reflected in the captive, and saving his life was an attempt at saving his own. I couldn't stand in his way.

I left the cell, Mirable on my heels. In the corridor, we stopped to listen for any sounds of human presence. The passageway forked left and right, each wrapped in the nightmarish stillness. I was about to head left when a hiss from Mirable stopped me.

'Can you hear that?' he asked, cocking his head to one side. The gesture reminded me of an animal listening for an approaching predator.

I strained my ears, catching nothing but silence. Shaking my head, I stepped forward.

'Someone's coming.'

'I can't hear any—'

Echoing voices that sounded like two men in conversation. I whipped my head left and right, but couldn't tell which corridor they came from.

Mirable pressed the prisoner tighter to his chest, eyes full of panic. 'What do we do?'

I turned on my heels. With no weapons and a sick man in our charge, we stood little chance against the armed guards. Judging by the cells we passed earlier and the choices of torture, the warriors of Shinpi weren't to be trifled with. Lumi offered us hope of escape, and I was determined to make the most of her gift.

'We'll wait for them in our cell. Hurry.'

We raced back the way we came. The passageway stretched on forever, and now I could hear a faint echo of footsteps as the guards closed the distance between us. At last, we reached the cell, and I urged Mirable through the door, shutting it behind him.

'We have to hide him,' I said, parting the soiled straw to make room.

Mirable placed the man on the ground, handling him the way one would a wounded child. We spread the straw over the captive, but it did little to disguise his presence, and I prayed that he'd stay silent for his own sake and ours. The lack of true light and taking the guards by surprise were the only things we had to our advantage.

I sat on the floor with my back to the wall and my hands between my legs to conceal the broken shackles. Mirable followed suit, and we lowered our heads to give the impression of exhaustion and sleep. The guards conversed in the foreign tongue that sounded like the snapping of twigs to my ear. Amplified by the stone, their words rose and fell, ending in sharp bursts of syllables. The air in our room turned so brittle that I was sure if I reached for it, it would snap between my fingers. Sneaking glances at the doorway, I clamped my sweaty hands together to stop them from quivering while my heart drummed in my chest. The wait seemed endless.

A hand banged on the bars, followed by a question.

I glanced at Mirable, but he didn't shift. His impression of sleep verged on real. Another, louder bang followed by a rattle of keys. It was our cue. I lifted my head to see the frown on the face of the first guard. To my left, Mirable let out a small snore. I cleared my throat and used my elbow to jolt him back to wakefulness. He jerked upright and shot me an apologetic glance. I couldn't believe he nodded off at a moment like this.

The guard said something to his companion, who shoved him aside and pushed the door open. It squeaked on its hinges. In a few strides, the man crossed the space between us and his green boot kicked mine. He pointed a gloved finger at the cell door and followed the gesture with a question.

'How many times?' I said through clenched teeth. They knew we couldn't understand them yet still expected a response. I had an inkling this superiority filled them with great pleasure.

The second man joined his fellow guard. He narrowed his eyes at me, and his hand came to rest on the hilt of his sword. Both of them resembled the guards that apprehended us at sea. The scales of their green armour shimmered with the light from the magic orb, and the jade crescents on their helmets reflected the glow. The colours fused to create a graceful illusion that concealed the ruthless warrior within.

I sprang to my feet and seized the first guard by the throat. With a roar, I forced him back into the wall. The Varl in Mirable coiled and leaped at the second man. They crashed to the floor, and the merchant throttled him. My opponent shoved me back and grabbed after his sword. I threw myself at him with all the strength I could muster. We wrestled for the weapon. The sparring sessions with Njall on the ship paid off, and I knocked the blade out of the guard's hand. It clattered to the stone, and we both lunged for it.

I got there first.

The weight of the weapon surprised me. It felt well-balanced in my grip, the hilt twice as long and the blade itself much lighter than my own. I didn't know how to wield it, but when the Warrior of Death stared you in the face, skill and grace mattered little.

I stabbed at the guard, but he moved sideways.

In the confines of the cell, it was difficult to manoeuvre. The guard opened his mouth as if to call for reinforcements, but Mirable sprang at him, knocking him to the ground. He fell with a thud, and the cry died on his lips. I drove the blade through his chest. Mirable heaved with effort. His kind and cheery disposition vanished, replaced by a set of animalistic features. His large, round eyes turned to slits, and his lips curled, exposing a set of wide incisors. What stood before me was half-man and half-beast. Images of the Vestern Varls flashed before my eyes, and I ushered them away, unwilling to accept that my friend was becoming one of them.

I lowered the blade and took a cautious step towards him. 'Mirable?' A pool of blood from the guard's body spread between our feet, and for a heartbeat, I thought the merchant would leap at me, but then, the wild look on his face faded, and he was Mirable again.

His chin dropped to his chest, and he stared at his hands. 'That name belonged to an honest trader. I'm nothing but a senseless killer.'

I placed my hands on his shoulders. His muscles rippled under my touch, but he refused to meet my gaze. 'You saved us. If not for your strength, we'd be the ones laying in a pool of blood. For all my training, I struggled to wield that blade. Your transformation is a curse, but we're alive because of it. Don't blame yourself. If anyone is at fault, it's me. I brought us here.'

'I've never killed anyone in my life. My mother would've been horrified.'

I wanted to point out that for as long as we stayed in Shinpi, there was a strong possibility we'd be forced to kill again, but the look of shock on his face stopped me. From a young age, Father trained me in the way of Stromhold warriors, but Mirable was a merchant taught to fight with words, not steel.

The prisoner moaned, and Mirable rushed to his side. He removed the straw covering his body and supported his hand with his elbow.

The man's eyes rolled in his sunken sockets, and he lifted his hand. Mirable grabbed and squeezed it.

'No more torture for you, my friend.' A tear rolled from Mirable's eye and splattered onto the gaunt cheek of the dying man. 'This is no place to draw your last breath.'

'Run. As far as you can. This place… is cursed…' The prisoner twisted his head to reach Mirable's ear. A shadow of dread crossed his face, and it had nothing to do with the fear of death. 'His terrible laugh…ter…' His head fell backwards, and his chest stilled.

Mirable sat, holding the man's hand. The sorrow of the man's death was an invisible boulder upon his shoulders, and even I could feel the weight of it. I searched for the right words, but each felt meaningless. How could I reassure a friend all will be well when life made an example of him the moment he risked his own trying to save a man? The best I could do was to find Goro-Khan and put an end to this endless suffering.

'We must go,' I said in a low voice.

Mirable let go of the man's hand and placed the captive's head onto the floor 'May Yldir welcome you into the Fields of

Life, my friend,' he whispered, pulling his eyelids closed. He got to his feet and crossed the cell without another word, but his pain followed him like a second shadow.

We retraced our steps to the fork in the corridor. The room where we found the dying prisoner gaped open and eerily quiet, and I was glad he spent his last moments in the arms of my friend.

We soon learned the prison was an oddly shaped maze, with walkways branching out in multiple directions. Some cells stood empty, while others held the remains of the lawbreakers who came before, but we didn't meet anyone who was still breathing. Mirable led the way, his nose twitching like that of a hound on a game trail. In the shadowy gloom, with his back hunched and the bones prodding the material of his shirt, he looked less human and more like a Varl, but as much as I loathed the idea of his transformation, having a guide with animal instincts had its advantages. Twice we ran into guards patrolling the corridors, and twice Mirable saved us from an open conflict by steering us away into the nooks and crannies of the darkened passageways. His nose detected the human scent long before the echo of their footsteps entered my eardrums.

Not knowing how to wield it, rendered the blade I took from the guard unreliable. Without proper training, I'd be outmatched in a face-to-face battle, but if I took the guards unawares, it'd serve me well. At one fork, a high-pitched cry echoed through the prison. It came from the left passage, but when Mirable started in that direction, I grabbed his hand.

He cast a glance over his shoulder.

I shook my head. I wanted to help the people trapped here, but we had our own people to worry about. My mind was full of grim visions of them being tortured and pressed to divulge the reasons for our presence in Shinpi. Njall and Fjola wouldn't break easily…

We came to another branch in the corridor, and Mirable halted. He scanned both directions, sniffed the air, and pointed right.

I followed without question. The hallway led us to a set of steps descending to the lower levels of the prison. As we made our way deeper into the bowels of this cursed place, more cells and devices of torture stared at us through the wooden bars. A smell of dust motes replaced the stink of mildew and bodily odours. This part of the prison felt less sinister and more ordinary.

'Jarin?' Fjola's green irises flashed at me from one of the cells. 'Praise Yldir, you're both alive.'

The honest concern in her voice brushed the edges of my heart. She was unharmed. I reached through the gap in the cell door and wrapped my hand over hers, feeling light with relief.

Her skin was warm to the touch, the ridges of her knuckles hard against my fingers.

Njall crossed the cell. 'This place is seething with magic.' His voice carried a note of disgust.

'It's a torture house,' I said, and put my hand out. 'Mirable, the keys.'

He fumbled within the folds of his shirt and handed them to me. I placed the blade at my feet and tried each key in the lock.

'Can you use it?' Njall asked, pointing at the sword.

'I can take a life, if that's what you mean.'

'They took our weapons,' Fjola said. 'We heard voices. The guardroom must be up ahead.'

'Voices could mean a number of things,' Mirable said, brushing a hand through his curls. His vacant eyes stared off to the side.

I tried the last key and cursed. None of them fit. One look at Mirable told me that asking him to break the bars would fall on deaf ears. He shared his secret with me, but Fjola and Njall hadn't seen him in his Varl form. I didn't want to push him over the edge by expecting more than he was ready to give.

I looked over my shoulder. 'With any luck, the guardroom is where you think it is. The keys should be there.'

'And a bunch of blood-thirsty guards,' Mirable said.

Fjola looked at him. 'How did you escape?'

I knew someone would voice the question sooner or later, but this wasn't the time to bring up Lumi. Suddenly, the possibility of fighting the guards became more attractive. 'Later. First we must get you out of here.'

'Please hurry,' Fjola said. She wrapped her hands around her stomach, her face pallid in the greenish light cast by the orb affixed to the wall beyond.

'Watch your step,' Njall said.

I offered a quick nod, then picked up the blade.

We stole our way along the corridor, in the guardroom's direction. This time Mirable stayed back, allowing me to lead. With blade in hand and the goal in sight, I was filled with a sense of purpose, which took my mind off the torture and pain that would surely follow if I failed. My scalp tingled and my hands were slick with sweat. Since our imprisonment we had no access to fresh water, and my mouth felt like tree bark. The light from the magical spheres illuminated the walls and the sword in my grip shimmered with the eerie green, but this part of the prison had none of the grimness from before.

Rounding the corner, muffled voices drifted our way. I turned to Mirable with a finger pressed to my lips. He rolled his eyes. Despite the display of his strength, I still treated him like a helpless merchant. With my back to the cool stone, I peered around the wall's edge into the room ahead.

Two guards sat on cushions, cross-legged, their helmets resting on a low table next to a pile of nuts and two cups. Judging by the square board laid out in front of them, the men played some kind of a game. Wooden pieces dotted the surface in distinct patterns, each holding a clear meaning to the players, but none to me. The guard pushed a piece across the board and those standing in its path fell off the table. He took a swig from the cup, his face full of glee. His companion slammed the palm across his thigh and glared at him. After a moment, they burst out laughing. The loser threw a chunk of silver onto the table and his opponent scooped it up with a grin.

Mirable craned his neck over my shoulder, his eyes fixed on the board and the heap of silver. To my astonishment, he made a move as if to join them. I kicked his foot and he stepped back, his eyebrows pinched together. Sometimes I wondered who was more difficult to control, the Varl or the merchant.

We backed away and crouched near the wall.

'Two guards and no means to ambush them without detection,' I whispered.

'Don't ask me to kill them,' Mirable said, rubbing his cheek. With dark shadows under his eyes and curls springing in all directions, he looked like a scarecrow.

'I didn't expect you to, but we need a distraction.' When he said nothing, I continued, 'I'll go, but when I rouse them, you best be ready. We can't afford them sounding an alarm.' I got to my feet, wishing it was Njall and Fjola at my side. The three of us would do what needed to be done, without pondering the morals of our actions. As warriors, we understood the price that had to be paid for freedom and we were willing to pay it. This was the way of the Nordern clans, but Mirable grew up in Vester, where different laws governed the land and its people. 'I'll stand in the doorway and lure them out. Once they're in pursuit, you take one, and I'll handle the other.'

Mirable averted his gaze.

'Do what you can to disarm him and leave the rest to me. I really wish there was a way to avoid blood spill.' I put as much candour into my words as I could muster.

The look in his eye told me he wished to be anywhere but here. I'd do anything to spare Mirable the need to use his strength. It was unnatural, and every time he called upon the Varl in him a slight change took place noticeable in the tilt of his head and the manner in which his eyes narrowed when the confrontation was at hand.

I left him in the gloom and crossed the corridor to the guardroom. The men still sat at the table, their heads lowered, eyes focused on the wooden pieces on the board.

I stepped into view.

One of the guards lifted his head. At the sight of me, his eyes widened, and he grabbed the sword propped against the table. His left hand caught the cup that went flying, spilling the contents across the floor. The second man barked a string of words before lunging after his own weapon. They leaped at me, blades gleaming. I backed away into the corridor, veering right and giving Mirable a clear view of the two guards. Their attention was on me, their backs exposed to the Varl crouching in the shadows.

Mirable sprang, wrapping his arms around the throat of the guard closest to him. The man's blade clattered to the stone, and Mirable dragged him back into the guardroom like a predator dragging a prey into its lair. The guard's gurgling noises followed them.

I used the momentary lapse in my guard's focus to slam into him. His back smashed against the wall, and I slashed at the hand holding the sword. The steel cut through the flesh and bone as though they were a block of lard. His severed limb, still gripping the weapon, fell to the floor. There was a moment of silence as the guard followed its descent. Blood leaked from the stump, and I pressed my palm against the man's lips to stifle his cry. He sunk his teeth into the meat of my hand. I swore, driving my sword through his chest. His eyes glazed over, the shock forever fixed into the pupils. After his body stilled, I removed my palm from his mouth and let him slip to the ground.

I rushed back into the guardroom to find Mirable wrestling with the guard on the top of the table. Nuts and board pieces littered the floor. Somehow, the man had managed to overpower Mirable—his left hand pinned the merchant to the table, while his right searched for something to hit him with.

I grabbed the plate of his armour and pulled him off. His head crashed against the stone with a dull thud. I brought the blade down. A few jerks later, his body grew still.

'What happened?' My breath came on ragged, my muscles shaking with effort.

Mirable massaged his throat, his face twisted into a grimace. 'I got distracted.'

'Distracted?' I followed his gaze to where the silver lay scattered across the floor. 'Your greed will get you killed.'

He jumped off the table and crawled to the chunks of silver. He picked one up and clamped his teeth on it. 'Such a strange way to shape coin,' he exclaimed. 'But I cannot dispute its value.'

My patience was wearing thin, and I had to stop myself from lashing out. 'When in battle, you must leave the merchant in you behind. The man had half of your strength, yet you let him overpower you. Your reckless actions put us both in danger.'

'You're the one to speak of recklessness. We use different ways to measure our worth. Whilst your father trained you to prove yourself in battle, mine taught me the value of coin.' He scooped up the pieces and stowed them into the pocket of his trousers. The weight almost pulled them off. 'I killed a man back in that cell because I let your warrior talk influence my mind, but no more. I'm not a killer.' He patted his bulging pockets. 'I'm changing, yes, but I'm trying desperately to hold on to the man I used to be.'

My irritation with him faded. Mirable was right. I pushed him to do things that went against his nature. What other choice did I have? The situation demanded his involvement, but that didn't make it any easier for him to justify his actions to himself. Mirable took a life, and no amount of silver would dull the self-loathing that followed such an act. The difference between us was that I'd learned how to live with that feeling.

'Let's search for the keys,' I said.

There was a timber box attached to the wall, with keys of various sizes hanging off the hooks inside it. I walked over and examined a handful of them, but there was no way to tell which one unlocked Fjola's cell. I swiped them all and stuffed the bunch inside my shirt pocket, the very same that held Lumi's heart before they took it from me. Her warnings echoed in my head, but I refused to heed them. To do so would mean letting Goro-Khan walk free.

'Mother be praised,' Mirable cried out. He was on his knees, clutching a piece of red cloth in his hands. I crossed the guardroom, and he lifted his treasured turban to me. A chest stood open before him and when I looked inside, my sword flashed at me alongside Fjola's daggers. Njall's spear stood propped against the side of the chest.

I dived after the blade, and when my hand wrapped around the hilt, it felt like a reunion of long-lost allies. Recovering it was like finding a missing gem and fitting it back into a necklace to form a perfect whole. I pulled the weapon from its scabbard, and the weight brought back the sensation of strength and order. The jewel fixed into the cross guard gleamed with green light, and the script running across the face of the blade shimmered in response to my touch.

Mirable's voice reached me through the hum in my ears. 'It looks like we both recouped our lost treasures.' I looked up to find his turban wrapped around his head. No more curls. He looked like his old self again, and the flush in his cheeks matched the colour of his headwear.

'Why is it so important?' I asked. 'The turban, I mean.'

A small smile stole over Mirable's lips. 'In my family, only grown men are allowed to wear them. My father chose a dark blue cloth for his. I looked up to him, impatient for the day I could match him by wearing a turban of my own.' His eyes glazed over. 'Father was so sure about the course of his life. Mind you, he wasn't a man to be admired. His heart was stonier than the rain-starved soil, but I desired his approval all the same.' He touched his left arm with his right hand. 'I never got it.'

I didn't want him to travel down that path. 'Your turban is back, and that's what matters. Besides, you're an accomplished merchant, the best in your trade. Something to be proud of, for sure. When our quest is over, you'll go back to your life and your coin, and all of this will be nothing but a distant memory.'

'Our future depends on *you*. In a score of months, the Night of Norrsken will be upon us, and the sword in your hand will reveal Valgsi's true heart.'

I slid the blade back into its sheath and fastened it around my belt. The resolve about my fate grew stronger. 'I was never fond of the gods, Mirable.'

'More the reason for you to take this seriously. You may not be fond of them, but this sword exerts a powerful influence over you. Even you can't deny that. Skaldir chose you the same way Hyllus chose me—by sheer chance. Your mother was in the wrong place at the wrong time, and so was I. Refusing to accept it won't change who you are, and doing so will only make you weaker and more susceptible to manipulation. Skaldir slept for too long, and you're her only chance at awakening. Do you really think your denial of this will change her intent?'

Even I couldn't refuse the wisdom of his words, but I didn't want to think about the gods and their magic. Mirable was unaware of my pact with the witches. Only Fjola and Njall were privy to that knowledge. In a strange way, the throbbing sensation of Trofn's mark strengthened my resolve. The witches wanted me to answer Skaldir's call because it would fill my soul with her magic. But I wasn't willing to give it up so easily. On the Night of Norrsken, I intended to be far away from that forsaken hill. Only by defying my fate could I keep my soul intact. 'One thing at a time,' I said. 'Let's go back to the others and find a way out of this wretched place.'

Mirable picked up Njall's spear and turned it over in his hands. 'A fine weapon, but how on earth can you use it to good effect?'

Sometimes I wondered about that myself. Norderners favoured blades and axes over spears, but Njall chose it as a weapon and proved very skilled at using it. His original spear was splintered by Antaya's giant, but as soon as we returned to Hvitur, Njall fashioned himself a new one. The long handle was made from oak and had no decorative patterns, but there was a grace to it, which was enhanced by the way he handled the spear in battle. One tip was longer and wider. Steel leaves of varying lengths encased it as if it was the head of a flower. A black ribbon tied at the base of the tip signified the owner's loss. In the case of Njall, it was his father, a fisherman, who perished at sea.

We hurried back to Fjola and Njall. Both of them stood vigil at the cell door, their faces awash with anxiety. At the sight of her daggers, Fjola squealed, while her brother only grunted in approval. I attempted each key and on the fifth try the lock clicked. As soon as the door opened, Fjola grabbed her daggers and pressed them to her chest. Mirable handed Njall his spear. He thanked him with a nod and ran his hand over the shaft.

'The guards?' Fjola asked.

I shook my head.

'How did you escape?' Njall said, scanning both ends of the corridor.

I shot a glance at Fjola. 'Lumi.'

'She was here?'

'She freed us,' Mirable said. 'I wager she broke a rule or two by doing so.'

'It sounds to me like she came to claim her property.' Fjola's voice was steel.

'The heart is gone,' I said, 'and no, she didn't ask for it. She warned me about Goro-Khan and told me that our ship is docked east of the harbour.'

Njall narrowed his eyes. 'A trap?'

'I don't think so.'

'So now we're trusting this demon?' Fjola asked.

'What other choice do we have?'

She drew breath, but Njall placed a hand on her shoulder. 'Jarin's right. The only way to know for sure is to get to the harbour. We need a safe place to regroup and decide our next move.'

She said nothing, but the flash of hurt in her eyes conveyed more than any words.

Mirable yawned a deep yawn. When we looked at him, he shrugged. 'For a band of mighty warriors the three of you sure know how to squabble. You would excel in the war of words.'

As was often the case, the merchant was right. We stood here, arguing, and putting our lives in danger. We escaped our cells, but our freedom was still out of reach.

'First, we need to find our way out,' I said. 'This prison is a maze.'

'And then?' Njall said.

'Then we'll head for the harbour. The sea is in your bones, we should have no trouble finding the water.' I hoped the smell of salt would guide us to the shore of the Great Atlantic. Once there, I'd see my friends safely on the ship. It was the only way to keep them from endangering their lives further. As for me, I had an audience with the laughing menace.

'It won't be easy finding the ship without drawing attention,' Mirable said.

Fjola examined him closely. 'You don't look so good.'

'I'm sick of this dungeon. Can we go now?'

I scanned both corridors. 'Which way?'

Before anyone else could answer, Mirable pointed to the right.

'How did you—' Fjola started, but I cut her off.

'He can tell you later. For now, let's follow his lead.'

Mirable shuffled back a step, as if to refuse, and I said in a softer tone, 'We need you, and you can do this well.'

He sighed and took a few steps forward. His head twisted from side to side and I could see his nose twitching. Maybe he caught the scent of the air outside because his face became alert and he followed the passageway without looking back.

* * *

Like thieves in the night, we snaked after Mirable, clutching the weapons and filling the silence with our rasping breaths. The corridor narrowed and the sense of entrapment intensified. As I clamped my teeth onto the soft of my cheek, a metallic taste flooded my mouth. I recognised the same wariness in my companions. They took one cautious step after another, their postures rigid and faces taut with tension. Njall held his spear in front of him like a protective barrier, and Fjola's gaze darted back and forth, scanning for threats. I couldn't see Mirable's face, but from the low slant of his shoulders I gathered he sought solace within, submitting to his varlish senses.

The spheres of magic cast shadows that looked like ghosts veiled in green, shifting along the walls in step with us. Our boots filled the corridor with faint echoes that stirred the hair on my neck. Silence amplified all sound. On each side of the passageway, empty cells lined the walls. A faint odour of blood, old and fresh, hung in the air, but with my father's sword firmly in my grip, I no longer feared the evils of this place.

Mirable halted at the corner, sniffing the air. 'This way,' he said, motioning left.

'Is your smell that good?' Fjola asked.

Her question brought back the memory of the broken Varl we had encountered in Vester. Alkaios. Mirable was lucky his transformation didn't stall, for if it did, his body would've turned into a heap of mutated flesh. Alkaios was a sad example of what happened to the Varls who failed their change.

'My nose distils the air, extracting various information in the process,' Mirable said. 'To my right, it smells stale, and to my left, there's a fresh quality to it. It's a skill I'd rather not possess.'

'We're lucky to have you,' she said.

The comment earned her a smile that didn't quite touch his eyes.

We followed Mirable along two more corridors, encountering no guards, and I felt myself relax, the hope of getting out alive growing stronger with each step to freedom.

The last corridor opened into a large room with a sturdy door. Just as I reached for the round handle, it burst open.

I found myself face to face with a man in a velvet cloak.

The encounter took us both by surprise. We stood there for a moment, staring.

The man drew a small blade, and it clashed with mine. Steel pressed against steel as we measured each other's strength. I could hear my friends, but the doorway was too narrow for them to aid me. The man's eyes turned to slits, and he bared his teeth.

I crashed my forehead into his.

Our swords parted with a ring, and he staggered against the wall.

I advanced, sure of my victory, when he started chanting a string of foreign words. A wave of green slammed into my chest, forcing me back through the doorway. I smashed into the stone, and the pain that shot through my back took my breath. Njall grabbed my shoulder and pulled me to my feet. I swayed in a daze, my hand pressed to my chest.

'Magic,' I croaked.

Mirable recoiled at the word and scrambled into the corner. There'd be no help from him. The cloaked man recovered and was walking through the doorway. Fjola moved to meet him, but the man uttered another incantation, and her daggers burst into flames of emerald green.

She screamed and dropped them.

They clattered to the floor, while Fjola watched them, frozen.

I grabbed her hand and pulled her back into the corridor that led us here. Njall retrieved her daggers and followed, with Mirable on his heels, chased by the voice of the cloaked man. He shouted something in Vestern that sounded like an order to stop. We broke into a run cut short a few strides later by two guards rounding the corner. They drew their weapons, cutting our only way of escape.

Clutching his turban, Mirable made a wailing sound.

'What now?' Njall asked, pointing his spear at the incoming guards.

If it wasn't for the magic, we'd best them, but against the force that sent me crashing through that door, we were powerless. The choice was to fight, or end up like the man Mirable tried to save, and I'd rather die with my sword in hand than be forced to endure an agonising torture. One glance at my companions assured me they shared my resolve.

We turned back and ran for the cloaked man. He opened his mouth to call on the spells again, but Fjola leaped into the air and threw a dagger his way. It didn't hit the mark, but it broke the man's concentration, giving us precious moments to close the distance.

Boots stomped behind us and the yells of the guards reverberated through the corridor.

Njall used the moment of confusion to impale the cloaked man on his spear, its tip tearing through the green of his robe. He drove the man through the door, roaring, and forcing the spear deeper into his chest. The man's arms flailed and blood gushed out of his mouth, turning his chin crimson. Njall pushed him to the floor with his boot and pulled the weapon free.

We bolted through the doorway, and the four of us raced the length of the next corridor to find another door. I slammed my boot into the woodwork, but it didn't give. Njall crashed into it with his shoulder.

'Hurry,' Mirable screamed as the guards closed the distance between us.

'Again,' I shouted, and the three of us rammed the door.

It gave way and the momentum threw us onto the streets.

'Gods have mercy on us all,' Fjola whispered.

A sonorous sound of a gong split the air, and we broke into a run, chased by waves of deep vibrations.

VII

'Where to?' Njall shouted over the shrilling of the gong. The alarm raised by our escape stirred Shinpi's residents to wakefulness. Green lights flickered in windows and doorways.

'Mirable, lead us to the harbour,' I shouted.

He nodded and pushed past us, the crimson of his turban a guiding light in the darkness. The white shield of the moon guarded the midnight sky, casting a glow that revealed the shapes and structures of buildings and converging paths. Strands of green fog weaved its way through Shinpi, waist high, shimmering like the jewel in my sword. A rich, heady smell of magic hung thick in the air, and my lungs struggled against it. Despite the night's coolness, sweat poured down my neck, and I found myself gasping for breath.

After a score of steps, Mirable stopped at the edge of a house, pressing a fist against his mouth, while his face contorted into a grimace. None of us relished wading through magic, and I suspected Mirable most of all. Even for a well-travelled merchant like him, to sail from a place that abhorred magic to a land where people embraced its power was too great of a leap.

'I can't do this,' he said, bending in half.

'We must get to our ship,' I said. 'Think of home.'

‘It’s easy for you to say. Her magic is in you, so you have nothing to fear.’

‘And neither have you.’ I tried to grasp the fine fog, but it slid between my fingers. ‘This is only a mist. It can’t harm you.’

‘You don’t know that.’

Fjola leaned close to him. ‘We need you. Shinpi is coming awake, the guards are on our trail, and we’ve no place to hide. The ship is our only hope.’ She cast a glance over her shoulder, then looked back at Mirable. ‘I’ve never been so afraid in my life, but I don’t want to die on this cursed island. And neither do you.’

Mirable nodded, and I exhaled. Since the moment he met Fjola, he had a soft spot for her, and her words could reach him in a way that mine never would. He squared his shoulders and thrust his chest out. ‘Follow me.’

We ran through the streets. Every structure surrounding us had a swollen roof with curved eves extending far beyond the curving walls. Twice we had to hide from the residents who peered into the night with spheres hovering above their palms, dispelling darkness from the front yards. In the greenish glow, I glimpsed faces that bore resemblance to Lumi’s. Behind us, the shouting of guards and the pounding of boots came from all directions. It would only take one wrong turn to fall into the arms of our pursuers. Never in my life had I felt so blind and directionless, but I had faith in Mirable and his sense of smell. The hue of magic here was thick, clouding my human senses, but the Varl among us seemed immune to the effects.

We ducked behind a wall and vaulted over a low fence.

'There!' someone shouted, pointing a ghostly finger our way.

More lights flickered in front of houses. Shouts and urgent voices drifted on the cool air, joining those of the guards. How long before the entire village would leap into a chase? Lumi said our ship was hidden in a cove, but with the guards on our heels, there was no way we'd lift the anchor unseen. We had to find a hiding place and wait for the pursuit to thin out. The guards wouldn't stop their search, I knew that much, but if Shinpi was anything like Hvitur, most people would have chores to do, which should divert their attention for a time.

I scanned the surroundings. Ahead, the paths criss-crossed. Some headed into the shadowy store buildings, while others lead deeper into the village. To increase our chances, we had to follow one that would take us to the outskirts.

'That way,' I yelled, pointing to a track leading away from the main path. Mirable flashed me a confused look, but there was no time to explain. Pushing my arms back and forth, I forced myself to greater speed, jumping over potholes and skirting around hedges. My breathing laboured and my heart hammered in my chest, ready to explode. The pounding of our boots filled my ears, and the thought of capture sent the surge of adrenaline into my limbs.

As we left the last houses behind, the shrilling of the gong grew more distant and so did the voices of the men tracking us. The night worked in our favour, enfolding her black wings around us, but away from the village lights, we faced natural challenges.

Njall tripped on a protruding rock and crashed to the floor.

Fjola dropped to her knees next to him. 'It's the wound. He's bleeding.'

The stab I'd delivered to his thigh in an attempt to save him from the serena scabbed over, but the chase tore it anew. Blood soaked through his trousers.

'It's nothing,' Njall said, and waved his hand at me. 'Help me up.'

I grabbed his arm and pulled him to his feet. 'Mirable, take his other hand.'

Together, we steadied him, while Fjola tore the sleeve of her shirt and tied the cloth around his wound.

'Why the change of course?' Mirable asked between breaths.

'They knew we were heading for the harbour.'

'But soon they'll discover our diversion.'

We stopped at the edge of a forest, but nothing about it looked familiar. Tall trees, with cylindrical stalks, grew in close proximity to each other, their crowns swaying high above like blades of grass. Narrow paths lined with long, tapering leaves, wound through the forest, seemingly directionless.

'We have to trust the nature,' I said. 'It's the only thing that doesn't take sides.'

'I'm not so sure,' Fjola said, looking up.

The night was fading, and soon, the light of dawn would make our escape that much harder.

Mirable cocked his head. 'We best hurry.'

His words stirred a shiver of gooseflesh. If the forest failed us, we'd be captured, tortured, and killed. I cast one last look over my shoulder. Away from the village, the green mist of magic thinned until it lost most of its colour. Windows twinkled in the distance, luring us back with a false promise of safety.

I adjusted Njall's arm around my neck. 'The only way is forward.'

When we walked past the first line of trees, the silence slammed into us like a wave. One moment we stood in the open countryside, listening for the faint echoes of the gong, and the next, we found ourselves in the stillness both eerie and unnatural. The trees towered above us, shedding their pointed leaves without as much as a rustle.

'I don't like it,' Njall said. The silence swallowed his words.

‘This place reminds me of Sur,’ Fjola whispered. ‘There’s no wind, only quiet.’

Trofn’s symbol throbbed under my skin like a second heart. If Shinpi had its own witches, I didn’t fear them, for I carried their mark wherever I went.

‘Must we always talk of magic?’ Mirable asked. ‘The witches of Sur are far away. We should focus on those who are coming for us. Which way?’

He aimed his question at me, as if I knew more than any of them. Four paths lay ahead, none too inviting, and something told me it didn’t matter which one we followed because the forest had a mind of its own, and regardless of our choice, it would lead us down its ancient trails into the heart of silence.

Kylfa’s voice echoed in my mind like a murmur of a long forgotten past. *‘There is only one true path for a Valgsi. Your choice means little in the face of destiny.’*

I shook my head at the false declaration. ‘We take the middle path,’ I said, guiding Njall towards the widest trail.

Mirable wrinkled his nose but said nothing. Fjola walked ahead of us, her daggers drawn, back curved in readiness to spring. Our feet brushed against the leaves and tiny stones that lined the path. Like an invisible hand, the silence pressed against my chest while the forest filled my nostrils with an overpowering mixture of damp moss and sweet grass. It smelled wrong to me, and the deeper we went the less I liked it. The night was fading, but under the canopy of trees, the everlasting gloom made it difficult to track the moon. I lost all sense of time, and the feeling was disorienting.

'Why can't we hear our pursuers?' I asked. They must've seen us heading this way, yet it felt like the forest cut us off from the outside world. Was it protecting those who entered its realm, or leading us to our doom?

'I can't smell them,' Mirable said. 'The odours here are overpowering my senses. Even the busiest markets, with their mixture of spices and herbs, were less of an assault on my nostrils than this place.'

'We shouldn't linger. Njall needs to calm the bleeding, and we must figure out our next move.'

Fjola turned. 'I thought we were going back to the ship.'

'We are,' I said. 'I want you back on the ship, and I'll see to it that we get there safely.'

Everybody stopped at once. 'What do you mean by that?' Njall asked. He stepped away from me and leaned on his spear.

I scratched the back of my neck, steeling myself for the blow of words. 'I want you to sail back to Nordur.'

Mirable gasped, and Fjola threw her hands in the air. 'I knew you'd say something like this. It doesn't matter how much reassurance we give you, you keep pushing us away.'

'Fjola's right,' Njall said. His voice was calm and free of emotion. It'd take more than one declaration on my part to shake him. 'The cause that brought us here is as much ours as it is yours. Yes, I'm willing to admit we don't always see eye to eye, but all of us want Goro-Khan dead. He allowed Hyllus to practice his art. He cannot walk free.'

'But things have changed,' I said. 'This wasn't what I had in mind when we sailed here. I was a fool for believing we could worm our way to Shinpi without notice. It's my lack of foresight that led us into these woods, with no clear way out. We have no food, water, or shelter, and only a vague idea where our ship is anchored.'

'When we followed you to Vester, we didn't know the cost of that ride,' Fjola said. 'But still none of us faltered.'

'It was different.'

She rounded on me. 'How was it different? Skari died because of the choices we made that day. You say Goro-Khan is responsible for everything that happened in the Citadel of Vester, and if that is so, then Njall and I have our own score to settle.'

The memory of Skari was a dagger to my gut. Fjola wasn't there to make the choice, but I was, and the one I'd made, killed her betrothed. For as long as I breathed the air, I'd never forgive myself for leaving him behind. 'This isn't a game. The dangers are real.' I swiped my hand in the direction of the village obscured by a firm wall of trees. 'These people are mages. You saw the way the magic flows here. Free and untamed. The forces we're up against are more powerful than we've imagined, and I refuse to lead you into the arms of Agtarr.'

'And what about you?' Mirable said. 'You made a promise, Jarin.'

Yes, I made promises. I'd promised Mirable to find the cure for his transformation. I'd promised my mother her death would be avenged, and I'd even made a pact with the witches to secure my father's place in Himinn. Many promises and only one of them fulfilled, but at what cost? In the prison, the witch mocked them, and maybe she was right. Everyone kept reminding me I held the fate of the world in my hands, but what did it matter if I couldn't even make good on one vow.

'I only wish to keep you safe from danger,' I said at last. 'The three of you are the only true friends I have. Until *she* came into my life, I was alone, surrounded by my father's warriors. I wanted to live up to everyone's expectations, but all I had achieved is disappointment. Goro-Khan is here, and it's my duty as a son, and the future Guardian of Stromhold, to find him and kill him. His death will mean no more Varls, no more magic, no more lies. Only my vengeance will set us free.'

'It's not for you to decide our fate,' Njall said. 'We may not have a say on how we fall, but we can choose how we stand.'

I looked at each of them in turn, knowing there was nothing I could say to change their minds.

'You all have reasons to press on, but so do I,' Mirable said. 'I'm changing into a beast of Hyllus's design. I've no control over the transformation, and my body is twisting in ways which are both painful and hideous to look at. Jarin can attest to that. Shinpi is magic, and as much as it pains me to say it, magic is the only force that can stop me from becoming a monster. I don't have anyone to avenge, and I don't want to kill people. My greatest desire is to live out my days practicing my trade. If Shinpi fails me, there's no place for someone like me in Vester, so this journey is my last and only chance at life.'

Fjola took Mirable's hand. 'We won't abandon you. We're going home together, all of us.'

Mirable wiped his eyes with the back of his hand, and sniffed.

'If Goro-Khan won't tell us how to stop the transformation, someone else will,' I said. 'We'll cut the knowledge out of them if that's what it takes, but you're coming home a whole man.'

Fjola's eyes met mine, and in them I spied a flicker of gratitude. 'Let's find the way out of this forest. The longer I'm here, the less human I feel.'

I nodded. I missed the sky, for it was the only way I knew how to tell time and find my way in the wilderness. I offered my shoulder to Njall, but he refused it.

'She'll keep me on my feet,' he said, sliding his hand down the shaft of his spear. He leaned on the weapon and hobbled ahead of us to set the pace. Mirable followed, his left hand pressed to his turban. Fjola and I walked side by side. The path was wide enough, but from time to time, her hip brushed against mine, and I enjoyed the sensation.

'When we're clear of these woods, where do we go?' she asked in a low voice.

'We find the tallest hill and study the surroundings. Without knowing the lay of the land, it'll be impossible to find our way.'

'Doesn't it strike you as odd that no one entered this forest but us?' She looked around, and her fingers curled over her daggers. 'It's as if they chased us here on purpose.'

'Maybe they did, but the only way to find out is to follow the path to the end.'

'And what is the end?'

The question was simple enough, but it held many answers. Would the end come when Goro-Khan lay dead at my feet, or when the witches took my soul? Fjola deserved the truth.

'I don't know,' I said. 'I came here to find Goro-Khan and stop the abuse of magic. The Varls plagued us for many years, and even though Hyllus is no longer alive to create them, who's to say Goro won't send another to take his place?'

'But is that all?'

Was it ever? The guards confiscated Lumi's heart, and I had no way to trace its whereabouts, but I hoped Lumi knew where to search. Her desire to recover it was powerful enough to betray me and slaughter my family. I did my part by freeing it from the depths of Antaya. The rest was up to her.

'I want answers,' I said.

'What answers can a demon give you?'

I fixed my eyes on Mirable's hunched back. 'Why must we talk about her?'

Fjola caught my sleeve. 'She stands between us. Your unwillingness to let her go is keeping us apart. I see how you look at me when you think I'm too busy to notice.' She pointed at my neck. 'And that pearl is driving me insane. I keep thinking it's a keepsake for the demon.'

I stopped, waiting for the others to walk out of earshot. Fjola dropped her head and stared at her boots.

'From the moment we met, you knew my destiny. I gave up the right to my soul when I accepted the power to kill Hyllus, I sealed my fate. Even if Lumi didn't exist, I could never pledge myself to you. Goro-Khan's death won't erase the mark on my wrist, and it won't silence Skaldir's call. Some of us are born free, while others wear shackles even as they grow in their mother's womb. I'm trying to break mine by thinking of ways to alter the prophecy, but I'm thwarted at every turn.' I lifted her chin, and she bit down on her lower lip. With my thumb, I brushed the softness of her cheek. 'I wish it was you whom my father brought to Stromhold on that fateful night.'

She closed her eyes. 'But it was *her*.'

Her sounded like a strike of a whip. 'Even Lumi can't change the fact that my soul is not my own. Whatever it takes, I must resist the call.'

Understanding mixed with hope dawned on her face. 'Without Skaldir's magic, your soul will be of little value to the witches.'

I nodded. 'But first, I must track down Goro-Khan. I can't let other worries cloud my mind.'

'That's why we're here. Skari died because Goro ordered Hyllus to commit atrocities in the name of Skaldir. This can't go unpunished.' Her jaw clenched. 'Magic is forbidden for a reason. Nothing good ever came from the abuse of power. It's time to end it and give peace back to our people.'

I thought of the war between mages and humans, as well as Antaya's fall to ruin because of the misuse of magic. History had a way of repeating itself, and I had a strong sense that Shinpi harboured evil that posed far greater risk to our world than all the Varls put together. The Goddess of Destruction was not to be trifled with.

‘Let’s catch up with the others,’ I said, and despite my earlier words, I took Fjola’s hand. The warmth radiating from it spread through my skin like the heat of summer, and the intense longing to feel the touch of her fingertips on my face turned the forest into a swaying blur. I could lie to myself about my true feelings, but such restrictions didn’t bind my body. Every time I was near her, it reminded me how much Skaldir took from me when I drew my first breath.

We hurried along the path. The dangers ahead were far from over, but holding Fjola’s hand took weight off my heart. The all-consuming Lumi, a blank page of mystery, a white canvas of confusion that drew me in as a boy... she had left me with nothing. When Fjola came into my life, she painted a world for me, a future infused with colour and life. In the face of the sun, I was a fool for letting winter into my heart.

Mirable waited at the edge of a clearing. He took one look at our joined hands and his lips quivered. He said nothing, but I didn’t need words to read his thoughts. Fjola blushed and let go of my hand.

‘What took you so long?’ he asked, a sly grin on his face.

I ignored him. ‘Where’s Njall?’ I walked closer to the edge where the path gave way to a pond.

‘Attending to his personal needs.’

Fjola flipped the hair away from her neck. ‘We shouldn’t stray from each other. His wound makes him vulnerable.’

'I'm sure some things are best accomplished in solitude.' At the scowl on her face, he hastened to add, 'He couldn't have gone far.'

'Is there a way around?' I asked.

'If there is, I can't see it,' Mirable said.

The tall trees surrounded the pond in a semicircle, packed so tightly together that even Fjola would have a job of squeezing through. Valgsi's path wasn't so true after all. I was about to suggest we try one of the other trails when a ripple on the water caught my eye. I inched closer to the edge. Like a layer of verdant skin, a thin film coated the surface of the pond, not so different from the hue of magic in the village. A faint smell of moss hung in the air, mixed with another, stronger odour I struggled to place. Everything about this forest felt unnatural. From the tublike trees swaying on the absent wind, to the dead water, and the silence that devoured the smallest of sounds.

'We shouldn't be here,' I said. Despite myself, I craned my neck to glimpse my reflection on the green surface. The man who stared back bore no resemblance to the boy who pounded the water with his fists, grieving his father's passing those months ago. I looked older and careworn. Like life rings of a tree, the lines on my forehead told tales of restless nights and thoughts filled with hurt and anger. I tied the hair Mother was so fond of away from my face, but strands still fell down my collar in lanky waves. My stubble looked in need of a pocketknife. I did a decent job keeping it trim during the voyage to Shinpi, but our capture, and the events that followed, left little time for such fancies. The look in my eyes spoke of grim determination, and the muscles of my jaw were tight with days of tension.

'The breaker of chains.'

The force behind the words made me stagger. It wasn't the witch who spoke this time but an unfamiliar voice.

'What is it?' Fjola said, pulling her daggers halfway out of their scabbards. Her eyes flickered from me to the pond.

I shook my head to clear it, but the words still hummed inside like a confused fly. The trees beyond the pond rustled and parted, giving way to a woman dressed in a velvet cloak of deep green. A stripe of malachite paint ran from her left temple to her right. Just above it, a jade crescent decorated the exposed part of her forehead. A green line ran from the lower tip of the crescent all the way down the bridge of her nose to her mouth, where it ended in a stain on her bottom lip. The eyes that bore into mine looked translucent like those of the serenas, but I knew the woman's sight was sharper than steel because of the way it cut through the depths of my soul. It was her voice that called out to me from the pond.

She knew we were coming.

Fjola took a step back and Mirable moved to stand behind me. I scanned the trees for Njall, but there was no sign of him. As if held by some invisible hand, the leaves suspended in midair, while the nature all around us took in a deep breath, waiting for a sign of release.

'Who are you?' I asked, reaching for my sword. The small pond separated us, but I knew it was no barrier for her magic. The thick smell of it came from the woman in waves.

She opened her hands wide. 'Welcome, Valgsi. You're home at last.'

VIII

When the initial shock of her appearance faded, I said, 'Do you always imprison your guests?'

'Do you let just anyone through the gates of Stromhold? I think not, Jarin Olversson.'

Her knowledge of my name, home, and language heightened my guard. The woman knew of my connection with the Goddess of Destruction, which meant any chance of taking Goro-Khan by surprise was lost. 'Where I come from, we aren't in a habit of torturing people,' I said.

Her blank eyes settled on Fjola. 'Your companions are trespassers, and as such, they're subject to Shinpi's laws.'

I raked my mind, desperate to find a way to escape. The pond separated us from the woman, which gave us a slight advantage. As far as I could see, she stood alone. If we scattered among the trees, she'd have to choose which one of us to pursue, and I was hoping it would be me. In an effort to bide my time, I said, 'You seemed to know a great deal about me.'

'But of course. You're the one Skaldir entrusted with the task of her awakening. Her vessel, drawn to magic like a moth to light.'

My arm jerked, and an urge to run her down surged through me. Only the pond and the fear for my friends stayed my hand. As if reflecting my anger, the water bubbled crimson.

Fjola gasped, and Mirable whimpered.

'What do you want with us?' I asked through clenched teeth.

The woman waved her hand. 'Nothing from them. Everything from you.'

'In that case, let them go, and you can have me. I won't fight you.'

Fjola grabbed my arm.

The woman laughed, as if amused by my offer. 'You may be a Valgsi, but a very artless one. There's no place for you other than Shinpi. None of you will leave this island unless the Laughing God wills it so.'

'If you know so much, then you know why I'm here. Let my friends go, and take me to your master. It's time he faced the destruction he unleashed by tearing down the gates of Stromhold.'

The woman curled her stained lips, and I caught a glimpse of her teeth. All of them were white apart from the two canines encased in golden crowns. They brought to mind the fangs of a wild vixen. 'Don't make idle threats, Valgsi.' She raised her left hand, joining her thumb and two middle fingers. 'You gave yourself to anger. It burns so bright it blinds what's right in front of you.'

She snapped her fingers.

The sound was a loud crack. Like a mirage in the heart of Eydimork Sands, the forest around us began to shimmer and dissolve. One by one, the trees faded, and the leaves above us curled and vanished. A small whirlpool formed in the middle of the pond, growing wider and wider, until the whole surface turned into a furious vortex. Fjola clapped her hand over her lips as the water spanned and vaporised, leaving only a faint mist in its wake.

I looked around, and my mouth dropped.

The forest was no more, and we stood in the field, surrounded by a tight circle of warriors. We entered the woods at night, but while we were trapped here, daylight washed away all traces of darkness. The sun stared at us through a veil of green hue. A dog howled in the distance.

'This can't be,' Fjola said. 'All this time we thought we were running…'

'An illusion, created to lure you into thinking you had a chance. Just like your pathetic escape. This is the power of Skaldir's magic. You cannot fight it, or hope to resist it.'

'We want no part of it.'

The woman wrinkled her nose. 'I'm not speaking to you, girl. Both you and your brother are less significant than a grain of desert sand. You've nothing to offer Skaldir.'

'Watch your tongue, witch,' I said, feeling the familiar tremor in my right arm. This woman tricked us, allowed us to believe there was hope, and now, she was mocking us. The warriors reached for their weapons, but the woman raised her hand.

'Don't compare me to those wretched creatures.'

'Those who embrace magic are all wretched,' Mirable shouted over my shoulder. 'You worship the Goddess of Destruction, yet it was her who doomed your kind to oblivion. Your precious city sank to the bottom of the Great Atlantic, and no amount of magic will change that.'

I wiped Mirable's spittle off my neck.

The woman narrowed her ghostly eyes. 'Ahh… the Varl. I was told you're Hyllus's greatest creation, but instead of welcoming your magnificence, you cower in the face of it. Tell me, how does it feel to know your human days are numbered?'

Mirable sprang from behind me and faced the witch. 'I hate it with every fibre of my being.'

'It's a pity, but that'll change soon. When you're no longer hindered by human weakness, you'll serve us well.'

'He'll serve no one,' Fjola said. Her hands balled into fists, and the warriors surrounding us shifted.

'It's his duty to obey. Once transformed, he'll be a fine weapon indeed.' The woman crossed the space between us and looked me up and down. Her tongue passed over her upper lip. 'I can see why the demon was in no rush to finish her task.' Her green nail traced down my arm. The heat spread through my skin, and it prickled at her touch. The witch was doing something to me, and I jerked away from her.

Her expression darkened. 'Seize them.' She turned her back on me. 'And find the brother. He can only run for so long.'

A dozen warriors scattered through the countryside, while two of the others confiscated Fjola's daggers and took away my sword. I let them. Struggle would only delay the inevitable. Goro-Khan knew I was coming, and there was something he wanted from me. Our capture only closed the distance between us.

'They'll kill him,' Fjola said, lifting her chin. In that moment, she looked fiercer than the warriors in my father's band.

'He's more skilled than any of us,' I said, wishing that my words proved true.

The warriors replaced our broken shackles with the new. Mirable wailed at the sight of them. My throat clenched, but I tried to control the heat burning in my soul. They chained us like animals for the last time. The witch would deliver us before the Laughing God, and justice would be served. The shackles binding my friends would fall with the weight of our triumph. This I swore.

* * *

The witch led us back to the main road that cut through the heart of the village and disappeared into the mountains beyond. The warriors flanked us on both sides, their faces expressionless, and the crescents on their helmets shimmering green. Further from the wilderness, the hue of magic grew thicker, its misty form settling on our clothes and skin like a morning dew. From time to time, Mirable made disgusted noises, shaking his hands as if trying to rid them of a sticky web. But in Fjola's face, I spied a flicker of wonder. She wove her fingers through the magic and brought them up for inspection. Her skin shone with a soft, wavering light, but when she saw me looking, she quickly wiped her hand on her trousers.

The witch cast a glance over her shoulder. 'It's a residue,' she said. 'The luxury of using magic comes at a price. Inhale too much, and it'll corrode your lungs.'

'Agtarr will banish you for this practice,' Mirable said, clutching his throat. 'Frankly, I'm surprised this place is still standing.'

'The same blessing runs through your veins, merchant. Instead of lamenting, kneel before Skaldir and accept her gift.'

‘I’d sooner see my kneecaps shattered than let destruction into my heart. You can’t force me to do your bidding.’

The witch laughed. ‘There’re better ways than force to bend your knees.’

Mirable tugged at my sleeve. ‘I think I’m choking.’ His mouth parted, revealing a darkened tongue.

I pressed my fingers under his jaw, and it closed with a snap. ‘If you keep gaping like that, you will.’

‘You have the protection of my shield,’ the witch said. As if to prove it, she made a wiping motion with her right hand. A green barrier flickered in front of her. ‘Be glad we captured you in time. The same cannot be said for your friend.’

I looked at Fjola, and the worry in her face reflected my own. I wondered about the side effects of the prolonged exposure to the residue, and I wished there was a way to warn Njall. A part of me wanted him caught just to keep him safe, but what safety could there be in the hands of the enemy? A faint jolt of hope ran through me. Despite the odds, there was a chance Njall would make it to the ship. Lumi said the vessel was docked in a cove east of the harbour, and I prayed she was telling the truth, for it was our only means to get free of Shinpi. I focused on the surroundings, trying to memorise the landmarks and calculate the best escape route. Once Goro-Khan was dead, it would be a race to reach the ship.

In the daylight, the island appeared less threatening, but the fog of magic made it seem like we were walking through a secret world created to worship the sleeping goddess. The village before us nestled in a valley, surrounded by grassy slopes. To the south, the expansive waters of the Great Atlantic guarded Shinpi from the rest of the world. As a warning to trespassers, dozens of green sails flashed on the horizon, and seeing them in numbers I realised we were fools for thinking we could breach this place unseen. To the north, like a giant wrapped in white furs, a high mountain kept watch over the island, and at the foot of it, as if trying to outmatch the mountain in height, a crimson tower reached for the sky. From afar, the structure was little more than a bloody stain on the snow, but I felt strangely drawn to it.

'I can't hear any birds,' Fjola said in a low voice.

I sharpened my ears to the sounds, only to discover she was right. Amid the whooshing of our boots in the grass and the clunking of the guards' armour, I couldn't catch one birdsong. The trees skewering the hills showed no signs of life.

'It's this foul magic,' Mirable said. 'If we don't contain it once and for all, it'll ruin the world. Mark my words.'

'Or make it better,' the witch said. She swept her hand at the village. 'Look around you, these people embraced the teachings of Skaldir, and they haven't laboured a day in their lives. Can you say the same?'

I followed her hand to find the residents hard at work, but their methods were far removed from those used by Norderners. In Shinpi, magic was a tool for everything. A woman stood in the front yard of her house, chopping wood, without a need for a physical axe. I watched as she placed a log onto the chopping block and sent a green wave of magic at it. The force split the log in two, and the pieces clattered against the pile of wood at her feet. To the right of the house, a man ploughed the field, but instead of an ox, he employed a deep-green force to loosen and turn the soil. Whichever way I looked, magic was everywhere. Even children used it to throw sticks at each other while engaged in a game of chase.

Mirable spat. 'It's unnatural. I'm surprised Yldir allows it.'

'He's too busy sleeping,' I said.

'We knew the mages fled east after the war, but no one really believed in Shinpi's existence,' Fjola said. 'It was merely a legend, spoken in taverns, in front of the roaring fire, with a mug of mead in your hand.'

Her curiosity about Shinpi was a brilliant contrast to Mirable's distaste of the place. Since our talk in the forest, I'd noticed a slight change in her demeanour. The crease of hurt faded from her face, replaced by a thoughtful wonder that reminded me of our trip to the Lost City of Antaya and the way she couldn't stop herself from touching the tunnel walls. I often wondered how it would feel to see the world through her eyes. My lips twitched. I was sure all parts of it would be awash with light.

Fjola eyed the man pushing a cart full of roots without the use of his hands. 'These people are so at ease in the presence of magic. If it was Hvitur, everyone would've fled by now, screaming prayers. But here…' she shook her head, 'people treat it like a gardening tool.'

'Why should they fear it?' the witch said. 'This power is a blessing.'

It unnerved me how the witch answered our questions in a manner of a parent lecturing her wayward children. I reached for the hilt of my sword, and my hand came up empty. Darkness spilled across my heart, infecting my mood. 'Why don't you ask the broken Varls how blessed they feel?'

She snorted. 'Hyllus was a puppet who lacked a true skill. His creations were as flawed as the creator himself. Except for the merchant, all his experiments ended in failure. Without another mage to keep him in check, his obsession grew out of control. By killing him, you did us a great service.'

'I didn't do it for you, witch.'

She stopped and turned her head. Her translucent eyes bore into mine. 'Don't call me that,' she hissed. 'My name is Galdra, and I'm nothing like those revolting creatures.'

‘You’re one and the same to me.’ Green flickered at the corners of my vision. I took a step forward. If I had my sword, I wouldn’t hesitate to strike her down.

Fjola caught my hand, and the warmth of her touch chased away the fury.

Galdra dipped her head to one side, considering Fjola for a moment. Her eyes narrowed. ‘I serve Skaldir, but even her magic pales in the face of the blackness worshipped by the witches of Sur. We don’t speak of it here.’

The mark on my wrist pulsed and twisted, and I could feel the eye livid with the poison of my covenant. ‘What blackness?’ I asked, pressing my hand against the symbol.

‘One that feeds on living souls and whose name is best left unspoken.’

Fjola blanched, and her eyes grew wide.

Galdra didn’t know about my pact with the witches. Among the folds of her distaste, I spied fear, and the realisation turned my stomach. To whom had I surrendered the most precious part of my being? The answer crouched in the dark, out of my reach. Galdra wouldn’t speak of it, but when all of this was over, I’d pry the answer out of her.

We resumed our trek, and the village houses enfolded us—wooden structures with elevated foundations and lintels supporting slanted roofs. In Nordur, builders chose stone, but here, the walls were a mixture of wood and thin material that bore semblance to parchment. In the confines of the settlement, the smell of magic was thicker, chaffing against the lining of my throat like loose grit. Light pebbles coated the road leading through the centre of the village, and our passing stirred the residents. Most abandoned their chores to witness our procession, their curious looks following us north. Their clothing looked nothing like the drab furs and leather tunics of my homeland. Here, women wore dresses embroidered with colourful flowers I had no names for and birds with wings that brought to mind the brilliant hues of sun and fire. Each dress was decorated with a velvet sash in a shade of malachite. The men seemed to favour green cloaks and simple trousers.

My eye fell upon two women holding hands. One had Lumi's features: eyes lifted at the corners, and coal-black hair, while her companion had dark skin and the curls of a Vesterner. They wore gowns of velvet green with red flowers blooming at the hem. Matching crescents were painted on their foreheads. My gaze shifted to their laced fingers. Shinpi defied Nordern traditions in every way, but the realisation didn't fill me with contempt. Quite the opposite, watching the two women, I felt a stab of envy. They were allowed freedom I could only dream of.

A girl with black ponytails wriggled free of the crowd and stretched her palm my way. It held a parcel made of something that resembled a sheet of seaweed. Brown rice formed a ball in its centre, with a large chunk bitten off. The girl smiled at me, then stuck her tongue out at Mirable.

I snapped my head away. These people were my enemies, and when they learned I'd slaughtered their master, they'd spare me no mercy.

'Do you think Njall is among them?' Fjola asked, scanning the crowd.

'Doubt it,' I said, knowing that Njall would follow his warrior's instincts and stay out of sight. 'But with everyone's attention on us, he'll have a better chance at getting to the ship.'

Mirable plucked at the strands of his turban, his shackles rattling with every pull. 'With Shinpi's guards after him, he'd be lucky to keep his freedom until sundown.'

'You're not helping,' I said.

Fjola sighed. 'I hope the gods are watching over him.'

'He's safer than us, that's for sure. We're heading into the maw of evil with no bargaining token.'

'We're not here to bargain.'

'Nevertheless, I feel better with a pocketful of coin.' He patted the silver he stole from the guardroom.

I clamped my lips to keep myself from saying something scornful.

We left the settlement behind in favour of a more rugged landscape. Trees, with a dome-like canopy and multiple trunks, skirted the pebbled path that led in the tower's direction. Red leaves lined the ground, giving the impression of low-burning fires.

Fjola bent down and picked up a star-shaped leaf. She turned it in her hands, then pressed it to her nose. 'Smells sweet. Like honey.'

I took a lungful of air, but the only thing I could smell was the magic. It wasn't as potent as in the centre of the village, and Galdra's shield blocked most of it, but it still sat heavy in my nostrils.

The cardinal trees gave way to rocks, and the vermillion tower flashed into view, glimmering amidst the white slopes like a bittersweet berry. A winding path lined with jagged stones led towards it. Ahead, my eyes fell upon a green gate made of two pillars united by a tie beam. A score of crescents hung from its lintel, chiming on the breeze.

Galdra raised her hand, and everyone halted. I looked up. The gate loomed above us, emanating with an invisible force that separated this world from the one beyond. A place of no return. My stomach fluttered, and I wiped my sweaty palms on my shirt. A whisper of warning sounded in my head, and suddenly, I was afraid to move. I had no choice but to cross the threshold, but my friends had no business here.

'Let my friends go,' I said.

'So they can warn your uncle in Hvitur? I think not. It took you long enough to find this place, and after two centuries we're tired of waiting.' Galdra looked at each of us. 'You're standing before the place of her birth. In the heart of this mountain, the giants forged Skaldir from steel to restore the balance between life and death. This is a sacred ground and even the most destructive hearts are welcomed here.' Her lips twisted. 'Unless, of course, they oppose the Goddess of Destruction.'

'What happens if they do?' Mirable asked.

'She may be asleep, but her servants have the power to cast judgement.'

'Then punish us if you dare,' I said, taking a step forward. The power emanating from the gate felt like a silken scarf against my throat, but it didn't choke me. My skin seemed to welcome the unfamiliar touch of magic.

'It's your task as the Valgsi to bring defilers to their knees.'

I laughed, but there was no mirth in it. It was an ugly sound, reserved for those whom I despised. 'Give me back my sword, and I'll gladly fulfil my duties.'

Galdra deflected my display with a shake of her head. 'You may be the Skaldir's chosen, but you're a child at heart. Do you think it matters what you want?' She crossed the space between us and leaned her head close to my ear. 'You cannot fight the desire burning inside you. No amount of resistance will change the course of your fate. From the moment you drew your first breath, you belonged to Skaldir. It wasn't the air of this world that filled your lungs but her sacred magic.'

Her lips brushed against my lobe, and my ear filled with her sensuous sigh that sent a shiver through me. She traced her fingernail up my left temple where it pressed against the Skaldir's mark. Her tone was the purr of a cat. 'In the months to come, you'll accomplish great things. They'll whisper your name in all corners of the land, as that of a man who restored glory to Antaya. The world will fall at your feet. You'll judge all living things with the power of her magic and the might of her sword. Destruction is the greatest force, and once unleashed, there'll be no man strong enough to resist its tide.'

I snatched her hand, and she hissed against the crush of my fingers. I pulled her closer, so the tips of her nose touched mine. Her translucent eyes made me think of the vicious serena. 'The day Skaldir grants me her power, you and your kind will be the first to get the taste of my blade.' I pushed her away from me with a force that made her stagger. 'Take me to your master, and let the judgement begin.'

Galdra pressed her fingers to her chest. 'You're a fool for thinking we need your permission to achieve what we want.' She waved at the guards. 'You four will accompany us to the pagoda. As for the rest of you, get back to the village and find the brother.'

The guards bowed deeply, then marched down the slope, while the remaining four pushed us through the gate. Galdra hastened forth, her cloak billowing around her like a green sail. As soon as I crossed the threshold, a wave of dizziness swept through me, and the slopes ahead bobbed in front of my eyes like rugged boats. Amidst the gentle chime of the crescents, a voice echoed in my head. The might of it filled every crevice of my being, and the Valgsi part of me hailed it.

'Come forth, Valgsi, and fulfil your calling.'

It was a welcoming order, and my first instinct was to refuse it. The idea caused a surge of pain that split my head in two.

'What's wrong?' Fjola asked.

I slapped my palm against Skaldir's mark, and the world came back into focus. I looked at the gate. The last time I walked through one, it took me to the ruins of my home. Where would it lead me this time? To victory, or a bitter defeat? With the numerous voices in my head vying for attention, I felt like a man on the brink of madness. I looked at Fjola. Her eyebrows were drawn together and dark circles marked the skin under her eyes.

'I'm losing myself.'

IX

The pagoda, with its many tiers and crimson walls, stood out like an angry gash against the brilliant white of the mountains. Galdra led us up the stone steps to a red doorway studded with gold, where she paused and looked up at the curved roofs stretching like wings overhead. Fjola followed her gaze, and a look of wonder stole over her eyes. No structure like this existed in Nordur, or Vester for that matter. Galdra seized the crescent-shaped handles and slid the door open. It parted with a rasp.

We stepped through to be greeted by a sharp and lingering scent of incense. The chill inside stirred the hair on my arms and legs, and the familiar touch of cold made me think of Stromhold with its stone walls that no amount of fire could truly warm. Supported by timber pillars, the square room gave the impression of stillness and calm. The Lost City of Antaya was painted on the ceiling, with Sirili—the school of magic—at its centre, as tall and glorious as I remembered. It was hard to imagine all this magnificence sank to the bottom of the Great Atlantic. A vermillion rug led to the back of the room where Skaldir's wooden figure presided over an altar littered with bowls and cups of various sizes. Candles moulded from green wax cast an eerie glow over a stone table, and thin wisps of smoke curled from the burners.

Galdra strode from the door to the sanctum where she bowed deeply before the statue. 'May the force of destruction prevail and cleanse our world of weakness.'

At the reverence in her voice, I rolled my eyes. She was nothing more than a puppet of her goddess, blinded by the days of glory long dead.

As if sensing my thoughts, Galdra turned and gave me a scornful look. In the candlelight, the crescent painted on her forehead shone a spectral green.

'Now, we climb,' she said, pointing at the staircase to the right of the altar. Her ghostly eyes searched mine. 'With each step you take, think hard about your reasons for being here.'

I held her gaze. 'I know exactly why I'm here. Lead the way.'

Mirable groaned. 'Is it really necessary for all of us to go up there?' A low rumble emanated from his belly, and he pressed his hands to it. 'All the pleasures of simple life lost because of this wretched magic.' His bottom lip quivered. 'No more feasts at the Merchant's Circle, no more debates about the best methods of generating profit, no more judging things by their weight in gold…'

‘A little dramatic, don’t you think?’ I asked. ‘If you want your future, you must make do with your past and keep your head clear about the present.’

‘What does it even mean?’ His foot caught on the first step, and he tripped.

Fjola grabbed his shirt and pulled him back. ‘Watch your step. What good is the future if your neck is twisted?’

Galdra climbed ahead, and we followed, flanked by the guards and surrounded by the hollow sounds of our feet striking timber. She ushered us from room to room, from one staircase to the next, without as much as a single glance over her shoulder. As we crossed each floor, I glimpsed the walls adorned with murals and tapestry, detailing various depictions of Skaldir, but there was no time to admire them.

Fjola stopped to touch an intricate flower carved into the handrail at each curve of the stairway. She ran her fingers over the pointed petals only to have the guard slap her hand away.

She whipped her head, eyes full of angry sparks.

Without thinking, I pushed the man, and if not for the guard standing behind him, he’d have tumbled down the staircase. He grabbed the handrail, uttering a string of harsh words. Fjola’s daggers hung at his hips, and my fingers itched to grab them and slice off the hand that slapped her.

Fjola touched my arm and steered me up the stairs. ‘It’ll be over soon,’ she whispered.

My shoulders loosened, and we resumed the climb. Silver snowflakes embellished the wall to my right, and the shape of them took me back to the day in the Stromhold hideout where Lumi brought the winter in my drawing to life with her magic. In those days, our greatest worry was how to get away with mischief and avoid punishment. Was Lumi here, hiding behind the walls of this strange pagoda? She gave us our freedom and urged me to sail back to Hvitur. Were these the acts of a bloodthirsty demon? Or maybe a ploy, created to mislead us and protect her master, the Laughing God? With Lumi, I could never be sure.

After what felt like an eternity of climbing, we came to a stop in front of a closed doorway. Galdra took a deep breath and smoothed out her cloak. She lowered her head for a moment, and I felt a twinge of unease. I was about to face the man who ruined my world and planned to destroy the whole of Nordur with his vengeful goddess. When I climbed the Citadel of Vester to confront Hyllus, I had Kylfa's box in my possession, but this time, I had no plan. Even my sword was out of reach. I sailed the breadth of the Great Atlantic for a chance at revenge, and the gods granted my wish, but at what price?

Kylfa's voice rustled in my head. '*Be careful what you wish for, Valgsi.*'

I rolled my neck, flexing my fingers to ease the pins and needles. I was ready for whatever lay in wait behind that door.

'Are we waiting for an invitation?' Mirable asked. The long ascent knocked the wind out of him, and he stood with his hands resting on his thighs, panting.

To my right, Fjola shifted uneasily.

Galdra straightened her back. 'Whatever you do, don't make him laugh,' she said and pushed the door open. It came apart without a sound.

It led us into a square room stripped of all decorations. Green orbs hovered in each corner, illuminating the simple woodwork. A rack full of swords of various lengths stood propped against the back wall, steel glinting in the afternoon light that streamed from the gap between two shutters. An altar shaped into a triangle occupied the opposite corner, with a small carving of Skaldir in its centre. Unlike the one on the floor below, it was free of clutter. A lone candle burned at the feet of the goddess, its flame matching those cast by the orbs, and next to it, a stick of incense sent a faint whirl of smoke into the air.

A man sat in the centre, cross-legged, his back to the window, wearing nothing but a pair of loose trousers secured at his waist with a green sash. His bare feet poked through the cross of his legs while his hands rested on his knees, palms down. He didn't stir when we entered; he simply sat there, eyes closed, his face a mask of peaceful concentration.

I stared at him. Was this half-naked man the much-feared enemy of Nordur? The Laughing God of Shinpi who issued orders that killed my family? A snort trembled on my lips, but I held it back, curious to see what welcome he'd give us. The ropes of dread that bound me during the long voyage to Shinpi fell away, and for the first time, my chest felt light. A sense of sureness washed over me—I was going to kill this man right in the safety of his own pagoda. I cast a sideways glance at the guard who held my sword. When the opportunity arose, I'd seize it back, and when I did, Goro-Khan's reign would end.

Galdra took a step forward and bowed. 'As per your orders, the Norderners are here. Unharmed.'

Goro's lids parted. Against the whites of his pupils, his irises looked obsidian. He regarded me with a keen and thoughtful gaze. 'One seems to be missing.'

'The girl's brother fled, but the guards are looking for him.' Her fingers tightened around the edge of her robe. 'He won't hide for long. He is wounded, and the prolonged exposure to the residue will make it difficult to breathe.'

'In other words, you didn't follow my orders.'

Galdra winced as if scalded. In one smooth movement, Goro rose to his feet. He was taller than me, but judging by the lace of silver in his bound hair, I had the vitality of youth on my side. He clasped his hands behind his back. 'Tell me, *Valgsi*, what brings you here, to this forgotten island in the middle of the Great Atlantic?'

I stood tall, filled with confidence my father would've been proud of. The moment of my mother's vengeance was at hand. 'I'm here to take your life.'

Galdra let out a small gasp, and I could hear soldiers behind me clasping after their weapons.

'Ah, vengeance then.' Goro-Khan seemed unconcerned by this revelation. 'I find it curious how the Goddess of Destruction chose *you* to set her free. A Nordern wolf without as much as a drop of magic to his name.'

My neck grew hot. 'I don't need magic to make you bleed.'

Goro's face betrayed no emotions, and I couldn't help but admire his self-control.

'The way you dispatched Hyllus tells me otherwise.'

'He was a broken coward, hiding behind the walls of his citadel while his Varls roamed untamed, killing innocent people.'

'No one is innocent.' Goro stroked his neatly trimmed beard. 'Come to think of it, you walk with a Varl of your own.'

I bared my teeth. 'Mirable is nothing like those creatures.'

'Of course not.' His piercing eyes shifted to Mirable. 'He's so much more than that. When his transformation is complete, you'll envy his power.'

‘I’d rather die than accept this fate,’ Mirable snarled, hunching forward. The tumours under his shirt rippled.

The guards unsheathed their weapons while Galdra brought her hands in front of her like a shield. The air in the room turned brittle, and it seemed everyone, including me, held their breath. Part of me hoped Mirable would launch himself at Goro, and in the commotion that would certainly ensue, I’d get a chance to reclaim my sword. I leaned forward, biting down on my bottom lip.

Fjola pressed a hand on Mirable’s shoulder. ‘Get a hold of yourself. Remember who you are.’

His breathing slowed, his muscles loosened, and his mouth closed over his teeth.

Goro-Khan clapped. ‘Remarkable. To control a Varl ruled by instinct is an impressive skill. It’s a shame you’re not one of us.’

‘I didn’t do it to impress you, and I’d never stand with those who wish for pain and destruction.’

Goro-Khan offered her a bemused smile. ‘Yet you love *him*.’

Colour drained from Fjola’s cheeks, and Goro-Khan dismissed her with a wave.

‘Shall we?’ he asked me.

I frowned.

'You came all this way to kill me, so it's only fair to give you a chance.' He snapped his fingers at the guard who held my blade. 'Give him the sword.'

'It's unwise,' Galdra said. 'Before they overpowered him, he ran down a score of guards.' Despite the warning, her ghostly eyes shone with pearly light.

'More the reason to test his mettle,' Goro-Khan said. 'It's a long time since I fought a worthy opponent. If Skaldir wants me dead, so be it. After all, everything starts with destruction.'

Mirable tugged at my sleeve. 'For Yldir's sake, don't fall for a trick like that.'

'He's right,' Fjola said. 'Look around. This isn't a fight you can win. Don't let your desire for vengeance cloud your judgement.'

Bolstered by the memory of my triumph back on the ship, I took my sword from the guard. 'I won't be fighting alone,' I said. When my hand closed around the hilt, the familiar feeling of rage sparked inside me, and I recognised it for what it was—Skaldir's need for destruction, restrained only by the magic of her brothers. The gods slept, dreaming their eternal dream, but I was awake. She lent me her powers before, and there was no reason why she wouldn't this time. It didn't matter how powerful Goro-Khan was, and it didn't matter he considered himself a god. He offered me a chance to fight him, and I wasn't about to refuse.

'The Laughing God is famed for his laughter,' I said, giving my sword a swing. 'Let's see how loud he can laugh in the face of Agtarr.'

Goro-Khan walked to the weapons rack. He picked up and tested two swords, weighing them in his hands. His choice was of no consequence because the blade of Stromhold Guardians wasn't made of earthly steel. Just holding it sent vibrations through my arm. If anyone tried to take it from me now, they'd find themselves cut to pieces. I crossed the Great Atlantic to make my stand, and my friends made sacrifices to get me here. Only the death of Goro-Khan would unlock the Fields of Life, allowing my parents to reunite. In response to my silent elation, the jewel in the cross guard came alive with green light. I assumed the warrior's stance, wishing Njall was here to witness this moment.

Goro made his choice and turned to face me. The blade in his grip was long and curved. 'Show me what you're made of, Valgsi,' he said, thrusting his left leg out wide. He brought the sword in front of him, and its sharp edge glinted a deadly warning.

My insides vibrated, and the hot wave of excitement surged through me, filling my mouth with a sweet taste of vengeance.

I charged.

Goro-Khan stepped sideways, but I wasn't about to engage in this predictable play of avoidance, so I turned in a flash and rushed him again. This time his blade met mine with a clang. Mirable yelped, and Fjola let out a small cry. I pushed against Goro's weapon with all my strength, but he stood his ground. My sword slid against his with a sharp peal that set my teeth on edge. Goro pushed me, and I staggered back. I braced my feet against the wooden floor.

'Your father taught you well, but not well enough,' Goro-Khan said, slicing the air with his blade. 'Again.'

I glared at him, my stomach churning with an erosive fury. 'You know nothing about my father.'

'The bond between a father and his son is most powerful.' His left eye twitched. 'Not even death can sever the ties of blood.'

I roared and charged him.

He sidestepped and started circling the room. I came at him again and again, trying every move that Argil ever taught me, but Goro-Khan evaded them with such ease that I was beginning to wonder about his true abilities. Could it be that he was a mind reader, and this little interlude was to shame me in front of my friends and strangers? He wanted me down on my knees, begging for mercy, but I'd sooner look into Agtarr's face before bending my neck for the Laughing God.

Our swords came together in another mighty ring that sent tremors up my arm. I managed to deliver four strikes against his steel, but in a series of fluid parries, he warded them off. I don't know how but I found myself staring at the wall with his naked foot pressed to the low of my back. Through the shirt, I could feel the impression of his toes and the hard crush of his heel. He pushed me forward, and I slammed into the wall.

'Don't ever turn your back on your opponent,' Goro-Khan said. 'Didn't they teach you this in that winter hovel you call home?'

I stood, heaving, my forehead pressed against the wall, wishing the timber turned to parchment so I could rip it open and throw Goro-Khan off his precious tower. Instead, I punched the wood with my fist, and the stabbing pain that shot through my knuckles sobered me up. Anger tore at the old wounds, and the images of my past rushed in a bloody surge. My father's name rang in my ears like an accusation, and my mother's mournful cries echoed in every beat of my heart. My inability to draw even the tiniest drop of blood from the man who ordered them killed filled me with shame. The hilt of my sword dug into the flesh of my palm while pulsing circles obscured my vision, casting a green veil over the world. The power of the goddess stirred inside me, and I welcomed it, savouring the bitter taste of her wrath. It was an ancient fury of a beast battering the bars of her prison with me as her only link to freedom. The lone candle that burned at Skaldir's altar hissed and flickered, its green flame like the erratic tongue of a viper.

Slowly, I turned. Goro-Khan lifted his eyebrows, and I revelled in a shadow of surprise that passed across his face. The duel was no longer between the two of us. My hands twitched at the thought of spilling his blood, and a burst of ugly laughter escaped my lips. Fjola's voice hummed from somewhere in the room, calling my name, but faced with the divine power, the actions of the living held no meaning.

'Come and test me then,' I said, sneering.

Goro's muscles tightened. He drew his head back and made a deliberate slash with his sword. 'Finally. Show me her power, Valgsi.'

He advanced.

Everything slowed. In three strides, Goro-Khan closed the distance between us. I stepped aside, bringing my sword down. The edge connected with his shoulder and sliced through the bared flesh. I pulled the blade back. Red droplets splattered my face, and I licked Goro's blood off my lips, savouring the metallic taste.

Goro-Khan clasped at the wound, and Galdra screeched.

I let out a deep, satisfying sigh. I slew Varls before, and I killed Hyllus, but nothing compared to this moment. My sword took on a life of its own, vibrating with energy fuelled by the freshly spilled blood while the green haze obscured all but the face of my enemy. 'Ready for more?' I asked.

Blood ran in rivulets from the cut on Goro's shoulder, but his face betrayed no signs of pain. His lips twisted, and the coals of his eyes gleamed. Seeing him this way infuriated me further, and I rushed him, letting the mist of rage guide my movements. This time, Goro-Khan was ready. His blade met mine in a flurry of slashes. I parried them all. It was the most exhilarating dance, and I never felt so alive in my life.

I didn't know how long we fought because I lost all sense of time. Goro-Khan began showing signs of fatigue: his cheeks turned crimson, his breath came on ragged, and the sureness in his step gave way to a stagger. I delivered another slash to his hip, but he lurched sideways in time to escape the worst of it. I refused him the chance to recover. Skaldir's sword chased the Laughing God across the room until I had him where he wanted to have me at the start of this duel—on his knees, with blood pooling from the numerous cuts on his body. I lifted my boot and pressed it against his wounded shoulder. He winced but uttered no sound.

Galdra attempted to come to his aid, but Goro stopped her with the flat of his palm.

'Anything you wish to say to your goddess?' I asked, pushing him on his back. I pressed the tip of my sword to his throat. 'Beg forgiveness for all the lives you took.' I cast a glance over my shoulder and some of my elation dissipated. I expected to see the joy in the faces of Mirable and Fjola, but instead, they stared at me wide-eyed. A fresh eruption of anger shook me. I just bested the greatest evil, so why did they still look so scared? 'We crossed the endless ocean to exact vengeance on the Laughing God. Rejoice with me!'

Mirable shuffled back a step, his left hand clutching at his turban while Fjola held onto his arm, her face as pale as that of the moon.

Low laughter rippled through the room, and I whipped my head back to Goro. He lay splayed on his back with an expression that showed no signs of remorse. The green veil in my vision drew back, and the world regained some of its colours. Suddenly all the strength that drove me fell in a heap at my feet like an invisible blanket. My sword arm trembled while my legs felt ready to collapse under me. Runnels of sweat ran down my forehead, pooling into the corners of my eyes. I wiped them away with the back of my hand.

The lone candle on the altar guttered and died.

'Stop it,' I said. Something was terribly wrong. The wretched Khan should be begging for mercy instead of making this… this noise that sounded like some horrible mixture of laughter and doom.

'Did you really think Skaldir would kill her mortal god?' Goro said in a voice full of triumph. 'She brought you here to show us her power and to strengthen our resolve. We hid in the shadows for far too long, shunned and despised by men like you. But no more.'

My sword felt impossibly heavy, but I kept it trained on his neck. 'Only Valgsi can awaken Skaldir, and I'll never answer her call.'

Goro-Khan slapped the blade away and sprang to his feet. 'But you already have.'

I wanted to come at him, but the weakness overwhelmed me, and I stumbled. My sword clattered to the floor, and the green light illuminating the script faded. I looked at my bloodstained hands. Rage welled up in me anew but stripped of the divine intensity it was merely a human anger, a feeble mixture of frustration and shame.

'Never,' I said, loathing the quiver in my voice. 'I'd rather die than see your goddess released from her dream.'

Goro-Khan uttered another bark of laughter. 'Only Agtarr can grant that wish, but you defied the gods all your life.' He wiped the blood off his chest. 'You came here to kill me, and you failed, so spare me your speeches.'

Galdra rushed to his side, dabbing at his wounds with a piece of white cloth that soon turned crimson. I didn't understand how he moved with such purpose after losing so much blood. Heedless of her efforts, Goro marched across the room to where Fjola and Mirable huddled together.

He picked a lock of Fjola's hair and turned it in his fingers. 'Do you know why they call me the Laughing God?'

'Don't touch her,' I said. My legs were two hunks of lead bolted to the floor, and even a thought of taking a step felt like an impossible effort.

Fjola lifted her chin and returned Goro's stare. Even though it was he who posed the greater threat, it was she who looked like a fearless queen issuing a challenge to a barbarian king.

'They call me that because I laugh in the face of my enemies.'

And then he did.

It started as a low and guttural chuckle, seemingly harmless yet highly contagious to those it was intended for. Fjola's jaw tightened, and her hands locked into fists, but this small display of resistance had no effect on Goro-Khan. His laughter became louder, more intense, and to my horror, Fjola's lips stretched and parted in response. She clasped her hand over her mouth as if to stifle a mischievous giggle, but at the same time, her eyes grew large and her forehead creased, turning her beautiful face into a mask of horror. Goro screeched like a barn owl in the dead of the night, and the sound pierced my eardrums. I made another attempt at movement but my legs refused to obey. Mirable fared no better. He stood with his mouth agape and his eyes transfixed on Fjola's face.

‘Do something,’ I screamed at him, but he didn’t flinch.

Goro’s laughter became deeper. The muscles of his torso jerked and twitched as if they belonged to a puppet animated by a madman. Fjola’s hand fell away from her lips and her laughter spilled in a wave of merriment I’d never heard before. For a brief moment, her joy mesmerised even me, and I found myself smiling at the pure brilliance that filled the room. But Fjola’s grotesque expression never changed. Her face contorted like that of a person fighting extreme pain. She bent in half and hugged her belly, laughing, laughing, laughing…

Clutching his turban, Mirable dropped to his knees, wailing and rocking from side to side. Galdra pressed her hands to her temples, and the guards plugged their ears with their fingers. I fought the force that held me in place while my helpless roars joined Goro’s laughter. At that moment, I understood why the magic was shunned along with those who wielded it—its capacity to do evil far outweighed its potential for good.

Goro’s laugh morphed into a shriek. Fjola fell to her knees, red tears streaming down her cheeks, and the Laughing God opened his arms wide in a call for more. Blood gushed from her nose as she collapsed to the floor in a convulsing heap. Like on that day in Sur, when the witch showed her the images of her dead father, foam frothed at the corners of Fjola’s mouth. And still, she laughed.

Mirable threw his hands wide, lifted his head, and uttered a doleful howl that sounded like a chorus of wolves baying their woes at the moon. A green wave of magic rushed from his fingers and wrapped around Goro's neck as though it was a noose, putting an end to his laughter. Still howling, Mirable curled his fingers, and the rope tightened. The veins in Goro's neck stood out, and his eyes bulged from his sockets as he clawed at the green cord choking his windpipe. Spittle gathered at the corners of his mouth while his face turned crimson from the strain. Fjola's laughter died, and her convulsions ceased.

Galdra's scream ripped through the silence, and she lashed out at Mirable with a green wave that sent him sprawling. His head hit the floor with an audible thud, and the expression of anguish fell off his face, replaced by the serene look of unconsciousness. His magic noose dissipated.

Goro-Khan fell to his knees, rasping for breath and clutching his swollen neck. Green lashes, similar to those we saw on the prisoner's back, marked his skin.

'How?' he croaked.

Galdra bent next to Mirable. 'I don't know,' she said. 'Without Hyllus, we can never be sure, but the creature called magic at will, which makes it rather dangerous if it's not on our side.' She twisted her hands into a circle, and a green orb of energy came to life between her palms.

With Galdra's attention on Mirable, the force chaining me to the spot fell away, and I lurched forward. 'Get away from him,' I screamed, groping after my sword.

She snapped around and threw the orb at me. It was like being hit with a ball of iron, and the force of it brought me to my knees. I was sure all my ribs shattered at the impact that knocked the wind out of me and filled my eyes with water.

'Enough!' a voice cried.

A chill blew across the room, and my nostrils filled with the sharp and wet smell of ice. My mind prickled with a recognition that took me back to the snowy peaks of Nordur, where the air burned the lungs like ice fire. This sweet and frosty scent of home infused me with a longing that touched the core of my soul.

In a flurry of snowflakes, Lumi stormed through the door.

The guards drew back, and Galdra pulled up her cloak to cover her mouth and nose. At the sight of the girl who ruined my life, my treacherous heart quickened, and heedless of the pain inflicted by Galdra, my lungs refused me a full breath. Lumi was no longer a girl I'd chased throughout the expanse of the Great Atlantic. She walked across the room with her shoulders back and her head high. Her dress floated around her like a sky blue breeze, and her black hair formed a stark contrast to her skin, which was as white as a snowbell. I searched the deep pools of her eyes, and the old wanting surged through me—to get lost in the sapphire vortex where time didn't exist and where Lumi's whiteout froze all rational thought. From the moment she set foot in Stromhold, I had no choice but to follow her into the eye of her storm. Long ago, the touch of her glacial lips encased my heart in ice that even Fjola's warmth failed to thaw. Lumi's ice burrowed deep under my skin, and looking at her, I knew that no amount of heat would melt it.

Lumi's deep-blue eyes bore into Goro-Khan. 'You stole something from me.'

The sound of her voice stirred the witch's mark and awakened the memory of my first trip to Sur and the way Kylfa laughed at my misguided desire to lift the spell that made Lumi mute. Except it was all a trick set in motion to lure me away from Stromhold so Lumi could execute her wretched deed. The notion sickened my stomach. After what happened, how could I still want her near me? I didn't understand myself anymore.

I pulled my gaze away from Lumi's slender form and crawled to where Fjola lay, her face stained with blood. The sight of her hurt took a dagger to my heart. It was my desire for revenge that caused this pain, and I loathed myself for failing to protect her from the laughing madman. Even Mirable, who despised magic, called upon the art to save Fjola's life while I remained rooted to the floor like an oak tree. I pressed my ear to her chest, and the faint beat of her heart brought on a surge of gratitude. 'Fjola, can you hear me?' I asked, patting her cheek.

Her mouth twitched.

I took her hand and pressed it to my lips. Her skin was warm and dry. 'I'm so sorry.' I choked on the word, for no amount of apology would change the simple truth that she almost came face to face with Agtarr. 'I should've never brought you here.'

Goro's voice reached me through the haze of my guilt. 'You forgot your place, ice demon.'

At the sound of him, my hair stood on end, and the muscles of my arms swelled with a monstrous desire to destroy. Goro-Khan. His name haunted me since I heard it from Lumi on that fateful day in Stromhold. I gave up everything to track him down, and now, I had him within my reach. I squeezed Fjola's hand. My quest to avenge Mother wasn't over yet. 'I won't be long,' I said, kissing her forehead. She moaned softly. I wanted to cradle Fjola close to my chest and stay with her until she regained consciousness, but to truly keep her safe, I had to silence the laughing evil.

I got to my feet and retrieved my sword. My legs didn't shake as much, and my arms recovered enough strength for me to wield my father's blade once more. The pain in my chest was still alive, and each breath came with a harsh stab, but I ignored it and walked to stand at Lumi's side.

'I have no place,' Lumi said. 'Hyllus made sure of that when he ripped my heart out of my chest.'

Goro sneered at me. 'Have you learned nothing?'

'I told you to leave,' Lumi said in a low voice. 'This isn't a fight you can win.'

'Listen to your demon, Valgsi.'

'I'm not going anywhere until I get what I came for,' I said.

Lumi pressed her lips into a blue slash. 'Give me back what's mine and let them go.'

Goro-Khan let out his vicious laughter, but Lumi was quick to react. With one swipe of her pale hand, she erected an ice shield that absorbed the sound, then cracked and shattered under the force of it.

'How many of them can you make before you run out of magic?' Goro asked.

'To silence you, as many as it takes.'

'I can laugh for eternity and never tire of it.' He cocked his head to one side. 'Tell me, what's so important about staying human?'

'The question reveals more than the answer. You hope to gain Skaldir's favour, but we both know that nothing can bring back the dead.'

Goro-Khan's eye twitched. 'Watch your tongue, or I'll carve it out for good.'

'Give me back what's mine.'

Goro pointed his stout finger at me. 'Your task was to bring him here. You know who he is and what he must do.'

'If you think I'll bring the Wrath of Skaldir upon the world, you're entertaining empty illusions,' I said, lifting my sword. 'No god or mortal controls my fate.'

'I'm growing tired of the same singsong.'

Lumi angled her head at me. The sapphire of her irises swirled and rippled like the surface of a mountain lake. 'I wish we had more time,' she whispered. 'The things I did—'

'There'll be time for that later,' I said.

I imagined this moment so many times—me confronting her—but never did I think she and I would be facing the same enemy side by side. In that instant, the doubts and hurts I harboured for so long melted like snow touched by sun rays. Yes, Lumi destroyed my home and killed my mother, and I didn't know if I could ever forgive her for that, but knowing Goro-Khan forced her hand made the idea of absolution possible. When this battle was won, and Lumi's heart was beating again in her chest, anything would be possible…

She held out her hand, and I took it, relishing the familiar chill that spread through my fingers. Her touch was home, and having her so close, I could almost feel the icy wind on my face as we rode my beloved Blixt across the planes of Nordur.

'Ready?' I asked.

Lumi nodded once, and together we faced Goro-Khan.

'How touching,' he said. 'A pity it cannot last.' He trained the gleaming steel on Galdra and the guards. 'Don't interrupt us.'

I assumed the warrior stance. 'Let's finish this.'

We plunged into battle anew, only this time, the Goddess of Destruction didn't cloud my vision. I fought like the man my father trained me to be. Every blow, every strike, was imbued with the force of vengeance that devoured my heart since the moment I'd learned about Goro-Khan's existence. It was pure emotion, untainted by the corrupt magic of the gods. Lumi's presence gave me a different kind of strength. In every flash of her ice, I glimpsed a promise of what could be if we emerged victorious. Old wounds would heal at last, and the snowy landscape of the future would stretch before us, ready for fresh footprints.

Goro-Khan was a master warrior. Despite the wounds I inflicted on him during our earlier fight, he moved like the wind, wild and fierce, striking with skill and trained precision. His pupils flared with the glee of battle, but his expression was that of pure focus as he assessed and reacted to our every move.

Lumi's crystalline magic shattered against the walls, filling the room with the crackling of ice. It took her years to master the power, but now she unleashed every inch of it. A whirlwind of snow advanced through the room, sweeping one guard into the white vortex. His piercing scream rang in my ears long after the man himself was a heap of broken limbs. Whenever Goro tried to laugh, Lumi silenced him with a shield of ice. Cut from his power and weakened by the existing wounds, Goro's vitality began to wane.

My sword caught his side, and blood splashed across the frozen floor in a series of blotches. A shard of ice slammed into his chest, throwing him off balance and creating an opening for another stab. Every successful strike released a fresh surge of adrenaline that suffused my aching muscles with new energy. No other fight brought me this much joy. When I battled Hyllus, Trofn's magic cast the finishing blow, but today, my sword carved its own way to victory.

Goro-Khan rushed to the opposite corner of the room. Lumi fell into a crouch and pushed her hands forward. A fresh sheet of ice trailed after the Laughing God, covering the floor with a slithery sheen and turning the highest chamber of the pagoda into a frozen lake. Goro slipped and crashed to the ground. His head bounced off the ice, and the impact wiped the composure off his face.

I brought my sword up.

'Galdra!' Goro-Khan shrieked.

Galdra ran to his side with her right hand outstretched. When I saw what was in it, all fight went out of me.

I froze, unable to take my eyes off the heart in her grip.

Goro's lips drew back in a snarl. 'Did you really think I'd let you and that frozen witch walk out of here?' He hefted himself into a sitting position, and Galdra helped him to his feet with her free hand. His bloody chest heaved with effort. He held up his palm, and Galdra dropped Lumi's heart into it. Goro's blood-stained fingers closed around the crystal, and Lumi took in a sharp breath. She bent forward, grabbing a fistful of her dress.

I lowered the sword. My heart thudded in my ears like the beating wings of Agtarr's ravens. Under the weight of this crisis, my mind crumbled. I stood frozen to the spot, unable to take my eyes off the crystal beating erratically in Goro's grip. I needed time to think, to consider my options, but I was afraid to move, to speak, to breathe for fear the mere sound of my voice would make Goro shatter the heart.

Slowly, I placed the sword on the frozen floor. The ice was already melting, giving way to the original trappings of the pagoda. I spread my palms in front of me in a gesture of surrender. It seemed like defeat was my middle name, for it followed me wherever I went. The exhilaration I felt only moments ago gave way to the bleakness of despair. My tongue stuck to the top of my mouth like a lizard dried out by the sun.

'Don't hurt her,' I said in a trembling voice. An irrational thought of bargaining for Lumi's heart with Mirable's coins crossed my mind, but Goro-Khan didn't need gold. To awaken his goddess he needed power, and only Valgsi could give him that. 'If you let her go, I'll do what you ask.'

Lumi grabbed hold of my arm. 'No,' she rasped. 'This is what he wants. If you surrender, the world will burn. Don't repeat my mistakes.'

Goro tightened his fingers around the heart, and Lumi sank to her knees, clutching at her chest.

'Last time your mages called for Skaldir, her wrath destroyed everything,' Lumi told him. A painful gasp preceded every word. 'What good is the world in ashes?'

'The humans started the war out of fear. Because they couldn't understand the force of magic,' Goro said. 'You should know better than to side with them.'

I squeezed my hands into fists. 'Can't you see that summoning Skaldir won't restore the mages to glory? If they cause destruction again, the world will hate them even more.'

'Let it. Humans or not, we're all children of destruction.' His left eye twitched. 'I've waited countless years for a sign, and now that you're here, I can set everything right.'

'You're a fool for believing Skaldir has the power to resurrect your son,' Lumi cried.

The pagoda fell silent, and it felt like everyone present drew breath, not daring to exhale it. Goro's face grew still. His obsidian eyes drilled into Lumi's, and blue clashed with black in the soundless exchange. My mind buzzed with tension, and sweat formed tracks down my neck. My fingers itched for the sword that lay at my feet, but I pressed them firmly to my thighs. Goro was a spark, ready to ignite at the tiniest excuse, and I didn't want to give him one. I bit on my cheek, hard enough to draw blood. My eyes shifted from Lumi to Goro and back to Lumi as I waited for a sign, anything to tell me she was ready for another strike. But Lumi just knelt there, glaring at the man who played a hand in her creation.

At last, Goro-Khan spoke, and if the voice alone could summon darkness, the room would turn into a pit of gloom. 'You were running wild for far too long, defying my will with your blizzards, pretending to live a human life. You think your useless heart will set you free, absolve you of your sins. But demons can never be humans, and so you shall melt like the ice you were made of.' He thrust the hand holding the blood-stained crystal at Lumi and loosened his fingers. Free from the pressure, the heart returned to its steady beat.

Da-dum, da-dum, da-dum, da—

Goro-Khan, as if reignited by the unyielding look in Lumi's eyes, closed his fingers around it and squeezed.

The tendons in Goro's hand bulged with the force of his crushing press. At first, Lumi's heart fluttered erratically, like a bird locked in a cage. I stared at it, mouth agape, feeling my own heart swell and writhe for freedom in my chest. I was back in Nordur again, facing the yawning gate of Stromhold, beyond which lay ruin and death; the same icy wind swept through my mind, freezing my soul with terror as I watched Lumi's heart, the one I had held so close to my own, lose the fight.

With a sound like thousand chiming bells, Lumi's heart shattered.

The pieces of crystal rained to the floor in gleaming droplets, not to be joined again. As each struck the floor, a new thorn of ice embedded in my heart, hooking through the flesh and giving rise to black lesions that would never heal. I pressed my knuckles to my mouth, stifling a sharp scream. My lungs refused to take another breath, and deprived of air, everything inside me turned to stone. I couldn't take my eyes off the pieces scattered at Goro's feet. It was Stromhold all over again, and I could almost sense Agtarr's Warrior of Death at my shoulder. Everyone told me I was Skaldir's chosen, but it was the God of Death who walked my path, casting black shadows in his wake.

Goro-Khan raised his foot and crushed the remaining fragments with his heel.

Lumi let out an agonising cry and collapsed to the floor.

The sound broke my paralysis, and I sank to my knees. I pulled Lumi into my arms, hugging her close to my chest. The pagoda and everyone in it disappeared as I found myself back in Nordur, surrounded by the precious white of the falling snow. I caressed her cool cheek while the weight of despair pressed down my shoulders like a giant anvil. With my shaking fingers, I traced Lumi's pale face and the faint blue of her lips, committing them to memory. Lumi's eyes found mine, but the sapphire in them lost all of its intensity. At that moment, I would've given anything to bring back the vivid colours that mesmerised me as a boy.

'I never wanted to hurt you.' Her voice was stripped of the enchanting ring, and each word came out brittle and hollow.

I choked back the tears. 'Say nothing.' My fingers tangled in her hair, and I stroked it, memorising the soft feel of the inky strands. 'It's all my fault. If I'd left your heart in Antaya, where it belonged…'

She grabbed my hand. 'My heart didn't belong in that chest. From the moment I set foot in Stromhold… it was yours to keep. When you pulled it free, you gave me the greatest gift. The whole time it was with you, I felt real. I felt everything. Every beat of your heart echoed in my chest as if it were my own.' She coughed, and it sounded like ice cracking underfoot. 'You shouldn't have sailed here.'

I pressed my finger to her lips. 'I sailed here… for you.' My ribcage caved in under the press of devastation, and the ache in my heart matched the one I felt holding my mother's frozen body. I squeezed my eyes to hold back tears, but it was like trying to hold a rushing river. I placed my hand against Lumi's chest. 'For as long as my heart is beating, so will be yours.'

A first crack appeared on the surface of her cheek, just below the left eye—a tiny web of lines on the porcelain skin of the girl I named Lumi. I wanted to rub at the fracture, polish it off her face, so it stayed unmarred, just as it was in my mind. To my friends, Lumi was a demon who stole into Stromhold under a guise of a lost girl, only to gain trust and repay the kindness of those who took her in with icy death. All of it was true. She did those things and more. But the girl in my arms was also my childhood friend who accepted my shortcomings and drew back the curtain of loneliness pulled shut by the hidden powers of my destiny.

'I miss Nordur,' she whispered. 'I miss the snow, the wind chill…'

I squeezed her hand, and it felt like carved ice in my grasp. More and more fractures appeared on her face, making it look like a mirror about to be shattered.

'Can you tell me about home?' she whispered. Her blue irises faded to grey, and a crack shot from the corner of her right eye, cutting through the pupil and fracturing the cornea.

I didn't bother disguising my tears anymore, and large drops splattered on her face. I pressed Lumi's hand to my cheek, and with the help of words and memories, I took her home. 'The snow is everywhere,' I said, fighting the tremble in my voice, 'blanketing the world as far as the eye can see. Dressed in their evergreen armour, the pines of Nordur defy the winter storms, answering each gust with a barrage of needles.'

Lumi's hand cracked in my grip, and a piece of me cracked with it. She was breaking in my arms, but there was nothing I could do. I rocked her gently. 'Blixt's lungs contract and expand as we ride through the open country, leaving hoof prints in the snow.'

'Blixt,' Lumi said weakly, and the memory tugged her fractured lips into a smile. 'He raced like the wind.'

The realisation that Lumi would never mount Blixt again caused a new inflow of pain. 'The night falls, and the sky is full of shimmering stars. They twinkle down at us. We're alone in the wilderness. Just you and me, riding together into the safe embrace of our home.'

Lumi's eyes grew still.

My voice died in my throat. I sat there, staring into her fractured face. 'Lumi?' I whispered.

Silence.

X

Fjola rubbed the corners of her eyes, which were glued by a sticky mixture of blood and tears. They itched and throbbed, and when she forced them open, the room was little more than a hazy blur. Her mouth was a husk. A merciless sickle of pain sliced through her brain while jumbled thoughts and memories resurfaced in disjointed pieces: their climb to the top of the pagoda, Jarin's madness, and that awful laughter, the echo of which still lingered inside her head.

'Where am I?' she croaked, but the question was drowned by the sounds of a raging battle. A terrible crash filled the room, and the volley of ice spikes pierced the pagoda's western wall.

Fjola blinked, and the world regained more of its focus. Using her elbows for support, she pushed herself up into a sitting position. Her body ached, as if crushed by a trunk of giant spruce. As she took in the scene, her hands rushed to her mouth.

Jarin fought Goro-Khan alongside a girl in a blue dress. The girl's black hair whipped about her as she evaded Goro's sword with grace and precision. At the snap of her fingers, snow fell in flakes, turning the room into a whirlwind of white. When she exhaled, the wind gusted from her lungs while her dress floated in her wake like a veil of blue mist. Her pale skin made Fjola think of ghosts from her childhood tales, and her dazed mind whispered the wretched name—Lumi. The revelation brought on a sudden urge to scream. This… *thing* stole Jarin's heart? This pale apparition that capered around the room, using the forbidden arts without fear of retribution? How could this be?

A wave of nausea turned her stomach, and heat crept into her cheeks. It was she, not Lumi, who followed Jarin to Sur and witnessed his oath to the witches. She was there when he ventured into the Citadel of Vester to confront Hyllus, and later when they barely escaped the raging waters of Antaya. Fjola shared in his grief, his anger, his despair. She crossed the Great Atlantic by his side. She'd done all that only to discover it wasn't enough. That *she* wasn't enough… A gut-wrenching current of shame ripped through her, and she jerked her head away. Let them fight, and let it be the end.

Fjola caught sight of Galdra, who stood in the far corner, leaning forward and shielding her face with her cloak, her attention on the battle raging a few feet away. Then, her gaze fell on Mirable laying on the floor, with his hands flung to either side of him.

Her chest tightened.

Gods no. Her brother was gone, and she couldn't lose the merchant as well. She braced her elbow against the icy floor and slid across to him. A gust of snow blew in her face, filling her nostrils with sharp flakes of ice. Spitting and snorting, Fjola grabbed Mirable's sleeve and tugged.

He didn't stir.

She pressed her ear to his chest, but against the maelstrom of battle, it was impossible to hear his heart. As a last resort, she slapped him hard.

'Wake up,' she pleaded. 'For Yldir's sake, wake up!' She delivered another slap that left a red handprint.

Mirable moaned, and Fjola whispered a prayer to the God of Life. 'You scared me to death, you fool.' She clasped his temples and planted a kiss on his forehead.

Mirable sat up, rubbing the back of his head. 'I can say the same about you. To laugh like that…' He shivered and glanced over her shoulder. His eyes widened. 'Is that…?'

Before she could answer, a large icicle crashed to the floor, showering them with ice chips. Fjola threw her hand over Mirable's shoulder and turned them both away so the ice struck them in the back.

Mirable yelped. 'What's going on?'

'Magic, that's what's going on.' She searched the room. 'Where are my daggers when I need them?'

'You're not thinking of joining them, are you?'

A few moments ago she'd have said no, but now, the warrior in her rushed to answer. 'I can't just sit here. Jarin needs my help.'

Mirable cast another look at the fray and grimaced. 'I'd say he's doing quite well on his own. Besides, your daggers will be of little help against this madness. To tell you the truth, I'm surprised to see you breathing after that wretched Khan almost laughed you to death.' There was a fever in his stare, as unnatural as the frost born of Lumi's hands. He rubbed the tips of his fingers. 'If anyone should go, it's me.'

'You?' A realisation struck her. In the eyes of the people gathered in this room, she was the odd one out. Aside from her, every person present had some connection to magic. Even Mirable, who constantly prattled on how much he despised the foul arts, was changing under the power of Hyllus's spell. It made her feel like an outcast. Maybe that's why Jarin chased after Lumi. Magic called to magic, and Fjola had no connection to it.

Just then, Goro-Khan slashed with his blade, almost catching Jarin on the shoulder. Only a well-timed leap saved Jarin from a wound that would have cut his hand in two. Instinctively, Fjola reached for her belt, but her hands came away empty.

She had to get her daggers back. And fast.

'Go. Help them.' She gave Mirable a gentle shove, and nodded at Galdra. 'I'll take care of the witch.'

He shrank away from her. 'They don't need a merchant—'

'You're not a merchant,' she snapped, then immediately berated herself. She hated the idea that Lumi fought by Jarin's side while she huddled in the corner incapacitated by… what? Laughter? Unthinkable. She put as much urgency into her voice as she could muster. 'If there was ever a time to call on the Varl, it's now. We can't let Goro-Khan win this fight.'

Mirable cast her a wounded look. 'I never asked for this.'

'And neither did I, but if we don't do something, we're as good as dead. Was it not your wish to go back to Vester, to your old life?'

'I have no life,' he cried out. 'I gave it up when I agreed to accompany Jarin to Sur.' He waved his fingers in front of her face. 'These wretched hands killed a man, and no amount of gold will bring him back to life.'

Fjola bit down on her lip, torn between her desire to comfort Mirable and her need to help Jarin. She looked over her shoulder at the door where the guards stood in a semi-circle, their curved blades at the ready. One of them had her daggers, but she struggled to see through the flurry of snow.

Lumi and Jarin joined forces in a whirlwind that made them look like skilled dancers, putting on the most magnificent display of their lives. They brought to mind a pair of lovers, charming their audience with magic and steel. The ice demon was an extension of Jarin, bound to him by an invisible thread of childhood memories. Fjola could never hope to compete with this kind of bond. Her shoulders slumped, and the eagerness to join the fray leaked out of her.

She wished for Njall. Her brother infuriated her more than she wanted to admit, but she missed his internal calm and his willingness to accept the bitter truth of life—it didn't always reward you for doing the right thing. More often than not, those who carved their own path through the forest of life were the first to feel the lashings of stray branches.

When Fjola's father insisted on taking a boat to sea in a raging storm, she begged him not to go, but it didn't matter how many times she told him she loved him, he still left her on the beach, crying and shivering in the cold. Her eyes followed his ship as it disappeared into the pouring rain, and when she asked her mother why she did nothing to stop him, she told Fjola that to love a man was to watch him go, safe in the knowledge he would return to his rightful place. She listened to her mother, and then watched her go mad with grief when her father's boat never returned to the shore. When her own time came, Fjola couldn't let Jarin go. She climbed aboard his ship, unable to watch another boat carry the man she loved into the unknown. And just like life punished her mother for being a dutiful wife, it was now punishing Fjola for her foolish devotion.

She sat beside Mirable, feeling numb all over, her eyes following Jarin and Lumi's progress as they overpowered Goro-Khan. Her friend was right—they didn't need her help. She watched as Jarin pinned Goro-Khan with his sword. His victory would mean a return to Hvitur, where Fjola would atone for her foolish desires and be forced to find a new purpose in life. Her head filled with drab images of the future without Jarin…

Wrapped in the grim of her thoughts, she ignored the exchange between Jarin and Goro-Khan, and only when Galdra hastened to her master's side, Fjola snapped back to the present. Cold fingers of dread pressed upon her heart, and she lurched to her feet. The room spun around in flashes of red and black, and she staggered.

Mirable was on his feet, supporting her with his arm. 'Steady. We don't know what he did to you.'

Fjola shook her head and swallowed against the nausea swimming up to her throat. The room was icy, but Mirable's hand felt unnaturally hot against her back. The exchange between Jarin and Goro came to her in a slur of broken words she struggled to make sense of. Whatever Goro-Khan did to her weakened her from the inside.

She closed her eyes, trying to focus on her core, just like Argil taught her when he trained her how to fight. The queasiness faded, and Fjola opened her eyes.

Her ears filled with a sharp chime of shattering crystal.

As the pieces of Lumi's heart rained to the floor in a crystalline shower, Fjola clapped her palms against her cheeks. Mirable's hands flew to his turban, and he made a sound between a bark and a cry.

The heart of the girl Fjola loathed for so long lay crushed at Goro's feet.

Fjola's first emotion was that of triumph. She wanted to lift her hands to the sky and sing praises to Agtarr. Jarin's mother was avenged, and he would know peace at last. No more chasing after shadows. The ice that encased his heart for so long would thaw, and she relished the idea of Jarin no longer a slave to his frosty desires. Her spirits soared at the possibilities.

But then she looked at Jarin's crumpled face, and the guilt set the wings of joy on fire.

His expression was that of utter shock and devastation. He dropped to his knees and cradled Lumi into his arms. Rocking her back and forth, he whispered words Fjola stood too far to hear while sobs raked his chest. Her eye caught the first of many tears, and she trailed its descent as it rolled down the bridge of his nose and splattered on Lumi's cheek. Lumi lifted one fractured hand and Jarin pressed it to his face like it was the most precious thing in the world.

Fjola's jealousy vanished without a trace, replaced by a feeling of love so fierce it made her light-headed. The intensity of it frightened her because, unlike her mother, who believed in the power of letting go, Fjola knew she could never stay rooted to the spot and let Jarin sail into the storm alone. Even now, when he grieved his beloved demon, every fibre of her being urged her to run to his side, enfold him into a warm embrace, and put the pieces of his broken spirit back together. Since the moment she met him at the hot springs, his name was in each beat of her heart, and no amount of rejection would change that.

On the heel of this awareness came a darker, more sinister thought. What if, like the passing of Fjola's father that brought on her mother's madness, Lumi's death would bring about Jarin's end? Her mind conjured up images of herself holding Jarin in her arms, knowing she was holding an empty shell. Her legs folded under the finality of the vision, and she sank to the floor next to Mirable.

Mirable sniffed and mopped his nose with the loose flap of his turban. 'She can't be dead…'

'But she is, and we did nothing,' Fjola whispered. Tears made rusty tracks down her cheeks, and Jarin's image blurred. She no longer knew if she cried for him or herself.

Did they really think they could outmatch Goro-Khan? Shinpi was magic, and they were fools for believing they could just climb to the top of his pagoda and take his power from him. The four of them walked into a trap without a backward glance.

With one furious swipe, Fjola wiped the tears. Feeling sorry for herself wasn't going to change anything. Jarin needed her more than ever now, and it was time to prove she was worthy of his trust. They would have to fight their way out of here.

She placed her hand on Mirable's shoulder. 'I need you to—'

'Seize him,' Goro-Khan ordered.

Two guards rushed to Jarin's side, and each grabbed one of his hands. They hauled him up. He didn't struggle, but his eyes never left Lumi's face.

'We can't let them take him,' Fjola cried, leaping to her feet.

Galdra's voice pierced the room. 'Stay.'

Like a pair of green fetters, magic coiled around Fjola's ankles, locking them in place. She strained against the force, but her struggle was in vain. It took one word from Galdra to immobilise her.

'Let me go,' Fjola screamed.

Mirable made a low, guttural sound, and took a step toward Galdra.

'What are you going to do, *merchant*? Kill me?'

The menacing sound in Mirable's throat died down, but he stood his ground.

Galdra's mouth twisted. 'You're more powerful than any here, but your reluctance to embrace the magic within you is pitiful. You, humans, are fools. Holding on to your ideals as if any of them would better your lives.'

Fjola bared her teeth, and her fingers curled into talons. 'And you? Cowering behind your magic. Why don't you give me back my daggers and face me in a fair fight, witch?'

Galdra raised her hand as if to deliver a powerful slap.

Mirable leaned forward, flashing his teeth. 'Touch her and see what the Valgsi does when he finds out. If you think Lumi's death broke him, think what will happen when you kill the only person he loves left alive.'

Galdra flinched but lowered her hand. 'I would watch my mouth if I were you.'

From the corner of her eye, Fjola glimpsed Jarin being dragged away from the room like a lifeless heap of meat wrapped in clothes. She wanted to call his name, tell him to snap out of it, fight back, but what good would it do? Just as she feared, the demon's death broke him, and Fjola's anger sparked anew—even in death, Lumi unleashed devastation.

'The God of Death, be my witness,' Fjola said in a voice shaking with fury. 'When this is over, I'll stab my dagger through your heart.'

Galdra laughed and cocked her head. 'You're such a loyal fighter, but still, he chose the demon over you.'

'Jarin will come to exact his revenge, for such is the way of our people, and when he does, even your Laughing God won't save you.'

'I have nothing to fear. After all, the Valgsi and I worship the same goddess.' She touched the crescent moon on her forehead. 'Days of glory are upon us. Your beloved warrior will lead the mages and take back what's ours. He'll restore the world to its proper order.'

Fjola kicked against the magical shackles. 'You mean destroy the world.'

'We only ask for acceptance. If your people offer it willingly, there'll be no need for war. But, if I've learned anything about humans from my days in Antaya, their fear will call for blood long before their reason has a chance to speak.'

'People shunned your kind, but it was Skaldir who destroyed your city. If you think she'll awaken from her sleep to bear gifts, think again.'

'With the Valgsi on our side, we'll appease the goddess.' Galdra's ghostly eyes bore into Fjola's. 'It is you who should be afraid.'

The ominous warning squirmed its way into Fjola's chest, and she stopped struggling against the shackles. What if Galdra was right? The vision of Skaldir burning Hvitur to the ground exploded in her mind, filling her ears with agonising screams of people dying under the shimmering skies.

Mirable tumbled to the floor. With his wide, unseeing eyes, he looked like a man caught in a daydream. His lips moved in quick succession, counting invisible coins out loud.

The string of words broke the illusion, and Fjola's worry vanished. Warm blood rushed into her face. 'What are you doing to him?'

'Making sure he stays in his place like the loyal dog he is.'

Fjola leaned forward. Unlike Galdra, she had no magic to defend herself with, but she was ready to stand for what she held dear. 'You can pull all the tricks you want, but mages will never rise.' And with that, she spat in Galdra's face.

Veins stood out on Galdra's shapely neck. 'You'll regret this,' she hissed, wiping the spit off her face. 'I may not be able to kill you, but I can make you wish you were never born.' The room filled with words of incantation.

A gaping hole opened under Fjola's boots, dark and bottomless. She wanted to scream that humans will never fall, but the pagoda caved in on itself, and she fell into the black abyss.

XI

My days turned into a blur of meaningless time as I sank deeper and deeper into that space between dreams and reality. It was a bleak land, full of damned shadows writhing in the empty fields littered with uprooted trees. I searched for a sign of light, but my efforts were in vain because the light vanished from this barren place long ago. The hair on my neck bristled, and my scalp felt like a pincushion stuffed full of needles. With each step I took, they pricked and prodded, each stab a reminder of my many failures.

I walked alone, awash with an intense feeling of being watched, but whenever I turned my head, I saw nothing but emptiness. Withered bones lined the edges of the path. I didn't know how, but I knew they belonged to all the people I'd lost. Dark laughter rippled through me. Everyone feared I would destroy the world, but the only world I'd decimated was my own.

It started with my father's death in Elizan, where I stumbled among the bodies, frantic to stop Hyllus before he accomplished his wretched task. The childish part of me believed my father was immortal, but his body was just like mine, weak and vulnerable. Next came the loss of my mother and the deaths of the Stromhold warriors. Yet again, I wasn't there to help them, trying to save a girl who didn't need saving. If only I went back with Argil that day… Everything would've been different. I'd have persuaded Lumi to join with me instead of believing the corrupt promises of the Laughing God. Instead, I found her heart and delivered it straight into the hands of Goro-Khan. I blamed him for her death, but the truth was, *I* killed her. From the moment I set sail for Shinpi, I headed for a fall, dragging my friends along with me.

I lifted my hands to the darkened skies, demanding Agtarr to show his face, so the last thread of my life could be severed. But the God of Death remained unseen. The gods never answered to free me of my burdens, and my disdain for them burned hotter and hotter until it consumed the last shreds of my piety.

From time to time, voices rose in my consciousness, agitated murmurs filled with concern and frustration. The conscious part of me wanted to cry out to them, but the wounded part, the one that lost everyone it held dear, silenced me. I vaguely remembered the sensation of cool liquid sliding down my throat as someone forced a cup to my lips. The water would only prolong my misery, so I struggled against it. I wanted to fade, to be forgotten, not brought back to face the ghosts of those I failed.

I existed in this state, neither dead nor alive, refusing the calls from the outside world, until one day the shadows dissipated, and I glimpsed a figure wrapped in a velvet cloak of dark green. It stood a distance away, waiting for me to follow. My instincts whispered a warning and urged me to hide, but I was alone for a long time, meandering among the broken bones of my past.

I picked up speed. The figure turned and walked ahead without a backward glance. I hurried on, but the distance between us stretched farther and farther. Who was this intruder, and how did they find their way into this realm? The need to know was all-consuming, and I broke into a run. The velvet cloak billowed ahead, daring me to catch it.

My heart thumped in my chest, and the thrill of the chase filled me with a sense of purpose. I sprinted as if my life depended on it. Maybe it did, or maybe it was another trick of my mind. To know for sure, I had to win the race. I pushed harder, the world whipping past in a haze of grey.

My chest slammed into a liquid wall, invisible to the naked eye.

Like a diver, I broke the surface with the force of the impact. The water sucked me in, then spewed me out into a world of snowy fields. When my feet struck the ground on the other side, the chill took hold, seeping deep into my bones. I closed my eyes, inhaling the clean winter air and savouring the familiar tingling in my lungs. The images of home filled my mind, and a sense of peace settled over me. For a heartbeat, I allowed myself to believe it was over. I'd reached the end of my journey, and here I'd stay, in the heart of winter, with no promises to keep and no thoughts of past or future.

The tension that gripped me for so long released its hold, and my muscles loosened. As if made of wet clay, the events of my past shaped and reshaped. An array of fingers inside my head sifted and changed the truths of my world. My brain resisted this invasion, but it was a weak effort. Lulled by the promise of release, I let the fingers do their work while I savoured the feeling of white calm. Maybe I had to empty my mind before I was allowed entry into the Fields of Life…

'One cannot enter without his soul,' Trofn reminded me in a rustling voice.

I snapped my eyes open.

The figure stood at the far edge of the field, its back facing me. The green cloak was gone, replaced by a sky blue dress I recognised instantly, and my heart shrank with the memory of Lumi's passing. I dropped my head, rubbing my eyes until they burned, but when I looked up, Lumi was still there.

My first reaction was to run away, but my heart ached with the need to see her one last time. I took a cautious step forward, knowing that if the cruel gods allowed me one touch of her, I'd *never* let her go.

My fingers trembled, and despite the cold, rivulets of sweat formed on my temples. Breath puffed in and out of my mouth, and the snow crunched under my boots as they took me closer to the blue dream. I thought of Lumi's mesmerizing eyes and their power to drown all my sorrows. The memory made me halt. What if, instead of the intimate pull, Lumi pushed me away? I was the reason why Goro-Khan shattered her heart, so why would she want to embrace the man who brought about her death?

I took another step. 'Lumi?' In the winter silence, my voice sounded dry and brittle. 'Is that really you?' I hesitantly reached out to touch her hair. What if she vanished? I'd be alone again, left to contend with my forbidding thoughts. I drew back my hand.

Slowly, Lumi turned.

Her face bore not a single crack. Lumi's lips were pressed into a frozen line, and her eyes swirled and glimmered like a pair of precious sapphires. She stood before me—the ghost wrapped in layers of blue silk—and my chest swelled with joy.

'How could this be?' I whispered while my mind sifted through possible answers. Another trick of the gods? Or Skaldir's way of punishing me for my disobedience?

Lumi didn't answer, merely stared at me. Through me.

The space between my ribs turned black and hollow. I touched her cheek, but instead of the cool softness, my fingers pressed against solid ice. I leaned away from her. She wasn't my Lumi but a phantom of the girl I used to love. Lumi's head tilted to one side, and her blue eyes continued to stare into nothingness.

'What jest is this?' I screamed. 'Wasn't her death enough punishment? Must you bring her back to haunt me?'

My teeth clenched so hard my jaw cried out in pain. I glared at the dead thing in front of me while the familiar darkness converged all around.

As if in response to my anger, Lumi's face fractured with a loud crack, and the sound stabbed like an ice pick through my heart.

I took a step back. 'Not again…' My ears pounded, and green spots flickered in the corners of my eyes. I balled my hands and roared at the white sky, 'I curse you, Yldir, the God of Life, for leaving me with nothing to live for.' As the words left my lips, something darker slithered through the gap and sank its fangs into my heart, befouling my flesh with its venom. The entity fed on my rage and rejoiced at my despair. 'I curse you, Agtarr, the God of Death, for refusing to show me your face.'

More cracks shot through Lumi's face, neck, and arms, fracturing her pale skin. It wasn't enough that I saw Lumi's heart shatter, now I had to witness her memory being desecrated right in front of me. I refused to suffer through her breaking the second time, so I shoved her away from me. Her chin struck the collarbone, and her head bounced back. She stood upright, her face concealed behind a curtain of black hair and her arms dangling to either side of her like two lifeless branches.

'I curse you,' I whispered, backing away.

She snapped her head up, and Galdra's translucent eyes stared into mine.

I gaped at her while the sensation of fingers leafing through my mind returned. Galdra reached out and trailed a long, green fingernail down the side of my neck. She leaned close, and my nostrils caught a whiff of winter. I closed my eyes and inhaled deeply. My nerve endings took up the scent and carried it to my brain, flooding it with the aroma of freshly fallen snow suffused with wet earth and pine needles. The explosion brought on homesickness so fierce it reduced me to tears. I wanted to go home, to walk the familiar corridors of Stromhold, listening for the echoes of my childish laughter as I chased Lumi through the stone rooms.

Except now, there was no Lumi…

Galdra's cool breath tickled my left ear. 'The power of destruction can bring her back,' she whispered. Everything about her reminded me of Lumi, and even her voice had a small chime to it.

'Nothing can bring back the dead,' I said, wishing it wasn't true.

'You can. With Skaldir's magic, there's no such thing as impossible. You're her Valgsi, and she'll never deny you. When the awakening is complete, those alive will bow at your feet, and the souls trapped within the halls of Himinn will be yours to command. But first, you must embrace your destiny…'

But how could I? I refused my fate for so long, strong in the knowledge that I made my own path in life. To answer Skaldir's call would be to acknowledge I never had any say. *And what about Lumi?* my heart whispered. Did she have a say when you delivered her heart into the hands of… I frowned. Who was it that shattered her heart? I searched my mind, but the answer was lost to the void.

Galdra uttered a string of incoherent words, and like the rain-starved soil, my brain absorbed each one. I stood frozen, unable to comprehend or deny them.

I opened my eyes. Galdra shifted and changed before me, taking on the shape of Lumi then transforming back to Galdra. Her eyes flickered from blue to white and back to blue, and all the while, the crescent on her forehead shone with green light. The two women merged into one, then came apart again, and every time Lumi's form took shape, my chest grew colder and colder. Clear tendrils of ice wrapped around my heart until they encased it completely.

'Who are you?' I asked.

‘I am who you want me to be,’ Galdra purred.

* * *

Two quarrelling voices echoed in my mind, and each sharp word took a nail to my skull. I couldn’t stand the pain. My consciousness searched for a way back to the white calm, where Lumi waited for me. This time she wouldn’t break, and together, we’d find our way back home. The space between my ribs felt like an ice cavern, and the sharp sting of cold made it difficult to breathe. Beneath the shut eyelids, my eyes flickered erratically, but I refused to open them. To do so would mean to leave the world of peace and embrace the chaos of reality, where I was sure the grief would consume me.

A female voice floated my way. ‘I don’t think he’s ready. A little longer, and he’ll follow your orders without question, but if I rouse him now, there’s no telling what his mind will do.’

It was Galdra—the witch who stole into my mind and… and did something to me… I struggled to recall what it was, but the sound of her voice made me want to call out to her. Galdra’s skin carried the frosty scent of Lumi, and a sudden need to touch her washed over me. She was real, alive, and she knew my mind like no one else in this world.

‘I will wait no longer,’ the male voice answered, and I recognised it at once. Goro-Khan. The name burned like acid, but I couldn’t remember why it filled me with so much hatred.

I fought this man, and he bested me, but there was something about his victory that rang false. The sensation swam away on the wave of doubt. None of this was true. In its attempt to wake me up, my brain imagined Goro-Khan and Galdra, that was all. I had to let the dream run its course, and when it did, I'd be free to go back to the white planes.

'We have wasted enough time,' Goro-Khan continued.

'You don't understand how—'

'No more delays. I have a war to win and the city to restore. This Norderner caused enough trouble. The fool doesn't understand what a privilege it is to serve the Goddess of Destruction.'

The contempt in his voice sent a hot flush up my neck. I wanted to remind him that I was the Valgsi, and to follow Skaldir's will was my destiny. My lips parted, but no words came out.

'He fought you well,' Galdra said.

Goro blew out a rattling breath. '*The goddess* fought me well. When it came to it, the boy couldn't even lift the sword without shaking like a leaf.'

'My magic is strong, but something is festering inside him,' she said. 'Something dark that interferes with my power. I need more time to understand its source and the way to banish it.'

‘You possess the knowledge of all your ancestors. Are you telling me you can’t control the mind of a puny boy?’

I tensed. Puny boy? Goro-Khan needed a lesson in respect. My true hand twitched, and in my mind’s eye, I reached for the hilt of my sword to teach him.

‘It doesn’t work that way, and you know it. Even my magic has its limits. His resolve is stone-hard, and his spirit is split in two. His memories are like an intricate web, connected by the emotions of every person he’s ever cared for. When I sever one, in its place springs another, weaving a new path through his mind and healing the broken strings. And there’s darkness in there too… like an undercurrent, tainting everything black. I must close all the gaps before we bring him back.’

‘I don’t care about that. We have one moon before we set sail, and I want results. There’s too much at stake, and I won’t let this boy interfere with my plans.’

‘He’s not just *any* boy, Goro. Skaldir chose him to bring us salvation. If I don’t do this right, his mind will unravel, and all will be for nought.’

Goro-Khan snorted. ‘Skaldir’s long dream muddled her mind. If an ox came along, she would’ve marked it. The boy doesn’t deserve her grace. Besides, there’s a better man for the task.’

‘You?’

Goro laughed—a dark and hollow sound that rattled my soul. 'My son wanders the Fields of Life, but he doesn't belong there. His place is by your side, in Antaya. Your powers combined will make the mages a force to be reckoned with. Together, you'll restore Skaldir to her former glory, and build new temples in her name.'

A brief silence followed, broken only by the soft patter of rain against the shutters.

'How can you be sure Yomu will want this life?' Galdra asked in a low voice.

'Am I not the closest thing to a god in this world? Just get it done and let me worry about my son, but if the Valgsi fails and I lose him again, you'll both face the consequences.'

'What about the others? The girl's brother is still missing, and Skaldir only knows how he's managed to hide this long.'

'Considering how the Varl almost strangled me, he might be of use when we reach the shores of Nordur. As for the others, do what you want with them. Employ the help of mages if you must, but don't fail me.'

'I won't.'

The door closed, and a blessed silence spread its wings over the room. The conversation made little sense to me. Was the girl Galdra mentioned Fjola? She and Njall sailed with me to Shinpi, but beyond that, I remembered little else. Thinking of Fjola brought on an odd mixture of warmth and betrayal, but to make sense of it, I'd have to wake up, and even the idea twisted my guts. Besides, Lumi was waiting for me, and I had to find my way back to her.

I fell into a troubled sleep.

* * *

Hands pressed against my temples, and a current of warm energy swept through my mind, awakening my senses. My eyes flew open. I hoped to see Lumi waiting for me at the gates of Himinn, but instead I found myself at the foot of the hill in Hvitur. I stared at the place of my birth, wishing to be anywhere but here. A powerful force settled on my shoulders, leaving me with no choice but to ascend. A pair of invisible hands pressed against my back, propelling me forth, step by agonising step. As I braved each one, I remembered Marus—the drunken scholar in my uncle's service—telling me that my life's story began with my mother climbing these steps to give birth under the green veil of Skaldir's magic. Aliya delivered me from one dark world into another. What did it matter if my soul was bleeding darkness? My whole life was tainted with it. Nineteen years ago, on the Night of Norrsken, the Goddess of Destruction made her choice, thus robbing me of my own.

'This is your path, and you must follow it,' a new voice whispered in my ear. It belonged to a female and vibrated with power that stirred the marrow in my bones. It was the voice of

destruction, the essence of Skaldir speaking to her Valgsi through a lattice of dreams, connecting one dreamer to another.

My first thought was that of defiance. 'And what if I don't?' I said, pushing against the force.

A shove forward was my reply.

The hill loomed above me, waiting for the Valgsi to complete his ascent. A green curtain of mist fell over the peak, obscuring the altar and the prophecy inscribed into the rock. Beneath the smell of moss and damp stone lay the faint scent of magic that intensified with every step I took.

'Why are we here?' I asked, and my mind supplied the answer. I had to welcome the light and pledge myself to my goddess. My purpose shone as bright as a star in the moonlit sky, and my steps quickened. The need to defy vanished, replaced by an urge to prove myself worthy. As if sensing my eagerness to reach the top, the force pushing against my back turned to weightlessness while my thoughts drifted to my first climb all those months ago when I walked the same path without knowing who I was. The steps seemed long and arduous then, but now, filled with Skaldir's presence, my feet conquered them without a single quiver. My friends told me again and again that only by embracing my destiny could I save the world. Perhaps they were right. Denying my fate as the Valgsi was foolish. We don't choose who we are. We simply become.

I scaled the final step. Atop the hill, the mist lost some of its density, allowing for an unobstructed view of the stone in its centre. The crest was just as I remembered it—flat and bare except for a tangle of weeds at the base of the platform that still resembled a crumbling coffin. My eyes found the inscription, and I read the words aloud.

'When my soul spills across the sky,
Heed my call and seek out the blade,
The power is yours to take,
The judgement is mine to make,
The end of mortal vanity
The beginning of divine eternity.'

When the last word left my lips, I became aware of Galdra's presence, and the fresh scent of ice crystals drifted up my nostrils. She stood at my shoulder, whispering a string of words into my ear. I understood none, but they vibrated through me, sinking deep into my brain. I placed my hands on the cold stone. The slit gaped at me, hungry for the sword of Skaldir, knowing I'd be the one to thrust it home.

I had both the power to awaken the goddess and the power to keep her dreaming. Or had I? My denial of the prophecy didn't ease the pull I felt whenever I took up her sword. I had a strong sense that to accept the summoning would bring about… what? Some terrible calamity? Like a star on a moonlit sky, the answer was out of my reach.

Galdra's icy breath hit the shell of my ear. 'To answer the call is to save the world. Only Valgsi can unite the mages and humans, and bring about the eternal peace.'

I touched Skaldir's mark on my temple, tracing the lines of the constellation that held the secrets. On the Night of Norrsken, Skaldir's power would fill my soul, and with it, I'd use the blade to sever the bonds that kept her captive. My father wanted me to succeed him as the Guardian of Stromhold, but I'd do better. I'd become the guardian of the goddess, a blade in the fight for a divine eternity of peace.

My mother's face flashed before my eyes, creased with sorrow. What would she say to me now? She tried so desperately to save me from the destiny I felt so compelled to embrace. The thought dazed me, and the tide of my resolve ebbed away. What was I doing on this forsaken hill, making pledges to the very deity I had sworn to refuse? The invisible grip on my mind loosened, and my thoughts broke free. Images came rushing back, words left unspoken, and faces of people I loved: Fjola's green eyes, Njall's solemn expression, and Mirable's cheery grin. I could sense them forming grooves, creasing and stretching my memories like fullers in the forge. Pain exploded inside my head, and the world turned into a series of bright flashes. Blood gushed from my nose, splattering the stone and the words of the prophecy. I groaned.

An icy hand pressed against mine, and the feel of it brought instant relief. The burning in my brain subsided, but my soul grew heavy with the ache of Lumi's passing. Her presence grieved me to the brink of madness.

I squeezed my eyes shut. 'I know you're a ghost.'

Lumi's fingers slid up my arm in a touch lighter than breath. I froze, afraid to hope and unable to stop myself. She was a dream, a figment of my imagination conjured up by the power of my guilt. Her fingers tightened around my shoulder blade, and she turned me to face her. I refused to open my eyes, sure that if I did, she'd vanish in a puff of snow. The silence stretched until it was thinner than a strand of hair. My breath coiled in my lungs as I stood motionless, waiting for the gods to punish me and put an end to this agonising moment. I felt her leaning over, and the chill settled in my chest.

I opened my eyes.

At the sight of Lumi's dark-blue irises, my heart lurched. 'This is a dream…' I whispered.

The girl who shattered in my arms tilted her head. 'I'm real,' she said in a chiming voice. She pointed her pale finger at the inscription. 'When the goddess awakens, all dreams will become a reality.'

I understood at once. Skaldir had the power to join the shattered pieces. She had the power to bring Lumi back to life.

I turned to the stone, letting go of the images holding me back. My past was a fading cloud of sand, my present an agonising battle of wills, but my future held the promise of relief, and it's to that future I looked. Standing on the hill of my birth, I released the latches on the door that kept me hostage to my false beliefs. With each one, the voice of reason faded until it became a distant hum. The words of incantation rose and fell in my mind, but I no longer questioned them. When the final latch lifted, I threw the doorway wide open, welcoming the flood of green light. The sharp smell of ice crystals infused my nostrils, and I took a deep breath, savouring the winter air.

'You have slept for too long, Valgsi. Wake up.'

XII

'Lay still,' Galdra said. Her cool hands cupped my temples as she tried to lower my head onto the pillow.

I jerked away. My mouth felt stuffed full of sawdust, my tongue so stiff I could hardly swallow. Breath wheezed in and out of my lungs in painful gusts, and my body shivered uncontrollably. The ache in my head was a blinding surge that made my eyes water. It was as if two bands of seafarers waged war with sabres and cudgels, cleaving and clubbing the flesh of my brain. Through the haze of tears, the room fell in and out of focus.

'Where am I?' I croaked. The words chaffed against the raw lining of my throat, which tasted of copper. The fragments of my dreams flickered back and forth like a pack of confused gnats. My mother told me once that dreams were blessings from the gods, for they allowed us to make sense of life, and if Yldir willed it, even a glimpse into the future. If that was true, the remnants of nightmares buzzing inside my head held little promise.

'Safe among your people,' Galdra said.

My people? I rubbed my forehead. My mind felt divided in two by something like a see-through mirror glued together in a skewed way. Some of my memories hovered on the other side, hazy and vacant, and there was no way of reaching them other than breaking the glass, but something warned me against it, so I turned to the things I could remember. The memories on my side of the mirror were strong and clear, but none of them felt true.

I recalled my voyage to Shinpi, and my brain insisted I sailed here in search of magic, but the art was forbidden in Nordur, so why would I break the laws of my people? Except, Galdra said my people were here…

Questions rose like warriors, eager to join the fray inside my head. I searched for the answers in the strange mirror, but the fractured glass distorted the images on the other side.

As if sensing my turmoil, Galdra said, 'You came here to liberate us. To prove yourself, you challenged Goro-Khan to a duel.' Her ghostly eyes shone with dim light. The creamy irises should've repulsed me, but I found myself drawn to them. 'It was magnificent. You truly are Skaldir's Valgsi.'

She picked up a cup from the bedside table and offered it to me. Water sloshed inside, and my thirst returned with a vengeance. I grabbed it from her, spilling some of the liquid onto the white sheets.

'Careful,' she cautioned, steadying the bottom of the cup with her long fingers.

I drank in greedy gulps. When the cup was empty, I handed it back to Galdra, wiping the chin on my sleeve. I cleared my throat. 'Did I kill him?'

'Kill him?' She laughed. The room chimed with the sound, and the memory of another laughter rippled through my mind. 'Skaldir would've never allowed it.'

I fell back against the headboard. 'I remember the forest, but beyond that, everything is fuzzy.'

'It's the exertion. Destruction is a force that requires a tremendous amount of energy. You gave your all, and now you're paying the price. Magic gives, and it takes.' She stroked the curve of her throat with her dyed green nails. 'My eyes are proof of that. They used to be iron-rich, but when I came of age and started using magic, each spell I cast absorbed some of the colour.' Her eyes shifted like a pair of ghosts. 'In return, Skaldir blessed me with the skill of enchantment.'

'It doesn't sound like a mighty gift,' I said, thinking of my sword and the speed with which it took lives.

Galdra tilted her head to one side. Free of the hood, her hair fell across one shoulder in an inky river. Even though they were nothing alike, I couldn't believe how much she reminded me of Lumi.

'Just because I don't bleed people with my magic doesn't mean my results are less fatal,' she said. A smile played on her green-stained lips, and a sudden urge to taste them came over me. The tips of my ears burned.

I dropped my eyes to my quivering fingers. To wield Skaldir's blade, I needed a pair of steady hands. 'Where is my sword?'

'Safe,' she purred. 'It's as precious as you are. Let me retrieve it for you.' She stood up in a rustle of skirts. Her dress was long and fashioned to enhance her body in all the right places, its colour matching the jade crescent painted on her forehead.

When she left, my headache subsided, allowing me a coherent thought. I looked around the sparsely furnished chamber. Across from my bed was a storage cabinet carved from solid oak, next to which stood a folding screen depicting images of vermillion birds in full flight. To the left of the screen was a dresser with an empty washbasin. My bed dominated the space—four wooden bedposts supporting a canopy embellished with delicate carvings of crescent moons. The only window in the room opened to the grey sky, letting in the cool breeze.

My fingers groped for the black pearl at my neck, and the familiar shape brought some comfort. Apart from the sword, it was the only trinket I had from Nordur. I scraped my hand across my face. Galdra said I challenged Goro-Khan to a duel. To prove… what? That I was worthy of his acceptance? I probed the strange mirror inside my head, beyond which the interlaced memories of past and present pressed like phantoms against the glass. I wanted them, but I also feared them. There was something else there—long threads of dark energy that weaved through every thought, memory, and feeling.

The door slid open, and Galdra entered the room with my sword in hand. At the sight of it, my spirits lifted. When she offered me the blade, I snatched it, relishing the feeling of oneness that came with it. My hand fastened around the scabbard. The blade of Stromhold Guardians passed down from my grandfather to his son, and from my father to me—the bridge between the mortal and the divine. Holding it close, I felt the familiar pull of the script inscribed into the steel by Skaldir herself.

'How long was I asleep?'

'Judging by your dazed look, not long enough.' She perched on the edge of the bed and held her palm against my forehead. At the cold touch, tingles erupted all over my skin, and I had to resist the urge to grab her hand. 'You're still running a fever, but it'll pass. As long as you don't exert yourself. I did all I could for you, but I'm no healer.'

'Is it true?' I asked.

'Is what true?'

My dreams were so real that I needed to hear the truth out loud. 'That she is gone.'

Galdra glanced sideways and gave a single nod, crushing my hopes. 'How much do you remember?'

'I know that she… that her heart…' I swallowed against the gall in my throat.

'I'm sure you have many questions, but they must wait until your mind is strong enough to accept the answers.'

'Just tell me.'

'As you wish,' she said with a sigh. 'You and Lumi fought Goro-Khan, but the girl you call Fjola couldn't control her jealousy.' Galdra's words were calm and measured. 'When Fjola saw her chance, she took it. It was *Fjola* who crushed Lumi's heart.' She tugged at the cuff of her dress. 'You ordered her locked in the cell along with the Varl.'

I imprisoned my friends? Even the thought of it seemed insane. All at once, my ears filled with the sound of breaking ice and the gusts of freezing wind. The fight was a clear image in my mind—Lumi using her crystalline powers, and I, with Skaldir at my shoulder. Then nothing but a gaping hole that stretched for eternity until it took on the shape of me sitting on the floor with my back crumpled, grieving Lumi's death.

A heavy sense of betrayal flared up in my ribcage. Would Fjola really do this? It was never a secret that she detested Lumi, but killing her out of sheer jealousy didn't sound like Fjola I knew. Inside my mind, the currents of memories coiled and uncoiled behind the fractured glass.

'Some things are difficult to accept, but when you chose your path, so did your friends,' Galdra said. 'Although calling them friends feels too generous. Even before you met Goro-Khan, Njall abandoned you by fleeing from his duties as your guardian. He's still hiding, ashamed to face you.'

'And Mirable?' Surely, the merchant wouldn't have deserted me so easily, but Galdra only shook her head.

'When Fjola shattered Lumi's heart, the Laughing God had to punish her, but Mirable intervened. He almost strangled Goro-Khan with the noose he forged with his magic.'

'Mirable is a Varl. He can't use magic in that way.'

'His gift came as a surprise to us all. We knew he was special, but we didn't realise how special.' She picked up a loose strand of my hair and coiled it around her fingers. 'The mages fled to Shinpi, but our number is dwindling. Every heart on this island longs to unlock the gates to our beloved city. And you are the key.'

'The magic protecting Antaya vaporised, and the city collapsed under the pressure of the ocean. There's nothing left but ruin.' My mind flashed with the images of rushing water and the whinnying horses as we rode to escape the angry currents. 'I was there when it happened.'

'We're well aware of that, but with Skaldir's magic, we can fish out the pieces and put them back together. Your people would rise anew.'

Her words stirred a powerful urge to know about the mages of Shinpi. 'You keep calling them my people, but I'm nothing like them.'

Her eyes searched my left temple, where my hair concealed Skaldir's mark. 'You may think of yourself as a simple Norderner, but your soul belongs to the Goddess of Destruction.'

In response to her words, dark fingers rapped against the glass in my head, followed by a distant cackle. I rubbed my forehead.

'What's wrong?' Galdra asked, shifting on the edge of the bed.

'I don't know,' I said as warm blood trickled from my nostril.

Galdra's eyes widened in alarm. 'Jarin, look at me,' she said, lifting my chin. 'If you insist on prodding your brain, you risk lasting damage. We have no healers on this island.'

'What happened to them?' I asked, trying to steer my thoughts away from the echo of that sinister cackle.

Galdra pulled a white handkerchief from the sleeve of her dress and wiped the blood off my face. 'The last healer perished trying to find his way back to Antaya. Goro-Khan ordered us not to leave Shinpi, but Saru defied him and laughed to death for his disobedience. Others died of natural causes.'

‘I thought the mages were immortal.’

‘Despite what the old tales might say, Skaldir blessed us with long lives, but she didn’t afford us immortality. Just like humans, we’re vulnerable. We age and die.’

Galdra didn’t look much older than me, and I found it hard to picture her as an old woman. ‘And you?’

‘I’m twenty-three years of age.’

‘How long have you been twenty-three?’

‘A while.’

‘I saw you in my dreams,’ I said after a brief pause.

Galdra fussed with the bloody handkerchief. ‘You did?’

‘You told me Skaldir could bring Lumi back.’

Silence fell, broken only by a light tapping of the shutters stirred by the autumn wind. I waited for Galdra’s answer, knowing it would change everything. If there was even a shred of possibility to revive Lumi, there was nothing I wouldn’t do.

‘She killed your family, yet you still care for her,’ Galdra said, tapping her chin with one long finger. ‘Agtarr commands the souls of the dead, but those with magic in their veins belong to Skaldir. The goddess can breathe life back into Lumi.’ She leaned forward, and the air shivered with the chill. ‘But first, you must wake her up.’

The familiar cold that radiated from Galdra whenever she was near me reordered my thoughts. I turned my back to the memories coiling behind the mirror. I came to Shinpi to find my people and restore them to their former glory. My duty as the Valgsi was to awaken the Goddess of Destruction, so she could bring Lumi back to life and unite the mages and humans. In the face of this calling, Nordur, with all its problems, looked little more than a white dot on the map of my mind—frozen and insignificant. My headache faded. The chaos turned to order and doubt to certainty. I inhaled, and the fresh smell of snow flooded my nostrils. The Laughing God had a plan that had me at its centre, and it was time I started acting like the man I was born to become. I swung my legs off the bed.

'Take me to Goro-Khan.'

XIII

After days in bed, my legs felt weak and ready to fold under me. I flexed my feet and knees to loosen the muscles and allow for the blood to flow. With Galdra's help, I washed away the sweat of fever and changed into fresh clothes. She replaced my worn Nordern shirt with one of silk, embroidered at the cuffs and collar with green lace. I discarded my bonded trousers in favour of a pair cut from soft brown leather, and to guard against the autumn chill, I donned a waist-long jerkin. Galdra tied my hair into a loose tail at the back of my neck. With my sword fastened to my belt, I felt like a man reborn.

'Thank you,' I said. Galdra stayed by my bedside without judgement. When I slept, ravaged by grief and grave dreams, she watered and fed me while her magic worked on the wounds left by Skaldir. Sharing one's mind with a god had its consequences.

'It's my duty to serve the Valgsi,' she said, adjusting the sleeve of my shirt.

I caught her hand, and the connection sent a light tingle through my fingers. Whenever we touched, I immediately thought of Lumi. Galdra was like my own conduit, and the more time I spent with her, the more I desired her presence.

'You're not my servant. Without you, I'd still be languishing in this bed, plagued by nightmares.'

A smile of pleasure spread across her lips. 'You're awake, but your mind is still recovering. Even if it fully heals, the scars will remain. The rage you feel in battle is divine, and when you give in to it, you're no longer in control. When Shinpi guards apprehended your ship, the goddess took over. The same happened when you fought Goro-Khan. After such frequent intrusions, confusion is only natural. I tried to take the burden off your mind, so it has space to heal, but to do so, I had to separate your memories.'

I nodded. The see-through mirror I sensed inside my head was proof of her work. 'How long before I remember everything?'

'I can't say, but until then, control your anger and refrain from thinking too much.' Her voice dropped to a whisper. 'Trust me on this.'

What other choice did I have?

Galdra examined my right arm, and her brows furrowed. 'What's this?' she asked, rolling up my sleeve. A circle, with a black eye in the centre, marked my wrist. The eye was closed.

I frowned. 'I don't know.' As soon as the words left my lips, something shifted behind the glass—a dark memory from before my time in Shinpi.

'Does it hurt?'

I rubbed the mark with my fingers. ‘No.’

‘I don’t like the look of it,’ Galdra said.

And neither did I. There was something sinister about the eye, and I had a strong sense of it looking at me through the closed eyelid. I pulled my sleeve down. ‘When I remember, I’ll tell you.’

‘Be careful.’

Like a long body of a snake, a black tendril of smoke coiled on the other side of the mirror, and my mind drew back from it. ‘Let’s not mention it again,’ I said, heading for the door.

Galdra followed me out without a reply.

Out in the corridor, I stopped. The pagoda looked striking from the outside, and I was curious about its purpose. Never in my life did I see a building with so many floors and roofs built to curve like ocean waves. ‘Tell me about this place,’ I said, hoping the change of topic would make us forget about the strange mark.

Galdra pointed to the ceiling. ‘This pagoda is a place of worship. We built it in Skaldir’s honour, and every floor tells a different part of her story. The highest one, where you challenged Goro-Khan, is called Desolation.’

The memory of that duel was still hazy, but I took a small satisfaction from the knowledge that Goro struggled to defeat me. And who knows, if Lumi never came to my aid, maybe I’d have bested him, and she'd still be alive. I remembered little of what I was trying to prove by fighting him and even less about how Fjola got hold of Lumi's heart. I wasn't sure I wanted to know.

'The Laughing God goes there to meditate for days at a time,' Galdra said. 'Among other sorrows that burden his heart, he mourns the Lost City of Antaya and the imprisonment of our goddess.'

'That's some devotion.'

She glanced over her shoulder as if afraid someone might be listening. 'He kept us together and alive all these years. Without him, the dream of restoring Antaya would've died long ago. Still, I advise you to stay away from that room. At least for a while.'

I looked up at the timber ceiling that separated me from the place where Lumi drew her last. 'I doubt I'll ever want to see it.'

'It's for the best,' she agreed.

'You seem relieved.'

'I am. Seeing how you gnaw at every thought that comes to your mind, it's best not to give you more reasons to lance your brain.'

We started down the corridor illuminated by green orbs. In the wake of our passage, the magic inside them swirled, brightening and dimming at the flick of Galdra's fingers. The light shone on several doors lining the left wall.

'The sleeping quarters,' Galdra explained. 'We built a score of rooms in-between floors to house the mages.' She halted at the neck of the staircase. 'During daylight hours, we help the inhabitants of Shinpi with their chores.'

'So not everyone here is a mage?' That would explain why we couldn't understand the guards when we first arrived.

'When we came to Shinpi, the village was a crumbling ruin. In exchange for sanctuary, we offered to restore it. Some humans bonded with the mages and gained the ability to wield a little magic.'

I grimaced at the thought of humans wedded to mages. 'Is that even possible?'

Galdra rolled her spectral eyes. 'Anything is possible if you open your mind to it. Unlike Norderners and Vesterners, the inhabitants of Shinpi held no preconceived ideas about us. They needed help, and we offered it. In time, they adopted our beliefs and began worshipping Skaldir along with us. Shinpi isn't so different from Antaya. Before the War of Mages, we made an alliance with humans and shared our art with anyone who desired to learn.'

'Nords would never accept that.'

'Luckily, we have your sword to convince them.'

'I doubt the steel alone would be enough.'

'You underestimate yourself.' She angled her head. 'Why? Do you really believe your Nordern brethren hold more power than you?'

'We follow our chosen leader. His word is final.'

'If that is so, then why are you here?' She pointed at the sword. 'You follow a divine destiny, which places everyone else beneath you. It is the Valgsi who will decide the order of the world.'

Her words didn't sit right, yet they empowered me all the same.

We took the stairs to the floor below, filling the pagoda with the hollow sounds of our passage. My curiosity about Shinpi grew along with my desire to learn about this world that was rapidly becoming my own.

'This chamber is called the Sleeping Goddess,' Galdra said, opening her arms wide. 'The mages come here to pray in silence. Sometimes they arrive in pairs to combine their magic and lull each other to sleep. In this state, they hope to share their powers with the goddess through the channel of dreams.'

'Does it work?'

'We believe the practice helps to keep Skaldir strong.'

The back wall depicted images of the slumbering gods. Skaldir knelt between her brothers with her head lowered and eyes closed, but even in her dream, the angry scowl twisted her face. The artist of this piece dressed her in a jade-coloured robe not dissimilar to Galdra's and painted her hair golden. It fell across her shoulders in a wild tangle. The God of Death wrapped his raven wings around Skaldir, and the God of Life spread his hands over her head in a blessing-like gesture.

'It's unnatural,' Galdra said, appraising the goddess with a sad expression. 'To be forced to dream against your will… It's a fate worse than death.' She rested her head on my shoulder.

The scent of ice crystals washed over me, and the chill cleared away some more of my confusion. Galdra smelled like Lumi, and her skin felt just as cold.

'She won't be dreaming for long,' I said. Staring into her colourless eyes, I wondered how she would look if her irises were blue.

The room below showed the goddess in shackles. Skaldir's face was a mask of seething rage as she strained against the bonds of sleep fastened around her wrists and ankles. Her eyes flared, and her bared teeth reminded me of Nordern wolves prowling the snowy planes in search of prey. I shuddered. It was merely a painting, but the fury radiating from it felt so real. Could unleashing this deadly force really bring peace to the world? The answer came as easy as sleep after days of hard labour. I touched the blade at my hip. With it, I'd sever the chains and restore the order. The mages depended on me, and so did Lumi.

Galdra found my hand, and her fingers interlaced with mine. We shared the same goal and had the means to realise it. My old life withered like parchment put to the flame, and the less I fought it, the better I felt. To think I'd waited this long to come here, to accept my destiny, to see the world for what it was—a place bereft of the divine rule. I defied the gods all my life, but standing in this chamber, holding Galdra's hand, I realised my disobedience came from contempt for their idleness. The gods created this world, and it was time they awakened and took responsibility for it.

On the floor below, Galdra pointed at the next set of paintings. 'The Day of Judgement,' she said, her face gleaming.

It was the only room with a window, but the red shutters were drawn. I looked at the images on the central wall, and the arrow of dread shot through my heart. Skaldir held her sword high above her head, bracing for the final strike. She swapped her simple robes for a warrior's armour. A crown embellished with green jewels sat upon her brow. Her braided hair billowed in the invisible wind as she surveyed the world of smoking ruin, scorched by the flames of her wrath. The gates of Antaya stood wide open, releasing a flood of people into the wastelands.

'Terrifying,' I said, but the word was too weak to give the images justice. Looking at the devastation, my resolve to awaken this wrathful being wavered. Skaldir almost destroyed Antaya. Who's to say she won't do the same this time around?

'Magnificent,' Galdra countered. 'Humans wanted war, and so they left us no choice.'

'A lot of mages died that day.'

'But we survived and inherited their legacy. We must ensure the sacrifice of our ancestors was not in vain.'

'Why would this summoning be different? Why would Skaldir show us mercy? Many might fall under the sword of her anger.'

She waved her hand. 'During the War of Mages, some of us sided with humans while others stood united in their belief that magic was the essence of the world and had to be preserved at all costs. To tip the scales in our favour, the mages called the Goddess of Destruction to help them win the war. She caused so much devastation because we had no one strong enough to guide her power. Back then, the mages had no choice but to accept the consequences. But this time will be different. We're not at war, and we have you, our very own conduit.'

'I hope you're right.' I looked at the wave of people rushing through the city gates, surrounded by a red hue. Their eyes bulged in their sockets. Some clawed at their cheeks, drawing blood, while others grabbed onto each other as if that would shield them from the divine wrath.

‘Where were you when Antaya fell?’ I asked.

‘In the heart of the city,’ she answered dreamily. ‘I was only a child back then, but I walked the burning streets, singing songs in Skaldir’s honour. I wanted to see the goddess with my own eyes.’

I swallowed hard. If that was true, it would make Galdra close two hundred winters old. Looking at her unblemished skin, the idea of her age was impossible to digest. ‘You were lucky to survive,’ I said.

‘Luck had very little to do with it. When the mages completed the calling ritual, Antaya plunged into chaos. Humans and mages alike cast aside their weapons and ran for the city gates to perish in blood and fire. I still remember the screams…’

‘No one tried to help you?’

‘I didn’t need help. I made myself invisible to them. Only one being saw through my illusion.’ Galdra reached out and brushed the image of Skaldir with her fingers. ‘She was glorious. Her anger cut through me like the edge of the sharpest blade.’

‘She let you live,’ I exclaimed.

‘And I swore to worship her to my dying day. I want to free her more than anything, and with you by my side, we can achieve the impossible. We’ll tear down the old ways and create a new world of possibilities. Antaya will rise again, and the mages will be free to worship the Goddess of Destruction.' She turned to face me. Her wish burned so brightly I could almost feel the heat of it on my cheeks. 'Just imagine the world where everyone is at peace, sharing knowledge, living how they wish, and loving whom they wish.'

I thought of the two women in the village, wearing matching dresses and holding hands. I hadn't seen such a union outside Shinpi, but come to think of it, it wasn't so different to my own love for Lumi. She was a demon, which was why Nords struggled to make sense of my affections for her. If Skaldir brought Lumi back to life, I could take her to Antaya where we would be free to live out the end of our days in peace. When I looked at the mural again, it no longer seemed so terrifying.

We descended to the fifth floor. Devoted to the summoning ritual, here the orbs of green shimmered with low light, and in the far corner, a lone mage bowed before the tapestry on the wall. I recognised the four towers of Sirili—the holiest structure in Antaya. Inside, a circle of mages surrounded an altar upon which a blue flame burned bright. My mind shifted uneasily. I tracked Lumi's heart to that very altar. I released the latches of the chest and brought the crystal heart to Shinpi, only to see it crushed. My fingers travelled to the pearl at my neck. I needed to see Fjola and ask her why. My spirit shrank at the thought of her locked away in that foul prison. Her and Mirable.

'Stop doing that.' Galdra's voice snapped me out of my thoughts like a whip.

'Doing what?'

'Retreating into yourself. I warned you about the repercussions. If you continue to vex your mind, it'll take twice as long to heal. The pieces will come together eventually, but you must be patient. Your weakened brain will offer limitless scenarios and reasons. Acknowledge them, then let them go.'

'It's easy for you to say. Your mind is sound, but mine is a jumble of senseless thoughts.' My words reverberated through the room, and the lone mage looked up with a startled expression.

'Lower your voice,' Galdra said. 'This isn't a place to flaunt your frustrations.'

I pressed my lips into a tight line.

'You should think less. Your heart and soul will share in Skaldir's magic, and you should prepare yourself for the calling. Instead of worrying about the past, look to the future.' She cupped my cheek. 'My magic has its limits, but I promise to do all I can to restore your mind. If you let me.'

I said nothing.

She cocked her head. 'Don't you trust me?'

I hesitated. There seemed to be no one else to trust. As far as I knew, Njall fled, Mirable lost control, and Fjola betrayed me, while Galdra gave me hope of saving Lumi.

'I'm sorry,' I said. 'I should be more grateful.'

She acknowledged my apology with a brisk nod, then gestured at the painting on the wall. 'The Calling,' she said in a low voice. 'It's a sacred rite known to a handful of powerful mages. Sadly, they all perished. Our people come here, hoping to learn the secrets of how to call a god to earth.'

'What about Goro-Khan?'

'You're the only living mortal who can summon Skaldir. Many would die in exchange for such honour, so wear it with pride. You may be confused about things, but you must never doubt your purpose.'

Galdra led me to the lowest floor, where a score of mages dressed in green robes prayed at the altar with Skaldir's statue at its centre. They pretended to ignore us, but even so, I caught a few curious glances. Galdra marched across the room, her skirts sweeping the floor behind her, and slid the main doorway open. I welcomed the whiff of fresh air. It felt like I spent half of my life confined to this pagoda, and my eyes resisted the natural light. I blinked a few times. The pale sun peeked through the clouds at the village below, obscured by a haze of green mist. To the left of me, a well-maintained path led deeper into the mountains, where the snowy peaks glittered like golden coins. The sight made me think of Mirable. Like a true merchant, he would've assigned value even to a trick of sunlight. The last time I saw him, the tumours did work on his chest and back.

'Is there any way to stop Mirable's transformation?' I asked as we took the higher path.

Galdra gave me a sharp look. 'Why would we want that? He's growing stronger with each passing day but continues to deny his nature. Any more of this, and he'll end up broken. But without Hyllus, it's impossible to say for sure.'

Hyllus—the mage who used his magic to turn Mirable into a Varl. 'Where is Hyllus?'

'He was… killed.' Galdra said, staring at the road ahead. 'He misjudged his quarry and paid a heavy price. It's unfortunate. He had the knowledge to guide Mirable through his change.'

'Maybe someone else here could help him?' It felt wrong to just leave Mirable to suffer. 'Whatever he did that day, the magic is to blame.'

'Let me remind you that your precious merchant tried to strangle Goro-Khan.' She stopped and faced me. 'I admire your concern, but it's safer to leave him where he is. He's well looked after, and you can visit him when the time is right. Once his change is complete, you'll have a powerful Varl at your side, but until then, his loyalty is questionable. Simply put, Mirable is still too human.'

'But what if he dies?'

'Then we know he was never one of us.'

A cold gust of wind swept across the path, but I hardly felt the chill. My head ached. Should I insist on helping Mirable, or should I let the magic do its work? The mirror inside my head beckoned, but Galdra warned me that to seek the answers beyond was to risk insanity.

I shook my head, and the world came back into focus. 'I did it again,' I said, feeling ashamed of this admission.

I expected Galdra to say something scornful, but she simply stood there, her face like a polished stone.

I opened my mouth to apologise, but what good would it do? 'Let's go,' I said. 'Goro-Khan is waiting.'

XIV

'You look well,' Goro-Khan said, scrutinising me with eyes as dark as charcoal. 'But Galdra tells me your recovery is not yet complete.'

His statement sounded like an accusation. I pulled back my shoulders. 'I don't see how my wellbeing has anything to do with the task at hand.'

'A sound mind is a necessary ingredient to success.'

'Are you calling me insane?'

Goro's eyes narrowed. 'Don't take that tone with me, boy.'

A retort sat ready on my tongue, but the touch of Galdra's hand on my shoulder made me hold it back. I returned Goro's stare. Except for the slight twitch to the left eye, his face remained still. It wasn't how I'd imagined our meeting. I hoped to find a mighty ally in Goro-Khan, so why did my body tense at the sight of him? A warning horn sounded deep within my troubled mind—this man was not to be trusted.

Galdra broke the taut silence. 'The mages wish to meet the Valgsi and hear him speak.'

Goro laughed, and the sound rasped in my ears like a blade against a sanding belt. The green orb in the ceiling flickered as if upset by a high wind. Galdra glanced up and clasped her hands until her knuckles turned white.

‘Tell me, boy, are you good at speeches?’

‘I’m not your *boy*,’ I said, taking a step forward.

Goro’s narrow lips curled. ‘I thought you *healed* him,’ he said to Galdra.

‘*Healing* takes time, as you well know.’

I wasn’t bedbound and my wounds were internal, so what did healing me have to do with mages and speeches? My hand found the hilt of my sword, but instead of steel, I drew a sharp breath. If I challenged Goro again, I’d lose the chance of winning over the mages who held the Laughing God in high regard. To dispute his right to rule, first, I had to prove myself worthy.

‘But of course,’ Goro said, eyeing my hand. ‘We can’t risk anything befalling our beloved Valgsi, can we?’ He motioned to a square table in the centre of the room. ‘Would you care to join me for my afternoon tea?’

A set of flat pillows lay on the floor beside the short-legged table that held two cylindrical cups with no handles. I pointed at them. ‘You’re short a cup.’

‘I prefer solitude, but since you’re here we should speak man to man, without needless distractions.’

The colour drained from Galdra’s face, but she inclined her head. ‘I’ll take my leave.’

‘She dines with us.’

‘It appears you’re quite smitten with our enchantress. Considering how skilled she is at healing, I’m not surprised. But don’t get too carried away. Her affections have already been spoken for.’ He clapped his hands, and a man in a dark-green robe entered the room. ‘Get another cup,’ Goro ordered him.

The servant bowed, his bald head glistening in the light from the orbs. ‘As you command,’ he said, glancing my way. Judging by his smooth and youthful skin, I thought him to be my age.

‘Shall we?’ Goro-Khan said, settling himself on the pillow.

He didn’t ask the servant for a third, so I offered Galdra my own. She made a gesture as if to refuse, then thought better of it and lowered herself onto the cushion. I unbuckled my sword and placed it within easy reach. I sat down next to Galdra. Goro watched us with his forehead creased but made no remark. I wanted to ask him what he meant by ‘her affections have been spoken for,’ but doing so would be giving in to his game.

‘Servants?’ I asked instead. ‘I thought all Skaldir’s children were equal.’

‘All Skaldir’s children will be equal,’ he said as if reading from scripture. ‘Netis wishes to ascend the ranks. It takes years of disciplined practice to control the magic, and it all begins with mastering the most important skill.’

‘Which is?’

‘Knowing your place in the order of things.’

This declaration went against everything Galdra told me, and my tongue itched to remind Goro-Khan that my arrival in Shinpi changed the order of things. Instead, I turned my attention to the room. Aside from the table and a weapons rack full of knives and short swords, it contained little to no furnishings. A rectangular mat woven from coarse material lined the floor, and a ceiling-high shelf stood propped against the right wall. It held volumes bound in soft leather alongside stacks of tightly pressed scrolls that reminded me of the ones in Stromhold’s library. I wanted to get up and read the titles on the vellums, but at that moment, Netis returned with the cup. He placed it in front of Galdra and started filling the three mugs with steaming water from an iron pot.

‘Any news on the brother?’ Goro-Khan asked.

The servant’s hand jerked, and he missed my cup, splashing water onto the table.

Goro’s eye twitched, and the hand resting on his thigh curled into a fist.

Netis pulled a cloth from the folds of his robe and mopped up the liquid. Sweat beaded his temples, and his eyes jerked to and fro like those of a lizard. When the table was dry, Netis mumbled an apology and refilled my cup. With a trembling hand, he added a handful of wilted leaves to each mug. They absorbed the liquid and sank to the bottom. I thanked him, but he only blinked and hurried out of the room.

'Nothing yet,' Galdra said. 'But it's a small island. No one can hide here for long.'

'Yet, he'd managed to evade capture for days now.' Goro leaned forward. 'Maybe it's time to employ a different strategy?'

Galdra lifted her chin but did not reply.

Goro picked up his mug. 'This tea is known for its restorative properties.' He drank and smacked his lips. 'It helps to ease a weary mind.'

I brought the cup to my lips, and the aroma of grass and fresh leaves hit my nostrils. I took a sip. The tea had a nutty taste and left a bittersweet tang in my mouth. I watched Goro over the rim.

'How long did it take you to cross the Great Atlantic?' he asked, adjusting the cuff of his loose-fitting grey shirt.

I wondered about the wounds from our duel, but I couldn't see any. 'Time flows differently when you're sailing without a clear course. We left the harbour when spring gave way to summer.'

'A season then, which means we have one moon to prepare. How much do you know about the ritual?'

'Enough to do my duty.'

He traced the rim of his cup with one fingertip. 'The ritual must be seamless. We have one chance… I'm not prepared to wait two more decades to restore Antaya.'

'Antaya is a ruin,' I said. 'The magic shield crashed, and now, the Lost City is truly lost.'

'What is lost can be found again. You proved as much when you retrieved the heart of our dear departed Lumi.'

'Don't call memories at will,' Galdra snapped.

Their eyes locked, and something passed between them. The exchange happened in the span of a heartbeat, but it was long enough to make me question this alliance. What was I doing here, on this island full of mages and their forbidden magic? My friends languished in the prison while I sat here, drinking tea and enduring Goro's insults. Despite my resolve to heed Galdra's warnings, I got dangerously close to the mirror again, and the familiar tendril of a headache reared its ugly head. My first instinct was to recoil from it, but my treacherous hand groped after the fractured glass. It was like touching ice. Dark shapes coiled on the other side, gathering in the spot where my fingers pressed against the cold surface. Whispers echoed like a long-forgotten song…

My right arm tingled, and I jerked away.

Whatever lived beyond the glass belonged to another man, the one who died in the Desolation chamber, holding Lumi's ruined body in his arms. I forced my mind to return to the present, and when it did, I found myself clutching the pearl at my neck. I let it drop. I snatched the cup and drank the rest of my tea in one gulp.

'Why is Antaya so important to you?' I asked, setting the mug back on the table with a light tap. Galdra explained her reasons to me and I wanted to hear Goro's. 'You're powerful enough to create a new city for the mages. Why not just stay here and make it your home?'

Goro-Khan gave me a wild look. 'On this forsaken island?'

'No one bothered you here all these years, and the mages are free to practice their art without fear of retribution. It seems like a safe enough place.'

'*Safe?*' His teeth drew back in a snarl, and tendrils of heat raced up his collar. His left eyelid spasmed erratically.

I leaned back, stunned by this sudden loss of control.

Galdra shot to her feet and grabbed Goro's shoulder. 'Get a hold of yourself.'

His feral eyes fell on her, and the cup flew from his hand, smashing into pieces. He seized her by the neck. 'Don't tell me to calm down when my boy is nothing but ashes.'

I snatched the blade out of its sheath, pointing the tip at Goro's neck. 'Let her go.'

'The Valgsi puppet to the rescue. If you're so devoted to each other, perhaps I should leave you both here to rot.'

‘He knows nothing of your loss,’ Galdra wheezed. Her face and lips turned bluish purple. She held up a hand. ‘Lower your sword, Jarin.’

I hesitated. My mind supplied images of Goro-Khan throttling Galdra to death, leaving me bereft of my only ally. I couldn’t let that happen. ‘Let her go.’ I repeated, pressing the tip against his skin. A tiny droplet of blood trickled onto the blade.

I thought he wasn’t going to listen. His thumbs pushed deeper into Galdra’s neck, and the grimace on his face grew more feral. But then his grip on her loosened, and he shoved her away. Galdra staggered against the weapons rack. It toppled with a crash, spilling swords and daggers onto the hardwood floor. She stood amidst the chaos, clutching her throat and gasping for air.

Goro-Khan slapped away my sword as if slapping a pesky insect, and the hideous scowl vanished from his face. I stared, unable to fathom how a person could transform from a raving maniac into a man of tranquillity in an instant.

‘Please, sit,’ he said, wiping at the small cut on his neck. His fingers came away bloody, but he paid them no mind. Instead, he wiped his hand on his cotton trousers, leaving a red smear. ‘Sometimes the grief gets the better of me.’

‘Better of you? You almost killed her.’

Galdra staggered back to the table, nudging the weapons out of the way. 'Loss is an inconsolable thing,' she said between breaths and sagged down onto the cushion. Some of the colour returned to her face.

He clapped his hands, and Netis reappeared. Goro pointed at the overturned rack and the shattered pieces of his cup. 'Clean it up.'

The mage bowed and set about his business.

Goro lowered himself onto the cushion, crossing his legs as he did so. 'First, we assemble the mages in the pagoda,' he said in a voice as calm as a lake on a windless night. 'They need reassurance you're indeed the Valgsi we've been waiting for. When their curiosity is satisfied, we'll make provisions for our departure. We must reach Hvitur before the year's cycle comes to a close.'

I ignored him. 'Aren't you going to say something?' I asked Galdra.

'The mages grow impatient. It's only natural—'

'I'm not talking about the mages.'

'Oh?' She arched one brow.

I stood up, knocking the table with my knee.

Netis looked up, his hands full of cup shards.

'He almost strangled you, yet you're acting as if nothing happened,' I said. 'This isn't the way to treat women.' I stared

Goro in the eye. 'For a man who demands respect from others, you should be ashamed.'

In one smooth motion, Goro rose to his feet, his eye twitching. 'You forget where you are. Your title doesn't permit you to insult me on my island, under my roof.' He stabbed his finger at the floor as he spoke.

Galdra grabbed my arm. 'We have to go.'

'I'm not leaving until—'

She tightened her grip. 'Jarin, please.' Her voice wavered, and something flashed in her translucent eyes.

'Do as she says,' Goro said, 'and don't come back until you've learned some respect.' His finger jabbed in Galdra's direction. 'I want him brought to heel. As for you, remember where your loyalties lie. You pledged yourself long ago. If you betray my son… no illusion will hide you from me.'

I saw green spots, and before my rage exploded, I let Galdra lead me out of the house.

Outside, I inhaled deeply, filling my lungs with the smell of earth and damp rock. Slowly, my anger receded. Standing on the mountain path, surrounded by the craggy cliffs, Shinpi almost felt like home. Gooseflesh stood up on my arms and legs at the thought. Maybe it was I who wanted to stay here for fear of facing Torgal? I knew my uncle would never grant me a free passage to the top of Skaldir's hill, and I had a strong sense our swords would cross. But even if it didn't come to that, Nords would never accept Lumi.

'Goro-Khan can be ruthless,' Galdra said, yanking up her collar. 'But it's his ruthlessness that keeps us safe.'

I couldn't believe what I was hearing. 'You defend him?'

'He wants to restore our city and awaken Skaldir. In that, we're of one mind.'

'We don't need him for that. Besides, what does it matter if Antaya is rebuilt if you become slaves at his command? To be ruled by a madman. This isn't the future you envisioned.'

She looked up to where the sun sought shelter among the soaring peaks. 'It's not that simple.'

'It *is* simple. There's only one Goro-Khan, but the mages are many. We have all we need to awaken the goddess and give them back their city.'

'You don't understand.'

I took her by the shoulders, forcing her to look at me. 'You follow a man who calls himself the Laughing God. But he is no god. That power was promised to *me*.'

'Goro-Khan is the strongest mage on this island. You saw for yourself how dangerous he is. Since the death of his only son he's become unstable, and it's getting worse.'

'What happened to his son?'

I let go of her, and we started down the path leading back to the pagoda.

'His son, Yomu, was twenty-six years of age when an earthquake shook Shinpi. When we first arrived, the residents warned us about the demons stirring in the bowels of the earth. We took no notice of what we thought to be some local legend.' Her voice grew distant. 'Nothing could've prepared us for the magnitude of that disaster…'

'When the earthquake subsided, Yomu was missing. Goro-Khan spent weeks searching the island for him. He stopped eating, and he prayed in the Calling chamber until the early hours of the morning.'

A shrill cry of a mountain quail interrupted her. As if to rebuke it, another bird answered with a low hoot. I thought of my desire to resurrect Lumi. Goro-Khan knew the same loss and shared the same wish. Suddenly, he and I didn't seem so different. The realisation didn't sit well with me, for it was easier to hate a man when you saw him in the light of pure evil.

Galdra resumed her tale. 'Goro found Yomu's body trapped under a rock. His skull was crushed, and birds made a feast of his eyes.'

I shuddered. 'What a gruesome way to die.'

'Before then, Goro never used his laughter for punishment. Quite the opposite. He and Yomu made us laugh when days grew dark and our hope of ever leaving Shinpi diminished. Even for a mage, two hundred years of exile is a very long time.' Galdra clenched and unclenched her fingers. 'When

Agtarr revealed his face to Yomu, the merry part of Goro died. On the day of his son's burial, he lost control and began laughing. The mages standing closest laughed with him. All five died that day while others fell to their knees, bleeding from their ears.'

'Yet you still follow him.'

Her hand drifted up to the dark bruises forming on her neck. 'When Yomu is back among the living, Goro will crown him Antaya's protector, and I am to become his wife.'

I halted mid-stride. 'What?'

'I'm the only enchantress left in our fold. When I breathe my last, my bloodline will be no more. Goro wishes to preserve my magic by the means of… an offspring.'

Goro's earlier words started to make sense. 'And you agreed to that?'

'When I pledged myself to Yomu, there was no one else.'

'And now?'

Galdra's eyes fell on the pearl at my neck. She leaned forward. The fresh scent of ice chased away the smells of nature until my nose and head knew nothing else. 'I don't want to be bonded to a dead man.'

She was so close I could feel her cold breath on my face. Her lips parted halfway, and an overpowering need to kiss them came over me again. I reached out to touch her hair. 'You know how I feel about Lumi,' I said, while everything inside me questioned that very statement. Maybe Skaldir's magic affected my body as well as my mind. If that was so, how could I ever distinguish truth from a lie?

Galdra pulled away. Her luminous eyes gazed into mine with a feverish intensity. 'Set us free.'

Despite my earlier words, a powerful image flashed in my head: Galdra and I side by side, my sword glowing green with Skaldir's power, as we bring about a new future. Something wet and dark coiled in my gut. I opened my mouth to remind her of Lumi, but instead, I uttered two words, 'I will.'

XV

Fjola placed her hand on Mirable's shoulder. 'Stay strong,' she said in a firm voice.

He bobbed his head up and down, but the trembling in his hands and knees didn't ease. After the events in the pagoda, the guards seized them both and dragged them down the many steps and through the wretched rooms, the Goddess of Destruction following their progress from the paintings and murals hanging on the walls. The mages were obsessed with Skaldir, and every floor of the pagoda reflected it. Fjola didn't understand how something so destructive could be treated with such reverence.

The guards led them down into the village, where the green smog shimmered like a veil spread above the ground. At first, breathing it in didn't bother her so much, but after a while, the heavy scent made her dizzy. Each breath caught in her chest, inducing a small coughing fit. She glanced at Mirable, but he seemed unaffected. During that disgraceful walk, the residents spat at them, screamed curses in Skaldir's name, and wished her judgement upon them. Fjola didn't care for the insults, searching the crowds for the familiar face of her brother.

But Njall was nowhere to be seen.

Maybe he'd managed to steal the ship and sail for home, she told herself, because the alternative meant he was long dead, be it from the exposure to the magical residue or at the hands of the mages. She forced the idea out of her head, for even a thought that she'd lost her only brother was unbearable. Hot tears stung her eyelids, but she blinked them away, refusing to give these wretches the satisfaction of seeing her humiliated. Fjola lifted her chin and strode tall, using her pride as a shield.

Mirable walked next to her, his body hunched forward and arms dangling on both sides of his body like thick branches. His eyes fixed on the road ahead as he muttered something that sounded to her like two men haggling over a reel of silk. Her heart went out to him. The moment his path crossed with Jarin's, his simple life was put to the axe.

Come to think of it, all their lives changed when Jarin passed through Hvitur on his way to Vester. Torgal ordered Njall to go with Jarin, and her brother obeyed without question. Fjola's own discontent with life made her follow them. Skari chased after her and paid with his life, leaving her to wrestle with the guilt.

Jarin was the catalyst. He endured the destruction of his home, placed his soul under contract, and found Shinpi, only to see Lumi shatter in his arms. Could it be that her death finally broke him? They all believed his strength was boundless, but it seemed even those favoured by the gods had their limits.

When the guards hurled them into the prison cell, Mirable slumped against the wall and wrapped his hands around his knees. Everything about his shape looked wrong to Fjola. She knew that with no one to stop the change, the Varl growing inside him would take over. When that happened, would Mirable turn on her, or would their strong bond be enough to save her? She didn't care one way or the other. Sooner or later, Agtarr's Warrior of Death would come for them all, and she'd made peace with that. But before then, she had to see Jarin one last time. There was no use in denying her feelings for him. Whenever she tried, she tripped over her own heart.

The chill from the stone seeped through Fjola's shirt, making her shiver. She pushed away from the wall and got to her feet. The cell was a square box with its floor lined by damp straw. She wondered how many poor wretches found themselves locked in here simply because they were unfortunate enough to chance upon Shinpi during their voyage across the Great Atlantic. Unlike the cell that she and Njall occupied, this one didn't benefit from the light cast by the green orbs, but Fjola preferred the shadows. The magic made her uneasy.

She walked across to the cell door and peered through the iron bars. The corridor to either side stood empty. Fjola rattled the bars. 'Where are you hiding, you cowards?' she shouted into the silence.

No answer.

She slammed her fist into the bars, sending echoes through the vacant hallways. The pain shot through her knuckles at the impact. She winced and shook her hand. Her fingers missed the familiar feel of her daggers. Without them, she felt like the girl she used to be before she found the courage to ask Argil to teach her how to fight. Like a cold stone, the memory of that day lodged in the pit of her stomach, weighing her down.

With a sigh, she slumped next to Mirable.

He twisted his head her way. The whites of his eyes looked as if someone cast a red web over them, and his full lips turned the colour of ash. 'My chest hurts,' he said, rubbing his ribcage.

'Show me.'

With a grimace, he pulled up his shirt.

Fjola's hand flew to her mouth. It was worse than she thought—Mirable's torso crawled with three throbbing pustules that appeared to be fusing. Coarse tufts of hair made rings around them, and the flesh beneath turned black. The bones of his spine stood out in sharp ridges, stretching the skin until it appeared translucent. Now she understood why his posture changed so much since they arrived in Shinpi. Maybe it was the accumulation of magic or the way Hyllus's spell did its work, but Mirable's transformation gained momentum. There was no way to tell how much time they had left.

'I'm sorry,' she said, folding her arms around his shivering form, careful not to touch any of the tumours.

She always despised the Varls for the destruction they'd caused in Nordur, but not once did she stop to consider their pain. Would this torment end when the change was complete? She recalled Alkaios and how he drooled and trembled while leading them through the streets of Vester. He failed his transformation, so Hyllus cast him aside like a used up ragdoll. If like Alkaios, Mirable resisted the change, he would turn into a broken Varl. If he gave in to it, he would become a senseless monster.

Her friend had no choice at all.

At the thought of Mirable's cruel fate, a sob escaped her lips, and the hate for the Laughing God engulfed her heart like a giant storm cloud. He took Jarin captive and put her and Mirable in chains. It was Goro-Khan who indulged Hyllus's mania by ordering him to create a demon to deceive the warriors of Stromhold. The muscles of her jaw twitched.

'We can't let him get away with this,' she said through clenched teeth.

Mirable sniffed. 'As much as I resent the idea, do you want me to kill the next guard who enters? If it helps you escape, I'll do it. My soul is damned anyway.' He looked up at the ceiling.

'To think I bought myself a slip to Agtarr's Chamber of Torments, the very place Jarin sent Hyllus. The irony.'

'I'm not leaving without you.'

He touched one of the black pustules and cringed. 'I'm an abomination. I don't know how you can stand to be near me.'

'If you're an abomination, so was Lumi, but that didn't stop Jarin from loving her.'

'When put through many ordeals, we often ascribe feelings to things, and people, that aren't necessarily true. Loving someone brings comfort and affords us a unique view of the world. *We* is a much stronger weapon against loneliness than *I*.'

'Are you saying Jarin never loved Lumi?'

'By the gods, no. Our hearts set their own laws.' He plucked a loose strand from his turban. 'My father was a wretched man who never cared for me or my mother. Her love was sincere, but it was his adoration I craved. It didn't matter how many beatings I took. I still wanted him to be proud of me, to recognise my accomplishments even if they didn't meet his expectations. You're beautiful and loyal. Deep down, Jarin knows this, but his heart has been badly wounded. Even if he refuses to admit it, he's still grieving his parents. We look up to him because of his tremendous courage and drive. It's compelling. But in the face of death, he's still only a man.' He squeezed Fjola's hand. 'If you truly love Jarin, stay true to him. No matter what happens.'

Fjola wiped her eyes with her sleeve. 'I don't even know who I am anymore.'

Mirable sighed and looked at his chest, where the tumours wrought havoc.

'I used to walk around my village, doing chores for my mother, or simply looking for something to do, but everywhere I went I heard Hvitur's girls chattering about the men chosen for them by their parents. Whenever they invited me to join in, I refused, thinking them silly for wanting such a boring life.'

'Some of us feel at home in the centre of a bustling market—' his bloodshot eyes softened at the word market—'while others are happy sitting by the hearth, weaving baskets. To each his own.'

'I had no interest in domestic life. As a girl of ten, I stared the world square in the face, ready to take it on if given the chance. I'd often climb the tallest hill in Hvitur, and gaze at the vast reaches of the Great Atlantic, imagining the lands beyond.' Her voice faltered, and she looked down at her boots. 'Perhaps I was the silly one all along.'

'You saw more of the world than any of those girls could ever dream of. Take pride in that. It takes courage to follow your heart.'

She wondered at that. For a lifetime with Jarin she'd happily sit by the hearth, listening to the crackling of the fire while the blizzard raged outside, safe in the knowledge the man she loved sat beside her. To touch him, all she had to do was reach out…

Fjola squashed the image. The ice demon took that life from her.

Her mind turned to the events in the pagoda. 'What did Goro-Khan do to me?' Fjola asked. After their horrific encounter, her belly still ached in the way it used to when she trained for endurance with Argil.

'He made you laugh.'

'How can you laugh against your will?'

'The same way you change into a monster.' Mirable rubbed the tips of his fingers. 'I stopped him… with my magic.'

Her eyes widened. 'You can cast magic?'

'It seems that way.' He coughed, and pressed a fist to his chest. 'Who knew a Varl can waggle his tongue so much. All this talk is making me dizzy.'

'Mirable, this is serious. Alkaios said nothing about magic.'

'Maybe I'm special.'

'Enough with the jests. You can't talk your way out of this one.'

A sly smile played on his lips. 'I was trained in a skill of persuasion. I'm quite good at it, you know.'

Fjola was about to say something reproachful when an idea struck her. She leapt to her feet and pressed her face between the cell bars. The corridor to either side was still vacant. Satisfied, she crouched next to Mirable. 'For as long as we're confined to this place, we can do nothing to help Jarin.'

'That's no revelation.'

She waved her hand, then dropped her voice to a whisper. 'Everyone knows you're changing. When you're a fully-fledged Varl, who's to say you won't turn on your friends.' Mirable's mouth flew open, and she hastened to add, 'Hyllus turned you, but even he understood little of his creation. We can use it to our advantage.'

'Merchants often rely on their sharp instinct, and mine tells me I won't like what comes next.'

'It's not the merchant we need for the task. It's the Varl.'

Mirable's shoulders sagged. 'Why am I not surprised?'

XVI

Since Lumi's death, my dreams felt more real than the waking hours, and this night was no different. I drifted off to sleep under the canopy of the watchful crescents only to be awakened by a voice whispering in my ear that I was cursed and blinded. It chased me straight into the wastelands of my mind, where Lumi stood on the other side of the mirror. The cracks in the glass distorted her features, but at the sight of her, my heart flitted like a moth trapped inside a glowing lantern.

'You're dead,' I said. 'But I can't remember how it happened.'

'You will,' she said, her voice lacking its usual chime. It was distorted like a peal from a cracked bell. 'Everything you need is inside you.'

I pressed my fingers against the glass. 'I'll bring you back.'

Lumi hung her head as if my intention saddened her.

A string of words I recognised as Galdra's incantation filled my mind, and Lumi's face blurred.

'Tell me how it happened,' I cried, scraping the glass with my nails. All I wanted to do was smash the mirror with my fist, but the might of Galdra's words held me back, whispering of madness and death. They hacked at my brain, ordering my thoughts and sifting through memories. The mirror's surface began to shimmer with green light, and I took a step back. The magic locked inside the glass gathered in its centre, then rushed at my ribcage. The force of it shoved me backwards. I flailed, trying to catch my balance, but there was nothing I could do to stop myself from falling…

I awoke with a scream, gripping the sweat-soaked sheets. My muscles trembled, and my chest felt as if a raging blizzard swept through it while I slept, freezing the ribs and frosting over my heart. I coughed like a man taking his first breath on a winter morning.

'Drink this,' Galdra said, forcing a cup to my lips.

I took a sip and cringed as the bitter taste flooded my mouth. 'Mugwort?' I asked, pushing the cup away. 'Why are you giving me this?'

'Don't be a child,' Galdra said. 'This mixture will help with the pain.'

At the mention of pain, my headache returned with a vengeance. 'Where I come from, mugwort is used to induce lucid dreams. My uncle banished it.'

'Is he aware that, if combined with other herbs, mugwort can help relieve anxiety and speed up the recovery of brain tissue?'

I said nothing, continuing to eye the cup with suspicion.

'I thought so,' Galdra said. 'Now, drink.'

Her assurance did nothing to ease the doubt, but the growing headache decided for me. Reluctantly, I took the cup from her. My stomach heaved, but I forced myself to drink the mixture. As I did so, I had a strong feeling more vivid dreams would come to haunt me. But what would Galdra gain from evoking nightmares even I struggled to make sense of? My suspicions were most likely the work of my vexed brain looking for an explanation.

Galdra brushed aside my sweaty hair and pressed her palm to my forehead. 'You're running a fever,' she said, leaning close. 'Tell me about your dreams.'

I looked through the only window in the room. Outside, the wind ripped holes in the grey clouds, exposing bits of the sky. 'My dreams are twisted. Nothing in them makes any sense.'

'Dreams are an extension of life. They reveal the inner workings of our mind.'

It sounded like something my mother would say.

Galdra caught my chin and turned my head away from the window. 'What do you dream of?'

The question came clad in the clean scent of freshly fallen snow. Like a man starved of air, I inhaled, and all at once, my head hummed with the sound of Galdra's name.

'I dream of Lumi...' I thought of how Galdra always interrupted my nightmares, but I kept this knowledge to myself.

Her upper lip twitched, and her fingers brushed the front of her collar, where the marks left by Goro-Khan had turned a deep-purple.

'I'm not scared of him,' I said.

'You should be. Everyone on this island is.'

With a sigh, I fell back onto the pillows. The jade crescents blinked at me from the canopy of my ornate bed. I was suffocating in this room, on this island, but a score of weeks still separated me from the journey home. From seeing Lumi.

'I should kill him for what he did to you,' I said.

'You can't stop the unstoppable,' Galdra said with a glint in her luminous eyes.

'You don't know what I can or can't do.'

'To challenge the Laughing God, you'll need more than your confidence. A powerful sense of hope drives him. To see Antaya rise above the waves, with Yomu on the throne, means more to him than all the magic in the world.'

Despite his son being dead, I found it hard to believe Goro-Khan didn't care about a single soul in the world of the living. 'What happened to his wife?' I asked.

'She opposed the summoning. The mages didn't take kindly to her interference.'

Her answer gave me pause. It seemed not every mage desired to see Skaldir face to face. It was an interesting thought, and it uprooted my belief that everyone with magic in their blood wished for the Day of Judgement. 'They killed her?' I asked.

Galdra shrugged. 'I don't know for sure. Everyone here thinks she died trying to flee the city. Goro-Khan never speaks her name.'

'I pity him,' I said.

'You shouldn't. He's lost everything, and he loves no one. This lack of attachments is what makes him so dangerous.'

Goro-Khan—the man who abandoned his wife and lost his only son to an earthquake. The man whose laughter could bring even the strongest of mages to their knees. 'I know a creature that would relish an encounter with such a man,' I said, thinking of the serena and how it enticed Njall and Mirable to jump off the ship. Mirable said the creature lured those with hearts free of attachments, men and women with formidable qualities… The thought planted a seed of an idea in my mind, but it felt too risky. I opened my mouth to share it with Galdra, when a brisk knock on the door interrupted me.

Galdra stood up and smoothed her hair and gown. 'Enter.'

The door slid open, and Netis stepped through, dressed in a robe of dark grey. He inclined his bald head. 'Everyone's gathered on the ground floor and Goro-Khan is asking for you.'

'Excellent,' she said. 'Tell him we're coming.'

Netis bowed again, and his large eyes met mine before he turned on his heel and left. There was something about him, the way he looked at me as if taking my measure. I resolved to find him after the speech and learn more about him.

Galdra clapped. 'Finally. The time has come for the mages to meet their Valgsi.'

* * *

'Do it,' I ordered.

Galdra picked up the shaving knife from the table. 'Are you sure?'

'If I'm to gain their favour, I must embrace that part of me. I must become the champion of my cause, and rather than hide it from them, I must display Skaldir's mark with pride.'

'Very well.' She plucked a strand of hair closest to my left temple and cut it off. The hair drifted to the floor to rest on the cap of my boot. Like an echo from an empty well, the voice of my mother reverberated in my mind, telling me how my brown locks made her think of Father.

'You're brooding again,' Galdra said.

I jumped, and the knife sliced the tip of my left ear. Hissing, I clapped my palm to it.

Galdra threw up her hands. 'How many times must I tell you—'

'They'd be better off following a corpse. How am I to lead people when I can't even make sense of my own mind?'

She placed the shaving knife next to a basin full of water and picked up a cotton towel. She dipped it in the bowl. 'From the moment we met, I tried to do what's best for you, yet you continue to ignore my warnings.' She wrung the cloth and dabbed at my ear. 'Your mind is an open wound. I did my best to stitch it up, but my magic has its limits. If you keep prodding before it's fully healed, you risk lasting damage.'

My jaw clenched.

'When I say damage, I don't mean a splitting headache. I mean madness.' She wetted the towel again, and the blood from it formed rivulets in the water. 'In time, your memories will return and make you whole again, but if your impatience gets the better of you… well, think of a blood vessel rupturing inside your brain. You'll spend the rest of your life incapable of sane thought.'

The strands of blood blended with the water, turning the liquid into a crimson pool. I wanted to snatch the basin and smash it against the wall. Never in my life had I felt so powerless, stripped of the familiar, and forced to depend on someone I barely knew. If only my friends were here, but Galdra insisted on reminding me that Njall abandoned me as soon as we reached Shinpi, Fjola played a hand in Lumi's death, and Mirable sided with her. Yet, I found myself resisting the idea. We had gone through so much together for them to simply turn on me like that. As soon as this audience was over, I'd go to the prison and speak with Fjola.

I closed my eyes. 'Carry on.'

Galdra resumed her task, filling my ears with clipping sounds. Each handful of hair fell to the floor, taking a piece of the old Jarin with it. Questions swarmed my brain, but I refused to acknowledge them, knowing they'd only add to my confusion. It was time to accept reality—I was a broken man with no recollection of the past and an uncertain future. The only sure thing in my mind was Lumi and my need to save her. For all I knew, without her heart, she was denied entry into the Fields of Life and instead cast into the darkest pits of Agtarr's Chamber of Torments, where the souls of the damned burned in eternal flames. For someone like Lumi, who feared fire, it was the worst imaginable punishment.

'It is done,' Galdra said, and she kissed my temple. Her warm lips lingered on the mark of Skaldir, as if seeking to memorise every groove of the constellation. 'Magnificent,' she murmured, reaching for the looking glass. 'See for yourself.'

I took the round mirror. The man with sunken eyes stared back. Dark shadows lined his sockets, and the skin of his cheekbones had a look of an overstretched vellum. The left side of his head was shaved clean, exposing a mark centred on four stars linked by two intersecting lines. It stood out above my temple like a livid scar. I pressed my fingertips to the spot, feeling the raised edges, too smooth and perfect to be anything other than a symbol of divine creation—the mark of Skaldir's Valgsi.

'I'm ready,' I said, hoping to avoid her scorn.

She gave me a crisp nod and headed for the door. Relieved, I followed her out and along the corridor. This time, the sleeping quarters to my left stood vacant not because the mages were busy helping the villagers but because they gathered on the lowest floor in anticipation of my coming. My skin prickled at the thought.

Galdra paused at the top of the steps. 'Today may be our only chance at undermining Goro-Khan's hold on the mages and turning things in our favour. Don't spoil it with your ceaseless brooding.'

I looked into her eyes, where the shadow of her irises shifted beyond the pearly whites. Irritation bubbled in my gut, but I forced myself to cool it. Goro-Khan used Galdra to further his own gains, and she was right to be upset with me. Unless I silenced the laughter that plagued Shinpi, she'd never be free of him and his dead son. What's more, the Laughing God could hinder my plans for Lumi.

I brushed her cheek. 'I'll make you proud.'

Her shoulders relaxed.

We descended. My stomach twisted with each step as my mind hunted for the right words to address the mages. They thought me a hero, delivered by the Goddess of Destruction to liberate them, but in truth, I felt less significant than kelp in the Great Atlantic. I fixed my eyes on Galdra's back as if the speech would magically appear in the space between her shoulder blades. Aside from the echo of our boots, the pagoda held silent. Skaldir watched our descent from the murals and paintings Galdra showed me days ago, and the passing moments felt dreamlike. Since my arrival in Shinpi, my inability to distinguish between dreams and the waking world deepened with each passing day. Maybe it was the effect of mugwort, or maybe this island was an illusion created by the residents to confuse those unfortunate enough to drift here. After all, everyone considered Shinpi a legend, but here I was, walking its shores and about to meet its people, some of whom witnessed the Day of Judgement.

A whisper stirred beyond the magical glass inside my head. I reminded myself that Galdra created it to keep me sane. There was nothing to be afraid of but so much to embrace. Skaldir wanted me to come here, to find her worshippers and curb their slide into obscurity. I lifted my chin. The mages would get their speech and the freedom to practise the arts without fear of retribution. They'd earn the right to celebrate the god of their choosing. As for me, I'd have Lumi back and a place in Antaya where no one would question my choices.

Galdra stopped at the foot of the final staircase.

I gasped.

Mages crowded the lowest floor, elbow to elbow. The main door stood wide, and green cloaks and colourful gowns filled the gap. More lingered in the open, craning their necks to see inside. Men and women who swore fealty to Skaldir and hid in the mountains, waiting for the day their goddess would awaken to liberate them. She answered their prayers by placing the mark upon my temple. My quivering fingers found the lines of the constellation I had no name for.

Goro-Khan presided on a dais erected for the occasion. He wore a grey shirt with buttons at the front and a pair of cotton trousers. His hair sat atop his head in a tight coil, and his silvery beard was trimmed to a point. Like some unearthly crown, several green orbs hovered above, bathing his features in a leafy glow. He acknowledged us with a nod. At the sight of him, anger flared up in me like an old ulcer. How dare he stand there, with his hands behind his back and chest puffed out like a peacock's, claiming the rights to the throne of Antaya. My fingers tightened around the banister.

Galdra placed her cool palm over mine and leaned close. 'Think about the future,' she whispered, and the smell of winter suffused my nostrils.

Like that day on the path to Goro's house, the images of me and Galdra ruling Antaya side by side pervaded my mind. I frowned, for this wasn't how I imagined my future, but the vision was too powerful to resist. It swept through me like a hurricane, wiping away all traces of my former thoughts. In it, Galdra's eyes were smokey and dark, and the green crescent on her forehead shone with pure brilliance. My life before Shinpi was a muddle, but my vision of the future was sharp and clear.

Galdra seized my hand and strode to the dais while people parted to make way. The air in the room was stretched like a string about to snap.

We came to stand at Goro's shoulder.

Goro-Khan appraised the assembly. 'Our day has come.' His voice sounded cool and poised, allowing no room for doubt. He stood tall, his body as straight as an arrow, and every eye locked on his face. The Laughing God was a man who kept them alive during their endless waiting. For those who crossed him, his laughter was the last sound that rang in their ears, and for those who put their faith in him, he vowed to restore them to their former glory. If I opposed Goro-Khan, how would the mages react? Would they rejoice or brand me a traitor?

'Our goddess did not forsake us. Her reward for our devotion stands before you in the flesh.' Goro grabbed my shoulder and squeezed. 'Our Valgsi is here at last, with her mighty sword at his hip and his soul starved for her magic.'

Whispers rippled and died as everyone's attention turned to me. This was the moment to win the mages over. My back dampened with sweat, and the room wavered.

Goro-Khan pushed me forward. 'Make your speech.'

The murmurs ceased. A hush fell over the pagoda, and I was sure everyone could hear my heart crashing against my ribs. My mind fumbled for the right words. I still knew precious little about the Night of Norrsken and even less of Antaya and the time before the Day of Judgement.

Clenching and unclenching my fingers, I appraised the assembly. The eager faces peered back at me, and it was impossible to distinguish between the mages and those with only human blood in their veins. Their veneration of Skaldir made them equal.

'My name is Jarin Olversson.' My voice sounded like that of a youth who'd lost his mother in a crowded market. I glanced at Galdra, but her face showed no emotion. This task I had to accomplish on my own.

I cleared my throat and tried again. 'Jarin was the name given to me by my father, but Skaldir named me long before I drew my first breath. When my mother pushed me out into the world, the magic of destruction shone brightly in the sky, and it marked me as the Valgsi.' I angled my head so everyone could witness the symbol on my temple.

The mages whispered and nodded. Bolstered by their approval, I relayed the story of my birth and how Father fought Torgal over the right to Skaldir's blade. Whenever I came across the gaps in my memories, I filled them with my convictions.

'The Norderner must die!' someone shouted. 'He bars the way to the sacred ground.'

They craved my uncle's death, and I couldn't blame them. From the very beginning, Torgal wished ill upon the people of Antaya. When my grandfather, Bodvar, challenged him, he paid with his life.

'I can't promise that all of you will live to see the Lost City of Antaya reborn, but I vow that Skaldir will awaken.' I unsheathed my sword and pointed the gleaming steel at the hopeful faces. Stirred by the might of my words, the script ignited with green light, evoking the sounds of awe. The relic of Skaldir united us.

'I promise to give you back your home,' I said, savouring the moment. While Goro-Khan could make people laugh until the vessels in their brains ruptured, I possessed the power to wake the gods. 'I promise you the Day of Judgement, so you can have your justice.' I shook my fist. 'I promise you freedom.'

The room erupted with prayers as people fell to their knees, chanting the name of Skaldir and her Valgsi. Once upon a time, Stromhold was my home and the warriors my family, but it all changed when I set foot on Shinpi. My true family knelt before me, and together, we embraced my destiny. I inhaled deeply. The sharp smell of frost hung heavy in the air, driving away other scents.

Goro-Khan clapped three times. 'Well done,' he said in my ear. 'Just don't let it go to your head. The magic barrier protecting Antaya shattered, and we both know why.'

'You call yourself the Laughing God, yet Skaldir chose a simple mortal to do her bidding. Aren't you afraid this alone will strip you of your divinity?' Goro's eye twitched. I sheathed the sword and called, 'Brothers and sisters, don't kneel before me. Rise and let us prepare for the Night of Norrsken.'

One by one, the mages got to their feet, eyes gleaming. Their excitement made me feel taller, stronger, and more capable than ever. If only my father could see me now. At the memory of him, a shadow fell across my heart. Eyvar learned the face of Agtarr, and so did my mother. But I still couldn't recall how they died. Something rippled across the surface of the mirror in my head.

A commotion outside jolted me back.

'Let me pass,' a voice cried. 'And if you touch my turban one more time—'

A loud thump cut the threat short. A moment of silence followed, broken by a deep growl.

I recognised both the voice and the growl.

Two Shinpi guards and a man in crimson headwear pushed through the crowd.

'Mirable,' I called. Seeing him unharmed, a strange giddiness surged through me. I wanted to leap off the dais and embrace him.

Galdra caught my upper arm. 'Don't make a fool of yourself.'

'Jarin!' Mirable exclaimed. 'Yldir be praised. I thought you dead you foolish boy.'

Galdra held me fast, and some of the joy at seeing the merchant evaporated. 'What are you doing here?' I asked.

One guard said something in his native tongue, and Galdra translated, 'The Varl wants to serve you.'

I wanted to rebuke her, to tell her Mirable was no Varl, but one look at him would make such a declaration foolish. The merchant's spine arched like limbs of a bow, forcing him to hunch over. This posture did nothing to disguise the sharp edges of the backbone poking through his torn shirt. His hands appeared longer, the knuckles of his right almost brushing the floor, and even from a distance, I caught sight of the dark shadows of his tumours. A coiled beard covered Mirable's chin and lower cheeks, and the eyes that bore into mine were wild and bloodshot.

I yanked my arm free of Galdra's grip. 'Is it true?' I asked him.

Mirable patted his turban—the only familiar thing about him. 'It is.'

'Or maybe he wishes the Valgsi harm?' Galdra said, evoking the murmurs of agreement from the mages who eyed Mirable with an expression of distaste and wonder. Varls were Hyllus's creation, plaguing Nordern and Vestern lands. The merchant must've seemed like a rare and curious exhibit.

'I only wish to serve my friend,' Mirable said. He pulled off his shirt, revealing the true face of his transformation. The three tumours on his chest joined into a growth that looked like a second heart with dark vessels pulsing in its centre, the one on his abdomen fused with the surrounding tissue, tainting it black. Mirable's body hair grew thick and coarse like those of the Nordern wolves. 'Hyllus created me to follow and protect the Valgsi.'

The guard said something again, and Galdra's brow furrowed. 'He attacked the girl,' she said. 'If not for a guard passing by, he'd have ripped her to pieces.'

Mirable shrugged. 'I can't help my nature.'

Acrid bile rose in the back of my throat. 'What did you do?' To think Mirable would harm Fjola was beyond me. Perhaps Goro-Khan did the right thing by locking him up… I rejected the thought at once. Mirable deserved better than to spend his days in the stinking cell. And so did Fjola.

'You assume the Valgsi needs protection,' Goro-Khan said, dragging his fingers along his pointed beard. 'May I ask from whom?'

Mirable twisted his head to look at Goro, and the gesture contorted his face into a painful grimace. 'The same men you're hiding from.'

'In other words, the men like you.' He paused, then added, 'But then again, you're no man.'

Mirable ignored him. 'Jarin, you know how I loathe this change, but I can't deny it any longer.' He clasped his hands. 'Don't let me turn into a broken Varl.'

I wasn't sure what I could do for him, but I couldn't bear the thought of leaving my friend to suffer alone.

'Allow the magic to run its course, merchant,' Galdra said. 'When it does, you'll be free of pain and more powerful than ever.'

Mirable's fingers curled into claws. 'I felt perfectly powerful as a simple human.'

'Those days are behind you. If you wish to make yourself useful, stop resisting and embrace your true potential.' She swept her hand at the assembly. 'Many here are curious about Hyllus's magic, and since the mage himself is no longer with us, your presence would serve as a great lesson of what can be accomplished if one isn't afraid to experiment.'

'He's not here to amuse them,' I said.

'Then why is he here?' Goro-Khan asked.

His question gave me a pause. Unlike Njall and Fjola, the magic in Mirable's veins bound him to the mages and our cause. He'd be a powerful ally, and together we could use his keen nose to solve the problem of the Laughing God. But until then, I couldn't give Goro any more reasons to doubt me. 'Fjola ended Lumi's life, and you sided with her. How can I trust you?'

Mirable's jaw flew open and closed like that of a fish while his eyes rolled from me to Galdra. 'Why would you think—'

'Answer the question, merchant,' Galdra snapped. 'Should the Valgsi place his trust in you?'

Mirable's eyes flared up, and his whites turned into balls of red. He took a hulking step forward, but the guard grabbed him by the neck.

The merchant jerked free without much of a struggle. 'Jarin, we've gone through much together. I showed you the path to the witches, and you saved my life in return. I owe you a debt, and this is my way of repaying it.'

The word 'witches' lanced my brain. With a giant cracking sound, a deep fracture shot through the surface of the mirror, and the dark tendrils seeped through the newly formed fissure, twisting fingers of smoke eager to get hold of me. At the same time, my right wrist exploded with a throbbing ache. The pagoda and everyone in it ceased to exist as I stripped my cloak and rolled up my sleeve. Dark lines pulsed under my skin like second veins, sending currents of pain. The source—a black eye in the centre of my wrist—was wide open, like an eye of some creature that ate its way into my flesh. I stared at it, and it glared back. Blood splattered onto the foul mark, and when I touched my nose, my fingers came away crimson.

Goro's voice boomed in my ears. 'Get him out of here.'

A hand tugged at my shirt. 'We have to go.'

My legs rooted to the floor, and I forgot how to use them. Someone slapped my cheek. A low cackle rose at the back of my head, wicked and oozing evil. It echoed through my skull and multiplied.

I shrieked.

Everything blurred. A lone howl mixed with words of incantation chased me into oblivion.

XVII

Voices, rising and falling like a curtain on some forgotten stage. Were they figments of a meaningless dream or fragments of reality, trying to force their way into my broken mind? Either way, I didn't pay them much attention. Like the phantoms of my past, the voices drifted in and out, and while I acknowledged them, I refused to give them any meaning. In this place, suspended between worlds, nothing made sense anymore.

'Why are you here? And do not lie to me, merchant.'

'I told you. I want to serve him.'

'Last time I saw you, you wanted to be a human.'

'Can you make me a human?'

Silence.

'I know she put you up to this. It's just like her to meddle with things she doesn't understand.'

'She has nothing to do with it. Actually, I'd send someone to tend Fjola's wounds. I lost my temper, and it turned nasty.'

'So you keep saying.'

'Why would I lie to you? It's not like Nords will welcome me in Hvitur with open arms. If I'm to survive, I need a place of my own. You speak of rebuilding the Lost City of Antaya and creating a home for the mages. Maybe I could find solace there? Besides, when I'm fully transformed, my magic will be stronger. If you teach me how to wield it—'

A single snort.

'Believe what you want, but let me stay by his side. That's all I ask.'

'I thought you and your friends didn't approve of his destiny.'

'Jarin is the only person who would have me.'

A repeated tapping of boots against the floor.

'If I let you stay, do you swear to serve Skaldir and do what we ask of you?'

'I'll do whatever Jarin wants me to do.'

'His mind is disturbed, and he needs reassurance from someone he knows. But. If you betray me, I'll cut you open, and your conniving friend will be next. Understood?'

'Oh, I understand. You confused him, so he'll do your bidding, but you saw what happened. You can't take someone's memories without asking for trouble. What happens when he remembers? Do you think he'll look kindly on you?'

'But he won't remember, and you'll make sure of that. Unless, of course, you want your precious little Fjola to burn for your defiance. I'll ensure she gets *special* treatment.'

A low growl.

'If you touch her…'

'You have nothing to worry about, as long as you do your part. But if you think of crossing me—'

'Do you truly believe he can love you?'

'What did you say?'

'I may be turning into a Varl, but I haven't lost my wit.'

'Shut your mouth, or I'll give you a taste of my magic.'

'No matter how many tricks you pull, you can't bind the soul that belongs to another. Your schemes won't save you from Goro-Khan.'

'But *he* will.'

The voices faded, then dissolved, leaving me in the arms of blessed silence.

* * *

I woke to the sound of pouring water. My head burned like a giant fireball, and my right arm ached—each throb a reminder of the stain on my soul. I forgot about the witches and our pact, and now, they exacted their vengeance. The shutters in the room were drawn, blocking out the hour of the day. I looked up to where the green carvings of the crescents formed a mock sky above. This bed was my world of late. Always brought here unconscious to sleep my days away while my spirit wandered the wasteland of my mind, searching for Lumi. The hope of seeing her alive was the only thing that kept me going, but I dreamt less and less of her, and it terrified me. To forget Lumi's face would be like forgetting my own name, and at times I came close to doing both. Only in Galdra's presence, my memory of Lumi was sharp and clear: the glacial smell of her, the way her skin felt cool to the touch, and even her voice with that slight chime to it…

A clatter of cups drew my attention, and I turned my head to meet Mirable's bloodshot eyes.

'Finally,' he said in a gruff voice that sounded nothing like the cheery babble of the merchant I chanced upon in Vester. 'Who knew you could sleep days at a time without uttering a single snore.' His long and darkened fingernails curved around the steaming cup. 'I was *told* you must drink this.'

I motioned at his nails. 'Don't they bother you?'

Mirable huffed. 'Of course, they bother me, but every time I trim the vile things, they grow back twice as fast.'

I reached for the cup, and the musky, sage-like odour wafted up my nostrils as I recognised the scent of mugwort. I drank. My throat felt as if someone took a skinning knife to it, each swallow more painful than the last.

When I started coughing, Mirable snatched the cup. 'Enough of this nonsense. I'm willing to bet my coins this stuff is doing you no good.'

'You have no coins.'

He slammed the cup on the bedside table, spilling the yellow liquid all over it. 'What's wrong with you? You were unconscious for three days.'

‘Three days?’ It felt to me as if my speech happened a few hours ago. Was it the same for Skaldir? Forced to dream against her will for eternity, with no hope of release. Suddenly, the idea of awakening her seemed more like mercy than destruction. I wanted to learn about the goddess, to understand the inner workings of her mind. Did she truly have the power to resurrect Lumi and Yomu?

Mirable nodded. His usually neat turban sat atop his head, wrapped into a series of messy folds that made it look like a nest of a harried pigeon. ‘Do you remember what happened?’ he asked.

‘Fragments. I recall the speech, and you, making a ruckus.’

Mirable waved his hand. ‘I’m not asking about that.’

Blurry images rippled across the surface of the cracked mirror, and my head began to pound. ‘I’d rather not talk about it.’

He slumped onto the edge of the bed. The space between his brows all but disappeared as they joined into a single strip above his nose. ‘How did we get here?’

‘This is my destiny. I was meant to find Shinpi and guide its people to freedom. I must follow the path Skaldir set before me and find out where it leads.’

‘You know where it leads,’ Mirable said, glancing at the door. ‘The Day of Judgement still burns hot in people’s memories. If you unleash Skaldir, the world will condemn you.'

My fingers found the witches' mark. The skin around it felt hot to the touch. 'I'm already damned.'

'You don't know that.'

'And you do?'

'I see that you're suffering.' His voice dropped to a hoarse whisper. 'I want to help, but first, you must search within yourself. The answers are there. You only have to open your eyes and ears.'

'Which side are you on, Mirable?'

'I'm here because I still believe in my friend. The Jarin who brought us here was a noble warrior seeking justice for his family. Maybe overly reckless, but never to be swayed by lies and trickery.'

I stared past him at the vermillion birds on the folding screen. With their wings in full flight, they looked free of all burdens, oblivious that the artist imprisoned them for eternity with one stroke of his brush. 'That man is dead,' I said. 'If you want to stay here, accept it. False hopes never did us any good.'

'I don't understand… After everything we've been through.'

Green spots flickered in the corners of my vision. I jerked forward, grabbed a fistful of Mirable's shirt. 'No, *you* wouldn't understand. You call me a friend, yet you sided with Fjola when she crushed Lumi's heart.' I shook him. 'Why? What did Lumi ever do to you? Fjola's jealousy got the better of her, but you…' I shoved him away and fell back onto the pillows. 'I expected better from you.'

Mirable's bulging eyes narrowed to slits, and his lips drew back to expose his elongated teeth. A guttural sound rumbled in his chest.

I opened my arms wide. 'Come then,' I shouted. 'Embrace the beast and let it rip me apart like it wanted to rip apart Fjola.'

Mirable flinched back as if scalded by boiling water. 'I never wanted to hurt anyone,' he cried. 'The people you cherish turned me into this. Have you truly lost all sense of self?'

'So tell me.' I pulled at my hair. 'Tell me what happened and let the madness take me. You'll be doing me a favour.'

'Pain, death, and destruction…' the witches hissed in unison, and the skin around their mark rippled. *'Follow the path… the path must be followed…'*

To silence that ancient voice, I took a fist to my temple, but the blow did nothing to rid me of the dark entity. The witches were no mere memory. They were real, and I would have to face them again.

I fell back against the pillows. ‘I’m sorry. I shouldn’t be taking my frustrations out on you.’

Mirable moaned. ‘I wish I could do more, but your life isn’t the only one at stake.’

The door slid open, and Galdra stepped through. Her dress fell to her ankles in a green cascade of lush velvet. The hem and the edges of its long sleeves were embroidered with golden vines. When she entered, the air in the room changed from stifling to that of the fresh winter morning. At the sight and smell of her, the fog and confusion brought on by the heated exchange receded. I took in a huge breath, but Mirable only wrinkled his nose.

Galdra smiled at me, but when her ghostly eyes shifted to Mirable, the smile died. ‘I warned you not to agitate him. His upset may be someone else’s pain. Your words have weight, merchant. You’d do well to remember that.’ Before I could ask what she meant, Galdra crossed the bedchamber and cupped my face. ‘I’m glad you’re awake,’ she said, leaning close. Her green-stained lips brushed against my cheek. ‘Is your wayward Varl causing you trouble?’ she murmured.

‘Let him be,’ I said, embracing the chill brought on by her touch. ‘His transformation has been rough on him.’

Galdra looked over her shoulder. ‘Your faith will be tested, creature.’

Mirable’s nostrils flared.

'Perhaps a brief history lesson would tame that varlish abandon.'

I groaned. 'A history lesson?' An old memory of the hours spent in Stromhold's library resurfaced, and the stern voice of my teacher, Marco, boomed in my ears, telling me to pay attention. 'I was planning on seeing Fjola.'

'It'll have to wait. I'm about to take you to the most sacred place in this world. It's my final gift to you before we set sail for Hvitur. After today, you'll never question the Goddess of Destruction and your destiny again.'

'Hearing the truth from Fjola is also important.'

Galdra straightened. 'I've already made the arrangements.' She swiped her finger at Mirable. 'Help him get dressed, and meet me at the entrance.' She glided out of the room, taking the feeling of calm with her.

'How can you be taken with…' Mirable paused, searching for the right word, 'with *that*,' he finished, shaking his head.

I swung my legs off the bed. 'Don't antagonise her. She took care of me when no one else did. After Lumi's death, I felt so lost and confused. Her presence brings me calm.'

'I can see that. She has made quite an impression on you.'

I stood up. The room swayed, and I clutched one of the bed poles. 'Think what you will, but Galdra is here to stay. Besides, it's Goro-Khan we should worry about.'

'I wouldn't be so sure,' Mirable said.

I walked to the dresser and pulled out a grey shirt. 'Here,' I said, tossing it to him. 'You need this more than I do.'

Mirable caught the garment and turned it over in his hands.

'What's wrong?' I asked. 'Is it not to your liking?'

He sighed. 'I wish some things were as easy to make right as donning a new shirt.'

* * *

Dressed in a fresh set of garments, Mirable and I headed for the lowest floor of the pagoda. The stairs proved a challenge, and he clung to the banister as he took one careful step after another, his bristled cheeks gusting in and out like a pair of bellows. Galdra waited at the entrance, with her back straight, looking out at the mountains. In her green dress and with her hair twined into a tight braid, she looked like an unbending blade of grass. A cluster of mages gathered at Skaldir's altar, chanting prayers, but when Mirable and I descended the staircase, their turned to appraise us.

'Valgsi,' a voice whispered, and I recognised Netis.

I raised my hand in greeting. I never got a chance to speak with him after that disastrous speech. Netis shot a glance at Mirable, then dropped his head, and the remaining mages followed suit.

Mirable snorted. 'I wonder if they hold me in equally high esteem. After all, you and I share the same letter in our *divine* names. The valiant Valgsi and his veritable Varl are a venerable vision to behold.' He winked. 'Not bad, ha? Beast or no, my way with words is as good as it used to be when I reached the peak of my vocation.' He emphasised the last word. 'Did you know that a quick tongue is one of the first skills you must prove to be accepted into the Merchant's Circle?'

'Those days are behind you,' I said. 'We serve a greater purpose now.'

He sighed wistfully.

'You took your time,' Galdra said when we joined her. She looked Mirable up and down. 'Soon, you will have little need of shirts.'

'I'm hoping that soon I'll have little need of you,' he snapped.

Galdra crossed her arms.

I grew weary of their squabbles. 'Where are we going?'

'Deep into the mountain,' she said in a frosty voice. 'It's time for you to learn how our goddess came to be.'

'Her brothers forged her from steel to keep the balance between life and death,' Mirable said. 'And what a divine mistake that was.'

'Blinded by a fog of ignorance. I didn't expect any different.'

'A bit like Jarin's mind then.'

'If my presence pains you this much, you can go back to the dungeon and rot your days away.'

'Enough,' I said. 'For the love of Skaldir, enough with your quarrels.' I pointed at Mirable. 'No more snide remarks. I've more pressing things to worry about than you aggravating one another.'

He spun away and stalked out the door.

I took Galdra's hand. 'For my sake, let him be. One way or another, he'll see the light.'

She rolled her eyes but said nothing.

From the corner of my eye, I caught the assembly watching us. 'Let's go,' I said, pulling her outside. I needed the mages to have faith in me instead of questioning the deepening rift between Galdra and Mirable.

The three of us followed the road leading up the mountain. Autumn began in earnest, turning the green forests into a riot of fiery maples. Stripped of the summer's warmth, the air pricked my nostrils like the sting of an insect. The path was clear of snow, and the cliffs on either side moulded in such a way as to prevent avalanches in winter. In Shinpi, even nature yielded to the force of magic.

'It wasn't always like this,' Galdra said. 'When the mages first arrived here, Shinpi was a wild place. We had to use a lot of power to clear the drifts and shape the ridge to allow passage.' A look of wonder stole over her face. 'It's a sacred place, for it was here our beloved goddess came to be.'

'What'll happen to Shinpi when we depart for Hvitur?' I asked.

'Some mages and the remaining guards will stay behind to tend the mountain. Goro-Khan wants us to hold a pilgrimage every year in Skaldir's honour. A journey across the Great Atlantic, with rites and rituals.'

The Goddess of Destruction was asleep, the Lost City of Antaya still underwater, yet Goro-Khan organised the future without any regard for the mages' wants and needs. 'It doesn't sound right. The mages waited years to see their homes again. Surely, Goro's decision will spark a rebellion.'

'We must preserve the mountain at all costs.'

'It's only a rock,' Mirable chimed from behind us. 'Grander structures fell into obscurity over the centuries. Not to mention nations far greater than a handful of magic-hungry people.'

The green crescent on Galdra's forehead creased, but before she had a chance to respond, I shook my head at her. It was best to ignore Mirable's outbursts.

We walked the rest of the way in silence. Away from the hustle and bustle of the village, the quiet encased us like a cocoon. Above, the peak soared into the cloudless sky, where the sun ruled supreme, drenching the crags in the golden light.

The path ended at the foot of the mountain with a cave-like opening fringed with icicles.

Galdra picked up a torch fastened to the rock. She cupped it with her hand and blew a gust of air that ignited the tip with green flame. She faced the entrance and bowed. ‘The Valgsi is here, my goddess. Shine your light and show him the wonder of your creation.’

Mirable took a step back. ‘I’d rather wait here.’

‘No,’ Galdra said. ‘Before you can serve the Valgsi, first you must learn the truth.’

‘I know the history—’

‘A fine line divides the truth from falsehood.’

Mirable groaned. His eyes wandered to the icicles. ‘Maybe it’s a trap,’ he whispered.

‘Don’t be a fool,’ Galdra said, stepping through the arch. ‘If Skaldir wanted you dead, you already would be.’

‘You mean if *you* wanted me dead,’ he called after her.

‘Stop it,’ I said, giving him a gentle shove forward. ‘Let’s get this over with.’

We followed Galdra into the depths of the cave. The ice walls on either side absorbed the light from her flame, glittering like emeralds. Our passage sent echoes through the cavern while our shadows clung to the walls, rising and falling with the motion of the torchlight. I breathed in the wet smell of ice, and my thoughts turned to Lumi. Kylfa, the witch from

Sur, told me that Lumi was created on the icy slopes of Shinpi. Could it be that this cave was her birthplace? As the days went by, the memories of Lumi grew hazy and distant, dampening the pain of her loss. If it was up to me, we'd be sailing to Hvitur at first light.

Mirable gasped. The noise pulled me from my thoughts and back into the cave.

'You stand in the centre of creation,' Galdra said, illuminating the walls with her flame. 'The holiest of places. Cast aside everything you've been taught before and watch your step, as well as your mouth.' She flashed her torch at Mirable. 'That goes for you too, merchant.'

'The mages built this?' I asked in astonishment.

We stood in a circular chamber supported by four crystal pillars holding the weight of the mountain above. The cavern walls were frozen into shapes of waterfalls cascading to form ice pools on the crystal floor. In the centre, encased in a thin shell of frost, stood the statue of sleeping Skaldir. The goddess dreamt, with her eyes closed and her hands locked on the hilt of the sword while her chest pulsed with the eerie, viridescent light that had no apparent source.

'It's our greatest accomplishment and took years to uncover,' Galdra said, flipping her braid back. The cavern resounded with the might of her voice.

I approached the statue and pressed my hand against the film of ice. My fingers prickled, but the sensation soon faded, replaced by a sickening vibration that emanated from Skaldir's ribcage, filling me with anger so great, the hair on my arms stood up. As my muscles swelled with a monstrous impulse to destroy, green specks flashed before my eyes, and the constellation on my temple began to throb rhythmically. My hand found my sword, and my fingers wrapped tightly around the hilt.

'She waited for so long,' Galdra whispered in my ear. Her fingers caressed Skaldir's mark. 'You're the only mortal ever raised to a divine rank. You'll be remembered for centuries to come. Your name will be chanted alongside those of Agtarr and Yldir. When your soul is carried to the gates of Himinn, our children will share in your legacy.'

At the words 'our children' I jerked away from the statue, and the green spots in my vision receded. I looked at Galdra. Her lips parted, exposing the white edges of her teeth. The sharp smell of ice crystals permeated every crevice of the chamber, making me light-headed. It felt as if my ribcage became home to Grand Isfjells—the huge ice formations south of Stromhold born from the depths of the Great Atlantic. Cold stiffened my lungs, making it difficult to breathe.

'Unbelievable,' Mirable grumbled from behind me.

The reproach in his voice broke the spell. I took a step back, and the intense chill melted away. 'You speak of the future, but my soul is no longer my own,' I reminded Galdra. 'I can't remember why I gave it up in the first place, but an oath is an oath.' I looked down at my boots, hoping the prize was worth the price, for my pact with the witches meant I wouldn't be there to watch over Lumi when Skaldir brought her back. My heart crushed under the heavy stomp of regret.

Galdra's hand lingered on my shoulder. 'Do not fear the witches. Once reawakened, Skaldir will release you from the oath.'

In response, a chorus of cackles echoed inside my head.

'I doubt that,' I said.

'Perish the doubt. If you stay true to your calling, the goddess will reward you tenfold.'

'But at what cost?' Mirable asked. 'Jarin's oath binds him to the witches, and who's to say when Skaldir destroys the creatures, he won't perish right along with them?' He tugged at my sleeve. 'Her cunning will be the death of you, mark my words.'

'You're quick to speak of deceit.' She pursed her lips. 'A man who made his living by cheating people out of their coin.'

'I'm an honest merchant,' Mirable said with a note of outrage. 'I'd never—'

I cut him off. 'You brought us here for a reason, so let's hear it.' I wanted to be out of this cave and on my way to the prison.

Galdra whipped around, illuminating the walls with her flame. She recited some ancient chant in a voice that rose and fell, and the chamber transformed before my eyes. A series of images marked the ice from floor to ceiling as if someone drew them using green paint. They shifted with the torchlight, giving the impression of life.

Mirable yelped as if pricked by a needle and skittered to the far corner. I wished he would stop being so squeamish. As a fledgling Varl, his reactions to magic were simply irrational.

'Before Skaldir's birth, Agtarr, the God of Death, reaped the souls of the living,' Galdra said in a tone of profound reverence. 'To replace the lost souls, Yldir, the God of Life, brought more into existence, but he could never set them free into the world, for when he tried, Agtarr's ravens devoured them one by one. Too many birds, but not enough souls to feed them. And so the war between life and death raged for centuries.' She passed me the torch.

I looked at it as though it was barbed with thorns. The flame burned bright but didn't give off any heat.

'Don't touch it,' Mirable said.

I reached out and grabbed the torch.

The temperature dropped, and the cold sank its glacial teeth into my bones. Mirable screamed, and I lifted my hand in front of my face to shield it from the green blaze that licked the cavern walls. They unravelled before us with no sound, like a loose thread from a woolly garment. I wanted to drop the torch and take to my heels, but my fingers wrapped tighter around the wooden stave.

When the walls fell away, I found myself in a long and dim hallway. Ahead, two shadows glimmered in the torchlight, one black and one white. I didn't need Galdra to tell me I was in the presence of the divine brothers, a sole witness to their acts of creation and eradication. Yldir's white silhouette stood surrounded by spheres of flickering souls. A flock of ravens encircled Agtarr in a dark cloud, screeching and flapping their wings. Each beat agitated the air that whooshed into my face, stirring the hair follicles. My torch fluttered. Life and death in chaos—two opposing forces, each set on gaining the advantage over the other.

One by one, Yldir's shadow cupped the spheres, blowing into their centres. As the souls flared to life, the ravens plunged down in a volley of obsidian arrows to feed. I stared in horror as their beaks stabbed through the heart of each soul, tearing it to pieces. The more of them they devoured, the bigger they grew until their immense wings enfolded the god himself in a living coat of black feathers.

Galdra's voice reached me from afar. 'You cannot see it, but in this oblivion, Agtarr did not hide his face behind a cowl. Many of our mages attempted to carve his true visage, but they all dropped dead upon completion of the work, and the god's features vanished straight after.'

Instinctively, I squeezed my eyes shut. Everyone knew Agtarr only showed his face to mortals right before his Warrior of Death cut out their souls. Even a glimpse of his features meant death.

'It was Agtarr who decided to seek balance,' Galdra continued. 'He understood there was no life without death, but watching his ravens devour the souls, he also realised there could be no death without life. They're entwined. In that everlasting chaos, the God of Death alone held the power to end life before its time, which stripped his brother of his purpose. Agtarr couldn't kill the ravens, as they were part of him, but he knew that to bring balance he had to make a sacrifice. He called forth the Star Forgers—the giants whose job it was to light the night sky by shaping stars.'

When her words faded, I opened my eyes to witness this moment of summoning. The hallway morphed into a circular chamber supported by eight stone pillars, each the size of a giant tree trunk. Agtarr and Yldir stood in its centre, still only shadows to my eye. The giants knelt before them—two great beings made of metal that shone brighter than all the stars put together.

Yldir voice echoed inside my head. 'Go forth and forge us a sister capable of restoring the balance between life and death.'

The giants rumbled and bowed their silver heads. A staircase appeared in the chamber's floor, and the Star Forgers descended. As each colossal foot hit the stone, the room filled with a sound like thunder.

'It was here the giants built a forge befitting their task,' Galdra said. 'And we're standing in the heart of it.'

The story of Skaldir was never told in the way Galdra told it. Most people refused to speak the goddess's name out of fear of misfortune they believed would befall them. I learned fragments of it from my tutor, Marco, but he never alluded to the early chaos and the Star Forgers. When asked, he simply recalled the Day of Judgement and the might of Skaldir's wrath.

The torch in my hand flickered, and the cavern transformed before my eyes into an ancient forge where the giants beat their strongest star steel to shape a female force. As they moulded her, the green fire roared, but like the flame in my hand, it released no heat. I tasted the metallic tang of molten steel while my ears rang with the sound of hammers bashing against the mighty anvils. Each strike sent an army of sparks into the night, and when I looked up, I saw green waves dancing in rays and spirals.

'The Night of Norrsken,' I whispered.

'When they accomplished the task, the Star Forgers brought Skaldir before the two gods,' Galdra said, and I found myself back in the cylindrical chamber.

The Star Forgers stood before Agtarr and Yldir, with a green shadow kneeling between them. I knew the events were conjured up by Galdra's magic—she was the enchantress and the mistress of illusions after all—but I felt Skaldir's presence as if the moment was real. I sensed no anger in her, only a powerful resolve to accomplish the task laid before her.

'How do you intend to restore balance between life and death, sister?' Yldir asked.

'With steel,' she answered.

'Where is your blade?' Agtarr asked.

The giants offered her the sword, the very same that hung at my hip. My trembling fingers sought the hilt. Made of star steel and shaped by the Star Forgers themselves, this relic drove my grandfather mad. It was a heavy weapon to carry, and I felt undeserving of it.

Galdra's voice drifted my way, and the images before me dissipated. 'To allow the souls to fully hatch, Skaldir's task was to slay all but two of Agtarr's ravens.'

The chamber was gone, and in its place came the hallway from my first vision. Skaldir's green shadow walked its length while the ravens cried and flapped their wings. Their powerful beaks stabbed at her only to splinter and break away. The Goddess of Destruction sliced through the screeching flock, and the black feathers lined the halls of Himinn.

As I watched the chaos, my mind fluttered with the memories of Hrafn and the way his beak plunged into the heart of Kylfa's eye. As if sensing my trepidation, deep inside my head, the witches cackled in unison, and the wretched symbol on my wrist throbbed with a sickening pain. I covered it with the flat of my palm. 'Were there any white ravens in Agtarr's flock?' I asked.

The vision wavered, and I could see Galdra again through the magical veil. She studied my face for a moment, then shook her head. 'Not that we know of. Why do you ask?'

I opened my mouth to answer when I glimpsed Trofn on the other side of the glass, shaking her gaunt finger as a mother would do at an unruly child. The witch wanted to keep her secrets, and I decided to let her. For now. 'No reason.'

At that moment, the flame in my torch dimmed, drawing Galdra's attention. She puffed her cheeks with air and blew at it. Green fire exploded into life, illuminating even the loftiest reaches of the cavern. Now the ceiling too glowed with depictions of the past.

‘For the life to flow, Skaldir had to cut down the ravens, but whilst doing so, she absorbed their need to destroy. She walked the halls of Himinn, the almighty goddess who brought even death to its knees. It was then that Agtarr opposed her, compelling Yldir to bind Skaldir and curb some of her wilfulness. Skaldir begged them not to do it, but their ears remained deaf to her pleas. The two gods summoned the Star Forgers from their home in the sky and ordered them to wake the fires in their mighty forge. The giants bent to their will and set about melting star steel and ringing their mighty hammers once more.’

I traced the new depiction of events on the walls. They appeared in time with Galdra’s words, then faded, making way for the next array of images. Now, the magical workshop in the core of the mountain came alive, spewing a mixture of green flame and smoke.

‘The giants softened the steel and mixed traces of light into the molten metal in the hopes it’d temper the goddess,’ Galdra said.

‘Why are you telling us this?’ Mirable asked, tilting his head. The story pulled him into the centre of the chamber, but now, the suspicion chased away the wonder. ‘For all we know, it’s a tale created by the mages to deceive us.’

Galdra peered down her nose at him. ‘Our magic comes from the divine, and so does our knowledge of the world.

Antaya is packed with historical scrolls. When Jarin recovers the city, we'll share the contents of our treasured libraries with everyone who wishes to learn the truth. We have always done so, but humans have a tendency to sneer at anything different to what they'd been taught by their mothers and fathers.'

Mirable muttered something under his breath.

'Did the Star Forgers fix her?' I asked.

'She was never broken,' Galdra answered with scorn, 'but full of scars. Unlike the original creation, which was painless, the ones that followed were sheer agony.'

The cavern echoed with Skaldir's screams. To reshape her, the Star Forgers had to melt her heart and hammer it anew. The pain was that of holding a hand over a burning stove and watching it singe. Unbearable to a mortal. I clutched my hand to my chest.

'Skaldir endured the pain, for it fed her strength and anger,' Galdra said. 'When she returned from the forge, she went back to her original task, but this time, she sliced through the souls, as well as the ravens. In their misguided attempts to make her more like them, Agtarr and Yldir destroyed Skaldir over and over. Eventually, they tamed her enough to restore the balance, but Skaldir's wrath lived on in her damaged heart.'

'And then your people summoned her and she brought that wrath on all our heads,' Mirable said. 'Even if your story is true, it doesn't change history. Many innocents died because

Skaldir was angry with her brothers.' He threw his arms up. 'It's… ungodly!'

'We *should* fear the gods,' Galdra snapped. 'The Day of Judgement was a display of her power. Skaldir proved she was more than steel to be shaped and moulded at their whim. Regrettably, the mages who summoned her had no means of taming her power. She was destruction in its purest form, and for that, Yldir and Agtarr chained her.' She dropped her head, her left hand curling into a fist.

'So why repeat the same mistakes and let Skaldir wreak needless havoc?' Mirable asked.

'It is not our intention to wreak havoc. We want to restore our home and worship our goddess in peace.' Her pearly gaze settled on mine. 'And we have the Valgsi to lead us now.'

'You don't need to awaken Skaldir to worship her.'

Galdra advanced on him. 'It's because of such thinking we're in exile. People like you are the reason why the war broke out in the first place.'

'You can't weave peace with a thread of destruction!'

I stepped between them. 'Nothing has been decided. You've said it yourself when mages came to Shinpi, they learned how to coexist with the natives to the point of sharing their beliefs and magic.'

Galdra snatched the torch away from me.

I looked at Mirable. 'I don't want another war, believe me. But I'm a Nord, and I know too well how fierce they can be if challenged.'

'Wouldn't you if you knew that everything you built is under threat?'

Galdra beat me to the answer. 'During those early days Skaldir kept some of the souls and imbued them with her magic, then released them among Yldir's souls. When he breathed life into them, he gave birth to mages.' She looked up, and her ghostly eyes searched the fading lines on the ceiling. 'She wanted to create a better world. We're divine beings, and humans are too simple to comprehend what it means to wield the power of the gods. They cower before the magic, embracing superstition over knowledge. It'll never change.'

'You hid on this island for far too long to make judgements.' Mirable started pacing the length of the chamber, his crimson turban bobbing up and down. 'Summoning a vengeful god is no way to earn freedom. What good would it do to turn the world into smouldering ruin? Everyone, including your precious kind, would suffer.' He looked at me, with eyes full of dismay. 'Tell me you don't approve of this foolishness?'

Galdra placed her hand on my heart. 'After all you've learned, tell me you'll fight to free her.'

When the echo of her words died away, the chamber fell silent. Even in my ignorance, I understood Mirable's concern, but the violence that broke out during the War of Mages wasn't caused by Skaldir but the mages like Goro-Khan who misused their power. Those who revolted were driven by the need to take some of that power back. The gods, Yldir and Agtarr, created Skaldir's need to destroy during the many nights of shaping and reshaping her. When mages called her to aid them, her rage burned hot, but this time it would be different. The goddess would listen to her Valgsi, and with any luck, she'd save my soul from being devoured by Hrafn and breathe new life into Lumi. Antaya would be restored, mages would return home, and the people would have their gods back. As if in response, a sharp smell of ice crystals suffused my nostrils, frosting over the glass inside my aching head.

I turned to look at Skaldir's statue encased in ice. No one deserved to dream against their will, least of all the Goddess of Destruction. Any doubts I had floated away like snowflakes on the wind.

'I will fight,' I said.

Mirable let out a deep groan. 'Then you have doomed us all.'

XVIII

'What are you going to do to her?' Mirable asked, toying with the loose strand of his turban. His red-rimmed eyes flicked from me to the door and back to me.

'I just want to hear what Fjola has to say,' I said, emphasising each word.

'You can't honestly believe she crushed Lumi's heart?'

Did I believe it?

Two days after our trip to Skaldir's cave, I requested to see Fjola, and to my surprise, Galdra agreed. My stomach lurched at the thought of facing Fjola and hearing her answer. Deep down, I hoped for an explanation that would clear her name and put the past behind us.

'Set her free,' Mirable begged. 'You owe her that much.'

I snatched the water pitcher from the bedside table and pointed at the dresser in the far corner. 'Pass me that cup.'

He hobbled across the room and watching his unsteady gait reminded me of the broken Varl, Alkaios. 'How long are you going to play this game?' I asked him when he returned.

'What game?'

I filled the cup with water. 'How long are you going to resist this transformation? I can see how much pain you're in.'

'Are you calling my efforts to stay human a game?'

‘And a dangerous one at that,’ I said, waving the cup at him. ‘You told me you didn’t want to end up like Alkaios. Your body is twisting because you resist the flow of magic. Maybe it’s time to let it finish its work?’

He looked at the floor, rubbing his misshapen ear. ‘Only the new Jarin would say something like this.’

‘The old Jarin made promises he couldn’t keep and sent everyone he cared for into the arms of the Warrior of Death. I have my reasons for following this path, and one of them is keeping you, the only friend I have left, alive. Nords will never accept you, and Vesterners will hunt you down. If I succeed in my task of awakening Skaldir, you will be free to live out your days in Antaya.’ I drained the water in one gulp.

‘And Fjola?’

‘What about Fjola?’ I asked, trying hard to keep the irritation from my voice. The idea of confronting her was difficult enough without Mirable’s constant reminders. Wondering how Fjola would react to learning of my decision to help the mages kept me awake most nights. She’d be furious, no doubt, but I hoped to appeal to her free spirit. Fjola was never one for the rules, and maybe she’d see how awakening the goddess could help to fix the wrongs. For one, Fjola cared about Mirable, and a place like Antaya would assure his safety. Two, if she indeed crushed Lumi’s heart, Skaldir would give her the chance to make up for it.

Mirable must've read something in my face when he said, 'You know better than to hope Fjola would side with the mages.'

'Let's say I set her free. Where would she go? Shinpi is an island in the middle of the Great Atlantic.'

'You can give her a boat. I'll go—'

I banged the mug on the table, and Mirable flinched. 'So you can warn Torgal of my coming? I don't think so.'

'Do you even know what happened that day?'

'I remember enough.' It was a lie, and we both knew it. I only remembered what Galdra told me, but since the visit to the cave, I stopped questioning the gaps in my memories. My course was set, and I intended to follow it until the end. 'All you see is the Day of Judgement, but we could accomplish so much if we worked as one.'

'These are Galdra's mutterings, not yours. I came here to save you, but maybe it's too late for that.' He shook his head. 'If I stay with you, I'll be forced to kill in Skaldir's name. Whatever I do, wherever I go, there's no peace to be found for the damned.'

I looked through the open shutter at the grey sky. The air smelled of damp soil—a sure sign a storm was on the way. I thought of the witch's eye on my wrist. 'In that, we're very much alike. We're both bound for the Agtarr's Chamber of Torments.'

Mirable raised his hands as if to ward off some unseen evil. 'Why didn't you tell me about the mark?' he asked in a gruff voice.

'It didn't matter then, and it matters even less now. The deed is done.'

'Do you believe Skaldir can release you from the oath?'

Despite Galdra's assurances, I had my doubts. The witches lived under Hrafn's rule, and it was he, not the gods, who granted the crones immortality. Whoever, or whatever Hrafn was, I had the feeling the white raven wouldn't be cheated of his gift—the gift of my soul imbued with Skaldir's magic. I detested the black eye on my wrist. It seemed to watch me through the sleeve day and night, throbbing with pain that made it impossible to forget it was there. I longed for those days when the memory of Sur was trapped behind Galdra's glass. Now I knew why she erected it in the first place, and I had little desire to spy through the cracks.

'Skaldir may be my only hope of getting rid of the mark,' I said, for telling Mirable otherwise would only make the bad situation worse.

As soon as the words left my lips, Trofn's voice rustled inside my head. *'Foolish… No god can release you from the black vow…'*

Mirable turned his back to me and dipped his head, displaying the jagged ridges of his spine. Since the day at the cavern, he grew restless, pacing back and forth like a caged animal, growling and snapping at anyone who dared to come close. Beads of sweat dotted his forehead, his bodily hair felt stiff to the touch, and his skin gave off a pungent odour of a wet hound. I'd wake at night to find him whining and shivering, and once or twice, the guards caught him circling the walls of the prison and howling at the full moon. Each time it happened, Galdra doused him with magic and dragged him back to my room. On some nights, he'd slink away only to return reeking of damp, mould, and fish guts. When Galdra began questioning his usefulness, I assured her Mirable played a vital part in my plan of dispatching Goro-Khan. After that disastrous visit to Goro's house, I thought long and hard about how to end the Laughing God's hold on the mages. Ideas came and went, but one lingered, and it had to do with the serena we encountered during our voyage to Shinpi, but I was yet to share my thoughts with Mirable.

'We may be cursed, you and I, but that doesn't change the fact that Fjola came here for you,' Mirable said, breaking my chain of thought.

This time, my irritation got the upper hand. 'You know, if you put half of the energy you exhaust lecturing me about Fjola into sniffing out Njall, we'd have found him by now.'

Mirable's neck jerked up, and he whirled around with a speed that was in contrast to his painful shuffle when he went to retrieve the cup. 'What makes you think he's still on the island?'

I cocked my head. 'Isn't he?'

He looked as if my question affronted him. 'How should I know? I'm not in the habit of hunting for bad smells.'

'I see your regard for Njall is as high as ever.'

'I was always more fond of his sister, and right now, it's Fjola who needs my help. *Our* help.'

'If it bothers you this much, stay here and let me and Galdra deal with her.'

'No! I won't leave her at the mercy of that wretched witch.' His nostrils flared. 'It's because of her we're at odds with each other.'

'That wretched witch is keeping me sane.'

'Your weakness for deceptive women is legendary.'

'Don't test me, Mirable.'

He lifted his hands high. Judging by the grimace on his face, the move caused him a great deal of pain. 'Don't tell me to stay.'

I sighed. 'Alright, but try not to interfere.'

'I'll be as quiet as a man contemplating a bargain.'

* * *

Galdra, accompanied by a score of mages, awaited us on the floor called the Day of Judgement. When Mirable and I descended, everyone, including her, inclined their heads, but this display of respect did nothing to relieve the suffocating sensation in my chest. I was about to face the person I cared about a great deal. Mirable insisted on Fjola's innocence, but whenever I pressed him for an explanation, he refused to offer one, saying he didn't want to cause Fjola more pain. I found it a curious declaration, for Galdra assured me the guards treated Fjola well, or at least as well as a prisoner could expect to be treated under the circumstances. She warned me that Mirable's transformation wrought havoc on his body as well as his mind, impairing his judgement. With the two of them at odds, I needed to see Fjola and decide her actions for myself.

Galdra crossed the chamber, and the crisp smell of freshly fallen snow filled the space between us. She took my hands and gave them a vigorous shake. 'Ready?'

The familiar chill raced up my arms, and I tasted ice crystals melting on my tongue. I craved to leave this room and seek refuge in Skaldir's cavern, where I'd listen to Galdra's chiming voice telling stories of the past. Instead, I had to confront the present.

'Let's get it over with,' I said.

The mages regarded me with solemn expressions—three men and three women ready to bear witness. I lowered my voice. 'Why are they here? I wanted to speak with Fjola in private.'

'Everything you do is for the future of Antaya,' Galdra said in a light tone. 'They must see and hear the depth of your devotion. Punishing a crime is the best way to win support.'

I struggled to shake the feeling that Galdra enjoyed this mock assembly way more than she had the right to. 'So we've condemned Fjola without a trial?' I said, forcing a smile at the mages. One woman clasped her fingers to her chest, her eyes shining pools of rich brown.

'To stand a trial, one must commit a crime,' Mirable rumbled. His nostrils twitched, as if Galdra's cool scent offended him.

'There's no greater crime than murder. Besides, it was Jarin's idea to bring her in. I simply provided the audience.'

'Which I didn't ask for,' I said.

A spot of red entered Galdra's cheeks. She laced her fingers in front of her and strode to the sole window. She threw open the shutters with more force than necessary. A gust of wind rushed at her, tangling the loose strands of her hair and sending the wide sleeves of her forest-green dress flapping. The chamber filled with a damp scent of the approaching rain. I turned my back to the brewing storm to appraise the smoking ruin painted on the wall before me. Skaldir held her blade high above the gates of Antaya, sneering at the men, women, and children fleeing the city, and the images looked more threatening than the first time I saw them. In the not so distant future, I'd be the painter with destruction for a brush and the world as my canvas. Was I really strong enough to tame this power?

I shifted my gaze away from the horrifying images to the mages assembled near the stairs leading into the room below. I didn't recognise any of them. Despite my willingness to lead the people of Shinpi to freedom, I made little effort to get to know them.

Mirable paced at the foot of the staircase, a pained expression on his face. He didn't bother with a shaving knife anymore, and his beard grew into a wild bush of curls.

Galdra stood at my right shoulder. 'Bring in the prisoner,' she ordered.

All moisture drained from my mouth, and I sensed the early onset of a headache. To stop my fingers from trembling, I sought the hilt of my sword, and the cool feel of metal encased in leather eased some of the tension that stretched my tendons to a snapping point.

A guard in scaled armour and a cone-shaped helmet mounted the steps. He halted at the top and turned sideways without as much as a twitch of an eyelid. Once, I asked Galdra about the men appointed to guard Shinpi, and she told me they were hand-picked by Goro-Khan and trained to strike fear into the hearts of trespassers with their presence alone. But I knew they bled just like the rest of us.

Fjola climbed next, her wrists shackled in front of her. She stopped at the foot of the stairwell.

My heart caught as if on a fishhook, and Mirable uttered a howl that made my skin prick with gooseflesh. I barely recognised the girl who sailed with me across the Great Atlantic. After weeks of confinement, Fjola's clothes turned to rags, and her once lustrous hair hung limply around her face, matted and caked with dirt. Streaks of soot marred her cheeks and forehead, and her lips reminded me of tree bark. Despite her ragged appearance, Fjola's expression was that of steel. Her jaw was set firm, and her eyes flared with a green flame that, if real, could burn this whole pagoda to the ground. The notion that Fjola crushed Lumi's heart made no sense, and the ache at the back of my head intensified. I felt movement behind the fractured glass inside my mind, and my old memories whispered through the cracks.

'I thought you said she was well looked after,' I hissed.

Galdra only shrugged.

A second guard came up behind Fjola. When she didn't move, he shoved her into the room's centre with a fist, earning a growl from Mirable. He ignored the Varl and assumed the same position as his companion on the opposite side of the staircase. The mages formed a loose semi-circle around Fjola. Two hooded men wrinkled their noses, and the woman with brown eyes pressed her hand to her mouth.

'Kneel before your Valgsi,' Galdra said.

Fjola's gaze never left mine as she answered, 'He's not my Valgsi.'

Murmur filled the chamber as the mages exchanged scornful glances. The man with hands gnarled by age kicked Fjola in the shin. Her leg buckled, and she fell to her knees in a rattle of chains. She didn't look up, but her soiled nails braced against the timber floor like talons. I moved to help her, but Galdra seized my arm in a vice grip.

Mirable rushed to Fjola's side, but the guard closest to him barred his way. Like a rabid dog, the Varl bared his teeth at him, but the man only drew his sword in readiness.

'Stop this before it's too late,' Mirable pleaded. 'She's *the one*, you fool!'

Something thick and slithery lodged in my throat, and I swallowed hard against it. This wasn't how I imagined our reunion. With Fjola locked in the prison, it was easy to plan the outcome, but seeing her face to face stirred old feelings and memories.

'Help her up,' I ordered the guard. 'Now.'

He might've been hand-picked by Goro-Khan, but the man did as he was told without a moment's hesitation. The Valgsi's word carried some weight.

Galdra blew out a rattling breath and let go of my arm. She pointed at Fjola. 'You're a murderer, and you continue to defy the Goddess of Des—'

'She did nothing wrong,' Mirable wailed from behind the guard.

'What is she talking about?' Fjola asked.

I pulled back my shoulders. 'I didn't bring you here to humiliate you. I just need to hear the truth. Why did you do it?'

She gave me a puzzled look.

'Her silence is our answer,' Galdra said, and the mages nodded. 'In Shinpi, murder is punishable by death.'

Galdra was getting under my skin with her hasty accusations. 'Stop it,' I told her. The confused expression on Fjola's face, and Galdra's urgency to condemn her, told me something was amiss. 'How to punish her is *my* decision.'

Galdra stepped in front of me, blocking my view of Fjola. Her cool fingers brushed against my cheek. 'She'll never admit her fault, but she'll undermine your position with her lies, or worse, confuse your fragile mind further. Judge her and earn the respect of all the mages. Show them you're just and fearless. The six in this room are loyal to me, and they'll spread the word among the rest. If we're to succeed, we need everyone to rally behind us. Don't let your misguided feelings of kinship ruin this. We're so close… so close to weakening Goro's hold and getting back what this girl stole from you.'

The words spilled from her lips one after the other, pressing in their intensity. Under different circumstances, the flow would've captivated me.

But not today.

Listening to Galdra's feverish speech, I felt only mild irritation, and for the first time, her wintery scent had no effect on me. At this moment, Galdra smelled more like spring sludge than freshly fallen snow, and the qualities she shared with Lumi were nothing more than a cheap imitation.

Fjola's brilliant laugh filled the chamber, melting the frost around my heart. Suddenly, I could take a full breath without stabbing pain.

'I see,' Fjola said. 'The witch told you *I* killed Lumi.'

Galdra whirled around. 'No one gave you permission to speak.'

'Jarin gave me permission when he asked for the truth, witch.'

Before she could say more, Galdra crossed the space between them in two strides and slapped Fjola with a force that made her head rock backwards. 'You address me with respect.'

A crimson petal bloomed on Fjola's cheek. 'You don't demand respect. You earn it.'

Galdra screeched, and a short knife flared to life in her right hand. The green blade was made of magic, but I knew it was sharper than steel.

Mirable grabbed the guard barring his way and flung him across the room. The man hit the wall just below Skaldir's image and went still under her sword. It looked as though the goddess was about to strike him down.

The Varl crouched at Fjola's feet. 'Not another step, witch,' he growled.

The guard by the staircase drew his weapon.

'Stand down.' I put as much authority into my voice as I could muster. 'We're here to make a fair judgement, not to kill each other.'

The guard halted his advance while the mages shifted on their feet. Me scorning Galdra was not the way to earn their allegiance, but her acting like an unbroken horse gave me no choice. Mirable's erratic behaviour didn't help either.

Galdra jerked her head at me. 'Judge her then,' she snapped, pointing the glowing knife at Mirable. 'And the creature will be next.'

I ignored her. 'All I want to know is why.' I said, clasping my hands behind my back so Fjola wouldn't notice the quiver in my fingers. 'Why in the name of Skaldir did you do it?'

Fjola appraised the exposed mark of destruction on my temple. 'Since when are you such a devout follower of Skaldir?'

'Answer the question,' Galdra said.

'The witch twisted his mind, and when I tried to help him, she threatened your life,' Mirable said to Fjola. 'I failed you both.' He dropped his head, and all signs of rage fled his face.

I looked at Galdra. 'Is this true?'

She rushed back to my side. 'Are you taking the word of a wild beast over mine?'

'We're here to seek the truth, are we not?'

The shackles rattled as Fjola joined her palms in front of her. 'Jarin, if you're there and if you can hear me, please try to remember.'

Her pleading voice stirred the memories beyond the glass, and an intense pain skewered the back of my skull. The images of Nordur flashed across the mirror's surface—the white plains, the seas raging below the precipice supporting Stromhold's fortified walls.

'We sailed to Shinpi to punish those responsible for your mother's death,' Fjola said. 'I don't need mortals to judge my actions, for I call Yldir as my witness when I say it was Goro-Khan who crushed Lumi's heart. And it was he who laughed in my face until I bled. For as long as he lives, your mother will never know peace.'

A lightning bolt of pain struck me, and in its wake, a deafening crack boomed in my ears. A new fissure shot through the glass inside my head like a fracture in the earth during a mighty earthquake. I pressed my palms against the surface, and the jagged edges sliced through my palms. Dark blood ran through the cracks, and I saw a reflection of my mother. She bore no resemblance to the Stromhold Guardian's brave wife. The skin on her cheeks stretched, exposing the bones of her skull. Her hair lost its golden hue and fell down her back in lanky strands of grey, and her vacant eyes stared into mine like those of a wraith. I lifted my hand away from the glass, leaving a bloody print.

'Mother?'

Her reflection rippled like water stirred by a stone.

'Fjola, don't!' Mirable cried from afar. 'He'll go insane.'

'What did you do to him?' Fjola demanded.

Someone shook my arm, and my head filled with chanting. At the sound of it, my mother recoiled, and her image blurred. I pounded on the glass, calling her name when a powerful slap jolted me back.

Aliya was gone…

'Breathe,' Galdra hissed into my ear.

I sucked in the air in great gulps, and the icy scent of it worked like balm. With each intake of breath, the chamber came back into focus, and the headache lessened.

A loud clapping filled the room.

'A display worthy of applause,' Goro-Khan said. He stood at the top of the staircase, striking his palms together.

At the sight of him, the mages scattered into the corners.

Galdra swiped the hair off her face. 'Goro-Khan… What are you doing here?'

'I should ask you the same question. Why wasn't I informed about this jest of a court?'

'We thought it best not to bother you with—'

'Spare me.' He crossed the chamber to stand next to Fjola. 'I can see all your enchanting work is coming undone, Galdra,' he said, staring me up and down.

Galdra stiffened. 'Nothing I can't handle.'

'Oh, I don't doubt you went above and beyond in taking care of *everything*.' He laughed, and every person in the room shrank back. A sinister shadow fell across Goro-Khan's face. 'I gave you the reins to guide the horse not to ride in the saddle.'

Galdra opened her mouth as if to respond but thought better of it and clamped it shut.

I shook my head to dispel the last tendrils of confusion.

'You're bleeding,' Goro-Khan said.

I examined my right hand, and an eerie sense of unreality settled over me. The glass inside my head was a mental image, so how could it be that my wound was true? I looked up to find Goro watching me.

'Magic is a wondrous force,' he said.

I put my hand behind my back. 'We gathered here at my request,' I said. 'I brought Fjola to Shinpi, so I should be the one to judge her actions.'

'I already cast the judgement.' Steepling his fingers, Goro gestured them at Mirable. 'But your creature interrupted the sentence. Perhaps all we need is to carry it out.'

Fjola threw her head back and laughed, and the clean sound of it thrilled my heart. The mages gasped in unison, and even the guard widened his eyes. Mirable shot a glance at Goro-Khan and grabbed Fjola's arm.

'The mighty mages with a long-standing feud,' she said. 'Skaldir would be honoured. After all, destruction is her name, so why not start by destroying her disciples?'

Goro-Khan tapped the side of his jaw. 'Now look at that. A Nordern girl with no fear of magic and the ability to control a Varl. Do you remember what happened when we first met?'

Fjola flashed him an icy smile. 'You killed Lumi, and then, you tried to kill me.'

'The ice demon served her purpose, but I might've been mistaken about you. You're not like the others.' He leaned close to her. 'There's a place for you among us, and who knows, if wedded to the right man, maybe you could learn to manipulate the elements.'

'And when I've outlived my usefulness, I'll meet the same fate as Lumi.' She pointed her grimy finger in my direction. 'You'll dispose of me the way you'll dispose of him. You ordered your witch to break his mind because you knew he'd never bow to you.' She laughed again. 'But the witch conspired against you, the *almighty* Laughing God.'

Galdra let out a blood-curdling shriek, and before I could grab her, she rushed at Fjola with the magical knife that burned green in her hand.

Everything happened so fast.

One moment she was within my reach, and the next, her glowing blade slashed across Fjola's left cheek.

Blood gushed from the cut.

Fjola clapped her palm against her cheek and swayed while her eyes took on a glossy sheen.

Mirable let out a long and doleful howl, then caught Fjola by the waist.

'I'll kill you,' Galdra screamed, and made a wide, sweeping stroke with her blade.

Goro-Khan backhanded Galdra across the face, and the knife in her hand dissipated in the way of flames doused with water. She hissed and lashed out at him, the wide sleeves of her dress flapping like bat's wings. Goro grabbed Galdra's wrists and shoved her back.

My head exploded. The careful control I exercised over my thoughts shattered into pieces. Memories of the past and present collided with an intensity that made my eyes burn. I pressed my hands to my temples, feeling the rush of air as

Mirable leapt through the window with bleeding Fjola in his arms.

XIX

The green blade slit Fjola's cheek open. She was aware of its burning edge as it caught on the cheekbone, then carved its way to just below her lower lip. A brilliant light burst behind her eyelids, and her tongue froze. She slapped her palm against the wound, feeling the hot flow of blood between her fingers. A dry coppery taste flooded her mouth, and an agonising scream rose in her throat, but Fjola refused to give it a voice. The room reeled like a waterwheel, going in and out of focus, and she swayed. Her brain repeated Jarin's name over and over. His face turned blurry, and an irrational fear swept through her at the thought she'd never see him again. She reached out with her right hand as if to touch him, but black spots obscured her vision, and her knees buckled.

A pair of powerful arms saved her from the fall, and her ears filled with the noise of snapping teeth. Unconsciousness lured her, but her mind wouldn't let go of Jarin. One witch took his soul, while another stole his memories, and now, even she failed him.

Fjola whispered Jarin's name, and then she was flying.

The chill and rain slammed into her, pulling her back from the edge of unconsciousness. Her cheek screamed as the cut stretched wide. An angry sound of thunder vibrated in her ears.

The grip on her waist tightened. 'Brace for a harsh landing,' a voice cried, and she recognised Mirable.

The merchant landed on his feet, and the impact sent a searing pain through Fjola. She was sure her ribs shattered, for all breath went out of her as her chest erupted with molten agony.

'I can't breathe,' she rasped.

'Hold on a little longer.' He crouched on three limbs, his fourth holding her close to his chest. Something snapped in his left arm, and the sound made Fjola wince. Next came a harsh pop, and now she felt his muscles expanding. A ripping noise tore through her ears and her nostrils filled with a musky odour of an animal fleeing from danger. A series of harsh sounds followed, each one a harbinger of a new change happening within the merchant's body. As his shoulders broadened and the palm supporting her back doubled in size, he uttered a harrowing cry between a human's wail and a wolf's howl.

Even at the threshold of oblivion, Fjola understood Mirable unleashed the beast to save her. Tears pressed against her lids while her throbbing heart swelled with gratitude and guilt. As if sensing her emotions, Mirable hugged her tighter.

Goro-Khan's voice boomed overhead. 'After them!'

The Varl broke into a run.

He raced down the mountain path leading to the village, and all Fjola could do was hold on to him while her mind sank in and out of consciousness. Mirable's body radiated heat, and his torso flexed beneath his shirt as each muscle expanded and contracted in time with Mirable's lungs that pumped the air in a regular rhythm. Fjola felt the pulsing tumours nestled inside the fibrous tissue of his chest and belly, and being so close to them stirred her innards. The Varl's shirt was torn, and the coarse hair poking through the holes scratched her face, aggravating her wound.

The world shot by, and in her dizziness, Fjola wondered how Mirable mustered such a speed. His limbs pounded against the ground, gaining momentum with each push and spraying her back with rainwater from the puddles. The wind snatched the loose strands of his turban that flapped about him like a crimson banner.

Urgent cries reached Fjola through her daze, but another roll of thunder drowned the words. She didn't need to hear them to know the mages so keen to condemn her wouldn't give up until they imposed Goro-Khan's sentence. Death by laughter sounded like nonsense until you experienced the punishment firsthand. Fjola would take a stab to her chest any day over being subjected to the Laughing God's insanity. But Shinpi was an island in the middle of the Great Atlantic. It didn't matter how fast Mirable ran, the only destination was the boundless ocean, with no means of crossing it.

A bolt of energy hit Mirable in the back, and the force sent him flying.

Jagged stones bit into Fjola's spine, and her head slammed against the ground. A fresh pain lanced through her cheek, and it felt like sharp fingernails digging into the wound and tearing the edges wide open. Her cry mixed with Mirable's raging howl, but he didn't ease his grip on her. Wrapped in each other's arms, they tumbled down the hill like a giant ball. The turban tore free of Mirable's head and caught on Fjola's fingers. Before the wind tugged it away, she seized the wet cloth as if it was a rope to freedom.

Another bolt of green struck the path, followed by the shouting of mages in pursuit. Maybe Jarin was among the hunters, believing Fjola killed Lumi and eager to avenge his demon. When Jarin summoned her, she was convinced that Mirable succeeded in their plan and the three of them would flee this forsaken place. But then she met Jarin's eyes, and the haunted look in them told her he was lost. While Fjola languished in prison, the witch worked her illusions, manipulating his mind to further her own gains.

Fjola stifled a sob. First her brother, and now Jarin. It seemed she was cursed to lose everyone who came into her life. Her face was ruined, and so was her heart. An overwhelming weariness spread through her limbs, and her grip on Mirable loosened. To face Agtarr would bring a blessed release…

Mirable was on his feet, dodging the bolts with inhuman agility. His body gave off a shimmering aura that enfolded them both in a protective shroud. When she realised what it was, Fjola's first instinct was to struggle out of the Varl's grip. The warm magic laced her in a live shawl, and an incessant urge to rip it off washed over her. Her skin crawled as if set upon by an army of ants.

Mirable must've sensed her disgust because he clutched her tighter to his chest. 'It's too late now,' he said, and the last trace of the merchant was gone from his voice. 'I am what I am, and if this wretched magic can help me save you, so be it.'

Still clutching the turban, Fjola fought back the revulsion and pressed her head against his muscular chest. Varl or no, Mirable would never hurt her, and maybe he was the last remaining person who still cared if she lived or died. Sooner or later, the mages would catch up to them, but until then, she'd spend her final moments chasing elusive freedom in her friend's arms.

The thought followed her into unconsciousness.

XX

'After them!' Goro-Khan shouted, leaning through the window. The rain pelted down on his head, soaking his hair and neck. In the distance, lightning flashed, followed by a resounding crack of thunder. The wind picked up speed, tossing the masses of dark clouds that obscured every inch of the sky.

The conscious guard and the six mages raced for the stairs in a flurry of cloaks. Their wide eyes and jerky movements told me that all were eager to escape the pagoda and its master's scrutiny.

When the echo of their boots died, Goro-Khan whipped around. 'What are you waiting for?' he roared at Galdra, who stood in the corner, nursing her wrists.

Her mouth curled.

Goro reached out as if to grab her by the throat but balled his hand instead. 'You made this mess,' he said, shaking his fist at her. 'Now fix it.'

Galdra's jaw twitched. Her colourless eyes searched my face, but when I didn't stand up for her, she gathered her dress and stormed off without a backwards glance.

'When this is over—'

‘What are you going to do, Valgsi? Kill me?’ He made an ugly sound that bristled the hair on my neck. ‘The only thing you’ll both do from now on is follow orders. *My* orders.’

I squared off my shoulders. ‘You’ll pay for what you’ve done.’

‘Don’t make me *laugh*. Instead of standing and blubbering, you’d be better off trying to catch your so called friends.’

I leaned forward, so our noses almost touched, but Goro didn’t flinch. He met my stare, and his angular face grew still. My fists tingled with the desire to slam into the space between his nose and forehead and to see him bleed. The urge awakened the rage of destruction, and green spots flashed in the corners of my vision, veiling Goro and the room in shimmering light. All I had to do was grab Skaldir’s sword and unleash her fury upon the Laughing God. But, the goddess failed me once before, and Lumi paid with her life. Now, Fjola and Mirable were in danger, and if I didn’t reach them first, the mages would apprehend them, or worse, Galdra would finish the job with her knife.

I drew in a long breath, and with the image of Fjola’s bleeding cheek fixed firmly in my mind, I stood down.

‘A wise choice,’ Goro-Khan said.

‘This isn’t over.’

He waved a hand, then strode past me and down the staircase.

I followed. My skull pounded as the headache rained blows into the back of my head. I took the stairs, three at a time, unable to decide which was worse, the physical pain or the claws of guilt that scraped across my heart. For whatever reason, Galdra withheld from me what had really happened, feeding me the lie that it was Fjola who shattered Lumi's heart. And the worst of it? I had believed her.

On the few occasions when Mirable alluded to the truth, I refused to listen, choosing to take Galdra's word over his. Did Fjola pose this much danger? I knew she would never follow me up the hill to awaken Skaldir, but that didn't make her a threat. Galdra thought otherwise, and her desire to dispose of Fjola brought on this disaster. It was never about my past but about me ending Fjola's life. Fjola, who never faltered in the face of my constant rejection. Fjola, whose bravery inspired even the battle-hardened Argil, and for whom Mirable cast aside the last shreds of his humanity.

I wrapped my fingers around the pearl at my neck. While I chased after the cold and ice, Fjola's existence warmed my heart from afar without asking for anything in return. Fjola, the girl with green eyes and a beautiful face, now ruined by my ignorance.

I reached the ground floor. Goro-Khan left the door wide open, and the torrent hammered the wooden boards while the wind stormed the room, blowing out the candles on Skaldir's altar. The gloom reminded me of the day I'd learned about the prophecy that shaped my life and led me to Shinpi. Another sliver of memory forced its way through the crack in the mirror erected by Galdra. This time, it was Hyllus's face. The headache flared, and I had to close my eyes to fight off the nausea. Trofn's mark throbbed in step with the pain in my head, reminding me why I allowed the witch to curse me.

I stepped outside. The storm assaulted me, and the rainwater soaked my shirt in an instant. A distant peal of a gong echoed through Shinpi, and the sound stirred a new memory. I'd heard this din before, and it filled me with an urge to run. Like a dog roused by his master's whistle, I sprinted down the trail in the village's direction. Cold air nettled my lungs, and several thrusts later, my calves began to tremble. Since my arrival here, I languished in bed for most of the time, and this inertia sapped my energy, turning me into a heaving bag of bones. To call myself the warrior of destruction was a mockery of the highest order.

The rain formed puddles on the path, and my boots splashed the water as I pushed myself to a greater speed. My breath gusted in and out, rousing a stinging pain in my left side. Red trees flashed past, and when I could make out the first slanted roofs, my ears caught muffled screams. An alarm bell resounded in my head at the possibility I was too late. The images of Fjola and Mirable lying dead forced my legs to work harder. I vaulted over the village boundary and raced along the main road, past a cluster of villagers heading for the harbour. The salty smell of the ocean filtered through my nostrils, mixed with that of freshly gutted fish. A few buildings later, I arrived at the docks and the scene before me brought me to a screeching halt.

Slammed by the waves, the Nordern vessel Torgal built to take me across the ocean was moored at the docks. Njall stood on the deck, holding the spear, and my chest swelled at seeing him alive. The wind whipped his sodden hair, and his always neatly braided beard was halfway undone, clinging to his bare chest. Just as I reached the harbour, a bolt of lightning tore through the clouds above Njall's head, making him look like a fearsome guardian of the Great Atlantic. Our eyes met, and his scarred face contorted into a grimace that made me draw back a step. Questions of his whereabouts raced through my mind, but the answer stood to his left in the form of Goro-Khan's slave, who served us tea not long ago. Netis's green cloak billowed in the storm, and his scalp, slick with rain, glistened like burnished brass. He was busy coiling the rope that kept the ship anchored. I scanned the deck for Fjola, but there was no sign of her.

Mirable paced the dock with his arms wide, guarding the gangway like some varlish champion in the king's retinue. His wiry beard covered most of his cheeks, exposing the reddish eyes and the single line of his eyebrow, now lowered in a feral expression. Through the holes in his shirt, his breasts bulged like miniature Volkans. Once crooked teeth turned into a set of fangs that snapped and gnashed in time with deep growls emanating from Mirable's chest. His turban was gone, leaving the wind free to ravage the shock of his curly hair.

'Bring me that treacherous wretch,' Goro-Khan screamed, jabbing his finger at Netis. During his mad race to the harbour, he lost all of his self-control.

When two mages rushed to obey, the Varl swiped his claws, catching one of them on the shoulder. Blood sprayed from the wound, and the man flew backward, crashing into a score of barrels stacked under a nearby stall. They overturned, burying the mage under a pile of silver-blue tuna. The other mage rolled his hands as if shaping a ball of dough, and a green sphere came to life between his palms, with a current of energy flickering in its centre.

He threw it at Mirable, but the Varl was quick to react.

His body lit up with a shimmering light that deflected the dancing orb of magic the way a shield would deflect an arrow in the heat of battle. The remaining mages followed suit, throwing the orbs at him, but their efforts met with the same result—Mirable's veil absorbed some of the magic and dispersed the rest.

'Mirable, climb aboard,' Njall shouted over the howling wind.

'Don't let them escape, you fools,' Galdra cried. She clasped her hands in front of her chest and started chanting. The roll of thunder engulfed the words, but Netis shrieked and fell to his knees, fists pressed to his temples.

'Go!' Mirable waved at the boat. 'Save her and warn the others.'

More mages appeared between the buildings leading to the docks, but with no one to explain or give orders, they stopped with their mouth agape, taking in the chaos.

'I'm not leaving you,' Njall screamed.

In response, Mirable grabbed the ship's hull and lifted it high above the water. His muscles swelled with strength, ripping through his sleeves. Njall crashed to the deck while Mirable strained and pushed the ship with a force that sent it away from the harbour and into the arms of the arching waves. The glimmering shield that protected the Varl from the magical onslaught drifted with the vessel. This feat must've cost Mirable a great deal of energy because his shoulders slumped, and he slid to his knees.

'You're all useless,' Goro-Khan bellowed at the mages. He marched across the deck, snatched the back of Mirable's shirt, and shoved him sideways. The Varl howled as his body smashed onto the dock in a heap. The Laughing God fell upon him, locking Mirable's chest between his knees. He seized hold of his neck.

My paralysis broke at the scene. With my heart thumping, I drew my sword and darted across the waterfront.

'Jarin!' Galdra screamed.

With my sword poised at Goro-Khan, I raced past her, but just as I was about to thrust my blade, my feet tangled in a wavering rope of green magic.

I lost my balance, nosediving into Goro's back.

My forehead connected with his spine, and the pain was like being punched in the face with brass knuckles. Stars burst behind my lids, and the force shoved Goro forward. He lost his grip on Mirable, who rolled away and out of his reach.

With a roar, Goro-Khan snapped around, his irises black holes against the whites of his eyes. He advanced with his lips pulled back and a foam building in the corners of his mouth. 'You dare to challenge *me*?' he shrieked.

Before I could react, his square hands fell upon my shoulders, thumbs digging into the flesh between my collarbone. Goro-Khan's glare pinned me to the spot, and I found myself powerless to look away. The left side of his mouth lifted, and my own lips twitched as if working a smirk of their own. Goro bunched his eyebrows while his lips stretched into a predatory grin. A rasping, scornful sound emerged from his throat. I tried to break free of his hold, but

I'd have better luck trying to bend an iron bar with my bare hands. My heart thrashed against my ribcage like a hawk trapped in a net, and I shook all over.

The rumble in Goro's throat turned into a mad chuckle that widened his eyes and expanded his chest as he drew air to fuel his glee. My breath caught in my throat, and I fought to stifle the laughter stirring inside my chest. The Laughing God's body rocked. He threw back his head, cackling at the dark, galloping clouds. His laughter roared in my ears while black dots exploded in front of my eyes. My blood turned to ice, and as my last effort at stifling this freakish mirth failed, I began to laugh with him.

Goro-Khan let go of my shoulders, waving his arms, stomping his feet, and dancing in step with a shrieking so loud it drowned the boom of thunder. My whole body vibrated with it, and despite the mounting panic, I sought to match his intensity. Every fibre of my being swelled with laughter that sparked my nerve endings and took over my thoughts until nothing remained but a single urge to laugh. Hot blood whooshed in my ears and pooled into the rims of my eyes. I folded my arms around my waist, howling at the docks in an uncontrollable fit of merriment. Acrid bile rushed up from my stomach. Gripped by violent convulsions and unable to stop laughing, I fell face first into my vomit.

'Stop!' Galdra screamed. 'For the sake of Yomu, stop this now.'

Silence spread across the harbour, and the maddening urge to laugh fell away. I found myself laying on the dock, twitching, with half of my face covered in vomit, and the rank stench of it made me gag. I sucked at the air, each intake of breath chafing against the raw lining of my throat. My eyes felt as if someone pierced them with hot needles, and my eardrums seemed ready to pop from the pressure.

Galdra was on her hands and knees. 'You need him,' she said in a trembling voice. 'We all need him.' She pushed herself up and swayed unsteadily. Runnels of blood dripped down her chin. She swiped at her nose, smearing the red across her left cheek.

Goro-Khan grabbed my collar and pulled me to my feet. The world spun like wagon wheels rolling down the slope, and I fell against him.

'You have Skaldir to thank today,' Goro whispered in my ear, then shoved me at Galdra. His dark eyes took in the small crowd that assembled at the harbour. 'This ends now. Anyone who thinks to conspire against me will suffer a fate worse than death.' He grabbed a fistful of Galdra's hair and pulled her close. 'No matter your lineage or abilities, if you speak of my son once again, his name will be the last word that comes out of your stained mouth.'

Galdra gave a single nod. The confident enchantress who dreamt of freedom and ruling Antaya under Skaldir's destructive gaze was gone. In the process of saving my life, she drew all her power, and the act left her bleeding and broken. Despite myself, I felt a pang of satisfaction—this is how it felt to stretch your mind beyond its limits.

Behind Goro, Mirable stirred.

'Lock him up,' Goro ordered Galdra. 'I want no Varls running loose on my island.' He strode past the cluster of guards attracted by the commotion and the alarm bell. 'Silence that cursed gong,' he snapped at them.

Everyone scurried back to the village.

Torgal's ship turned into a dark dot on the horizon, and my chest expanded with relief. Njall and Fjola were safe.

I turned my attention to Galdra. 'Why?' I asked, licking the rain off my lips. Mixed with blood, it left a coppery taste on my tongue. 'Why did you lie to me?'

Galdra brought her hand to her nostrils, and it came away crimson. She rubbed the blood between her fingers until the rain washed it away. 'Trying to interrupt his mania almost killed me,' she said in a distant voice.

'A bleeding nose is hardly a death sentence,' I said.

Her vacant eyes beheld the waves. 'In all the years following the Day of Judgement, I haven't shed a drop of blood.'

'That doesn't answer my question.'

She snapped her head at me. 'I didn't want you to remember because I knew how you'd react. You'd throw yourself at him and die attempting to avenge the demon.'

'And that's your excuse?'

'Apart from the Laughing God, I'm the most powerful mage in Shinpi, and look at me.' Galdra took another swipe at her nose and lifted her bloodstained hand. 'Today was a test of my skill, and I failed. My magic is useless against him.' She looked around the empty harbour. 'Those pathetic fools… they couldn't even stop the Varl, who understands nothing of true power. This island corroded our abilities. The longer Skaldir dreams, the more our magic fades.'

'So you toyed with my mind to ensure her awakening, is that it?'

'I did what I had to.'

'Then you're no better than Goro-Khan,' I said, turning my back on her.

Mirable sat on the deck. With the hair hanging in his face and sagging shoulders, he reminded me of a dog put out in the rain for bearing teeth at his master. He wasn't like the Varls I fought in Elizan. For all his varlish appearance, he retained sound logic and a sense of right and wrong. My throat clenched. Despite his unbending resolve to stay human, he had to embrace the monster in the end.

'Mirable, are you hurt?' I asked.

Mirable's right hand went up to touch his head, but instead of the turban, his fingers found wet hair. His bloodshot eyes shifted to Galdra, and a low growl emanated from his chest.

Galdra grabbed my hand. 'Wait,' she pleaded. 'This is what Goro-Khan wants. To drive the wedge between us.' As she spoke, the smell of ice crystals drifted up to my nostrils, so faint I wasn't sure if it was real or imagined. 'I never meant for any of this to happen. I erected the barrier inside your head to ease your grief. Nothing more.'

I rubbed Skaldir's mark on my temple. 'So, why did I forget so many things?'

'I merely separated you from your emotions, so you wouldn't go mad. I warned you about Skaldir's power and what it could do to a mortal mind. My barrier keeps you sane, but if you wish to reunite with Jarin from Stromhold, then go ahead and break it. I can't promise it'll be painless, but you'll bring back those broken pieces of yourself. But before you do, think about Hvitur and what will happen to your people… to Fjola when Goro-Khan gets there. He'll laugh everyone you love insane.'

Galdra's translucent eyes looked eerie in the encroaching nightfall, and the smell of ice grew more intense. I knew she couldn't be trusted, but I needed her magic to kill Goro-Khan.

A dog barked somewhere in the village. The rain turned into a drizzle, and the roll of thunder faded on its way north.

'We all failed, but there's one thing we have in common. Our desire to see Goro-Khan dead.'

Galdra let out a huge breath. 'I'm all out of magic. I'll need time to recover.'

I thought of the sacrifices we were ready to make for those we loved. To bring Lumi back, I was prepared to rouse the Goddess of Destruction from her dream. At the sound of his mother's voice, Mirable came close to jumping into the serena's arms. What would the Laughing God give to hear his son speak again?

XXI

After the events at the harbour, I spent my time shut in my room, pacing the length of it or staring at the green crescents. Galdra rarely came here, and when she did, Goro-Khan's guard appeared at my door soon after. Having a set of ears listening in on our conversations made it difficult to relay my plans to her. My hatred of the Laughing God wormed inside my gut like a leech, feeding on my anger and swelling with my need to destroy the man who caused me so much misery. The hill in Hvitur pulled at me from afar, and the closer the day of Skaldir's awakening drew, the more restless I felt. The Jarin from Stromhold had a mind to refuse the call, but the Valgsi part of me had a single purpose—to wake Skaldir and let her power infuse his soul.

I sensed the old Jarin shifting beyond the fragile barrier in my head. But I refused to acknowledge him, knowing this reunion would prevent me from doing what was necessary, or worse. Jarin from Stromhold would question my every move, debate right from wrong, and allow the grief to break him. On this quest, I was better off without him. Whilst before, Galdra was here to reinforce the glass separating my two halves, now, I had to rely on my mental will, and my headache worsened.

Some days it was so strong it drove me sick, but having the end in sight, I endured.

When Mirable let Njall's ship get away, Goro-Khan ordered him imprisoned until we sailed for Hvitur. I had to stand my ground and demand he stayed with me. At first, Goro flew into a rage, but when the mages reasoned with him, he agreed to my request. I suspected the men and women of Shinpi feared the Varl but they respected the Valgsi. In the end, Galdra locked Mirable in a cage that was put in my chamber and reinforced with magic. I came to regret my decision, for it left me exposed to his constant barrage of assaults on my conscience. He might've looked like a Varl, but his tongue was definitely human.

'If I had a purse full of coin, I'd whack you upside the head with it,' Mirable growled from the cage in the far corner of the room, but his voice lost its human quality. If a wolf tried to speak, it would sound like Mirable. 'With any luck, the blow would knock some sense into you. How long are you going to waste away in that bed?'

'Enough with your constant baying,' I said, rubbing my temples. After a night of this excruciating headache, my patience was thinner than parchment. Galdra would kill the pain in one whisper, but after uncovering her lies, I didn't want her magic anywhere near me. Besides, she was regaining her strength after her attempt to silence Goro-Khan's laughter.

Mirable's claws clicked as he wrapped his hands around the metal bars. 'Then let me out of this cage.'

'So you can run wild and cause trouble?'

'If not for my quick thinking, Fjola would be dead.'

His accusation was a hornet's sting, and I leapt to my feet. Another ball of agony exploded at the back of my head. I clutched the bed pole to steady myself. Fjola's face flashed before my eyes, but I ushered it away. Her memory called to the old Jarin, who grew restless behind the mirror, pounding on the glass and demanding to be released from his mental prison.

'Your witch cut Fjola open while you stood there like a dolt and did nothing to stop her. She stripped your memories, twisted your thoughts, and poisoned your heart with magic.' Mirable rattled the bars. 'I don't know you anymore.'

'The same magic flows in you, and you had no problem using it to save your hide.'

'I used it to save my friend. The Jarin from Stromhold would've done the same.'

I tightened my grip on the bed pole, and the carvings dug deep into my palm. Mirable was dangerous because he knew me like no one else on this island. With Fjola safely out of reach, Galdra had no hold on his tongue, and he ran it to remind me of things I wanted to forget. His words stressed the brittle glass that kept me sane, and I feared it would shatter before I put my plans in motion. 'The *old* Jarin was weak and weighed down by grief,' I said. 'I need the Valgsi to finish what he started.'

'Listen to yourself.' Mirable let go of the bars and flopped back on his hairy buttocks. 'Maybe it is too late for you. We all strike bargains in life. I embraced the Varl to save Fjola.' He scratched his chest and scowled. 'But I'll loathe myself until my dying breath. What's your excuse?'

'I don't need one. I'm simply trying to right my wrongs.'

'By unleashing destruction upon the world?'

'We don't know what will happen on the Night of Norrsken. Everyone expects another Day of Judgement, but we're not awakening Skaldir to fight a war. After years of exile, the mages deserve a place to call home, and they'll need Skaldir's magic to restore Antaya.'

'Do you presume to know the mind of a god?' he barked and started panting. 'This cage feels like a cooking pot.'

I walked to the window and pushed open the shutters. The wind cut through the room with a sharp edge, bringing in the faint scent of sea salt. In a few days, we would take to the ocean and find the answers to all our questions.

I sat down in front of the cage. 'How did you find Njall? And how on earth did you persuade him to accept help from a mage?'

'I used my wretched nose to sniff him out.' His wide nostrils twitched. 'Njall was fortunate not to be there when the witch accosted us in that forest. I followed his trail from there.'

'Galdra said the residue would kill him.'

At the mention of her name, the Varl's lips drew back from his teeth, and his expression turned feral.

'Don't do that,' I said, leaning away from the cage.

Mirable ran his tongue over his upper lip. 'I rarely got angry before,' he said in a rough voice. 'But now, I feel like tearing down Shinpi and all its mages.'

I thought of the fury that swept through my mind when I fought Goro-Khan and his own fits of rage. Skaldir's magic was forged from destruction, and it spread like a fever, infecting those it touched. Hyllus used it to turn humans into Varls, but the ruin was always at the heart of his perverse creation. If Mirable lost control, he'd bring terror worse than the one I witnessed in Elizan. The Varls that attacked the village were nothing more than bloodthirsty beasts acting at the behest of their creator, but Mirable had cunning and wit as well as strength and speed—advantages that made him a lethal weapon. The Lost City of Antaya was his only hope.

'Njall stayed out of sight, and when the witch took us hostage, he fled,' the merchant resumed in a calmer tone. 'His thigh wound weakened him, and so did the magical residue, but he limped his way to the cliffs. He wanted to steal the ship and get it ready for us. But with the guards on his heels, he had to jump into the sea. Netis found Njall washed up on the rocks, bleeding and unconscious. He offered him shelter, mended his wounds, and looked after Njall until his consciousness returned.'

I frowned. 'Why would the mage help him?'

'That's for the gods to say. Maybe not all mages are alike? Whatever his reasons, Netis saved Njall's life, and in return, Njall took him to Hvitur.'

'Torgal will kill the mage on sight.'

Mirable nodded. 'Nords can be bull-headed, but your uncle may listen to Njall. Having a mage at their disposal would even out the odds.'

After what happened to Fjola, I didn't want to get anyone else hurt. 'I'm hoping to avoid the confrontation.'

'And how will you do that? Hvitur will be on high alert. They won't let you pass.'

'If all goes well, they won't see us coming,' I said, remembering Galdra's illusionary forest.

'If you think Goro-Khan would miss the opportunity to burn Hvitur to the ground, think again. You may be the Valgsi, but he's in charge of the mages, and that includes your witch.'

'She's not *my* witch,' I said. 'Mirable, we have our differences, and you don't approve of my decision to awaken

Skaldir. But I know you hate the Laughing God as much as I do.'

Mirable arched his single eyebrow. 'Why have you decided on this path?'

I thought of Lumi, and the sound of her heart shattering into pieces rang out in my ears. My throat closed up, and for a while, I struggled to answer. The shadow of the old Jarin stirred behind the glass, and I sensed his profound sorrow. Galdra dulled my emotions with her magic, but it was my decision to keep them sealed. If I reunited with my lost self, the grief would drive me mad, and there would be no one left to stop Goro-Khan from destroying Hvitur.

I cleared my throat. 'Lumi died, and Fjola got badly wounded. All because of me. There's nothing I can do for Fjola, and besides, she's safer without me.'

Mirable groaned and banged his forehead against the cage. 'Like I said, bull-headed.'

'Let me finish. Lumi deserved to experience life with her heart in her chest. Her longing to be like us is something you should understand. If there's even the slightest chance Skaldir could undo what Goro-Khan so carelessly destroyed, I have to try.'

As if affronted by my declaration, a gust of wind rattled the shutters. The crisp air washed over me, drying the sweat of my temples. I kneaded the spot at the back of my neck from which the headache radiated. How I wished to be free of this constant pain.

Kylfa's voice rustled inside my mind. *'Soon, Valgsi… soon your soul will be devoured, and your torment will end.'*

'There's no talking you out of it, is there?' Mirable asked.

The witch's words faded, and I shook my head.

'What do you want me to do?'

'When we set sail, I need you to sniff out the serena's lair and lead us to it.'

He frowned. 'Now, why would you—' He tilted his head.

I let the silence do the talking. After a few long moments, Mirable's eyes widened as the understanding donned. 'How do you know the Laughing God will hear the song?' he asked.

I didn't, but all my previous attempts at fighting Goro-Khan ended in failure, and the creature was my only hope. The serena desired Njall's valour and Mirable's wealth, and with their hearts free of love affairs, they were easy targets. The Laughing God's abilities would attract the serena, and since he cared for no one left alive, I was hoping the creature would lure him in.

'Just do as I ask and leave the rest to me,' I said.

Mirable wrapped his hands around his shoulders. 'I will, but under one condition.'

'Name it.'

'I'll sniff out the serena if you fulfil your original promise to me.'

I searched my troubled mind but came up blank. 'You have to do better than that. What was it?'

Mirable pursed his lips. 'The witch sure sank her hooks into you. When the guards captured and threw us into prison, I asked you to kill the Varl. You promised you would, and I want you to make good on that promise.'

A tendril of recollection squeezed through the crack in the glass, causing a fresh explosion of pain. I squeezed my eyes and seized hold of the memory. My mind filled with the images of the prison cell where Mirable and I stood facing each other. His turban sat atop his head, and more or less, he still looked like a merchant from Vester.

'When the time comes, use your sword to cut me down.'

'If, and only if, it comes to that.'

I let out a harsh breath. 'Why?'

'I did right by Fjola, and after I find the serena, I'd have fulfilled my duty to you as well. I'd rather not witness the world in ashes.'

'But you could live safely in Antaya.'

'The dreams of Antaya aren't mine, and they aren't yours, either. Our journey brought us to Shinpi, and we proved the legends are true. But we both lost parts of ourselves along the way.'

‘Just think of all the treasure buried beneath the ocean,’ I said. My throat was dry, and the words came out in a series of croaks.

He reached through the bars and patted my shoulder with the hand that radiated heat. ‘Only humans see the value in gold, my friend.’

We sat there for a while, lost in our own thoughts. Mine were like snakes in the grass—elusive and dangerous. I wanted to smash my fist through the mirror and let the true Jarin decide the right course. Would he carry out his promise? After all, he was the one who made it. Skaldir’s mark on my temple bound me to my destiny, and the witches’ eye made certain I’d never see the gates of Himinn, but Mirable didn’t suffer from such limitations. He could live out his days among the mages in Antaya, and who knows, maybe with Skaldir awakened, even find a way to become human again. But who was I to decide Mirable’s fate? He was a friend who stood by me until the end, and granting his wish was the least I could do.

I swallowed against the bitter lump that formed in my throat. ‘When the serena’s song is done, I’ll fulfil my promise.’

* * *

‘Are you excited about tomorrow?’ Galdra said in a drawling voice. ‘I know I am. To cross the Great Atlantic and see my birthplace was a dream since the city was sealed after the War of Mages.’ She gazed through the window at the cloudless sky.

Her long hair was tied at the base of her neck with a black ribbon, and the dress she wore looked nothing like the elaborate skirts she donned in the days before the harbour. It was grey and buttoned up at the collar. Even her nails were scrubbed clean of their usual polish. Watching her, I felt a prickle of uncertainty. Goro-Khan wanted Galdra to sit beside Yomu on Antaya's throne, but that was before Fjola accused her of conspiring against him. The Laughing God stripped Galdra of the right to wear green—the colour revered by all mages, but I feared there was more to his punishment.

I glanced over my shoulder at the partially slid door where the guard stood with his hand wrapped around the hilt. He was poised there to listen and pass on every word to his master. 'I'm not fond of open waters,' I said. 'Without proper navigation, it's easy to get off course.'

'Lucky for you, you have a stray who's dying to see home,' Mirable growled from his cage.

'Trying to redeem yourself?' Galdra asked.

He uttered a long howl and rattled the bars, providing a much-needed distraction.

I took Galdra's hand, and it felt like parchment in my grip, dry and brittle. 'Now,' I whispered into her ear.

She turned and closed her eyes, smudged by dark shadows. A narrow line creased the spot on her forehead where a green crescent used to be. Her pallid lips moved, and as she spoke the silent incantation, a current of warm energy whooshed past me. I studied the guard, but he didn't change his stance.

Galdra's eyes flew open. Bleached of colour, they seemed glasslike. 'I don't know how long I can hold him.'

This was my only chance to share my plans with her, so I put as much urgency into my voice as I could muster. 'I need you to follow my instructions exactly. When I give the signal during the voyage, use your magic and make everyone on the ship deaf. Everyone *except* for the Laughing God. Can you do that?'

'Goro-Khan is taking two vessels with him,' she said with a slight quiver in her voice.

I cursed. I didn't want any of the mages to suffer Goro's fate, but having to watch over two ships full of people would put Galdra under a greater strain, and so far, she struggled to control one man. 'Are you strong enough to shield them both?'

Galdra frowned but nodded her assent.

'Whatever happens, the illusion must not be broken until it's over. If it fails—'

'Tell me your plan,' she said.

I was about to when a fat drop of blood spouted from Galdra's right nostril. She pressed her fingers to it and blinked.

The guard jerked and shook his head.

I let go of her hand. 'No time for that now. Just do as I ask, and we will be free of him.'

She didn't move, only stood, with her fingers cupped around her nose.

The guard poked his head through the door just as Mirable started barking and kicking at the bars.

'What's going on here?' the man asked, pulling the sword free of its sheath. He looked from Galdra to the Varl. 'Do you need me to silence him?'

'Come if you dare,' Mirable snarled. 'Let's see how tough you are when your manhood is between my teeth.'

The man spat and backed away from the door.

'Galdra,' I hissed.

She looked up. Her upper lip was streaked with blood. 'We sail at dawn,' she announced and walked past me.

'What's wrong with her?' Mirable asked when the echo of Galdra's steps faded.

I raked the fingers through my hair. 'I don't know.' The only thing I could think of was Galdra's clash with Goro-Khan. She exerted an inordinate amount of energy to stop his laughter, and it affected her magic. During one of her previous visits, she assured me that as long as she got her rest, her strength would recover in no time. But today, she seemed worse, not better.

'Let's hope she's up to the task,' Mirable said.

'You do your part, and let me worry about Galdra.'

XXII

Dawn came shrouded in mist that descended from the hills like a pale shade. It snaked through the village and between houses, where it entwined with the magical residue to form a silvery-green braid. Rolling clouds obscured the leaden sky, spraying my face with a fine drizzle that sapped my body heat. Pushed by the chilly wind, the waves scaled the shore only to break against the docks and the hulls of two ships ready to set sail.

The mages rushed around the harbour, swiping the soggy ground with their robes. They called out instructions while stacking crates and boxes filled with water, food, and other supplies necessary to sustain us during the long voyage to Hvitur. The commotion reminded me of the day I left my homeland in search of Shinpi, and the ache at the back of my skull reared its nasty snout. I winced—every memory was a harbinger of pain these days. The choking calls of seagulls mixed with the noise of the cargo being hauled onto the vessels were all sounds of yesterday. I remembered my uncle, Torgal, and the firm and dry feel of his hand as it gripped mine in a farewell shake. Now I was on my way to greet him with steel and magic. Before Fjola and Njall fled Shinpi, I'd hoped for a chance to explain to Torgal my reasons for climbing the hill. If I told him about Lumi, would he not understand? After all, my mother broke his heart when she accepted the black pearl from my father and followed him to Stromhold.

'Tell him… tell him you wish to bring back the demon who killed his beloved…' Trofn crowed, and the dark eye on my wrist rippled in response.

The crones made a home inside my mind, mocking my every thought. I wanted to carve them out, piece by blackened piece, but this silent desire only induced more cackles. I shook my head. There was no point worrying about the witches when I had my confrontation with the serena to look forward to. The old hags were harmless for now, but the malevolent creature lurking in the depths of the Great Atlantic could pull us all beneath the waves.

A rattling noise rang through the docks as two mages carried Mirable's cage aboard on a green cloud of magic, but the Varl didn't make it easy for them, snapping and snarling through the bars. Those charged with loading the pen jerked their heads and muttered something in Shinpi's tongue, leaning as far from the bars as their shoulders would allow. Goro-Khan gave strict orders to stow Mirable's cage on the upper deck, where the mages could keep a close watch—the request which worked in my favour. The Varl's job was to sniff out the serena, and for that, he needed to be in the open. Mirable promised he'd direct us to the nest, but despite his assurances, worry gnawed at me. I feared the creature would sneak up on us as it did during our first voyage, or worse, it wouldn't be there at all. The Great Atlantic was vast and deep. Who's to say the serena always nested in one place? My idea had more weaknesses than strengths, and I shuddered at the thought of Goro-Khan disembarking in Hvitur. His laughter would mark the end of every Nord.

'It's time,' Galdra said.

I didn't hear her coming, and her soft voice startled me. Whilst before, the scent of snow would alert me of her presence, now, I smelled nothing. 'Are you well?' It was a foolish question, for her sunken cheeks and pasty complexion were answer enough.

She fixed her ghostly gaze on Goro-Khan, who stood on the deck with his hands behind his back, barking orders. Galdra's hand drifted to her forehead where the green crescent used to be, and her face tightened. 'I want to see him dead.'

I almost felt the fever of her hate—a sensation I knew well from my encounter with the witches. To realise my vengeance on Hyllus, I relinquished my soul. 'I need to know you're up to the task.'

'Do you doubt me?'

I appraised the green sails mounted on the tall masts. Once unfurled, they'd harness the winds that would drive the ships towards their destiny. 'My plan puts everyone at risk, and the last time you used your magic—'

‘Stop questioning my abilities,’ she snapped and stalked off to the gangway, splattering rainwater with her boots.

I cast a final look at the village and the pagoda beyond. In the light of dawn, it was a silhouette against the mountains, but my heart clenched all the same. Lumi drew her last between those walls, and only my refusal to reunite with the old Jarin kept the crushing grief at bay. He was the one who witnessed her heart shatter in Goro’s grip, and it broke him. To right this terrible wrong, I needed a clear head and a firm resolve, which meant separating myself from his feelings. With the weak part of me sealed behind the glass, I was free to focus on eliminating Goro-Khan. But as I walked to the ship, the unshakable sense I was dicing with the God of Death settled on my shoulders. I adjusted my collar to guard against the wind, then followed Galdra up the gangway, and each dull step felt like a nail pounded into the planks that were to become my coffin.

When I strode past the Laughing God, he sneered. Like the rest of us, he put on a wool-padded coat and knee-high boots lined with fox fur. He tied his hair into a warrior’s tail and strapped a curved blade to his waist. The weapon was for show because his laughter cut deeper than any steel. There was a glint in Goro’s shadowy eyes, and his voice turned hoarse from shouting orders all morning. Seeing him in charge filled me with distaste.

I came to stand at the bow where Skaldir's figurehead stared out into the sea. I remembered looking at it from my ship when the guards had sailed to apprehend us. Only a few of them made it back to the shore. My lips twitched at the memory, and from this angle, it looked like Skaldir's wooden lips twisted in response. The Goddess of Destruction and her Valgsi, setting off on their greatest voyage. I touched the sword at my hip, and a warm current of energy seeped into my fingers. Before my trip to Shinpi, I regarded it as a precious relic, but the venture to the goddess's birth cave convinced me the blade was so much more. It felt alive and thrummed with the desire to be awakened. The Night of Norrsken was fast approaching, and Skaldir's magic stirred my soul. It was like having a rope strapped to my chest with someone holding the other end and tugging rhythmically, each pull more insistent than the last.

There was no resisting it.

'She knows we're coming,' Goro-Khan said. He reached out to caress the wooden lock of hair. 'Skaldir's green eye is set upon the hill of her rebirth.'

His presence punctured the bubble of anger, and my grip on the hilt loosened. 'We haven't crossed the Great Atlantic yet,' I reminded him, thinking of the serena and her needle-sharp teeth. If all went as planned, Goro would never see Hvitur's shores.

He surveyed the waves. 'I'm not afraid of the deep. With the goddess guiding these ships, nothing can touch us. But you've always lacked faith.'

'My faith is none of your concern.'

He leaned close. 'Don't think for a moment that I didn't know about your desire to turn my people against me.' He cast a look over his shoulder at Galdra, who stood with her hands on the handrail and eyes fixed on the second ship. 'I misjudged her, but I think she knows not to cross me again. My son will need her abilities to rule Antaya, but you—'

'But *I* am Skaldir's chosen.'

He uttered a quiet laugh that sent my heart racing, then turned his back on me.

I licked my lips and the taste of salt bit into my tongue. I wondered what kind of father Goro-Khan was before Yomu's tragic end. Had his son feared him? Or was he eagerly waiting for Himinn's gates to unlock so he could reunite with him?

'Weigh the anchors,' Goro called.

I drew in a lungful of briny air. Unlike Njall and Fjola, I was never fond of ships and open water. The constant rocking made me dizzy, and the constant headaches wouldn't make this crossing any smoother. I missed Blixt and his sure step. My trusted horse waited for me in Hvitur, and when I realised my calling, I'd mount him for my final journey to Sur.

XXIII

The gods didn't favour us with the weather. In the weeks that followed, the Great Atlantic tested our ability to stay above the water, assailing us with storms and calling forth the billowing clouds that blotted out the guiding stars. Like a violent captain, the wind charged across the deck, snatching coats, tangling hair, and blowing rain into the grim faces of mages who worked hard to reduce the strain on the green sails. The waves slammed at the ships, and watching them come and go made me think of horses with white manes and foam frothing at the corners of their mouths. As the ship rose and fell, my stomach churned and heaved, and many a time I tossed its contents into the raging sea. Never have I wished so much for solid land.

Goro-Khan and Galdra kept mostly to their cabins, leaving the mages to brace the storms and maintain the course. Ironically, their magic was of little use, and their lack of navigation skills put the whole voyage into question. When they turned to me for help, I shrugged my shoulders. I was a Nord, yes, but I didn't have Njall's knowledge. The man at the helm was no captain, and neither was I, which left us with the Varl and his superior sense of smell.

Mirable huddled in his pen, with his arms wrapped around his legs and his head stuck between his knees, but every so often, he'd get up to shake off the water trapped in his coarse hair. I shared in his desire to feel dry again, but with the ceaseless torrents, there was no hope of that. My skin itched, and the constant damp caused a rash to spread.

'This is worse than Agtarr's Chamber of Torments,' Mirable growled.

I squatted in front of the cage. 'I doubt that.' I had to shout over the wind. Seeing him locked up and at the storm's mercy, I wanted to break the magic seal that reinforced the cage.

The old Jarin stirred behind the glass inside my head. *'So why don't you?'*

'Because to do so would put me at odds with Goro-Khan,' I muttered. 'I need his attention as far away from me and Mirable as possible. I want to give him no reason to suspect us. The Varl understands this.'

'Since when did Mirable become a Varl to you?'

I rubbed the Skaldir's mark on my temple. Mirable was a Varl, wasn't he?

'What are you muttering on about?' Mirable asked.

I jerked my head up. 'Nothing. What can I do?' The question was born out of guilt rather than any desire to hear the answer. Jarin from Stromhold would oppose Goro-Khan and set the Varl free, but I couldn't take that risk.

Mirable flashed me a wild look. 'Make the rain go away.'

I laughed. ‘I don’t have that kind of power. Are we still on course?’

‘I can hardly make out your face in this torrent, not to mention the stars. We haven’t seen a clear sky in weeks.’

I chewed the inside of my cheek. If the storm didn’t let up, and if Mirable’s senses failed him, we could be drifting for months or until the food barrels ran empty. The idea of being stuck on the ship with the Laughing God and a starving crew bristled the hair on my neck.

Mirable must’ve spied something in my expression because he said, ‘I can smell them.’ His wide nostrils twitched, and he thrust his tongue out. ‘The stench of rotten fish. It’s faint, but it’s definitely there.’

All I remembered from the night with the serena was the scent of flowers and spice. ‘How far?’

‘You’ll know when we get there.’

I wiped my face—a wasted effort since, as soon as I stood up, a fresh surge of rain slammed into it. Far to the right sailed the second vessel, but if not for the dotted lights from the green spheres, I wouldn’t know it was there. I looked up at the clouds billowing like smoke puffed out by giant chimneys. There was no break in them. Could it be Yldir and Agtarr sensed my approach and this tempest was a warning to stay away from the hill?

'You'll need to do better than this,' I muttered at the sky, then louder to Mirable, 'I'll check on you later.'

'You know where to find me,' he called.

I walked back to my cabin, but when I opened the hatch leading below deck, I hesitated. With its musty odour seeping through the walls and a round window staring out onto the raging waves, my room felt like a tomb. Even at night, the air inside was stifling. I let the hatch fall. The ship lurched, and my stomach lurched with it as I staggered to the bow and the figurehead. Skaldir regarded the storm with her usual scowl chiselled into her face by the sculptor's magic. Standing next to the goddess eased some of my anxiety. I touched the sword at my hip. 'I can't do it all by myself.'

A hand fell on my shoulder, and a voice cried in my ear, 'You're not alone.'

I whirled around with the blade half-drawn to find the 'captain' watching me with eyes darkened by the storm. His hood was pulled back, and the water plastered his cropped hair to his forehead. Judging by his smooth face, the 'captain' was close to my age, if not younger. Although I could never be sure. The lifespan of a mage was three times that of an average human.

'I'm sorry if I startled you,' he said, lifting his palms. 'You carry a heavy burden, and I wanted you to know that not all of it rests on your shoulders. We're as divided as you are.'

I studied his expression, but all I saw was a creased brow and pulled down lips. 'What's your name?' I asked, feeling a tingle of shame for not remembering.

'Solas,' he said, wiping his face on a sleeve.

'Well, Solas, I can't say I understand.'

He looked over his shoulder, but the deck was a grey sheet of rain. I could just make out a solitary figure hunched up high in the crow's nest with the shining orb for company. Despite my assurances that I hadn't encountered a single ship during my first voyage, Goro-Khan insisted on keeping watch at all times and in all weather.

'My mother was a human, without a drop of magic in her blood,' Solas said into the wind.

'Is she here?'

'No, she learned Agtarr's face when I was twelve.'

This simple admission filled me with a sense of kinship. I understood his loss, and we both sailed into the uncertain future. 'May she know peace in the Fields of Life,' I said.

Solas blinked against the rain. 'My father was a mage, but he wished for a truce with humans. To honour my mother, he tried to leave Shinpi and sail back to Antaya to seek others like him. This act angered the Laughing God.'

I remembered the healer Galdra told me about who disobeyed Goro's orders and paid with his life. 'What was his name?'

'Saru.'

I nodded, thinking of Hyllus and how the dead wouldn't find peace until the living avenged them. 'My father died protecting me and his homeland. I made sure his killer got what he deserved.'

Solas licked his lips and cast another glance over his shoulder. His desire was written all over his face—he wanted to avenge his father, but his enemy was untouchable. Or so everyone thought. 'Many of us don't want another war,' he said at last.

The exchange filled me with a sense of unreality. I was brought up to think of mages as magic-thirsty demons who sacrificed their city to win the war, but time in Shinpi proved me otherwise. From Netis, who sided with a Nord and betrayed his kind, to Solas, who wished to honour his parents, and Galdra, who dreamt of restoring Antaya. Except for the magic that afforded them unique abilities, the mages were as diverse and flawed as humans.

'The Goddess of Destruction will awaken not to judge but to restore and give life,' I said, emphasising every word. I needed to believe it as much as I needed Solas to believe me.

Solas offered a hesitant nod.

I put a hand on his shoulder. 'Listen closely. Manning the helm in this weather is no simple task, but you *must* do as

Mirable says. His job is to get us to Hvitur on time. And, if Skaldir wills it, you may yet find justice for your father.'

I could feel his body tense, but he didn't ask how or why, and for that, I admired him. Defying Goro-Khan cost Saru his life, and now, I was asking his son to commit the same sin.

'Will you do as I ask?'

'Yes, Valgsi,' Solas said.

'Call me Jarin.'

* * *

More weeks passed, and I thought the storms would never end. Some days, the clouds thinned, allowing a glimpse of the sky, but just when the crew started to relax, they'd gather again to flood us with fresh rain. The mages combined their talents to keep each other dry and repair any damage to the sails. When the wind let up, they used magic on the oars. It was a curious sight to see the blades moving without a man or a woman to drive the poles. From time to time, minor scuffles broke out between the mages, and the mood on the ship grew bleaker by the day. Most of the arguments centred on the use of magic—Goro-Khan ordered everyone to conserve their powers until we reached Hvitur. Some, including Solas, thought little of his edict. As much as it pained me to admit, I shared Goro's concern. The more time I spent with the mages, the more I understood their abilities and the fragility of their power. When I first arrived in Shinpi, I believed it was infinite, and using it was like tapping into a thriving well. But it wasn't so. The well allowed them to haul only so much magic before it ran empty and had to be replenished through rest. Even Galdra, the most powerful enchantress, learned its limits.

'Our magic isn't as strong as it used to be,' the Laughing God said when a young man challenged his order. 'A band of bloodthirsty Nords is waiting for us in Hvitur, and we'll need every drop of power to win that battle.'

'We have the numbers,' someone countered.

Drawn by the commotion, the crew dropped their tasks and gathered on the upper deck. Even the man charged with keeping watch up in the crow's nest abandoned his post and joined the meeting. Seeing so many green cloaks together made my stomach flail. The last time the mages gathered, Fjola got hurt, and Mirable turned into a Varl.

'Numbers alone won't afford us victory,' Goro said. He stood with his hands clasped behind his back, speaking like a father who took it upon himself to lecture his rebellious children. 'Nords are known for their battle prowess.' He looked at me, and the corner of his upper lip lifted slightly. 'Even if we have witnessed little of that lately, we must not underestimate them.'

'How do we know they want to fight us?' a female voice called.

I searched the crowd, but I couldn't pinpoint the woman who asked the question.

Goro's eye twitched, and a mirthless sound escaped his lips.

The mages drew closer together. A man with a huge wart on his nose cleared his throat, and a girl wearing a jade necklace uttered a nervous laugh.

'Netis is with them,' the same voice cried, perhaps bolstered by the group's size. But I spent enough time with the Laughing God to know that once provoked, the numbers wouldn't stay his hand.

Goro-Khan's eyes narrowed. 'Don't just hide behind your cloak. Step forward and speak your mind.'

The mages shifted uneasily, and my armpits broke out in sweat. I prayed the foolish woman would stay silent, but she elbowed her way out of the group. Her green cloak was undone, and silver threads laced her brown hair. As she crossed the deck, her bare feet curled inward, and two badly healed stumps replaced her large toes. She stopped in front of Goro-Khan with her chin up and shoulders pulled back.

'Nora,' Goro said, tilting his head. 'I see that losing your toes was too gentle a punishment.'

'I'm not scared of you,' Nora said, but the quiver in her voice told me otherwise.

Goro's eyelid jerked again, but his expression didn't change. 'You should be.' He grabbed her arm, and Nora didn't resist when he dragged her to the railing.

The mages gasped, but none rushed to Nora's rescue. I stood frozen to the spot while the Jarin inside my head screamed for me to stop this madness. I wrapped my hand around the sword but didn't move to obey. Nora's defiance put everyone at risk. What's worse, it would increase the Laughing God's vigilance in the upcoming days.

'If you're so willing to follow Netis, it would give me a great pleasure to help you on your way,' Goro-Khan said, and his lips stretched into a sinister grin. He seized Nora by the collar and hurled her over the railing.

My breath caught in my chest while the Jarin behind the glass accused me of being a heartless coward.

Nora let out a sharp scream before the angry waves swallowed her.

'Anyone else?' Goro-Khan asked, looking from person to person until his dark gaze settled on me.

The mages murmured and dropped their eyes, for none dared to oppose the mighty god who ruled them with insanity. Before I came to Shinpi, I associated the word laughter with joy, but now, the sound became a precursor of pain and terror. I balled my hands into fists. The day of reckoning would come, and when it did, Goro-Khan would have no one to laugh at but himself.

* * *

Two full moons passed since we left Shinpi, and the serena remained as elusive as the sun. As the nights went by, doubt crept into my thoughts. I couldn't let Goro-Khan disembark in Hvitur, but without the serena's song, I'd be forced to call on the mages, and according to Solas, the crew stood divided. If I confronted the Laughing God in the middle of the Great Atlantic, and if he got the upper hand, I'd risk the lives of those who sided with me. Mirable still assured me he smelled the creature's presence in the air. He worked his nose, sharing his insights with Solas, who steered the ship in what we hoped was the right direction.

On one of the rainless days, I sat in front of the Varl's pen. He looked unwell. Yellow tinged the rims of his eyes, and his bulging muscles trembled as if gripped by a high fever.

'You're sick,' I said.

He made a wet sound with his tongue. 'Maybe I'm not such a perfect creation after all. I wonder what our broken friend Alkaios would say about me.'

'We need to get you out of this cage.'

Mirable grabbed the bars and pulled himself up. His long nails clicked against the steel. 'The Laughing God would never allow it. Besides, he fears me.' When he said the last, I caught a note of triumph in his tone.

'This is serious, Mirable. If anything happens to you—'

'You won't be able to find your precious serena, I know.'

'This isn't about the serena.'

He cocked his head. 'No? So what is it about?' His dense hair grew twice as quick, furling upon itself and obscuring most of his forehead. Even if he recovered his turban, I doubted the simple cloth would've been enough to restrain the shock of curls. 'Don't tell me you're having second thoughts. A promise is a promise, Jarin.'

The reminder stirred the old Jarin, and he resumed his endless pounding and scratching at the glass. My headache flared up. With all the fissures in the mirror, I feared it would shatter long before the Night of Norrsken.

'This promise goes both ways,' I said. 'You're no good to me sick.'

Mirable coughed. It was a dry, hacking sound. He glanced at Solas, standing at the helm. His hands were on the ship's wheel, but the green aura surrounding it told me it was magic that propelled the vessel. 'Get some rest. The youth and I will find the way.' He scratched his cheek. 'He's kind to me, you know.'

‘When Antaya is restored, there’ll be others like him. If you weren’t so set on dying, you could have a new life that’s even better than your old one.’

‘I don’t have a life.’

I shrugged. Mirable wouldn’t change his mind even if Yldir himself asked him to. ‘At least let me bring you more water and blankets.’

‘Like that would do me any good,’ he grumbled. ‘Useless human comforts.’

I left him and walked back to the hatch leading below deck. The wind brought a fresh and earthy smell to my nostrils, increasing my longing for the solid land. I didn’t want to die at sea, my body tossed by the waves and my flesh picked by the saltwater fish. I wanted to breathe my last with Nordur’s soil under my boots and the winter air in my lungs. Jarin from Stromhold shared in my desire, staring at me through the mirror with his lifeless eyes. He stopped the incessant hammering, and his arms hung limp.

‘Your weakness got us into this mess, and my strength will get us out,’ I muttered, thinking of my parents, who died apart from each other, of Fjola and her bleeding cheek, and Lumi, with her heart crushed under Goro’s heel. ‘If I set you free, your grief will destroy everything I’m trying to accomplish.’

The old Jarin said nothing.

I fixed Lumi's pale face in my mind's eye to remind me why I was willing to answer Skaldir's call. Her death was the only thing I had the power to undo. 'I'm doing this for Lumi,' I said out loud.

'Do not be a fool, Valgsi,' Trofn hissed from the depth of my troubled mind. '*None can deny the force of destruction. Your wish to resurrect the demon is merely an excuse, for all paths lead to the hilltop.'*

I jerked the hatch open, and the musty smell wafted up from the ship's bowels. My thoughts followed me down into the dim corridor leading to my cabin. Inside, I stripped off my wet coat and boots. The sword I placed on the berth, within easy reach. Whilst before, I'd often leave it in my room and go about my business, now the idea filled me with trepidation. I'd become one with my blade. Regardless of whether I needed it or not, I brought it along wherever I went, for leaving it would be like slicing off my arm.

I lay on the bed with my eyes closed. My right hand stroked the scabbard, while my left held onto the pearl at my neck. Green light shone behind my eyelids as my mind led me back to the hill in Hvitur. The ship creaked and groaned, battling the frantic waves and pushing against the wind. Before long, the sleep seized me, and I dreamt of the Night of Norrsken and Lumi, alive and well, running into my arms.

XXIV

My eyelids flew open, and my instincts warned me of danger. After the last threads of sleep fell away, the first thing I noticed was the absence of sound, as if everyone abandoned the vessel while I slept. The heavy weight of this ominous hush pressed down on my chest like a load of wet sheets. I could no longer hear the patter of rain against the hull, and even the wind stilled. My scalp tingled, and my skin crawled with an eerie sensation of invisible eyes watching me.

I grabbed my sword and swung my feet off the berth. Visible through the round window, the ocean resembled a lake covered in shallow waves that barely rippled the surface. The water took on the familiar shade of pink, and I thought of my first encounter with the serena. Back then, it announced itself with a song.

But not tonight.

I fastened the blade around my hip and donned my coat. It was still damp from yesterday and weighed me down. As I nudged the door wide, it creaked on its hinges, and instead of the light from green orbs, I faced utter darkness. Spiders of dread scuttled down my back, stirring the hair with their tiny legs and filling me with an overwhelming need to rip off my clothes and shake them free. I rubbed my arms.

I stepped out and into the lingering odour of mould and wet timber. With my hands outstretched, I patted the walls, feeling my way to the hatch. As if coated by a layer of moss, the wood was slick to the touch. An image forced itself into my mind that this ship sank to the bottom of the Great Atlantic long ago, and I was nothing but a corpse, shuffling along its empty hallways. I shivered and chided myself for the foolish thoughts. The corridor stretched on forever, and I stumbled twice before I finally reached the square door leading to the upper deck.

I pushed the hatch, and the clear moonlight spilt into the hallway.

The smell struck me—the sweet and creamy scent of cloves mixed with flowers in full bloom. It was faint, but it couldn't escape my heightened senses. Sweat covered my palms, and my pulse quickened while all the nerves in my body whizzed back and forth like a swarm of crazed hornets.

I clambered out and was relieved to see the mages. A handful leaned over the taffrail, searching the waters, while others stood in small groups, conversing in hushed voices. Anxious cries drifted from the second ship, and the green lights flickered on and off as the men signalled each other from the crow's nest. I made my way across the deck.

A woman grabbed my sleeve. Her gaping eyes looked ready to pop out of their sockets. 'Valgsi, something stirs in the night,' she whispered.

'Don't be afraid,' I said, prying open her fingers. 'Skaldir is watching over us.'

She licked her lips. 'Agtarr's Warrior of Death rides this vessel, Valgsi. I can smell his rotting flesh… hear the hollow footsteps—'

'Enough,' I told her. 'Get hold of yourself before you infect others with your fear.'

She gave me a wounded look and drew back.

I reached Mirable's pen. Solas squatted in front of it and turned his head up at me. His face was pallid, and beads of moisture settled on his broad forehead. The Varl sat on his hunches in the centre of the cage—a dark shape against the moonlight.

'What's going on?' I asked, crouching next to Solas.

He motioned at Mirable with his chin. 'I think he's sick.'

I seized the Varl's hand through the bars. It felt hot and huge in my grip, more like a bear's paw than a human hand. His fingers curled around mine, and his sharp nails pinched my skin. I jerked free. 'Mirable, what is it? What's wrong with you?'

He twisted his neck, and I saw that Solas was right. Mirable's whites changed from red to yellow, and pus gathered in the corners of his eyes. His wide nostrils flared, as if struggling to bring in ample air while his lungs rattled with each exhale.

'I found them,' he rasped, and the rancid stink that wafted from his mouth made me gag. It brought to mind bloating corpses left to rot in the heat. 'As promised.'

Solas moved away, pressing his palm to his nose.

'What do you mean *them*?' I said.

Mirable tapped a finger against his blackened lips. 'Shhhh… All you have to do is listen…'

I strained my ears, but apart from the Varl's laboured breathing, I couldn't hear a thing. 'I don't—'

Solas shot to his feet. He leaned forward with his head cocked and his palms flattened against his thighs. A thick vein throbbed in the centre of his forehead.

'Are you sure it's the serena?' I whispered, but Mirable only stared at me with those yellowing eyes.

I got up, and dizziness surged through me. If it was the serena, why didn't I hear the song? Lumi was dead, and my heart was free, which should've made me vulnerable. I scanned the deck to find Solas's look of concentration on other faces. The mages stood with their mouths ajar, and their necks stretched as if trying to catch some subtle note. But not everyone listened. Those with no romantic attachments, exchanged glances, asking questions of each other. If the Varl was right and the creature was upon us, I had to act fast.

I searched for Galdra and caught her standing by the stern, hands folded across her chest. The silver light of the moon reflected in her luminous eyes. In her grey robe and with her dark hair floating down her back she resembled a phantom from my childhood tales. As I walked towards her, an old rhyme echoed in my head.

The ghost is here.
The ghost is near.
It floats to your right.
It floats to your left.
It follows your every step.

It was a silly little rhyme my mother used to recite before a game of chase when Stromhold's walls vibrated with our laughter as we tried to outrun each other. When the last verse faded from my mind, the hatch banged open, and Goro-Khan climbed onto the deck. Seeing him and knowing what was about to happen tightened the noose of panic around my neck. From the moment I woke up and opened my ears to the silence, ghosts invaded my thoughts, and I sensed the gods shaping our future even in their sleep.

‘I think this is it,’ I said, wiping my sweaty hands on my trousers.

Galdra gave me a haunted look. ‘Is this part of your plan?’

I wanted to say yes, but something still didn’t feel right.

‘What in Skaldir’s name is this?’ Goro-Khan roared into the night. From afar, a resounding crack answered. The sound woke another memory of me laying in my bed in Stromhold and listening to Grand Isfjells shedding ice chunks that struck the sea with a thundering noise.

Goro marched to the nearest group. ‘Is this secret gathering your way of trying to make me laugh?’ he asked. ‘Because if it is…’ Something caught his attention, and he trailed off.

The shallow waves dissipated, and the ocean’s surface turned into a shell-pink mirror, reflecting the light back at the moon. A veil of yellow mist rose from the ocean, shimmering like snow crystals hit by the sun. It slid across the deck, weaving between the mages who stood mesmerised, their eyes transfixed on the water. The fog settled on my skin, and the sensation was that of walking face-first into a sheet of silken web. When the air grew rich with the smell of cornflowers, I knew the creatures had found us.

The Varl let out a deep and mournful howl.

Terror worse than I experienced watching Haamu crawling free of Trofn’s box gripped me. My heart rushed to my throat, blocking the airways and making it difficult to draw a clean breath. An urge to empty my bladder came over me, and I had to fight the impulse to run and hide in my cabin. My mouth dried out of all moisture.

'Now,' I told Galdra.

'But—'

'Do it now!'

For a heartbeat, I thought she'd refuse. I was about to grab her by the shoulders and give her a shake when she closed her eyes. The eerie light bathed her features, and the yellow hue caught in her eyelashes, making them sparkle. Galdra tipped her head back and uttered a string of words I hoped would be our salvation.

A current of warm energy whooshed into my face. My skin absorbed it, and I felt it tingling and looping through my bones. Some mages gasped, others cast questioning looks our way. Galdra's magic filled my ears, drowning out all sounds, including my voice. My head swam. The green lights still flickered on the second ship, but I could no longer hear the crew. Sweat stood out on Galdra's brow, and her lips trembled. I prayed to all three gods to give her strength to hold the spell.

I marched across the deck to the first group of mages and signalled them to step clear of the handrail. Most of them answered with a frown. A man with his long hair tied in knots scratched his temple and tried to speak. His lips moved, but I was deaf to the sound. A woman with crescent earrings tapped her left ear as if to expel excess water. Despite their confusion, they let me steer them away from the edge. As long as Galdra chanted her spell they were safe from the serena, but I didn't want to take chances.

The only person who would die tonight was the Laughing God.

I dashed from group to group while scanning the waves for the creature, but apart from the shifting mist, I couldn't see any movement.

I grabbed the mage with a pointed chin, gesturing for him to follow the others. He glared at me, then pulled free of my grip and hastened to Goro-Khan's side. The Laughing God stood with his left hand resting against the mainmast. He tipped his head to the side, and his face had an expression of a man trying hard to remember some important detail. His eyes narrowed, and his right foot tapped the deck in a steady rhythm.

When the mage patted him on the shoulder, Goro jerked as if stabbed by a hot poker, then swatted at the man's hand. Spots of colour entered the mage's cheeks. I crossed my palms in front of him, hoping to convey that he should leave Goro alone. He grimaced and hesitated, but after a few moments, spun on his heels and strode away.

I cast one more look at the Laughing God. Everything about his posture made me think of Njall before he dropped his spear to answer the creature's call. My lips curled. Solas would have his justice, and so would I.

I walked back to Mirable's cage while the mist snaked around my ankles like a yellow serpent. I tapped Solas's arm and pointed to the mages standing in a loose group near the stern.

He frowned and attempted to speak.

I twisted my head from side to side, pointing at my ears. After a few failed efforts at explaining, Solas gave a sharp nod and hastened across the deck to join the mages. I looked at Mirable, who sat in his pen, scratching and poking at his ears, as deaf as the rest of us.

Satisfied, I turned my attention to Goro-Khan.

His left hand still rested against the mainmast, and he clutched his chest with his right. Near the stern, the mages formed a semi-circle—dark silhouettes draped in green cloaks, looking from Goro to the ocean and back at him. Some examined the yellow hue clinging to their fingers as if seeking to determine its nature. No one seemed to notice Galdra, who stood to the side, with her palms facing the sky. I could just make out her face in the moonlight—her lids were closed, and she appeared to be in a deep trance.

Someone pointed at the translucent shapes of pinks and yellows, shifting on the waves and glistening like dewdrops on a glass. I counted at least six, and it chilled my blood. I tried telling myself it was an illusion spawned by the serena to drive fear into us. I waved at the mages to keep their distance. A few of them ignored me and edged closer to the taffrail, but to my relief, no one looked ready to jump.

Goro-Khan stared at the water with wide eyes. The mist fused with his cheeks, turning his skin waxen. His eye twitched rapidly. A single thought swished through my mind that maybe Goro's magic made him immune to the song. I wrapped my fingers around the hilt of my sword. My hands were sleek with sweat, and my muscles tensed in readiness. I sent a prayer to Skaldir. She was a fickle goddess who helped and hindered me in equal measure, but to fight and win this battle, I'd need both her rage and her strength.

My eardrums popped like a bubble burst with a pin.

The song exploded in my ears—a rich ensemble of voices and instruments. Panic bolted my feet to the deck, and my heart hammered against my ribs.

Something snapped—a harp string strained to its limits, and the night filled with jarring sounds as though the choir of expert musicians turned into a band of children who couldn't strike a pure note. I clapped my palms to my ears.

Galdra cupped a hand around her nose. I glanced from her to the ocean, my jaw dropped.

The Varl indeed made good on his promise, for instead of one serena, he'd found a whole nest of them. At least a dozen surrounded our ship, and more writhed near the second vessel. Seeing all those milky eyes and wide maws full of needle-shaped teeth filled me with a powerful urge to scream. The creatures, coated in shimmering scales, twisted and twined, filling the air with the clatter of sea shells trapped in their sandy hair. The pink water reflected the shapes as though each had a twin lurking beneath the surface.

Galdra's magic no longer shielded me, but instead of Lumi singing from the depths, my ears rang with ugly music. Why wasn't I leaping into the serenas' deadly embrace?

Goro-Khan's voice reached me through the cacophony. 'My son,' he called, leaning forward. Against the whites, his dark irises looked like nubs of obsidian. 'This cannot be…'

I watched him, afraid to breathe for fear of breaking his illusion. The ship with its crew faded into the background as all my attention focused on the self-proclaimed god who crushed Lumi's heart. The moment that would mark the end of his reign had come at last. My pulse quickened, and I had to force myself to stillness.

The Laughing God took a hesitant step and licked his lips. 'Is it truly you?' he asked in a hoarse whisper, blinking at the writhing creatures.

The musical notes grew darker, and the change stirred the hair on my arms and legs. Goro-Khan bit into his knuckles, as if stifling a cry. His mask of self-control shattered, and he aged right in front of me. Gone was the cruel twist to his mouth and the twitch in his left eye that everyone came to recognise as the harbinger of pain. In his crumpled face, I glimpsed the man he used to be before Yomu's tragic end. The leader who kept the mages together and made them laugh on the days when the hope dimmed and the longing to reclaim Antaya threatened to overwhelm. Instead of the cruel tyrant who made people laugh with fear, I saw the father, ready to destroy the world to get his son back.

The old Jarin's voice drifted through the cracks in the glass. *'Not so different from you then.'*

My whole body tensed. 'I'm nothing like him,' I said through clenched teeth. The air became too hot to breathe, and I felt the beads of sweat forming on my chest.

'You're more alike than you think.'

I wanted to draw my sword and charge him, to prove him wrong and carve him out of my brain.

'You can keep me away, but you cannot silence me. The mages, you, the Laughing God… we're all the same. You only need to look at me… at yourself to see it. There's a reason you chose the mirror as my prison.'

'It was Galdra who chose it, not me.'

The Jarin in my head laughed, and he sounded like a man mocking his own insanity.

The flames of fury seared through me, and I jabbed a finger at my reflection. 'You let everyone die!' I screamed. 'You didn't stop Hyllus from murdering our father. You left Mother to freeze alone. It was you who shattered Lumi's heart. You're the reason Mirable is rotting from the inside, and Fjo—' My voice caught. I was unworthy of speaking her name. She was my only source of light, and I extinguished it by following the Valgsi's path.

'You're asking yourself why you can't hear the music. While you're chasing phantoms, she's saving your life.'

'Yomu, is that truly you?' Goro called again. He curled his arms over his head. 'Answer me!'

The elation I felt moments ago drained away. As the heavy weight of exhaustion pressed down on my shoulders, my legs wobbled. I wanted to crawl to my musty cabin, lie down on the berth and sleep for eternity.

Goro-Khan tipped his head back and laughed at the sky. It was a pure and joyful sound without a drop of malice in it. The mages stared at him, but Galdra's magic spared them from having to listen to Goro's emotion-choked voice. I wasn't so lucky, and I knew it would haunt me for the rest of my days.

'Death breeds more death,' the old Jarin said. *'It doesn't have to end this way.'*

'Skaldir be praised,' Goro cried while tears flowed freely down his cheeks. 'I'm coming, my son. We'll laugh together again.'

I don't know if it was me or the old Jarin, but when Goro-Khan ran past me, I made a move as if to grab him. But then my ears filled with the echoes of Lumi's heart shattering between Goro-Khan's fingers, and I let my hand fall.

'This is *exactly* how it should end,' I said, turning my back to the mirror.

The Laughing God wiped the tears off and seized the ship's railing. I watched him as he climbed, laughing and calling Yomu's name. He missed his left shoe, and his naked foot slid on the metal.

When he reached the highest rung, he paused.

It was as if some ancient instinct, or maybe a warning from the Goddess of Destruction, stopped him in his tracks.

The yellow mist rose and fell to the beat of the sinister song while the serenas shifted above water, clicking their teeth.

An inhuman screech tore the air.

The melody wavered, and a deep frown replaced the joy on Goro's face.

Galdra raced across the deck with her hands outstretched and fingers curled like talons. Her nose and chin were all bloody.

The mages screamed in unison, and similar cries drifted from the neighbouring ship.

The spell was broken.

Galdra dashed past me, and I caught a fistful of her dress. She yanked free. The dress ripped in my grip, and I was left holding a piece of grey cloth.

Before I could do anything else, she uttered another terrifying scream and pushed Goro-Khan.

His bare foot slipped, and he banged his shin on the taffrail. He flailed, lost his balance, and went over. The last word that came out of his mouth before he hit the water was his son's name.

Pink scales flashed, teeth snapped as the serenas dragged him under the surface.

XXV

There was another giant splash. I whirled around to witness the chaos.

The mages climbed over the taffrail, laughing and thanking Skaldir for bringing them home at last. Some cried names, others jumped into the pinkish depths in silence, their faces beaming. As each person took their deadly dive, the serena closest to them sprang up, wrapped its shimmering tail around their waists, and pulled them under. The song turned even more frantic, and the fetid odour replaced the creamy scent of cloves and flowers.

I seized Galdra's shoulders and shook her. 'What did you do?'

She bared her bloodstained teeth and laughed. The madness in that sound iced over the marrow in my bones. I let go of her.

Her translucent eyes rolled in her sockets, and she collapsed onto the deck, unconscious.

I ran to a mage with a greying beard and tried to pull him off the railing. He gave me a wild look, then kicked me in the stomach. The breath went out of me, and I doubled over. With a chant, the man launched himself at the waves.

The song was so distorted now it caused me physical pain. Each jagged note sliced through my brain like a blunt saw. I pressed my hands to my ears, shouting at anyone who would listen to stop this insanity and see through the deception.

But I was screaming at the dead.

All around me, the mages threw their lives away without a backward glance. Only a handful remained unaffected. A group of them huddled near Mirable's cage, their horror-stricken faces turned to the east, where their loved ones awaited their return. Judging by the sounds coming from the second ship, the other crew fared no better.

I glimpsed Solas amidst the chaos.

His robe was undone, and he gazed at the ocean, oblivious to the world around him. He raised his hand and waved at someone that existed only in his mind.

I ran to him and slapped his face. 'Solas, look at me! Whatever you think is out there, it's an illusion.'

The yellow mist danced in his pupils. 'All these years, I believed my parents to be dead…' He raked his fingers down his cheeks.

I shook him. 'Your parents *are* dead.'

'You're wrong.' He pointed at the serena that stretched its hideous maw in welcome. 'They're alive. Can't you see?' His earnest eyes met mine. 'Isn't there anyone waiting for you, Jarin?'

My vision blurred, and the pain that gripped the back of my throat had nothing to do with the music. 'No,' I whispered and let go of him.

Solas opened his arms wide. 'Mother. Father. I'm coming.' And with that, he jumped.

I balled my fists and screamed at the sky. 'They believed you were watching over them! They sailed to witness your awakening.'

'But it was you who led them to their deaths…' the old Jarin said.

His emotions seeped through the cracks in the glass, saturating my heart with grief and guilt. Yes, my desire for vengeance killed them like it killed Skari and Lumi. When the female mage spoke of the Warrior of Death riding this ship, she was right. I was the warrior marked by destruction, holding the sword of death.

I unsheathed Skaldir's blade and lifted it over the water where the serenas feasted on the loveless hearts. Their shining scales reflected in the steel. Every fibre in my being screamed at me to toss it into the ocean and get rid of this curse once and for all. The witches in my head cackled while the old Jarin begged me to smash the mirror and set him free. My arms trembled, but like on the day I'd learned about my destiny, I couldn't bring myself to do it. The pull of destruction was stronger than my will, and no matter how hard I tried, I couldn't win this battle.

Skaldir called, and my duty was to answer.

Mirable's growl snapped me back to the present. 'Let me out,' he snarled, rattling his pen.

I shoved the sword back in its sheath. 'Close your ears,' I told Mirable. 'You fought off these creatures before, and you can do it again.'

The Varl slammed his body against the bars. 'Let me out!'

I went down on my knees by the cage. The eyes that glared at me were no longer human. The whites turned the colour of putrid flesh, and yellow liquid oozed from the corners. Mirable's lips were pulled back, exposing the black tongue that brought to mind a blood-swollen leech. The stink of spoiled meat wafted from his mouth. Everyone thought he was special, and even Hyllus called him his greatest creation. But the magic that transformed Mirable into the Varl came from the corrupted source, and nothing healthy could grow from corruption. My friend, who crossed the Great Atlantic, hoping to find the cure, decayed right before my eyes, and I didn't know how to help him. To save Fjola, he let the monster in, and it was eating him from the inside.

Mirable flung himself at the cage, again and again, howling and gnashing his teeth. In response to his lunacy, the song grew more erratic as though the musicians plucked the strings at random without caring much for the harmony. But I knew that to Mirable's ear, it was the sweetest creation. During our first encounter with the serena, the creature conjured up a beautiful maiden to lure him into the inky depths. What illusion did they weave this time to induce such frenzy?

'Get a hold of yourself,' I pleaded with him. 'We'll fix this, find the way to—'

'There is no way,' Mirable snarled. Blood covered his forehead from the constant bashing. 'You made a promise, so release me.' He grabbed the bars, threw his head back, and howled.

Yes, I promised to end his life, but how could I?

I slammed my fist into the metal, and my knuckles exploded with agony. 'I can't do it!'

Mirable pressed his face through the gap. His right eye bulged hideously. 'You can, and you will.' Some lucidity came back to his voice, and he sounded almost human again.

'But you're my friend. Maybe the only one I have left.' Hot tears filled my eyes. 'What am I saying? You're more than that. You're my family.'

He yelped like a wounded cub. 'And nothing will ever change that. Death is but a stall on the market of life, and we all must trade there. Today I wish to trade my pain, and I need you to keep your end of the bargain.'

He barked and succumbed to the madness once more.

The thrashing resumed.

I hid my face in my hands while the world around me crumbled. The old Jarin watched me through the glass, and reflected in his eyes were my own tears. I slid down in front of the mirror, and he followed suit. I entrusted him with my emotions, and some trickled through the fissures.

'If you do as he asks, you'll never forgive yourself.'

'And if I don't, he'll never forgive me.'

The old Jarin reached through the crack and squeezed my hand. The connection awakened memories of Vester and my first meeting with Mirable. How he barged into the tavern, waving a jug of wine, asking if I minded company. He was dressed in colourful garb and had his crimson turban wrapped around his head. Later, when I promised to ask the witches about his future, his brown eyes glinted with excitement. I was born under the lucky star, he told me. If only we had known…

A sob racked my chest. Nothing was left of that merchant. The magic destroyed him the way it destroyed Antaya and all its mages.

'Yet here you are, trying to awaken the Goddess of Destruction once more,' the Stromhold Jarin said.

I struck my temple, where Skaldir's mark held me to my fate. 'She's too powerful. I can't resist her.'

'Her power is the key…'

I looked at myself through the mirror—red-rimmed eyes, mouth shaped like a down-turned crescent, tangled hair, and quaking shoulders. I was my biggest enemy, and I erected the mirror to save me from myself. But no glass was thick enough to contain the memories and emotions that made me who I was. My dear friend was dying, and my heart wanted to prolong his life for as long as possible. To listen would be a selfish act, and I'd be repaying Mirable's kindness with suffering. I had no magic to heal his wounds, but I could give him the gift of release. My father trained me how to fight. My mother showed me how to love. From Fjola, I'd learned the power of devotion, and from Njall, loyalty. But Mirable taught me the greatest lesson of all—knowing when to let go.

I straightened my back. 'I'm ready.'

'What about me?'

'I'll come back for you.'

The old Jarin seemed to understand because he nodded and said no more.

I removed my hands from my face. Mirable still struggled against the cage that held him hostage to life. I dried the last of my tears with my sleeve.

I stood up. 'You,' I said, pointing at the few remaining mages. 'I need you to break the seal.'

They looked at each other as if my request was a madman's rave.

‘Open the cage,’ I ordered.

Two men rushed to obey. They placed their palms on the top of the pen and recited the spell in trembling voices. A light weaved between the bars like a green scarf, and it was followed by a soft click. The mages jumped back as if the enclosure was set on fire.

Mirable crashed into the bars once more. The door flew off its hinges and clattered across the deck. The Varl scrambled out of his prison and bolted for the ship’s railing.

‘Mirable!’ I called after him.

He skidded to a stop.

I held my breath, hoping against hope he’d refuse the bargain and choose life.

The moonlight illuminated his varlish silhouette, and the mist plucked at his fur with its yellow fingers. Mirable threw his head back and uttered one last howl. My heart echoed the lonely sound before the night carried it away into the arms of silence.

The Varl scaled the taffrail and jumped.

The song died.

I thought of Agtarr’s Chamber of Torments, where all soulless creatures met their end. ‘I’ll see you soon, my friend,’ I whispered into the darkness.

XXVI

I stood at the ship's bow, watching the horizon. At first, it was a grey strip wedged between Nordur and the Great Atlantic, but as the vessel closed the distance, it took on the shape of mountain ranges that separated my homeland from the rest of the world. The jagged peaks draped in snowy capes presided over Nordur like ancient sages born when the land was still in its cradle. I glanced up. The sun had set less than an hour ago, but stars dotted the sky, shimmering a soft green.

The Night of Norrsken was fast approaching, and so was my return home.

With each passing day, the divine call grew more intense, and the need to answer was impossible to resist. I was a fool, thinking I could free myself from Skaldir's hold and stop the unstoppable. I rubbed the Valgsi's mark on my temple. It felt hard and hot to the touch, throbbing under my fingers like a vein filled with magic instead of blood. This night, the stars would align, and Skaldir's essence would spill across the sky. The sword would absorb it and infuse my soul with its power. This fusion would sever the chain of dreams and bring about the awakening. I held on to my hope that Skaldir would restore Antaya and give back lives taken away with such cruelty. First Lumi's, and then Mirable's. I couldn't just abandon them. To think of Mirable locked away in Agtarr's Chamber of Torments to suffer for eternity tore at my soul. If there was even a slight chance of saving him, I had to take it.

My hand strayed to the hilt. Torgal and his warriors would be guarding the harbour, but only death would prevent me from climbing the hill and breaking the bonds of sleep. My muscles thrummed with the force of destruction, and whoever barred my path would face Skaldir's rage.

As the nightfall stretched its wings over the world, Nords sought to burn the darkness away with torches and lanterns. From afar, they looked like glowing embers scattered along the shore. It seemed a lifetime ago when I departed Hvitur hoping to discover the mysterious Shinpi. None believed I'd find it, and on some nights I wished I never did. My original crew was gone, replaced by a handful of grieving mages and an enchantress driven mad by vengeance. Hardly a force to be reckoned with.

Before the serenas and Galdra's breakdown, I hoped to use her illusion to slip through Hvitur unseen. But since the night of Goro's death, Galdra changed from the powerful enchantress to a woman confined to her cabin, muttering to no one and laughing at nothing. The few attempts to reason with her ended in her trying to claw my eyes out while raving and shrieking. Whenever she got agitated, blood gushed from her nose in crimson runnels. She refused food and drank only water offered to her by a female mage who made it her duty to care for her. I left them to it and planned for the worst.

The few mages who survived the encounter with the ocean creatures lost all interest in restoring their precious city and tried to talk me into sailing back to Shinpi. When one of them suggested it the first time, I laughed so hard it brought on tears. After all the sacrifices and years of waiting, they wanted to return to their desolate island, where they could waste their magic on chopping wood and ploughing fields.

'No wonder you lost the war,' I said in between bursts of laughter. 'Your Laughing God gave his life to get you here, and all you do is whine.'

The woman called Annis folded her hands across her chest. 'We only wish to see our families.'

'I thought Skaldir was your family.'

Dion, the man with a long face and silver hair, bowed. 'I say this with respect, Valgsi, but when we left Shinpi, we had Goro-Khan and two ships full of mages. Now look at us. Our enchantress doesn't make a word of sense, and we spent our magic navigating this vessel. We don't stand a chance against a village of Nordern warriors.'

'I don't expect you to fight,' I said to Dion. 'But I need you to hold them off until I reach the hilltop. If you fail, our sacrifices will have been for nothing.'

‘We’ll do as you ask, Valgsi,’ Annis said, inclining her head. ‘May Skaldir illuminate your path.’

I remembered my friends who crossed the Great Atlantic without fear and how I failed them all. I betrayed Njall by putting Fjola in harm’s way. The flat look he gave me before his ship took to the ocean conveyed more than any words—in exchange for his unbending loyalty, I almost got his sister killed. Mirable trusted me to find the cure for his sickness, but all I did was open the cage and deliver him into the arms and jaws of the serenas. And Fjola… the Jarin trapped behind the glass whispered her name over and over.

As the evening deepened, an eerie hush fell over the ship. The cold burned the tips of my ears, and the air formed a foggy cloud in front of my mouth. Closer to the shore, the snow drifted in tiny flecks, and the biting wind lashed my face and hair. From time to time, a green ribbon of light travelled across the sky, weaving through the glowing stars. My mind hummed, and if I listened hard enough, I could make out a female voice calling me forth to claim the power.

On the day of Mirable’s death, Jarin from Stromhold told me Skaldir’s power was the key, but in my nineteen years, all the keys I’d ever found unlocked the doors to grief and misery. Even the door to Hyllus’s citadel led to loss as I watched the Varls rip Skari into pieces.

I tightened my grip on the sword. I was born on the Night of Norrsken, and Skaldir marked me as her Valgsi. On the hour of my twentieth birthday, the world would change, and my life as Jarin Olversson would come to an end.

Voices drifted on the wind, and dark silhouettes moved about the harbour, waving their torches and bracing to defend Hvitur with their lives. My uncle, Torgal, would be among them. And Njall, if he made it back. Inside my leather gloves, my fingers grew slick with sweat. I didn't want to fight any of them, but if they stood in my path, Skaldir would force my hand. There was no denying the Goddess of Destruction, for tonight was her night, and her sword would carve the way to the hillside.

'Prepare for docking,' Dion called.

Boots slapped against the deck as the mages rushed to obey, shouting commands and readying the ropes.

The time for thinking was over.

With the help of magic, the mages stirred the vessel into the slip. Nords watched them manoeuvre the ship, but none offered to help—we were the enemy. As the ship glided into the gap between the dock and another barge, it chafed against the wharf with a crunch and a thud. Laughter rippled through the shadows, and I cringed, thinking of Njall and his exceptional navigation skills. To those assembled on the beach, my mighty crew must've looked like a bunch of children at play.

When the vessel was moored, I turned up my collar and stepped onto the gangway. The night was in full flight, and Skaldir's magic formed green wavelets across the sky. If not for the grim circumstances, I'd have stopped to admire this celestial display. The bridge swung back and forth, and my stomach churned with each sway while my feet urged me to break into a run. The need to reach the hilltop was so overwhelming I had to force myself to calm down.

Nords, my uncle among them, waited with hands on their weapons and shadows dancing across their hardened faces. The wind gusted around them, eager to extinguish their torches. Torgal stood at the head of the assembly, with his legs apart and his hand resting on the axe. During my absence, his hair grew longer, reaching past his ears, and he gained a fresh scar on his forehead. With his broad nose and sharp jaw, he was a spitting image of my father. Torgal and Eyvar were blood-brothers, and seeing him after all these months brought on a new tide of grief. When Father was alive, they were at odds, but Torgal was the only family I had left.

When I reached the end of the gangway, my fingers refused to let go of the rope. I drew a deep breath, filling my lungs with the harsh winter air. It was the smell of home, my childhood, and Lumi… As the old Jarin stirred behind the glass, I scanned the shadows, looking for the only person who mattered to him now. Was Fjola among the warriors, waiting to sink her dagger into my heart?

I stepped onto the dock, and the mages filed in behind me. During the months of sailing, I wished for the solid land under my boots, and I took a minute to savour the feeling. No more rolling waves, wobbling knees, and nausea. In this rare moment of gratitude, I made a silent promise to never board another ship.

'Nephew,' Torgal called. His voice cut through the night like a razor blade. 'I can't let you pass.'

I halted halfway down the deck, meeting my uncle's eyes. They were grey, like Father's. 'I'm not asking your permission.'

His men turned their heads and murmured.

I pushed back my shoulders. Every Nord present on the beach would look for any signs of weakness.

'This is my land, and I won't let you destroy it,' Torgal said. 'Surrender your sword and tell your mages to stand down.'

'You know I can't do that.'

A green veil shrouded the sky, bathing the village in an unearthly light. Behind me, the mages uttered a sound of awe.

My uncle looked up, and his hand tightened around the long handle of his battle axe. 'You bring destruction to my door.' His gaze shifted from the sky to my face. 'It's Agtarr's mercy my brother isn't here. It would shame him to no end to see his cherished son, whom he protected all his life, embrace the vengeful goddess.'

My cheeks grew hot. 'You're one to speak of shame. Father knew of my destiny, and so did you. When I first arrived here, you had the chance to kill me the way you killed my grandfather.'

'I did not kill Bodvar,' Torgal said through clenched teeth. He jabbed his finger at Skaldir's sword. 'My father sealed his fate with this cursed blade. It drove him mad like it's driving you mad. The gods made a sacrifice so we could live. Eyvar understood this, and so did your mother. Aliya gave up everything to keep you from harm. She even moved into the tower of cold stone to shield you from the prophecy.'

My mother's name stirred the old sorrow, but only Jarin behind the glass had to endure the true weight of it. 'Mother tried so hard to save me from myself she forgot why the goddess chose me in the first place. It was your feud with my father that made her climb the hill and give birth under the green sky.'

'I went up the hilltop to stop Bodvar from destroying the world, and now, you defile his memory by embracing those who practice the foul arts.'

'My mages have no wish to fight you. Let us pass without bloodshed.'

Torgal laughed. It was a bleak sound that told me this exchange could only end one way. 'You're a dreamer, Jarin, and dreamers have no place among the living.'

Green spots swam in my eyes, and I wrapped my fingers around the hilt. It felt alive to the touch, vibrating with mysterious energy. The hour of awakening grew near. I needed to get to the hilltop and slit the sword into the stone before it was too late. 'We're all dreamers, Uncle. You dream of my mother, and I of the ice demon who killed her.' I swept my hand at the warriors. 'Your men dream of battle, while my mages of a city to call home. The gods themselves are plagued by nightmares.'

I released the blade from its sheathe. The script was glowing with celestial light, giving the illusion of being on fire. I brought it out in front of me. 'It's time for us to wake up and see the world for what it is. A place ruled by the beings whose actions divided us from the beginning of time. I've learned much in Shinpi, and the stories I was fed as a boy were the makings of men like you, set in the old ways and unwilling to speak the truth. You can't create a peaceful world while asking others to live a lie. Our gods are the proof of that.'

The ethereal light shifted across Torgal's face, making him look more like a ghost than a fierce warrior ready to take on his last living relative. He freed his battle axe from its holder. 'I ask again. Turn back and take your mages with you.'

Behind me, Dion whispered, 'What do we do?'

I angled my head. 'When this fight is over, strike back with your magic and hold them off until I reach the hillside. Try your best not to kill anyone.'

He responded with a snort.

'Jarin, I suggest you listen to your uncle,' a familiar voice called.

I snapped my head up to see a warrior pushing through the crowd. He came to stand at Torgal's side and planted his spear in front of him.

The sword trembled in my hand. 'You made it.'

'No thanks to you,' Njall replied, scanning the dock. Metal bands bound his long beard, and he fastened his hair into a thick braid at the back of his neck.

My eyes felt gritty, and I had to stifle the urge to rub at them. Njall was like a brother to me. He joined me on my quest to kill Hyllus, and he stayed at my side until fate separated us in Shinpi. I admired him for his strength and loyalty, but none of this mattered tonight.

'Where's Mirable?' he asked.

I did my hardest to keep my voice from trembling. 'Not here.'

Njall's expression hardened. 'So you killed him too.'

I wanted to explain, to assure him I had nothing to do with the merchant's death, but it would've been a lie. Mirable died because I let Galdra into my mind.

He glanced up at the dancing lights. 'It's not too late. Surrender your blade and leave the gods to sleep in peace.'

Njall could never understand how impossible his request was. Skaldir would never allow me to obey him. Tonight I was her Valgsi, and my feet would carry me to the hilltop even if Njall gouged my eyes out. 'You told me to fight my destiny, I must accept it first, and you were right. No more running.'

'After everything that happened, are you really going to choose destruction?'

'The choice was taken from me twenty winters ago.'

Njall spat. 'You're a coward, and to think my sister wasted so much time loving you.'

His words drove the air out of me, and the old Jarin gasped. 'Where is she?' I asked, no longer caring if I sounded afraid. 'Is she dead?'

Njall said nothing.

'Is Fjola dead?' I screamed. A giant crack echoed inside my head, and I realised it was the mirror. Jarin from Stromhold smashed his fist into the glass, and new fissures split the surface.

'She's dead to you,' Njall said, pointing his spear at me.

My sword arm jerked up, but it wasn't me who guided the blade. Skaldir's rage turned my vision green, and my blood simmered with suppressed fury. The time was running short, and the goddess felt threatened. Sweat trickled down my temples, and my birthmark pulsed in a steady rhythm.

Torgal placed a hand on Njall's shoulder. 'This fight is mine and mine alone.'

For a heartbeat, I thought Njall would refuse, but his discipline and respect for Nordur's laws prevailed. The leader had the right to first battle, and if he exercised it, no man was allowed to interfere. Njall stabbed the spear into the sand.

Nords formed a loose circle around Torgal.

'Be ready,' I told Dion before striding across the deck to face my uncle.

The warriors let me through, then closed the circle behind me.

Torgal hefted his battle axe. It looked huge and heavy in his grip—a weapon worthy of Nordur's ruler. 'May the God of Death have mercy on your soul.'

I planted my feet firmly on the sand. The notion of fighting him made me sick, but like on my birth night, Skaldir left me no choice. 'Agtarr holds no power over my soul.'

'You have well and truly lost your way,' Torgal said as he advanced.

XXVII

Fjola strained against the rope until the searing pain in her wrists made her cry out in frustration. She fought the restraints for what seemed like hours, with no luck. Her dark thoughts turned to her brother and his foolish attempt at protecting her. Njall told her he wanted to discuss Jarin's imminent arrival in Hvitur and the steps they needed to take to stop him from climbing the hill.

'I have a plan,' he said. 'And you may be the only person who can carry it out.'

Fjola followed him into Eyvar's old room, eager to hear what Njall had to say. She didn't like the look in Torgal's eyes whenever she mentioned Jarin and considered her brother her only ally. Njall knew how she felt about Jarin, but when she turned, he snatched her daggers, and locked her arms behind her back.

'It's for your own good,' he told her.

At first, she pleaded with him, but when that fell on deaf ears, she'd put up a fight, kicking and cursing as Njall forced her into the chair and bound her wrists with a thick string.

'I'll untie you when this is over,' her brother said. Then he left.

Fjola called after him, but the only answer was the echo of his heavy boots as he crossed the hallway on his way out. When the silence fell, she broke it by screaming and swearing until her voice went hoarse. Her struggles were in vain. When Njall made up his mind, there was no way of changing it, and no one would dare to aid her out of fear of offending him. Fjola had to escape on her own.

She looked around the chamber. Apart from a single bed in the corner and a worn iron shield on the wall, there was little else. This room was as dead as Eyvar. She never met Jarin's father but often wondered about the man who became the Guardian of Stromhold, set to protect Nordur from the Varls. Jarin thought highly of him, but she noticed a faint note of resentment there too. It was to do with the lie about his birth and how Eyvar withheld the story of Skaldir's blade from his son to keep him safe. What was it with families and their need to do wrong things for the right reasons?

Fjola wriggled her hands repeatedly. Her wrists burned from the rope chafing against her skin, but she gritted her teeth and kept on turning and twisting. She only needed to loosen the bond on one wrist to pull it free. The chair creaked under her weight, and she was sure the worn legs would splinter. How much time did she have? There was no window in the chamber, so no way of knowing the hour, but she thought she heard voices coming from the beach, or maybe it was her vexed brain playing tricks on her. Either way, the day was fading, and if she didn't get out of this room, Jarin would die, or worse, release the Wrath of Skaldir upon the world. If that happened, none would be left standing.

Fjola squeezed her eyes shut and redoubled her efforts. Her brows knitted together, and sweat stood out on her forehead as she rotated her wrists, wiggling and pulling at the same time.

She uttered another curse and clenched her jaw. Her brother infuriated her like no one else. Since their return to Hvitur, he refused to leave her side. After the healer stitched her cheek, Fjola developed a fever. She lay in bed, falling in and out of consciousness, vaguely aware of Njall pleading with Yldir to spare her. In her darkest hours, she prayed herself, not to the God of Life but to Agtarr, asking him to send his Warrior of Death to end her suffering. But Jarin was right about one thing—the gods were fickle creatures who seldom cared about the woes of mortals. Eventually, the fever broke, forcing Fjola to contend with life once more.

A sharp pain told Fjola she'd torn the skin. Blood seeped into the threads, and each movement became pure agony. Her mouth trembled, and the wound on her cheek rippled under the dressing as the strain pulled at the edges. Galdra's cut was deep, and the stitches were still fresh. She couldn't afford to rip them, but she couldn't afford to stay prisoner to this chair.

With a desperate sob on her lips, she blew the hair away from her face and wrestled with the rope. Her aching cheek made her think of Jarin, and how his hand felt against her skin during their trek through Galdra's forest. The realisation that he would never want to touch her ruined face again overshadowed the memory. Her heart crumbled inside her chest, and she cried out in anguish.

The bonds gave way, and her right wrist slipped free.

Gasping, Fjola leapt to her feet and unlaced the rope from her other hand. When the cord fell to the floor, she laughed. The skin on her left wrist was raw and stung as if set upon by nettles, while blood oozed from the right. She removed the scarf from her neck and stood there for a moment, holding the crimson cloth. It was Mirable's turban—the only thing she had left of her varlish friend. He called forth the beast to save her life. By aiding their escape, Mirable defied the almighty Laughing God, and Fjola remembered too well how it felt to laugh against your will until your eyes bled and your stomach felt ready to explode. Worry for him twisted her guts.

Fjola wrapped the crimson cloth around her bloody wrist and tied it. It would have to do for now.

Cradling her hands to her chest, she hurried to the door only to find it locked.

'I swear to Yldir you'll regret this, Njall,' she yelled as she slammed into the wood with her left shoulder.

The timber groaned at the jolt, and her arm flared up.

'Please,' she begged under her breath and tried again.

The wooden frame was moth-eaten, and the bolt on the other side was old and rusty. Fjola heard it rasp at the impact, but it didn't give. After a few unsuccessful thrusts, she crossed the room, grabbed the chair by its leg and smashed it at the door. Once, twice, three times…

The chair shattered into pieces, but the timber frame held fast.

Fjola slammed her fists against her thighs, and her wrists rewarded her with another spark of pain. She scanned the bedchamber, and her eyes fell upon Eyvar's shield.

Fjola snatched it off the wall.

The iron felt cold and solid in her grip, and she held it in front of her, the rusty studs poised at the door. She inhaled deeply and charged the frame with a battle cry. Timber creaked at the impact, and the bolt bulged outward. Fjola retreated to the far corner, braced against the shield, and ran at the door again.

There was a splintering sound as the latch tore free of the wood.

She went flying into the corridor, while the shield crashed against the opposite wall. Fjola hit the floor with her cheek, and the stitches, so painstakingly applied by the healer, snapped, reopening the wound. The resulting agony was so great it paralyzed her. She lay on the chill stone, unable to move and helpless to stop the tears. Her breath came in shudders, and the taste of rusted metal flooded her mouth. She sensed the blood, hot and sticky, soaking through the dressing on her face.

A memory of Argil rippled through her mind. He was the only warrior who understood her need to be more than a village wife, and when she asked him to teach her how to use her daggers, he did not refuse her. It was a sunny day, and they practised on a barren stretch of Hvitur's beach when Argil overpowered her. She struck her forehead on a protruding rock, and the excruciating pain took away her will to fight. She lolled on the sand, moaning, but Argil showed her no sympathy.

'Get up,' he ordered. 'After the battle is over, you can weep all you want. The pain is your ally because it means you're still breathing, so embrace it.'

The memory faded, but the strength of Argil's words lingered.

Fjola pushed herself up. The corridor tilted, and she stumbled against the wall. When the dizziness passed, she pressed her hand to her cheek. The lint was wet and warm under her fingers, but she would have to take care of it later. First, she needed to get to the stables.

Fjola broke into a run.

XXVIII

Torgal swung his battle axe.

I ducked, narrowly avoiding the fatal blow.

We faced each other anew, gripping our weapons in front of us. Skaldir's magic weaved patterns in the sky, flooding the beach with green light and turning the men into ethereal heroes from legends past. Beneath the natural odours of sea kelp and saltwater, I recognised the same scent that permeated Shinpi—the rich and heady smell of magic. Prolonged exposure would affect our lungs and make us dizzy, this much I knew, but I hoped it would weaken Torgal and slow down the warriors during my race to the hill.

My uncle came at me again, but I countered. My blade connected with the axe handle, and the impact sent vibrations through my arms. Like my father, Torgal was a warrior hardened by years of rides against the Varls, and he proved his strength with every chop of his battle axe. I sensed Skaldir's rage simmering in the hollow of my gut, but the voice of the old Jarin kept it at bay with his incessant pleas to stop, to surrender. Despite my growing urge to reach the hilltop, the part of me I had imprisoned wanted to afford my uncle a fair chance.

Torgal took another swing at me, going for my sword arm.

I rolled away.

The axe cleaved through the air, missing its mark. My blade afforded me agility, but the blunt force behind the battle axe was more deadly. One hit would put me down.

'What's the matter, nephew? Have you lost your skill along with your memories?'

His question stopped me in my tracks. He knew about Galdra, which meant Fjola lived long enough to tell him. At the thought of her, the Jarin in my head made a mournful sound. The loss gnawed at the edges of my heart with chisel-like teeth, but I refused to give in to it. *'Not now,'* I chided him. *'This isn't the time for grieving.'* This pain was meant for Jarin from Stromhold, and I would feel it soon enough.

'I don't want to kill you, Uncle,' I said.

The warriors laughed.

'You should've thought about it before you set sail. Only one of us is walking out of here alive, and by the gods, it won't be you.' He coughed, and I knew it was the magic from the sky stirring in his lungs.

I tightened my grip on the hilt, which was slippery with sweat. Green spots danced at the edges of my vision, and the pulse pounded in my ears. The Goddess of Destruction demanded a way in, and my time to finish this fight on my terms was running short.

I rushed at Torgal.

Metal clanked against metal in a flurry of strikes. My uncle's eyes widened at this sudden onslaught, but his lips stretched into a satisfied smirk. If not for the circumstances, I'd think his expression was that of pride.

I delivered another blow, but Torgal pivoted, and the sword glanced off the toe of his battle axe, inches from his shoulder. He bared his teeth and shook his axe twice. The warriors roared a battle cry, banging their weapons against their shields. Skaldir answered the challenge with her own fury, turning my world green. Her presence slammed into me like a door ripped off its hinges.

The invisible hand took charge of my sword, compelling me to follow its command.

The true battle had just begun, and neither I nor my uncle had any say in how it would end.

Blade crashed against blade, sparks flew, Torgal staggered.

I thrust at the space between his ribs.

He parried, but his axe wavered, giving me an opening. I struck his side with the pommel. My uncle fell onto the sand, snatching at a breath.

He realised something had changed. I could see it in his eyes.

As Skaldir's rage rolled through my veins, her mark on my temple writhed and throbbed. The Goddess of Destruction fused with her Valgsi to cut down those who barred her path, and Jarin was no more.

Torgal leapt to his feet, wiping sweat from his brow. I glowered at him while flames of anger consumed all sounds. The roaring men faded, replaced by the thudding of my heart, each beat slow and clear in my ears. Alternating stripes of green and crimson flickered in my vision, and I could feel my hair follicles springing to attention like soldiers commanded to assault.

'Don't give in,' the old Jarin said. *'Fight her!'*

I laughed. Did I stand a chance against the raging cyclone? The moment I set my foot on the shore, I surrendered myself to the power of destruction. When Fjola's life force and my only guiding light winked out, it left me alone in the dark. My world was empty. No one was waiting for me. My only home the forsaken hill.

'Fight her!'

The battle raged anew, and Torgal threw his best skills at me, but he could never match the destruction driving my sword. Like the sky above, the symbols etched into Skaldir's blade radiated green, and so did the jewel embedded into the rain-guard. The power locked inside the script rippled through my muscles, goading me to soak the sand with blood. I had the strength to cut down every single man on this beach, and the realisation was as frightening as it was exhilarating.

'Fight her!'

This violent dance inside the warrior's circle took its toll on Torgal. Clash after clash, strike after furious strike, and my uncle's energy began to wane. His arms trembled under the axe's weight, and his hits were less controlled. Beneath the sky's light, his face blanched, and sweat soaked through the hair on his forehead.

As for me, the divine force charged my body, making me immune to mortal exhaustion.

My blade found my uncle's thigh.

He hissed. Blood gushed down the leather in a dark runnel.

Like a bull enraged by the sight of crimson, Torgal charged me.

I kicked sand into his face, and he cursed.

Blinking, he hefted his axe in front of his chest, but I knocked it from his hand with a hard strike.

I slammed my boot into his gut. He lost his balance and crashed to the ground.

Njall's cry reached me from somewhere far away. I searched my uncle's upturned face. There was no fear in it. He lived a warrior's life, knowing Agtarr rode close behind. To learn the face of death, all it would take was a turn of his head. Now the moment was here, and Torgal was ready.

'Fight her!' the voice of the old Jarin—*my* voice—screamed inside my head. His fist pounded against the mirror,

opening new fissures in the glass. He knew the cost of losing someone dear to him, and like my mother before him, Jarin from Stromhold desperately tried to save me from myself. I trapped that grieving part of me, but I could never fully separate myself from it because as much as it was broken, it was also pure.

The snow fell in great flakes, and I could see my breath billowing in and out. Torgal's face flickered from green to pallid while his eyes narrowed, and his mouth set into a tight line.

I shook my head to dispel the magic, but it was like trying to dispel fog on an early autumn morning with a flick of a finger. Trembling, my arm rose of its own volition to deliver the final blow.

'What's the matter with you?' my uncle said through gritted teeth. 'Take my life. You've earned it.'

I let the sword fall.

Perhaps it was the old Jarin who changed the blade's course, for instead of driving the sword through my uncle's heart, I stabbed his shoulder. The weapon's edge tore through the muscles and sinew, splintering the bone but sparing his life. Before I pulled it out, we looked into each other's eyes. Torgal's were the eyes of my father, bulging with shock as his brain scrambled to understand why he was still breathing. I hoped mine conveyed remorse and a warning that he should stay out of my way.

I yanked the blade free. Torgal's blood filled the edges of the script, obscuring the green glow. 'Dion, now!' I called.

Feet pounded against the dock, followed by a mass chanting.

Torgal's warriors, Njall among them, rushed at me, but the faint threads of magic bound their arms and legs. Their eyes, filled with rage, stared at me as I elbowed my way through the circle. The men shouted curses, fighting the invisible bonds. I didn't know how long I had, but the mages afforded me precious minutes, and I intended to use every single one to my advantage.

I darted across the beach, my boots crunching on the shingle, past the village houses, and out onto the road leading to the Ulfur Valley and the hilltop of my birth. A lone wolf howled in the distance, and I remembered riding this trail for the first time, oblivious to the web of secrets my parents had woven around my life. Away from the settlement, Skaldir's light seemed more vibrant as it painted green patterns in the sky. The Goddess of Destruction illuminated my path to the hill where I'd fulfil the ancient riddle inscribed into the stone.

As I ran into the heart of destruction, voices from the past echoed through the Ulfur Valley like ghosts, haunting my every step.

Fjola's voice, full of longing, rang in my ears. *'I always wanted to see the fort and the Grand Isfjells.'*

Pain rattled my chest. Just like Lumi's wish to recover her heart and become human, Fjola's dream of seeing Stromhold would never come true. I raced through the open country, yet the air was in short supply as I struggled to fill my lungs.

As if in response to my anguish, Fjola's whisper drifted on the wind. *'It seems love and loss are entwined.'*

I snatched the pearl at my neck, fighting tears induced by the old Jarin. The black orb felt cool and smooth to the touch. To my ancestors, it represented a promise. To offer the pearl was to offer one's heart, but now…

'There is no one left to give it to,' the old Jarin whispered.

Through the blur, I recognised the trees we had tethered our horses to on our first visit to the hill. It seemed an age had passed since I'd warned Blixt about the wolves prowling the nearby hillocks. The horse was a gift from my father and quickly became my trusted companion. Many a time Lumi and I explored Nordur's plains on Blixt's back, thrilled by the snowstorms and charmed by the jagged peaks. Now, all that remained was Lumi's name, and even that was borrowed from a childhood tale…

If anyone deserved Skaldir's judgement tonight, it was me. The old Jarin tried to save everyone he loved, but they died, and he continued to blame himself. He was a fool who believed by fighting the divine force, he could avoid bloodshed.

I ran into the Heilagt Passage, and blackness swallowed me. The place smelled of soil and musty rock. Without a torch to illuminate my path, I unsheathed Skaldir's blade and let its glow guide me as I stumbled on the uneven path, sending echoes through the cave. My fingers found the wall for support, rough and wet from the constantly dripping water. Above, wings fluttered as the intruder's presence stirred the bats roosting in the crevices.

Marus's voice reverberated from the walls. *'Ancient Nords climbed here to worship Skaldir. They hoped to pacify her and stop the upcoming doom.'*

Was the drunken scholar still in Hvitur, waiting for the Night of Norrsken? He was the one who'd deciphered the script that irrevocably altered my life. Did he take pleasure knowing his predictions were about to come true?

At last, the verdant light filtered through the opening ahead, and I welcomed it. Anything was better than this dank cave. I stopped in front of the steps cut into the mountain. A mere three hundred separated me from my fate. I cocked my head, listening for the sounds of pursuit, but the hilltop stood silent, like a maiden in mourning. Maybe the mages had enough magic in them, after all.

My stomach felt weightless, and my skin prickled all over. Snow swirled all around me, but the flakes were slow to hit the ground. One by one, they drifted down, only to melt on the wet stone. The sword in my grip thrummed with divine energy, eager to reunite with its goddess.

I took the first step, and the voice of my uncle whispered in my ear, *'Fate chose you and no matter how far you run, you can't escape it… You can't change what's written in the stars.'* These were the words he spoke on the hill, after I had learned about my destiny. But I told him I'd never follow a path I didn't choose for myself. The memory sparked off a bitter laugh.

I ascended, taking the steps two at a time, each one bringing me closer to my fate. By the time I reached the final step, sweat drenched my hair and clothes, and my calves trembled from the effort. I crossed under the looming arch.

The mountaintop was just as I remembered it—flat and barren, as if nature refused to grace it with life. Skaldir's magic fully claimed the sky, caressing the platform erected in the centre with its green fingers.

I walked up to it.

Chiselled into the top was the narrow opening, clear of moss and filled with magic that lapped like waves. Ancient symbols made lesions in the stone:

'When my soul spills across the sky,

'Heed my call and seek out the blade,

'The power is yours to take,

'The judgement is mine to make,

'The end of mortal vanity

'The beginning of divine eternity.'

Marus's voice echoed through the hilltop. *'On the Night of Norrsken, heeding the goddess's call, a child will come into the world, Valgsi, marked by Skaldir herself. She will bestow upon him the greatest power, the magic to pull her from her dreams. Together, the god and the mortal, will face her brothers in battle and bring the Day of Judgement upon the world.'*

I lifted the blade high above my head, fixing my gaze on the shimmering sky. The world grew still, the only sound that of my breath flowing in and out. I could feel the blood travelling through my veins—the everlasting river, rushing to fill my heart and lungs with life. The moment was charged with an otherworldly power that amazed even me, the Valgsi, whose purpose was to awaken the divine.

'You called, and I answered,' I said out loud. 'It's time to wake up.'

I plunged the sword into the narrow slit.

XXIX

Fjola spurred Blixt through Hvitur and towards the Ulfur Valley. Snow fell all around her in fat flakes, and the bitter wind whipped her face, biting into the gash on her cheek. Blood, sticky and jelly-like, clotted beneath the healer's dressing, but when she tried to remove it, it felt as though her skin would peel off with the lint, so she left it in place. If she survived the night, she'd ask the healer to clean the wound and replace the stitches. Fjola pressed her fingers to the ruined side of her face.

Blixt galloped across the market square, hooves skidding on the wet stone. Lights flickered in the windows, and Fjola imagined the women and children huddling inside, praying to the God of Life to help their warriors prevail and stop the impending doom. When she led Blixt out of the stables earlier, she heard agitated voices coming from the beach, but she had no time to check if Jarin was among them. She wanted to get to the hilltop before him, but she'd lost precious hours trying to get free.

Fjola gripped the reins with stiff fingers and dug her heels into the horse's sides. Whenever she strained her tendons, her wrists ached from the rope injuries, but she clenched her teeth against the pain and rode on. There'd be plenty of time to suffer later. For now, she had to reach Jarin before it was too late.

Fjola left the village behind and galloped up the path that would take her to the Heilagt Passage. Away from the settlement, the chill intensified. Her earlobes burned, and it seemed the only place warm was inside her mouth. On an ordinary night, the valley would've been pitch black, but not tonight. The magic flooded the hills with a green light that shifted above the peaks in perfect spirals. If not for the source of this display, the sight would've been one to behold, but Fjola had no intention of marvelling at the power that corrupted the man she loved. Skaldir marked Jarin as her Valgsi, but Fjola refused to give him up without a fight. Perhaps she was foolish, but as her father once told her, the hearts of fools lived by their own rules.

When they reached the Heilagt Passage, Fjola dismounted and tied Blixt to a nearby tree. As if in protest, he shook his head and whinnied. But she had no choice—the path ahead was too treacherous for a horse.

'I'll bring Jarin back,' she said, kissing the white blaze that earned Blixt his name. 'I promise.'

Fjola walked up to the entrance and hesitated. Darkness spilt out of the cave, pooling at her feet, and she wished for a torch. The opening made her think of a malevolent beast with a blackened maw—the moment she stepped inside, it would devour her whole.

'You're a warrior, so start acting like one,' she berated herself. She followed Jarin across the Great Atlantic, survived the Laughing God's madness and Galdra's burning blade. One darkened cave would not hold her.

She drew a deep breath and entered the passage.

Blackness engulfed her while the familiar smell of fresh earth and wet rock hit her nostrils. She stretched her hands and used touch to find her way. The feel of solid stone under her fingers brought strange comfort. Bats flapped their wings in the gloom, seeking to protect their nesting place, and Fjola imagined them plunging from above to tangle in her hair. Gooseflesh pricked her skin, and she had to stop herself from breaking into a run. To do so would result in a fall and maybe a broken ankle or two. When the leafy glow filtered through the opening ahead, she uttered a prayer of thanks.

Three hundred steps loomed before her, and the few boulders on either side brought to mind lichen-covered guardians slumbering below the overhanging rocks. Fjola remembered how in the daylight hours the neighbouring hills burned with many colours, but on the Night of Norrsken, green dominated the world. Skaldir's magic illuminated the path to the hilltop, while the steps carved by Fjola's proud ancestors challenged her to take them on. She touched the crimson cloth folded around her aching wrist. Mirable sacrificed his humanity to save her life, and she'd honour him by honouring her heart.

She lifted her chin—the challenge was accepted.

By the time Fjola conquered the stairway, her chest was on fire, and her skin flushed with heat. Blood pounded in her skull, and her tongue felt too big for her mouth. Her muscles punished her with a stabbing pain for putting them through such an ordeal.

Panting, Fjola stepped under the stone archway, and the flames turned to ice as she beheld the sight in front of her.

Jarin stood facing the platform with the blade of Stromhold Guardians raised high above his head. He had his eyes fixed on the sky, and the wind tangled his long hair. The magic gathered all around him, and the green tendrils coiling up his arms and legs looked like some noxious weed trying to feed off his life force. The sword absorbed the light, and the script inscribed into the steel shone with divine power. Even the air surrounding Jarin was different—thick and viscous, it shimmered like the residue in Shinpi. Fjola could feel it trickling up her nostrils and stifling her lungs.

She took a step forward, her right hand outstretched.

Jarin plunged the sword into the slit.

Fjola gasped, then screamed his name.

XXX

'Jarin!'

At the sound of that voice, my fingers froze around the hilt. I stared at it, afraid to move… After a few moments of stillness, my brain came up with a reason. Fjola died on the journey back, but the Jarin trapped behind the glass still mocked me with her voice. That was all. I promised him a reunion and failed to make good on that promise, so he punished me the only way he could—by conjuring up the people I had lost.

But then she spoke again.

'Jarin, it's me.'

I let go of the hilt and turned slowly. Fjola stood under the arch, with her right arm outstretched. Her rusty hair, damp and tousled by the wind. Drops of sweat glistened on her forehead, and her chest heaved in and out, each exhale forming a billow of mist. When our eyes met, Fjola's other hand drifted up to the dressing on her cheek. A cloth was wrapped around her wrist, and at the sight of it, my throat clenched. It was Mirable's turban, worn and stained but as crimson as ever.

'This can't be,' I whispered, taking one staggering step.

She glanced at the sword, then back at me. 'Am I too late?'

Too late for what? In Shinpi, Galdra told me Skaldir possessed the power to resurrect the dead. Was it possible the Goddess of Destruction raised Fjola out of pity to allow us this final farewell? By bringing myself and the blade to the place of her awakening, I had fulfilled my destiny. Perhaps this goodbye was my reward?

I took another hesitant step and lifted my hand. Fjola's own was still suspended in the air as if daring me to touch it. I wanted to, but the fear of shattering this beautiful illusion was greater than my need to know the truth.

Fjola chose for me. She crossed the space between us, and our fingers touched.

My consciousness slipped away.

The hill disappeared, and I found myself looking at my distorted reflection in the mirror. The glass I erected to keep my grief and memories at bay was fractured beyond repair, held only by the strength of my will. One purposeful strike would smash it into pieces.

'What are you waiting for?' the old Jarin asked, and it didn't surprise me when my lips moved in time with his question. After all, we were one and the same.

'I'm afraid,' I said in a quivering voice.

'You should be. The future of our world hangs in the balance.'

'I caused so much suffering, and in the end, I didn't make up for any of it. Worse, in my desperation to reach the hilltop, I almost killed my uncle. I was too weak to resist the call. I still am.' The admission turned my stomach. 'It's too late to turn back. The sword is in place. Agtarr and Yldir's power is fading, and I can feel the goddess stirring in her sleep.'

My upper lip curled in the mirror. 'How long are you going to wallow in self-pity?' the old Jarin asked. 'It's not your destiny that makes you weak but your unwillingness to accept and let go of the past.'

I frowned. 'I don't understand.'

'And you never will unless you stop blaming yourself for the choices you made. Before Goro-Khan crushed Lumi's heart, you asked yourself if you could forgive her for what she did. But the real question is, can you forgive yourself?'

'How?' I cried, balling my hand into a fist. 'My father is dead because I was too weak to stop Hyllus. My mother froze in her bed because I wasn't there to save her. Lumi died because I couldn't let her go. Mirable spoiled from the inside because I failed to find the cure. And Fjola.' I pointed behind me. 'Maybe she climbed the hill seeking justice for her injuries?'

'Or maybe she climbed the hill because she loves you.'

My own declaration stunned me, and I pulled away from the mirror. 'Loves me? After everything I've done? She must hate the very sight of me.'

'Stop being a fool, Jarin. You're turning us both into one.'

'Then tell me what to do!'

'The power is yours to take, and only you can choose how to use it.'

I pressed my forehead against the glass. 'You've said this before, but it still makes no sense to me.'

'To understand, you need to become whole again.'

'But what of the madness Galdra warned me about?'

'Isn't living as half a man the very definition of insanity?'

I didn't know how long I stood there, wrestling with my thoughts. The mirror cooled my forehead, and my warm breath coated the glass with tiny droplets. The old Jarin said no more, but I was keenly aware of his presence, his pull as powerful as the one that drew me to the hilltop. He held all my sadness and all my tears, and to reunite with him would mean reliving those agonising moments from my past. For a heartbeat, I considered leaving that part of me in its glass prison, and walking away, but then my fingers found the black pearl at my neck. The old Jarin was a broken man, but he also harboured Fjola in his heart.

When I lifted my head, the fractured Jarin nodded his agreement. I took a step back to create an arm's length distance between myself and the mirror. I raised my hand. 'Don't make me regret this,' I said, drawing back my arm. My heart thundered in my ears as I braced myself for the pain.

I smashed my fist into the mirror.

The glass shattered in a rain of jagged pieces that sliced through my knuckles. I hissed and bit down hard on my lower lip. The physical pain was only the beginning. I wiped my hand on my shirt, leaving bloody marks. The shards crunched under my boots as I stepped through the opening. Like freshly sharpened arrows, the memories pierced their way into my heart. I clenched my teeth and welcomed the pain, knowing that with acceptance came forgiveness, and forgiveness brought peace.

The first arrow took me back to Elizan and the moment of my father's death. Somewhere beyond, the battle with the Varls raged on. But it sounded far away as if some unseen force encased Father and me in a bauble. The old Jarin was kneeling next to Eyvar's crumpled form, watching the black bruise spread across his breast and swearing vengeance on the mage who killed him.

The grief I nursed for so long awoke, kicking and screaming in the crib that was my rib cage, each strike a reminder of the anguish I felt at Eyvar's passing. I lowered my head.

'I'm sorry I couldn't reach you in time,' I said in a thick voice.

I sensed Father's spirit at my shoulder. *'You couldn't have saved me even if you had, son,'* he whispered into my ear. *'Look there.'*

I turned, and through the bauble, saw my father on the battlefield, fighting a monstrous-looking Varl. Eyvar thrust out with his sword, but the creature brought up its arm, and the blade went through it. Gore splattered both of them. When Father tried to pull his weapon free, the Varl snatched a needle-like implement from its belt and stabbed Eyvar's exposed side with it.

Instinctively, I understood the Varl dealt him a deadly blow.

'Agtarr marked me long before Hyllus twisted my heart,' Father said. He squeezed my shoulder. *'The Warrior of Death waited in Elizan to cross swords with me in my final hour. I have no regrets, and neither should you.'*

When I accepted his words as the truth, the memory dissolved like smoke in the wind.

Another arrow shot through my chest, and I found myself in Aliya's bedchamber. My mother lay frozen on the bed, her mouth contorted in a grimace I could never erase from my mind. Two sisters—silence and stillness—branded the room with the absence of life.

The long-harboured sorrow seized my arm and led me to my mother's bed. During the few strides, my limbs threatened to crumble, and my shoulders sagged under the weight of the loss I'd experienced when I returned to Stromhold, only to be greeted by a deafening hush.

I took Aliya's freezing hand, and the chill from it seeped into my bones. 'Forgive me, for I wasn't there when you needed me, Mother. I…' The grief sucked the words right out of me.

My mother came to stand at the foot of the bed. Her hair was just as I remembered it—a golden wave cascading down her back. A black pearl hung from her neck on a silver chain. *'Nothing would have stopped her. Not even you, my son. I thanked Yldir you were away, but my soul ached for what you'd find upon your return.'*

It was difficult to accept her words. My initial impulse was to tell her how I could've persuaded Lumi to abandon her plans and kept everyone alive, but doing so would've been the same as re-treading the old paths, hoping they'd lead me to new places.

'There isn't a thing you can say or do to change the past, so let it go,' the old Jarin echoed inside my head.

I closed my eyes in a vain effort to hold back the tears.

When I opened them, my mother was gone, and in her place came another arrow. This one guided me to the ship and the moment when I released the Varl from his cage. The Great Atlantic lapped at the ship's hull, and the serena's song weaved yellow patterns through the air. When I called Mirable's name this time, he turned.

'I'm sorry I couldn't save you, my friend,' I said.

Mirable regarded me with his rummy eyes. *'The rot took hold the instant Hyllus finished his wretched spell. I wanted to believe there was a cure, but the transformation was irreversible. Kylfa told you as much.'*

I searched for the memory, and there it was, blinking at me like a wicked eye.

'I feel pain... great pain. I smell freedom and I see transformation. Challenge lies in his way and he shall follow his path until he will be no more.'

The witch knew Mirable's fate years before we lived to experience it.

I didn't speak, but Mirable nodded all the same, then raced to the taffrail, fading even as he did so.

I buried my face in my hands, bracing for the last arrow.

It fell with a whoosh and carried me back to Stromhold, planting me in front of Lumi's old bedchamber. The door stood ajar, and I glimpsed the bare floorboards and a section of the frost-covered window frame. I placed my hand against the doorway, reluctant to step inside and afraid not to. The last time I stood here was on the day of my mother's death, seething with the urge to throttle Lumi for destroying my world. Was she standing on the other side? And if she did, was I ready to let go of my childhood dreams?

Doubt crept into my heart. I'd lost her once when Goro-Khan shattered her crystal heart, and it almost broke me, allowing Galdra to take control over my grieving mind. There was a big difference between believing I could do something and having the strength to do it. But then I remembered Fjola waiting for me on the hilltop, her anxious eyes, and how tired I was of living in the cold.

I held my breath and pushed the door open.

As I stepped through, the cold hit me, so deep it felt as though I plunged through an ice hole into the harsh waters of the Great Atlantic. The hair in my nostrils prickled, and my toes curled inside my boots. I cupped my hands in front of my mouth and puffed air into them. Rubbing my palms together, I looked around the room.

I spent much time here as a youth, and it was like stepping into childhood's comforting embrace. The old fireplace had never been lit since Lumi took up residence, and it gaped at me accusingly. Lumi's presence was everywhere—from the crystalline patterns on the glass to the frozen flowers lining up the ledge.

Hurled by the wind, the shutter banged against the wall, making me jump.

My gaze shifted to the bed and the blue dress hanging off the footboard.

I crossed the chamber. A floorboard creaked under my heavy footfalls. I ran my hand over the lustrous material, and my chest exploded with the familiar ache. Lumi wore this gown on the day I departed for Elizan. I went to bid her farewell, and we shared our first kiss that chilled the blood in my veins. Back then, I still believed her muteness was the working of a curse and that my purpose was to break it. My numb fingers folded over the silk.

I picked up the dress and pressed it to my nose. The scent of ice and freshly fallen snow suffused my senses, and I closed my eyes. When I was a boy, this smell held endless possibilities. Every snowflake and a footprint promised a new adventure.

'You came back,' Lumi said, and her voice chimed in my ears like tiny bells.

I replaced the gown, smoothing out the creases. 'It's so cold here,' I said.

'It's always cold in my world.'

I turned to face her.

Lumi stood in the doorway, watching me with her sapphire eyes. In her snowy dress and hair the shade of charcoal, she resembled a bride from distant shores about to pledge her crystal heart.

'You wish to say goodbye,' she said.

That one word stabbed like a thorn. I closed the space between us in two strides and folded my hands around hers. 'By delivering your heart to the Laughing God, I condemned you to this place.' I pressed her slender fingers to my lips. 'Forgive me.'

'Like Mirable, I was never meant to be, and in the end, the magic killed us both. The difference is, he never betrayed those he loved…' Her forehead creased, and her blue mouth quivered.

I caressed her cheek. 'I got lost so many times, I forgot where I was going. But in the end, I always found my way back.' I looked into her shifting eyes that mesmerised me as a boy. 'Before my father brought you home, my life was empty.'

'But I destroyed your world,' she cried.

'You did what you were created to do,' I said. 'You broke me, but I loved you anyway. By accepting your destiny and doing what you had to, you prepared me to face my own. I'm finally ready.'

Lumi pressed one chilled hand against my chest. 'When I was dying, you told me that for as long as your heart was beating, so would mine. I'll keep you to this promise, Jarin Olversson.'

The memory of her breaking in my arms was too much to bear. My resolve to leave her vanished, replaced by a compelling need to stay in this chamber and dream the frozen dream in the safety of her icy embrace.

I cupped her face. 'You were my life, my home…'

Lumi shook her head and looked pointedly at the window. '*She* is your home.'

I frowned.

'Listen,' she whispered.

I cocked my head. At first, there was nothing but that peculiar hum the silence made when it was too quiet, but then I heard a distant voice. It was faint, but the more I focused on it, the louder it grew. I followed Lumi's gaze to the window, listening to my name being repeated over and over. The wind swept through the bedchamber, dusting the floor with snowflakes.

When I turned, Lumi was gone.

'Jarin!' the female voice cried. Urgent and persistent, it seemed to be coming from the lower floors.

'Fjola?'

'Jarin, can you hear me?'

I ran into the corridor, leaving the icy room and its ghosts behind. My body felt weightless as I raced along the hallway, sending echoes through the still tower. Fjola… her name tasted like summer berries, and I whispered it over and over. I reached the staircase and flew down the steps. With each one, the ice that encased my chest for so long melted, and by the time I arrived at the entry hall, my heart was free. Each powerful beat warmed my muscles, pumping hot blood that washed away the last traces of winter.

I approached the doorway leading to the courtyard. Fjola's voice was sharp and clear now.

'I'm coming,' I said, and I threw the door wide open.

The sunlight that spilt through was so bright it blinded me. I inhaled, and for the first time, my lungs allowed me a clean breath. I laughed and stepped into the warmth.

XXXI

My lids snapped open, and I experienced a moment of utter confusion.

Fjola threw her head back. ‘Thank Yldir. To collapse like that, I thought you died! What happened?’

I rubbed my left temple. I didn’t know where I was nor how we both came to be here. A deep rumbling noise arose from behind me, and I glanced over my shoulder. My sword, still embedded in the stone, glowed brighter than a freshly lit torch. Drawn by the script inscribed into the steel, the magic from the sky gathered above in a sinister maelstrom. The blade absorbed it through a vortex of shimmering energy.

I leapt to my feet, and the hill swayed. ‘Stand back,’ I told Fjola.

She grabbed my arm. ‘Don’t touch that thing.’

I untangled her clammy fingers. ‘I have to go.’

The green magic reflected in Fjola’s wide and pleading eyes. Her face was pale, and dark shadows pooled under her sockets. Blood soaked through the dressing on her cheek. The right corner of the lint peeled off, revealing the wound that looked angry and swollen. A powerful urge to stay with her washed over me. I wanted to throw my arms around her, hold her close, and shield her from all danger. But it was a foolish impulse, for the only way to keep her safe was to answer the goddess's call.

Her entire face tensed. 'Why?' she cried. 'What are you going to do?'

It was time for me to shake her. I seized her in a vice grip. 'I need to do this, and I need *you* to wait here. Promise me that whatever happens, you'll keep your distance.'

Her lower lip curled, and I caught that glimmer of defiance in her eye I'd learned to recognise from our travels together.

I put as much determination into my voice as I could muster. 'You have to trust me.'

She looked from me to the sword. 'But—'

I gave her another shake. 'Promise me!'

Fjola winced, but after a moment's hesitation, she nodded.

With a quiet exhale, I let go of her. I knew the victory was short-lived, and she'd be furious with me, but I could deal with that later. *If* I came out of this alive…

I turned to face my destiny.

Skaldir's blade vibrated with magic, and as the script absorbed the last of it, the world plunged into darkness. Even the stars and the moon shied away from the sky, as if afraid they too would be pulled into the whirlwind of destruction. I pushed back my shoulders, and an unexpected calm filled me. Twenty winters ago, on the Night of Norrsken, my mother gave birth to me under the shimmering skies, and the Goddess of Destruction marked me as her own. Tonight she called, and I answered. Her sword beckoned me to claim the power and fulfil the words etched into the stone.

The power is yours to take, so take it.

And I did.

I strode to the platform and wrapped my fingers around the hilt.

The magic rushed up my arm in a green current, and the pain that followed set my skin on fire. Skaldir's power burned, searing its way into my soul with an excruciating intensity. I clenched my jaw shut, refusing to give voice to this torment. Spittle flew from the corners of my mouth, and my head felt ready to explode, but I swallowed the agony and held onto the blade. The power was meant for me, and my soul would be strong enough to hold it.

Or so I believed.

I sensed the magic rushing through my veins. My muscles expanded with it, my lungs drowned in it, and my blood boiled in the wake of this inferno. The tendons in my neck stretched so tight I was sure they'd sever. My vision flickered from black to green, and Skaldir's mark on my temple pulsed and squirmed like a parasite jabbed with fiery needles.

Just when I thought the suffering would never ease, the pain dissipated. The sensation that remained was a dull throb in my rib cage as if some beast made of tremendous energy nestled there. My limbs trembled, and my heart raced the way it did when I scaled the three hundred steps.

I clutched at my chest, then yanked the sword free.

The hilltop was gone, and I found myself in a cylindrical chamber. I recognised it at once. It was the same room to which the gods had summoned the Star Forgers and ordered them to create a divine sister. Eight stone pillars towered over the main floor, but unlike those from Galdra's visions, these were real and embellished with an ancient script that mirrored the one on my blade. When I glanced up, I saw nothing but darkness. The pillars glowed, each casting a ray of silver light, and in the heart of it, the three gods knelt in a circle, with their hands joined. My breath stalled at the realisation I shared the space with the divine. At first, my legs grew heavy and refused to move an inch, but then I reminded myself the gods were asleep, and only I had the power to awaken them.

My nerves jangled as I walked around the three celestial beings, my footsteps impossibly loud in this stone tomb. Time and imagination eroded our idea of the gods, for they looked nothing like the statues and drawings in the scrolls.

The God of Life—my mother's beloved—knelt to Skaldir's right. I always thought him to be an elder, with withering features and a silvery beard, commanding the living souls from his high chair in Himinn. But the Yldir sleeping in this chamber looked more like a celestial warrior than an old man.

His skin was smooth and clear of wrinkles. The God of Life wore white armour, with matching bracelets and shoulder plates decorated with golden flames. The sphere of life hovered at his shoulder, radiating with energy that gave birth to human souls. To my surprise, I desired to move closer and touch Yldir's white and silky hair that gleamed in the silvery light.

To Skaldir's left knelt the God of Death, and as I approached, the hair on the nape of my neck bristled. To stand close to the god who had the power to end all life with his look alone almost unmanned me. Agtarr's cloak was made of black feathers wrapped so tightly it was impossible to tell what lay beneath. Perhaps nothing but void…

I leaned over to peek inside the shadowy cowl that guarded the secrets of death.

The three-headed raven that perched on Agtarr's shoulder screeched.

I jumped back, heart thrashing in my throat. I didn't think the bird was real, but the six beady eyes shifted in their sockets, following my every move. I remembered Galdra's tale about the ravens devouring the souls of the living in a never-ending cycle until Skaldir slaughtered them in her quest to restore the balance between life and death.

I turned my attention to the real reason for my being here. The Goddess of Destruction slept, but her breast wasn't moving up and down, the way it would if she were a mortal.

She donned a gown woven from green threads of magic that caused her skin to shimmer like emeralds. A golden circlet rested upon her head with the jewel matching the one embedded in my sword. Skaldir's hair was braided, each braid interlaced with white and black feathers. The only thing unchanged was her scowl. Her perfectly shaped eyebrows met at the bridge of her nose, creasing the skin above, and the twisted line of her upper lip reminded me of Mirable in the grip of a snarling fit. I didn't have to touch her to feel the anger burning deep within her still chest.

I traced the green chains that held the goddess captive—two magical fetters linked by a series of glowing rings. The power radiating from the God of Life charged the ones binding Skaldir's right wrist, while Agtarr's magic shackled her left. The three dwelled in this hall, locked in their eternal dream while mortals spun tales about them that changed with each passing age. I defied the gods all my life, questioning their existence and refusing to bow before their mighty idols. But here they were, reshaping my worldview even as they slept.

I lifted my sword.

Forged from the star steel and burdened by the fate of the world, it felt heavy in my grip. Nords called it the Blade of the Stromhold Guardians. It came to my grandfather's possession long before my birth, but the responsibility to use it, and use it well, rested with me—the Valgsi whose destiny it was to 'end the mortal vanity and bring about the divine eternity.' Skaldir imbued my soul with her destructive magic, so I could free her from the chains her brothers used to contain her wrath.

I brought the sword down, cutting through the bonds of sleep.

I expected a mighty rattle, a roar of thunder, or some other terrible calamity, but once severed, the green fetters simply dissipated.

A great hush fell over the chamber. I waited with the blade pointed at the floor, my hands shaking. My stomach felt hollow, as though someone took a spoon to it and scraped my guts out. All moisture leaked out of my mouth. My lips parted, but no air filtered in or out. As I fixed my gaze on the sleeping goddess, my imagination ran wild, feeding me the images of her pouncing and tearing me to shreds with her feral teeth.

Minutes passed, and fear turned to unease.

Maybe magic alone wasn't enough to undermine the gods of Life and Death? My muscles relaxed, and the sword's tip hit the stone with a resounding peal.

Skaldir's eyelids snapped open.

I anticipated this moment, but it still gave me a jolt, and before I could stop myself, I let out a harsh cry.

The Goddess of Destruction lifted her head, and our eyes met. Hers had no whites. Her emerald-green irises encased the silver pupils that shimmered like the stars she was made of.

Staring into them was like staring into the heart of all creation, a place beyond the stars where nature's laws did not apply, and time ceased to exist. The secret knowledge of how the world began and how it would end lurked deep within her shifting gaze, but deeper still, burned the primal rage.

Skaldir rose to her feet. 'You served me well, Valgsi.' Her words came at me from all directions and in multiple languages that sounded so ancient, I doubted I'd find any mention of them in the scrolls. Her infinite eyes scanned the chamber and fell upon her sleeping brothers. She sneered, then opened her shimmering palm. 'My sword.'

Although the urge to obey was powerful, I didn't move.

Her feathery braids bounced as she jerked her head my way. 'Surrender the sword.'

My hand twitched, eager to hand over the blade, but I tightened my grip on the hilt. 'No.'

Something flickered in her face, a mixture of dismay and confusion that seemed completely out of place—it was clear the Goddess of Destruction didn't take 'no' for an answer. 'The divine judgement is at hand.'

'Mages do not wish to war with humans. They want to restore the Lost City of Antaya and be free to worship you.'

'The beings I had imbued with life relinquished me to my prison. They must be judged with the rest of the faithless.'

'You call them faithless?' I thought of the mages throwing themselves off the ships in the dead of the night, and those alive, keeping Torgal and his warriors at bay to allow me passage to the hill. 'They sacrificed everything to be here this night.' I stood up straight but still couldn't match Skaldir in height. 'You don't want to judge the world, you wish to destroy it.'

She flicked her fingers, and the gesture appeared oddly human. 'You are here to obey, Valgsi.' She glared down at her brothers who now knelt at her feet. 'The bringers of their own demise. The cleansing shall begin tonight. When the cull of all beings is complete, the world will begin anew.'

I knew the moment had come, and whether I lived or died, was of little consequence. My parents laid down their lives to stave off the second Day of Judgement. Mirable turned into a beast, and Lumi saw her heart shatter. Not to mention Galdra who succumbed to madness in pursuit of the divine future. Those touched by magic paid a heavy price. I remembered the tapestries in Goro-Khan's pagoda and the terror on the faces of people fleeing through Antaya's gates. We all believed the Valgsi could tame Skaldir's wrath and channel her power to restore the lost city. The mages believed her awakening would bring an end to their exile, and I hoped it would gift Lumi a second chance at life. But there was no compassion to be found in the goddess's damaged heart.

Skaldir's power and her blade were connected, and I was a conduit between the two. Every fibre of my being demanded I surrender the sword. It was my duty. The magic—my only weapon against the celestial force—burned brightly in my soul, but instead of relinquishing this destructive force, I channelled it into the sword. The goddess planned to cleanse the earth of mages and mortals alike, and if she was allowed to live, the green flames of her wrath would devour the world. I was the only one who could stop her.

'The judgement is yours to make, but the power is mine to take, remember?' I said. Skaldir's mark on my temple throbbed and it took all my mental and physical strength to break Skaldir's hold on me.

Clutching the pearl in one hand and the sword in the other, I charged the goddess.

Skaldir raised her hands as if to answer the incoming blow with her own magic, but her fingers came up empty. She entrusted me with her power but misjudged human nature. When the gods fell asleep, we venerated them, carving idols and singing prayers in their name. In the divine eyes, our duty was to worship and obey, not to challenge and defy. But as the years went by, the fear of judgement diminished, and many left the gods to their dreams, choosing to walk their own paths. I wanted mine to lead me to a future with Fjola, and no god would take that away from me.

The sword went right through her, as if her body was made of air. I let go of the hilt and staggered backwards.

Skaldir looked at her chest and the blade sticking out of it.

For a moment, nothing happened, and I sensed the first onset of panic. Maybe it was I who misjudged her by assuming I could kill the goddess with her own magic.

Skaldir grabbed hold of the pommel, and her hands burst into green flames.

Her shriek filled the chamber, each note a needle piercing my eardrums. I clapped my palms over my ears, running for the closest pillar. A scorching wave of heat slammed into my back, and I gasped at its intensity. With my chest pushed against the stone, I watched the goddess with one eye.

The feathers in Skaldir's hair caught on fire, and the golden circlet on her forehead was ablaze. The air turned rich with the odour of singed brass that took me back to when I was a boy, sneaking into Einir's workshop. I had stared in awe as the blacksmith fed the flames that transformed the metal in the massive cauldron into a thick liquid of bubbling orange. The heat was immense, but it paled in comparison to the blistering inferno spreading through the chamber. As I watched the writhing goddess, my cheeks burned and my lungs pumped the acrid air like bellows.

Skaldir began to melt.

Molten star steel ran down in silver runnels, forming into a pool at her feet. The sword buried in her breast liquefied. Father wielded this blade until the moment he drew his last, and as it melted, a small part of him melted away with it. My fingers travelled to the empty sheathe at my hip, and the ache deep in my throat had nothing to do with the heat.

As Skaldir's face dissolved, her screams died away. The Goddess of Destruction chose me as her saviour only to find herself reduced to a pool of silvery metal that shimmered like the stars on the midnight sky.

I stared at it, mesmerised.

The bond connecting us dissipated, but I could still feel Skaldir's presence. Her magic filled my soul, and so her essence lived on even after the goddess herself had perished. In the silence that followed, a terrible fear gripped me. I killed a god. Could such an act go unpunished?

As if in response, the other two gods stirred.

The script carved into the pillars ignited with golden light. It matched the sun in its brilliance, forcing me to shield my eyes. A low rumble resonated from somewhere beneath the chamber. The stone floor began to tremble, and with it my whole body. My chest swelled with terror so great I thought my heart would explode. My mouth opened in a silent scream. I pressed my back against the pillar and wrapped my hands around my knees.

A flapping sound drifted from behind me, and a whoosh of air hit my face. Something sharp stabbed the centre of the witch's symbol on my wrist, and a voice older than the time itself sounded in my ear.

'Your soul is mine.'

XXXII

The stabbing ache in my arm jolted me awake. I lay in a room with bare walls and the fire crackling softly in the hearth. The chair and the shield were missing, but I recognised my father's old bedchamber. I didn't remember how I got here, nor what happened after that ancient voice that still echoed in my ears. The memories of the hill and Skaldir's final moments flashed through my mind, but I pushed them aside.

There would be time to consider the gravity of my actions later.

I swung my feet off the bed and folded up my sleeve. The eye blinked at me while the black lines surrounding it twisted and throbbed like roots of an ancient tree. The pain emanating from it was stronger than before, more urgent, and not one to be ignored. I placed my palm against my chest—the magic of destruction burned deep inside, and the witches demanded I bring it to them.

Kylfa's words rustled in my head. *'The pain is a reminder of your oath. When the time comes, it will guide you back.'*

And the time had come.

I reached for my sword, but my fingers came up empty. The blade had perished with the goddess, leaving behind a peculiar sense of loss.

I got up. My muscles ached as if exhausted by a week's long battle. I flexed my arms and stretched my back best I could, but it did little to ease the stiffness. Hobbling like a village elder, I crossed the room. The lock on the door was splintered, and the frame hung askew on its hinges.

I started down the corridor, halting briefly at the altar. The statues of the three gods towered over it, as hollow as the wood they were carved from. Now that I knew their story, I trusted them even less. My lips curled at the sight of Skaldir and her angry scowl. All that rage didn't save her, and soon, all her idols would meet with the same fate. I turned and walked the length of the hallway without a backward glance.

The main hall stood empty.

I pushed aside the curtain leading into the small hallway where I had waited with Skari and Njall to meet Torgal for the first time. It seemed an age had passed since that day. Outside, the sound of crashing waves greeted me, and it felt good to breathe in the clean and salty air. I glanced at the shore, and a flash of red caught my eye.

As I recognised Fjola, warmth filled my chest.

I descended the steps to the waterfront lined with Nordern vessels. Some were finished, their hulls pointing proudly at the ocean, but others still awaited completion, with their keels jutting out like antlers on a stag. I limped across the beach, my feet sinking into the sand.

Fjola waited at the water's edge, gazing at the horizon. The waves rushed at her boots, then drew back, pulling tiny shells and pebbles with them. I came to stand next to her, and we said nothing for a while. The seagulls glided on the wind that tugged at our hair, and Mirable's turban wrapped around Fjola's neck. This simple moment filled me with peace, and if not for the throbbing pain in my wrist, I'd remain here for hours.

I broke the silence. 'Where is everyone?'

'Getting ready for a celebration. The night is over, and the Day of Judgement is no longer a threat.'

Indeed. The people had the right to celebrate. I'd vanquished the Goddess of Destruction, but I couldn't share in their joy. The memory of Skaldir's liquefied form induced a hollow pang. The dark force that chased me for twenty winters was gone, leaving emptiness behind. I rubbed my chest. 'What about the mages?'

Fjola shrugged. 'Netis is in charge of keeping them under control until Torgal decides on the punishment.'

'Punishment? They did nothing wrong.'

'Says a man who ordered them to attack the warriors.'

'I ordered them to keep Torgal's men at bay to buy me time.' What I said next, surprised even me. 'They're *my* people, and Torgal has no right to judge them.'

Fjola arched her eyebrows at me. I readied myself for a blow of scornful words, but instead she pointed to my temple. 'Your mark, it's gone.'

I touched the spot where Skaldir seared her symbol into my flesh, marking me as her Valgsi. The scar gave way to smooth skin. It was as if the constellation was never there to begin with. But my destruction of Skaldir burned fresh in my mind, never to be forgotten.

'Look Jarin, what happened up there?'

I opened my mouth to explain, but then I checked myself. Like her brother, she trusted the gods, and I didn't want to ruin her image of them. Her faith was strong, and who was I to take it from her? 'I did what my father trained me to do. Guard Nordur and keep my people safe.'

'And Mirable?'

I shook my head.

She closed her eyes briefly while her fingers drifted to the red cloth around her neck. 'Was it you?' The question came as a whisper, and Fjola's chest stilled as she waited for an answer.

Mirable's gruff voice echoed in my ears, begging for release. 'He wanted me to end his suffering. I opened the cage, but he took the leap.' I shifted, so we faced each other. 'Fjola—'

She sighed. 'I know. It's your oath to the witches.' Her chin trembled, and she bit down on her lower lip.

'Yes, there is that. But it's not what I was going to say.' My mind buzzed with all the things I wished to tell her, but my tongue twisted into a knot.

Fjola rolled her eyes, and I had to curb an urge to laugh. It was so like her to grow impatient in the space of a few heartbeats.

'When I lost myself on that hill, it was your voice that brought me back.'

'I didn't do—'

'Let me finish. After Lumi, I built walls around my heart, my very own Stromhold, and I fortified them with my most agonising memories. Despite my best efforts to keep anyone from breaching them, you found a way. No matter how hard I pushed you and how much pain I caused you, you never gave up. And for that, I'm eternally grateful.'

Fjola shrugged and looked down at her boots.

I lifted her chin. The dressing was gone from her cheek, and fresh stitches closed over the wound. The surrounding skin puffed up, but the angry crimson from the night before turned a soft red. I wanted more than anything to go back in time and take the dagger in her stead, but even the gods didn't have that kind of power. If they had, the world would've been a very different place.

I must've lingered on it for too long because Fjola covered the cheek with her hand. 'The healer told me it needed to breathe. It'll leave a scar but…'

My chest swelled. Here she was, trying to apologise for the injury that was my fault. I removed her hand. 'You're beautiful,' I whispered, then I gently kissed the stitches.

Tears flashed in her eyes, and now they truly looked like forest pools. I reached back and undid the string that secured the black pearl around my neck. I held it in front of her.

Fjola's eyes widened.

I spoke the vow. 'With this pearl, I pledge myself to you and entrust my heart to your keep. Will you have it?'

Fjola looked from the orb to me and back at the orb. She closed her eyes briefly, and when she opened them, the hurt vanished, replaced by a glint of joy.

'I vow to stay true and cherish your heart until Agtarr does us part.' Here she paused and added, 'And even after, I'll wait for you in the Fields of Life.' The last wasn't part of the tradition, but I treasured every word.

I tied the black pearl around her neck. It rested on top of Mirable's turban—a midnight jewel in a crimson pool. I promised myself to never offer it to anyone, but standing here, looking at the pearl and knowing it bound me to Fjola, I was never gladder of breaking a vow. I was lost in a blizzard for so long, I went without truly 'seeing' her, and now, all I wanted was to memorise every inch of her perfect face, to know her sorrows and deepest desires. Seeing her smile was the most precious gift, and I wanted to find reasons to keep it alive.

I leaned in and kissed her.

Fjola's mouth pressed warmly against mine, and the sensation filled me with the images of summer. After a long journey in the cold, I was finally home.

When our lips parted, Fjola picked up the pearl and turned it in her fingers. 'What now?'

I thought of the glaring eye on my wrist and Hrafn's terrifying declaration. 'Now, I'm going to reclaim my soul.'

Fjola scanned the waves as if searching for someone, but after a few moments, she shook her head and took my hand. Her grip was firm. 'I'm going with you.'

We left the Great Atlantic and its mysteries to the wind and walked across the beach hand in hand.

Bonus Content:

Get your free fantasy adventure!

"An emotionless warrior.
A journey across four lands.
A quest to uncover the power of the human heart."

Visit ulanadabbs.com to subscribe and receive your free copy of:

Storms of Tomorrow

Note from Jarin:

Thank you for reading *Lumi's Heart*.

So, how did I do? I would appreciate your feedback! Please leave me an honest review on Amazon or Goodreads, so I can use it to prepare myself for my next quest. The journey to reclaim my soul won't be easy, but with a band of fearless readers like you at my side, I fear no witches.

—Jarin, the Guardian of Stromhold

Acknowledgements

I would like to thank Philip Athans for his editorial advice, and for encouraging me to stay true to the story I wanted to tell.

Lauren Nicholls, your feedback was invaluable and made the story that much stronger.

Rebecca Reed, for your comprehensive proofreading. You went that extra mile, and your comments helped me polish the story further.

Inghild, for being such a good friend and writing buddy. Without you and your exceptional eye for detail, this book would have landed in a digital drawer. I'm forever grateful for your support, enthusiasm, and encouragement.

Mario Wibisono, for bringing Jarin to life with your magnificent cover art. Your skills are remarkable, and my characters are lucky to have you as their artist.

Printed in Great Britain
by Amazon

79937507R00267